IN DUBIOUS BATTLE

BOOKS BY JOHN STEINBECK

Journal of a Novel, 1969

America and Americans, 1966

* Travels with Charley in Search of America, 1962

The Winter of Our Discontent, 1961   Once There Was a War, 1958

The Short Reign of Pippin IV, 1957   Sweet Thursday, 1954

* East of Eden, 1952   * The Log from the Sea of Cortez, 1951

Burning Bright (a play in story form), 1950

A Russian Journal, 1948   * The Pearl, 1947

The Wayward Bus, 1947   * Cannery Row, 1945

The Portable Steinbeck, 1943   Bombs Away, 1942

The Moon Is Down (novel), 1942   The Moon Is Down (play), 1942

Sea of Cortez (in collaboration with Edward F. Ricketts), 1941

The Forgotten Village, 1941   * The Grapes of Wrath, 1939

* The Long Valley, 1938   * The Red Pony, 1937

Of Mice and Men (play), 1937   * Of Mice and Men (novel), 1937

Saint Katy the Virgin, 1936   * In Dubious Battle, 1936

* Tortilla Flat, 1935   To a God Unknown, 1933

* The Pastures of Heaven, 1932   Cup of Gold, 1929

* Available in Compass editions

In Dubious Battle

JOHN STEINBECK

PUBLISHED BY THE VIKING PRESS

NEW YORK

First published in 1936
Published in 1949 by The Viking Press, Inc.
625 Madison Avenue, New York, N.Y. 10022
New edition completely reset in 1963
Viking Compass Edition issued in 1963 by The Viking Press, Inc.

SBN 670-39523-4 (hardbound)
670-00132-5 (paperbound)

Library of Congress catalog card number: 36-2209
Distributed in Canada by The Macmillan Company of Canada Limited

Seventh printing November 1970

M   B   G
Set in Janson types. Printed in the U.S.A.
by The Murray Printing Co.

Innumerable force of Spirits armed,
That durst dislike his reign, and, me preferring,
His utmost power with adverse power opposed
In dubious battle on the plains of Heaven
And shook his throne. What though the field be lost?
All is not lost — the unconquerable will,
And study of revenge, immortal hate,
And courage never to submit or yield:
And what is else not to be overcome?

— PARADISE LOST

The persons and places in this book are fictitious

1

AT LAST it was evening. The lights in the street outside came on, and the Neon restaurant sign on the corner jerked on and off, exploding its hard red light in the air. Into Jim Nolan's room the sign threw a soft red light. For two hours Jim had been sitting in a small, hard rocking-chair, his feet up on the white bedspread. Now that it was quite dark, he brought his feet down to the floor and slapped the sleeping legs. For a moment he sat quietly while waves of itching rolled up and down his calves; then he stood up and reached for the unshaded light. The furnished room lighted up—the big white bed with its chalk-white spread, the golden-oak bureau, the clean red carpet worn through to a brown warp.

Jim stepped to the washstand in the corner and washed his hands and combed water through his hair with his fingers. Looking into the mirror fastened across the corner of the room above the washstand, he peered into his own small grey eyes for a moment. From an inside pocket he took a comb fitted with a pocket clip and combed his straight brown hair, and parted it neatly on the side. He wore a dark suit and a grey flannel shirt, open at the throat. With a towel he dried the soap and dropped the thin bar into a paper bag that stood open on the bed. A Gillette razor was in the bag, four pairs of new socks and another grey flannel shirt. He glanced about the room and then twisted the mouth of the bag closed. For a moment more he looked casually into the mirror, then turned off the light and went out the door.

He walked down narrow, uncarpeted stairs and knocked at a door beside the front entrance. It opened a little. A woman looked at him and then opened the door wider—a large blonde woman with a dark mole beside her mouth.

She smiled at him. "*Mis*-ter Nolan," she said.

"I'm going away," said Jim.

"But you'll be back, you'll want me to hold your room?"

"No. I've got to go away for good. I got a letter telling me."

"You didn't get no letters here," said the woman suspiciously.

"No, where I work. I won't be back. I'm paid a week in advance."

Her smile faded slowly. Her expression seemed to slip toward anger without any great change. "You should of give me a week's notice," she said sharply. "That's the rule. I got to keep that advance because you didn't give me no notice."

"I know," Jim said. "That's all right. I didn't know how long I could stay."

The smile was back on the landlady's face. "You been a good quiet roomer," she said, "even if you ain't been here long. If you're ever around again, come right straight here. I'll find a place for you. I got sailors that come to me every time they're in port. And I find room for them. They wouldn't go no place else."

"I'll remember, Mrs. Meer. I left the key in the door."

"Light turned out?"

"Yes."

"Well, I won't go up till tomorrow morning. Will you come in and have a little nip?"

"No, thank you. I've got to be going."

Her eyes narrowed wisely. "You ain't in trouble? I could maybe help you."

"No," Jim said. "Nobody's after me. I'm just taking a new job. Well, good night, Mrs. Meer."

She held out a powdered hand. Jim shifted his paper
bag and took her hand for a moment, and felt the soft
flesh give under his fingers.

"Don't forget," she said. "I can always find room. People come back to me year after year, sailors and drum-
mers."

"I'll remember. Good night."

She looked after him until he was out the front door
and down the cement steps to the sidewalk.

He walked to the corner and looked at the clock in a
jeweller's window—seven-thirty. He set out walking
rapidly eastward, through a district of department stores
and specialty shops, and then through the wholesale produce district, quiet now in the evening, the narrow streets
deserted, the depot entrances closed with wooden bars
and wire netting. He came at last to an old street of three-
storey brick buildings. Pawn-shops and second-hand tool
dealers occupied the ground floors, while failing dentists
and lawyers had offices in the upper two flights. Jim
looked at each doorway until he found the number he
wanted. He went in a dark entrance and climbed the narrow stairs, rubber-treaded, the edges guarded with strips
of brass. A little night light burned at the head of the steps,
but only one door in the long hall showed a light through
its frosted glass. Jim walked to it, looked at the "Sixteen"
on the glass, and knocked.

A sharp voice called, "Come in."

Jim opened the door and stepped into a small, bare
office containing a desk, a metal filing cabinet, an army
cot and two straight chairs. On the desk sat an electric
cooking plate, on which a little tin coffee-pot bubbled
and steamed. A man looked solemnly over the desk at
Jim. He glanced at a card in front of him. "Jim Nolan?"
he asked.

"Yes." Jim looked closely at him, a small man, neatly
dressed in a dark suit. His thick hair was combed

straight down on each side from the top in a vain attempt to cover a white scar half an inch wide that lay horizontally over the right ear. The eyes were sharp and black, quick nervous eyes that moved constantly about —from Jim to the card, and up to a wall calendar, and to an alarm clock, and back to Jim. The nose was large, thick at the bridge and narrow at the point. The mouth might at one time have been full and soft, but habitual muscular tension had drawn it close and made a deep line on each lip. Although the man could not have been over forty, his face bore heavy parenthetical lines of resistance to attack. His hands were as nervous as his eyes, large hands, almost too big for his body, long fingers with spatulate ends and flat, thick nails. The hands moved about on the desk like the exploring hands of a blind man, feeling the edges of paper, following the corner of the desk, touching in turn each button on his vest. The right hand went to the electric plate and pulled out the plug.

Jim closed the door quietly and stepped to the desk. "I was told to come here," he said.

Suddenly the man stood up and pushed his right hand across. "I'm Harry Nilson. I have your application here." Jim shook hands. "Sit down, Jim." The nervous voice was soft, but made soft by an effort.

Jim pulled the extra chair close and sat down by the desk. Harry opened a desk-drawer, took out an open can of milk, the holes plugged with matches, a cup of sugar and two thick mugs. "Will you have a cup of coffee?"

"Sure," said Jim.

Nilson poured the black coffee into the mugs. He said, "Now here's the way we work on applications, Jim. Your card went in to the membership committee. I have to talk to you and make a report. The committee passes on the report and then the membership votes on you. So you see, if I question you pretty deep, I just have to." He poured milk into his coffee, and then he looked up, and his eyes smiled for a second.

"Sure, I know," said Jim. "I've heard you're more select than the Union League Club."

"By God, we have to be!" He shoved the sugar bowl at Jim, then suddenly, "Why do you want to join the Party?"

Jim stirred his coffee. His face wrinkled up in concentration. He looked down into his lap. "Well—I could give you a lot of little reasons. Mainly, it's this: My whole family has been ruined by this system. My old man, my father, was slugged so much in labor trouble that he went punch-drunk. He got an idea that he'd like to dynamite a slaughter-house where he used to work. Well, he caught a charge of buckshot in the chest from a riot gun."

Harry interrupted, "Was your father Roy Nolan?"

"Yeah. Killed three years ago."

"Jesus!" Harry said. "He had a reputation for being the toughest mug in the country. I've heard he could lick five cops with his bare hands."

Jim grinned. "I guess he could, but every time he went out he met six. He always got the hell beat out of him. He used to come home all covered with blood. He'd sit beside the cook stove. We had to let him alone then. Couldn't even speak to him or he'd cry. When my mother washed him later, he'd whine like a dog." He paused. "You know he was a sticker in the slaughter-house. Used to drink warm blood to keep up his strength."

Nilson looked quickly at him, and then away. He bent the corner of the application card and creased it down with his thumb nail. "Your mother is alive?" he asked softly.

Jim's eyes narrowed. "She died a month ago," he said. "I was in jail. Thirty days for vagrancy. Word came in she was dying. They let me go home with a cop. There wasn't anything the matter with her. She wouldn't talk at all. She was a Catholic, only my old man wouldn't let her go to church. He hated churches. She just stared at me. I asked her if she wanted a priest, but she didn't answer me, just stared. 'Bout four o'clock in the morning she died. Didn't seem like dying at all. I didn't go to the funeral. I guess they would've let me. I didn't want to. I guess she just didn't want to live. I guess she didn't care if she went to hell, either."

Harry started nervously. "Drink your coffee and have some more. You act half asleep. You don't take anything, do you?"

"You mean dope? No, I don't even drink."

Nilson pulled out a piece of paper and made a few notes on it. "How'd you happen to get vagged?"

Jim said fiercely, "I worked in Tulman's Department Store. Head of the wrapping department. I was out to a picture show one night, and coming home I saw a crowd in Lincoln Square. I stopped to see what it was all about. There was a guy in the middle of the park talking. I climbed up on the pedestal of that statue of Senator Morgan so I could see better. And then I heard the sirens. I was watching the riot squad come in from the other side. Well, a squad came up from behind, too. Cop slugged me from behind, right in the back of the neck. When I came to I was already booked for vagrancy. I was rumdum for a long time. Got hit right here." Jim put his fingers on the back of his neck at the base of his skull. "Well, I told 'em I wasn't a vagrant and had a job, and told 'em to call up Mr. Webb, he's manager at Tulman's. So they did. Webb asked where I was picked up, and the sergeant said 'at a radical meeting,' and then Webb said he never heard of me. So I got the rap."

Nilson plugged in the hot plate again. The coffee

started rumbling in the pot. "You look half drunk, Jim. What's the matter with you?"

"I don't know. I feel dead. Everything in the past is gone. I checked out of my rooming house before I came here. I still had a week paid for. I don't want to go back to any of it again. I want to be finished with it."

Nilson poured the coffee cups full. "Look, Jim, I want to give you a picure of what it's like to be a Party member. You'll get a chance to vote on every decision, but once the vote's in, you'll have to obey. When we have money we try to give field workers twenty' dollars a month to eat on. I don't remember a time when we ever had the money. Now listen to the work: In the field you'll have to work alongside the men, and you'll have to do the Party work after that, sometimes sixteen, eighteen hours a day. You'll have to get your food where you can. Do you think you could do that?"

"Yes."

Nilson touched the desk here and there with his fingertips. "Even the people you're trying to help will hate you most of the time. Do you know that?"

"Yes."

"Well, why do you want to join, then?"

Jim's grey eyes half closed in perplexity. At last he said, "In the jail there were some Party men. They talked to me. Everything's been a mess, all my life. Their lives weren't messes. They were working toward something. I want to work toward something. I feel dead. I thought I might get alive again."

Nilson nodded. "I see. You're God-damn right I see. How long did you go to school?"

"Second year in high-school. Then I went to work."

"But you talk as though you had more school than that."

Jim smiled. "I've read a lot. My old man didn't want me to read. He said I'd desert my own people. But I read anyway. One day I met a man in the park. He made lists of things for me to read. Oh, I've read a hell of a lot. He made lists like Plato's *Republic*, and the *Utopia*, and Bellamy, and like Herodotus and Gibbon and Macaulay and Carlyle and Prescott, and like Spinoza and Hegel and Kant and Nietzsche and Schopenhauer. He even made me read *Das Kapital*. He was a crank, he said. He said he wanted to know things without believing them. He liked to group books that all aimed in the same direction."

Harry Nilson was quiet for a while. Then he said, "You see why we have to be so careful. We only have two punishments, reprimand and expulsion. You've got to want to belong to the Party pretty badly. I'm going to recommend you, 'cause I think you're a good man; you might get voted down, though."

"Thanks," said Jim.

"Now listen, have you any relatives who might suffer if you use your right name?"

"I've an uncle, Theodore Nolan. He's a mechanic. Nolan's an awful common name."

"Yeah, I guess it is common. Have you any money?"

"About three dollars. I had some, but I spent it for the funeral."

"Well, where you going to stay?"

"I don't know. I cut off from everything. I wanted to start new. I didn't want to have anything hanging over."

Nilson looked around at the cot. "I live in this office," he said. "I eat and sleep and work here. If you want to sleep on the floor, you can stay here for a few days."

Jim smiled with pleasure. "I'd like that. The bunks in jail weren't any softer than your floor."

"Well, have you had any dinner?"

"No. I forgot it."

Nilson spoke irritably. "If you think I'm chiseling,

go ahead," he said. "I haven't any money. You have three dollars."

Jim laughed. "Come on, we'll get dried herrings and cheese and bread. And we'll get stuff for a stew tomorrow. I can make a pretty good stew."

Harry Nilson poured the last of the coffee into the mugs. "You're waking up, Jim. You're looking better. But you don't know what you're getting into. I can tell you about it, but it won't mean anything until you go through it."

Jim looked evenly at him. "Did you ever work at a job where, when you got enough skill to get a raise in pay, you were fired and a new man put in? Did you ever work in a place where they talked about loyalty to the firm, and loyalty meant spying on the people around you? Hell, I've got nothing to lose."

"Nothing except hatred," Harry said quietly. "You're going to be surprised when you see that you stop hating people. I don't know why it is, but that's what usually happens."

2

ALL DURING the day Jim had been restive. Harry Nilson, working on a long report, had turned on him several times in exasperation. "Look," he said finally, "you can go down to the spot alone if you want. There's no reason why you can't. But in an hour I'll go down with you. I've got to finish this thing."

"I wonder if I ought to change my name," said Jim. "I wonder if changing your name would have any effect on you."

Nilson turned back to his report. "You get some tough assignments and go to jail enough and change your name a few times, and a name won't mean any more to you than a number."

Jim stood by the window and looked out. A brick wall was opposite, bounding the other side of a narrow vacant lot between two buildings. A crowd of boys played handball against the building. Their yells came faintly through the closed window.

"I used to play in lots when I was a kid," Jim said. "Seems to me we fought most of the time. I wonder if the kids fight as much as they used to."

Harry did not pause in his writing. "Sure they do," he said. "I look out and see 'em down there. Sure they fight."

"I used to have a sister," Jim went on. "She could lick nearly everybody in the lot. She was the best marble shot I ever saw. Honest, Harry, I've seen her split an agate at ten feet, with her knuckles down, too."

Harry looked up. "I didn't know you had a sister. What happened to her?"

"I don't know," said Jim.

"You don't know?"

"No. It was funny—I don't mean funny. It was one of those things that happen."

"What do you mean, you don't know what happened to her?" Harry laid his pencil down.

"Well, I can tell you about it," said Jim. "Her name was May. She was a year older than I was. We always slept in the kitchen. Each had a cot. When May was about fourteen and I was thirteen, she hung a sheet across the corner to make a kind of a little closet to dress and undress behind. She got giggly, too. Used to sit on the steps downstairs with a lot of other girls, and giggle when boys went by. She had yellow hair. She was kind of pretty, I guess. Well, one evening I came home from playing ball over on Twenty-third and Fulton—used to be a vacant lot, there's a bank there now. I climbed up to our flat. My mother said, 'Did you see May down on the steps?' I said I hadn't. Pretty soon my old man came home from work. He said, 'Where's May?' My mother said, 'She hasn't come in yet.'

"It's funny how this whole thing stands out, Harry. I remember every bit of it, what everybody said, and how everybody looked.

"We waited dinner a while, but pretty soon my old man stuck out his chin and got mad. 'Put on the food,' he said. 'May's getting too smart. She thinks she's too big to get licked.'

"My mother had light blue eyes. I remember they looked like white stones. Well, after dinner my old man sat in his chair by the stove. And he got madder and madder. My mother sat beside him. I went to bed. I could see my mother turn her head from my father and move her lips. I guess she was praying. She was a Catholic, but my father hated churches. Every little while he'd growl out what he'd do to May when she did come home.

"About eleven o'clock both of 'em went into the bedroom, but they left the light burning in the kitchen.

I could hear them talking for a long time. Two or three times in the night I woke up and saw my mother looking out from the bedroom. Her eyes looked just like white stones."

Jim turned from the window and sat down on the cot. Harry was digging his pencil into the desk top. Jim said, "When I woke up the next morning it was sunshiny outside, and that light was still burning. It gives you a funny, lonely feeling to see a light burning in the daytime. Pretty soon my mother came out of the bedroom and started a fire in the stove. Her face was stiff, and her eyes didn't move much. Then my father came out. He acted just as though he'd been hit between the eyes—slugged. He couldn't get a word out. Just before he went to work, he said, 'I think I'll stop in at the precinct station. She might of got run over.'

"Well, I went to school, and right after school I came home. My mother told me to ask all the girls if they'd seen May. By that time the news had got around that May was gone. They said they hadn't seen May at all. They were all shivery about it. Then my father came home. He'd been to the police station on the way home, too. He said, 'The cops took a description. They said they'd keep their eyes peeled.'

"That night was just like the one before. My old man and my mother sitting side by side, only my father didn't do any talking that second night. They left the light on all night again. The next day my old man went back to the station house. Well, the cops sent a dick to question the kids on the block, and a cop came and talked to my mother. Finally they said they'd keep their eyes open. And that was all. We never heard of her again, ever."

Harry stabbed the desk and broke his pencil point. "Was she going around with any older boys she might've run off with?"

"I don't know. The girls said not, and they would have known."

"But haven't you an idea of what might have happened to her?"

"No. She just disappeared one day, just dropped out of sight. The same thing happened to Bertha Riley two years later—just dropped out."

Jim felt with his hand along the line of his jaw. "It might have been my imagination, but it seemed to me that my mother was quieter even than before. She moved kind of like a machine, and she hardly ever said anything. Her eyes got a kind of a dead look, too. But it made my old man mad. He had to fight everything with his fists. He went to work and beat hell out of the foreman at the Monel packing house. Then he did ninety days for assault."

Harry stared out the window. Suddenly he put down his pencil and stood up. "Come on!" he said. "I'm going to take you down to the house and get rid of you. I've got to get that report out. I'll do it when I get back."

Jim walked to the radiator and picked off two pairs of damp socks. He rolled them up and put them in his paper bag. "I'll dry them down at the other place," he said.

Harry put on his hat, and folded the report and put it in his pocket. "Every once in a while the cops go through this place," he explained. "I don't leave anything around." He locked the office door as he went out.

They walked through the business center of the city, and past blocks of apartment houses. At last they came to a district of old houses, each in its own yard. Harry turned into a driveway. "Here we are. It's in back of this house." They followed the gravelled drive, and in back came to a tiny cottage, newly painted. Harry walked to the door and opened it, and motioned Jim inside.

The cottage contained one large room and a kitchenette. In the big room there were six steel cots, made up with army blankets. Three men were in the room, two lying on cots and one large man, with the face of a scholarly prizefighter, pecking slowly at a typewriter.

He looked up quickly when Harry opened the door, and then stood up and came forward smiling. "Hello, Harry," he said. "What's on your mind?"

"This is Jim Nolan," Harry explained. "Remember? His name came up the other night. Jim, this is Mac. He knows more about field work than anybody in the state."

Mac grinned. "Glad to see you, Jim," he said.

Harry, turning to go, said, "Take care of him, Mac. Put him to work. I've got to get out a report." He waved to the two who were lying down. " 'Bye, boys."

When the door was closed, Jim looked about the room. The wallboarded walls were bare. Only one chair was in the room, and that stood in front of the typewriter. From the kitchenette came an odor of boiling corned beef. He looked back at Mac, at his broad shoulders and long arms, at his face, wide between the cheekbones with flat planes under the eyes like those of a Swede. Mac's lips were dry and cracked. He looked at Jim as closely as he was being inspected.

Suddenly he said, "Too bad we're not dogs, we could get that all over with. We'd either be friends or fighting by now. Harry said you were O.K., and Harry knows. Come on, meet the boys. This pale one here is Dick, a bedroom radical. We get many a cake because of Dick."

The pale, dark-haired boy on the bed grinned and held out his hand.

Mac went on, "See how beautiful he is? We call him

the Decoy. He tells ladies about the working classes, and we get cakes with pink frosting, huh, Dick?"

"Go to hell," said Dick pleasantly.

Mac, guiding Jim by his arm, turned him toward the man on the other cot. It was impossible to tell how old he was. His face was wizened and battered, his nose crushed flat against his face; his heavy jaw sagged sideways. "This is Joy," said Mac. "Joy is a veteran, aren't you, Joy?"

"Damn right," said Joy. His eyes flared up, then almost instantly the light went out of them again. His head twitched several times. He opened his mouth to speak, but he only repeated, "Damn right," very solemnly, as though it finished off an argument. He caressed one hand with the other. Jim saw that they were crushed and scarred.

Mac explained, "Joy won't shake hands with anybody. Bones are all broken. It hurts Joy to shake hands."

The light flared in Joy's eyes again. "Why is it?" he cried shrilly. " 'Cause I've been beat, that's why! I been handcuffed to a bar and beat over the head. I been stepped on by horses." He shouted, "I been beat to hell, ain't I, Mac?"

"That's right, Joy."

"And did I ever crawl, Mac? Didn't I keep on calling 'em sons-of-bitches till they knocked me cold?"

"That's right, Joy. And if you'd kept your trap shut, they wouldn't have knocked you cold."

Joy's voice rose to a frenzy. "But they was sons-of-bitches. I told 'em, too. Let 'em beat me over the head with my hands in 'cuffs. Let 'em ride over me! See that hand? That was rode over with a horse. But I told 'em, didn't I, Mac?"

Mac leaned over and patted him. "You sure did, Joy. Nobody's going to make you keep quiet."

"Damn right," said Joy, and the light went out of his eyes again.

Mac said, "Come on over here, Jim." He led him to the other end of the room, where the typewriter stood on a little table. "Know how to type?"

"A little," said Jim.

"Thank God! You can get right to work." Mac lowered his voice. "Don't mind Joy. He's slug-nutty. He's been smacked over the head too much. We take care of him and try to keep him out of trouble."

"My old man was like that," said Jim. "One time I found him in the street. He was walking in big circles off to the left. I had to steer him straight. A scab had smashed him under the ear with a pair of brass knuckles. Seemed to affect his sense of direction."

"Now look here," said Mac. "Here's a general letter. I've got four carbons in the typewriter. We've got to have twenty copies. You want to get to it while I fix some supper?"

"Sure," said Jim.

"Well, hit the keys hard. Those carbon sheets aren't much good." Mac went into the kitchen calling, "Dick, come out and peel some onions if you can stand the horrible smell."

Dick got up from the couch; after rolling the sleeves of his white shirt neatly above his elbows, he followed Mac into the kitchen.

Jim had just started his heavy, deliberate typing when Joy eased himself off the couch and walked over. "Who produces the goods?" Joy demanded.

"Why—the workers," said Jim.

A foxy look came on Joy's face, a very wise and secret look. "And who takes the profits?"

"The people with invested capital."

Joy shouted, "But they don't produce nothing. What right they got to the profits?"

Mac looked in through the kitchen door. He walked quickly over, a stirring spoon in his hand. "Now listen to me, Joy," he said. "Stop trying to convert our own people. Jesus Christ, it seems to me our guys spend most of their time converting each other. Now you go back and rest, Joy. You're tired. Jim here's got work to do. After he finishes, I'll maybe let you address some of the letters, Joy."

"Will you, Mac? Well, I sure told 'em, didn't I, Mac? Even when they was smackin' me, I told 'em."

Mac took him gently by the elbow and led him back to his cot. "Here's a copy of *New Masses*. You just look at the pictures till I get dinner ready."

Jim pounded away at the letter. He wrote it four times and laid the twenty copies beside the typewriter. He called into the kitchen, "Here they are, all ready, Mac."

Mac came in and looked at some of the copies. "Why, you type fine, Jim. You don't cross out hardly anything. Now here's some envelopes. Put these letters in. We'll address 'em after we eat."

Mac filled the plates with corned beef and carrots and potatoes and raw sliced onions. Each man retired to his cot to eat. The daylight was dim in the room until Mac turned on a powerful unshaded light that hung from the center of the ceiling.

When they had finished, Mac went into the kitchen again and returned with a platter of cup cakes. "Here's some more of Dick's work," he said. "That Dick uses the bedroom for political purposes. Gentlemen, I give you the DuBarry of the Party!"

"You go to hell," said Dick.

Mac picked up the sealed envelopes from Jim's bed. "Here's twenty letters. That's five for each one of us to address." He pushed the plates aside on the table, and from a drawer brought out a pen and a bottle of ink.

Then, drawing a list from his pocket, he carefully addressed five of the envelopes. "Your turn, Jim. You do these five."

"What's it for?" Jim asked.

"Well, I guess it don't make much difference, but it might make it a little harder. We're getting our mail opened pretty regular. I just thought it might make it a little harder for the dicks if all these addresses were in different writing. We'll put one of each in a mailbox, you see. No good looking for trouble."

While the other two men were writing their addresses, Jim picked up the dishes, carried them into the kitchen and stacked them on the sinkboard.

Mac was stamping the letters and putting them into his pocket when Jim came back. Mac said, "Dick, you and Joy wash the dishes tonight. I did 'em alone last night. I'm going out to mail these letters. Want to walk with me, Jim?"

"Sure," said Jim. "I've got a dollar. I'll get some coffee, and we'll have some when we get back."

Mac held out his hand. "We've got some coffee. We'll get a dollar's worth of stamps."

Jim handed him the dollar. "That cleans me," he said. "It's the last cent I have." He followed Mac out into the evening. They walked along the street looking for mailboxes. "Is Joy really nuts?" Jim asked.

"Pretty nuts, all right. You see the last thing that happened to him was the worst. Joy was speaking at a barber shop. The barber put in a call and the cops raided the meeting. Well, Joy's a pretty tough fighter. They had to break his jaw with a night stick to stop him; then they threw him in the can. Well, I don't know how Joy did much talking with a busted jaw, but he must have worked on the doctor in the jail some, 'cause the doctor said he wouldn't treat a God-damn red, and Joy lay there three full days with a broken jaw. He's been screwy ever since. I expect he'll be put away pretty soon. He's just taken it on the conk too often."

"Poor devil," said Jim.

Mac drew his bundle of envelopes from his pocket and collected five in different handwritings. "Well, Joy just never learned to keep his mouth shut. Look at Dick. Not a mark on him. And that pretty Dick's just as tough as Joy is when there's some good in it. But just as soon as Dick gets picked up he starts calling the cops 'sir,' and they got him sitting in their laps before he gets through with them. Joy's got no more sense than a bulldog."

They found the last of four mailboxes on the edge of Lincoln Square, and after Mac had deposited his letters the two of them strolled slowly up the brick walk. The maples were beginning to drop leaves on the path. Only a few of the benches along the walks were occupied. The high-hung park lights were on now, casting black patterns of the trees on the ground. Not far from the center of the square stood a statue of a bearded man in a frock coat. Jim pointed to it. "I was standing up on that pedestal," he said. "I was trying to see what was going on. A cop must've reached up and swatted me the way a man swats a fly. I knew a little how Joy feels. It was four or five days before I could think straight. Little pictures went flying through my head, and I couldn't quite catch them. Right in the back of the neck I got it."

Mac turned to a bench and sat down. "I know," he said. "I read Harry's report. Is that the only reason you wanted to join the Party?"

"No," said Jim. "When I got in jail, there were five other men in the same cell, picked up at the same time—a Mexican and a Negro and a Jew and a couple of plain mongrel Americans like me. 'Course they talked to me, but it wasn't that. I'd read more than they knew." He picked up a maple leaf from the ground and began carefully stripping the covering from the hand-like skeleton.

"Look," he said. "All the time at home we were fighting, fighting something—hunger mostly. My old man was fighting the bosses. I was fighting the school. But always we lost. And after a long time I guess it got to be part of our mind-stuff that we always would lose. My old man was fighting just like a cat in a corner with a pack of dogs around. Sooner or later a dog was sure to kill him; but he fought anyway. Can you see the hopelessness in that? I grew up in that hopelessness."

"Sure, I can see," Mac said. "There's millions of people with just that."

Jim waved the stripped leaf in front of him, and spun it between his thumb and forefinger. "There was more than that to it," he said. "The house where we lived was always filled with anger. Anger hung in the house like smoke; that beaten, vicious anger against the boss, against the superintendent, against the groceryman when he cut off credit. It was an anger that made you sick to your stomach, but you couldn't help it."

"Go on," said Mac. "I don't see where you're getting, but maybe you do."

Jim jumped up and stood in front of the bench and whipped the leaf skeleton across his palm. "I'm getting to this: In that cell were five men all raised in about the same condition. Some of them worse, even. And while there was anger in them, it wasn't the same kind of anger. They didn't hate a boss or a butcher. They hated the whose system of bosses, but that was a different thing. It wasn't the same kind of anger. And there was something else, Mac. The hopelessness wasn't in them. They were quiet, and they were working; but in the back of every mind there was conviction that sooner or later they would win their way out of the system they hated. I tell you, there was a kind of peacefulness about those men."

"Are you trying to convert me?" Mac asked sarcastically.

"No, I'm trying to tell you. I'd never known any hope or peacefulness, and I was hungry for it. I probably knew more about so-called radical movements than any of those men. I'd read more, but they had the thing I wanted, and they'd got it by working."

Mac said sharply, "Well, you typed a few letters tonight. Do you feel any better?"

Jim sat down again. "I liked doing it, Mac," he said softly. "I don't know why. It seemed a good thing to be doing. It seemed to have some meaning. Nothing I ever did before had any meaning. It was all just a mess. I don't think I resented the fact that someone profited from the mess, but I did hate being in the rat-cage."

Mac thrust his legs out straight before him and put his hands in his pockets. "Well," he said, "if work will keep you happy, you've got a pretty jolly time ahead of you. If you'll learn to cut stencils and run a mimeograph I can almost guarantee you twenty hours a day. And if you hate the profit system, I can promise you, Jim, you won't get a damn cent for it." His voice was genial.

Jim said, "Mac, you're the boss in the joint back there, aren't you?"

"Me? No, I tell 'em what to do, but they don't have to do it. I can't issue any orders. The only orders that really stick are the ones that come down after a vote."

"Well, anyway, you've got some say, Mac. What I'd really like to do is get into the field. I'd like to get into the action."

Mac laughed softly. "You want punishment, don't you? Well, I don't know but what the committee'll think a hell of a lot more of a good typist. You'll have to put romance off for a while—the noble Party assaulted by the beast of Capitalism." Suddenly his tone changed and he turned on Jim. "It's all work," he said. "In the field it's hard work and dangerous work. But don't think it's so soft at the joint, either. You don't know what night a bunch of American Legioners all full of whisky and drum-corps music may come down and beat hell out of you. I've been through it, I tell you. There's no veteran like the man who got drafted into the army and served six months in a training camp punching a bayonet into a sack of sawdust. The men who were in the trenches are mostly different; but for pure incendiarism and brass knuckle patriotism, give me twenty training camp ex-soldiers. Why, twenty of 'em will protect their country from five kids any dark night when they can get a little whisky. Most of 'em got their wound stripes because they were too drunk to go to a prophylaxis station."

Jim chuckled. "You don't like soldiers much, do you, Mac?"

"I don't like the ex-soldiers with the gold hats. I was in France. They were good, honest, stupid cattle. They didn't like it, but they were nice guys." His voice sobered down. Jim saw him grin quickly in embarrassment. "I got hot, didn't I, Jim? I'll tell you why. Ten of the brave bastards licked me one night. And after they'd licked me unconscious they jumped on me and broke my right arm. And then they set fire to my mother's house. My mother pulled me out in the front yard."

"What happened?" Jim asked. "What were you doing?"

The sarcasm came back into Mac's voice. "Me? I was subverting the government. I'd made a speech saying there were some people starving." He stood up. "Let's go back, Jim. They ought to have the dishes washed up by now. I didn't mean to get bitter, but somehow that busted arm still makes me mad."

They walked slowly back down the path. A few men on the benches pulled in their legs to let them by.

Jim said, "If you can ever put in a word, Mac, so I can get out in the field to work, I'll be glad."

"O.K. But you'd better learn to cut stencils and run a mimeograph. You're a good kid; I'm glad to have you with us."

3

JIM SAT under the hard white light typewriting letters. Occasionally he stopped and listened, his ears turned toward the door. Except for a kettle simmering huskily in the kitchen, the house was still. The soft roar of streetcars on distant streets, the slap of feet on the pavement in front only made the inside seem more quiet. He looked up at the alarm clock hanging to a nail on the wall. He got up and went into the kitchen and stirred the stew, and turned down the gas until each jet held a tiny blue globe.

As he went back to the typewriter he heard quick steps on the gravelled path. Dick came bursting into the house. "Mac's not here yet?"

"No," said Jim. "He hasn't got here. Neither has Joy. Collect any money today?"

"Twenty dollars," said Dick.

"Boy, you sure do it, I don't know how. We could eat for a month on that; but Mac'll probably spend it all on stamps. Lord, how he goes through stamps."

"Listen," Dick cried. "I think I hear Mac now."

"Or Joy."

"No, it's not Joy."

The door opened and Mac entered. "Hello, Jim. Hello, Dick. Get any money out of the sympathizers today?"

"Twenty dollars."

"Good boy!"

"Say, Mac, Joy did it this afternoon."

"Did what?"

"Well, he started a crazy speech on a street corner and a cop picked him up, and Joy stuck the cop in the shoulder with a pocket knife. They got him locked up, and they got felonious assault on the book. He's sitting in a cell right now, yelling 'son-of-a-bitch' at the top of his lungs."

"I thought he was screwier than usual this morning. Now listen, Dick. I've got to get out of here tomorrow morning, and I've got things to do now. You run to a public phone and call George Camp, Ottman 4211. Tell him the works, and tell him Joy's nuts. Tell him to get down there if he can and say he's Joy's attorney. Joy's got a sweet record if they put it on him—about six incites to riot, twenty or thirty vagrancies, and about a dozen resists and simple assaults. They'll give him the works if George doesn't get busy. Tell George to try to spring him for a drunk." He paused. "Jesus! If a sanity board ever gets hold of that poor devil, he's in for life. Tell George to try to get Joy to keep his mouth shut. And when you do that, Dick, you make the rounds and try to pick up some bail money—in case."

"Can't I eat first?" Dick asked.

"Hell, no. Get George down there. Here, give me ten of the twenty. Jim and I are going down to the Torgas Valley tomorrow. After you call George, come back and eat. And then start rounding up the sympathizers for bail. I hope to God George can get out a writ and get bail set sometime tonight."

Dick said, "O.K.," and hurried out.

Mac turned to Jim. "I guess they'll have to lock poor Joy up pretty soon, for good. He's a long way gone. This is the first time he ever used a knife."

Jim pointed to a pile of finished letters on the desk. "There they are, Mac. Three more to do, that's all. Where'd you say we're going?"

"Down the Torgas Valley. There're thousands of acres of apples ready to pick down there. Be damn near two thousand fruit camps. Well, the Growers' Association just announced a pay cut to the pickers. They'll be sore as hell. If we can't get a good ruckus going down there we might be able to spread it over to the cotton fields in Tandale. And then we *would* have something. That'd be a fuss!" He sniffed the air. "Say, that stew smells swell. Is it ready?"

"I'll dish it up," said Jim. He brought in two bowls half full of soup, out of which arose a mound of meat squares, potatoes and carrots, pale turnips and steaming whole onions.

Mac put his bowl on the table and tasted it. "Christ! Let it cool. It's like this, Jim, I always said we shouldn't send green men into trouble areas. They make too many mistakes. You can read all the tactics you want and it won't help much. Well, I remembered what you said in the park that night when you first came, so when I got this assignment, and it's a nice assignment, I asked if I could take you along as a kind of understudy. I've been out, see? I'll train you, and then you can train new men. Kind of like teaching hunting dogs by running them with the old boys, see? You can learn more by getting into it than by reading all you like. Ever been in the Torgas Valley, Jim?"

Jim blew on a hot potato. "I don't even know where it is," he said. "I've only been out of town four or five times in my life. Thanks for taking me, Mac." His small grey eyes were ashine with excitement.

"You'll probably cuss hell out of me before we're through if we get in a mess down there. It's going to be no picnic. I hear the Growers' Association is pretty well organized."

Jim gave up trying to eat the hot stew. "How we going to go about it, Mac? What do we do first?"

Mac looked over at him and saw his excitement, and laughed. "I don't know, Jim. That's the trouble with reading, you see. We just have to use any material we can pick up. That's why all the tactics in the world won't do it. No two are exactly alike." For a while he ate in silence, finished off his stew, and when he exhaled, steam came out of his mouth. "Enough for another helping, Jim? I'm hungry."

Jim went to the kitchen and filled his bowl again.

Mac said, "Here's the layout. Torgas is a little valley, and it's mostly apple orchards. Most of it's owned by a few men. Of course there's some little places, but there's not very many of them. Now when the apples are ripe the crop tramps come in and pick them. And from there they go on over the ridge and south, and pick the cotton. If we can start the fun in the apples, maybe it will just naturally spread over into the cotton. Now these few guys that own most of the Torgas Valley waited until most of the crop tramps were already there. They spent most of their money getting there, of course. They always do. And then the owners announced their price cut. Suppose the tramps are mad? What can they do? They've got to work picking apples to get out even."

Jim's dinner was neglected. With his spoon he stirred the meat and potatoes around and around. He leaned forward. "So then we try to get the men to strike? Is that it?"

"Sure. Maybe it's all ready to bust and we just give it a little tiny push. We organize the men, and then we picket the orchards."

Jim said, "Suppose the owners raise the wages to get their apples picked?"

Mac pushed away his finished second bowl. "Well, we'd find another job to do somewhere else soon enough. Hell, we don't want only temporary pay raises, even though we're glad to see a few poor bastards better off. We got to take the long view. A strike that's settled too quickly won't teach the men how to organize, how to work together. A tough strike is good. We want the men to find out how strong they are when they work together."

"Well, suppose," Jim insisted, "suppose the owners do meet the demands?"

"I don't think they will. There's the bulk of power in the hands of a few men. That always makes 'em cocky. Now we start our strike, and Torgas County gets itself an ordinance that makes congregation unlawful. Now what happens? We congregate the men. A bunch of sheriff's men try to push them around, and that starts a fight. There's nothing like a fight to cement the men together. Well, then the owners start a vigilantes committee, bunch of fool shoe clerks, or my friends the American Legion boys trying to pretend they aren't middle-aged, cinching in their belts to hide their pot-bellies—there I go again. Well, the vigilantes start shooting. If they knock over some of the tramps we have a public funeral; and after that, we get some real action. Maybe they have to call out the troops." He was breathing hard in excitement. "Jesus, man! The troops win, all right! But every time a guardsman jabs a fruit tramp with a bayonet a thousand men all over the country come on our side. Christ Almighty! If we can only get the troops called out." He settled back on his cot. "Aw, I'm looking ahead too much. Our job's just to push along our little baby strike, if we can. But God damn it, Jim, if we could get the National Guard called out, now with the crops coming ready, we'd have the whole district organized by spring."

Jim had been crouching on his bed, his eyes shining and his jaws set. Now and then his fingers went nervously to his throat. Mac continued, "The damn fools think they can settle strikes with soldiers." He laughed. "Here I go again—talking like a soap-boxer. I get all worked up, and that's not so good. We got to think good. Oh say, Jim, have you got some blue jeans?"

"No. This suit's all the clothes I own."

"Well, we'll have to go out and buy you some in a second-hand store, then. You're going to pick apples, boy. And you're going to sleep in jungles. And you're going to do Party work after you've done ten hours in the orchard. Here's the work you wanted."

Jim said, "Thanks, Mac. My old man always had to fight alone. He got licked every time."

Mac came and stood over him. "Get those three letters finished, Jim, and then we'll go out and buy you some jeans."

4

THE SUN was just clearing the buildings of the city when Jim and Mac came to the railroad yards, where the shining metals converged and separated and spread out into the great gridiron of storage tracks where line after line of cars stood.

Mac said, "There's a freight train supposed to go out at seven-thirty, empties. Let's go down the track a way." He hurried through the yard toward the end, where the many tracks drew together into the main line.

"Do we have to get it on the move?" Jim asked.

"Oh, it won't be going fast. I forgot, you never caught a freight, did you?"

Jim spread his stride in an attempt to walk on every other tie, and found he couldn't quite make it. "Seems to me I never did much of anything," he admitted. "Everything's new to me."

"Well, it's easy now. The company lets guys ride. In the old days it was tough. Train crews used to throw the stiffs off a moving train when they could catch them."

A great black water tower stood beside the track, its goose-neck spout raised up against its side. The multitude of tracks was behind them, and only one line of worn and mirror-polished rails extended ahead. "Might as well sit down and wait," said Mac. "She'll be along pretty soon now."

The long, lonely howl of a train whistle and the slow crash of escaping steam sounded at the end of his words. And at the signal, men began to stand up out of the ditch beside the track and to stretch their arms lazily in the cool morning sun.

"We're going to have company," Mac observed.

The long freight of empties came slowly down the yard, red box-cars and yellow refrigerator cars, black iron gondolas and round tank cars. The engine went by at little more pace than a man could walk, and the engineer waved a black, shiny glove at the men in the ditch. He yelled, "Going to the picnic?" and playfully released a spurt of white steam from between the wheels.

Mac said, "We want a box-car. There, that one. The door's open a little." Trotting beside the car he pushed at the door. "Give a hand," he called. Jim put his hand to the iron handle and threw his weight against it. The big sliding door screeched rustily open a few feet. Mac put his hands on the sill, vaulted, turned in the air and landed in a sitting position in the doorway. Quickly he stood up out of the way while Jim imitated him. The floor of the car was littered with lining paper, torn down from the walls. Mac kicked a pile of the paper together and forced it against the wall. "Get yourself some," he shouted. "It makes a nice cushion."

Before Jim had piled up his paper, a new head appeared in the doorway. A man flung himself in and two more followed him. The first man looked quickly about the car floor and then stood over Mac. "Got just about all of it, didn't you?"

"Got what?" Mac asked innocently.

"The paper. You done a good clean job."

Mac smiled disarmingly. "We didn't know there was guests coming." He stood up. "Here, take some of it."

The man gaped at Mac for a moment, and then he leaned over and picked up the whose cushion of papers.

Mac touched him gently on the shoulder. "All right, punk," he said in a monotone. "Put it all down. If you're going to be a hog you don't get none."

The man dropped the paper. "You going to make me?" he asked.

Mac dropped daintily back, balancing on the balls of

his feet. His hands hung open and loose at his sides. "Do you ever go to the Rosanna Fight Stadium?" he asked.

"Yeah, and what of it?"

"You're a God-damn liar," Mac said. "If you went there, you'd know who I am, and you'd take better care of yourself."

A look of doubt came over the man's face. He glanced uneasily at the two men who had come with him. One stood by the doorway, looking out at the moving country. The other one elaborately cleaned his nostrils with a bandana and inspected his findings. The first man looked at Mac again. "I don't want no trouble," he said. "I just want a little bit of paper to sit on."

Mac dropped on his heels. "O.K.," he said. "Take some. But leave some, too." The man approached the pile and picked up a small handful. "Oh, you can have more than that."

"We ain't goin' far," said the man. He settled down beside the door and clasped his legs with his arms, and rested his chin on his knees.

The blocks were passed now, and the train gathered speed. The wooden car roared like a sounding-box. Jim stood up and pushed the door wide open to let in the morning sunlight. He sat down in the doorway and hung his legs over. For a while he looked down, until the flashing ground made him dizzy. And then he raised his eyes to the yellow stubble fields beside the track. The air was keen and pleasantly flavored with smoke from the engine.

In a moment Mac joined him. "Look you don't fall out," he shouted. "I knew a guy once that got dizzy looking at the ground and fell right out on his face."

Jim pointed to a white farmhouse and a red barn, half hidden behind a row of young eucalyptus trees. "Is the country we're going to as pretty as this?"

"Prettier," said Mac. "It's all apple trees, miles of 'em. They'll be covered with apples this season, just covered with 'em. The limbs just sagging down with apples you pay a nickel apiece for in town."

"Mac, I don't know why I didn't come into the country oftener. It's funny how you want to do a thing and never do it. Once when I was a kid one of those lodges took about five hundred of us on a picnic, took us in trucks. We walked around and around. There were big trees. I remember I climbed up in the top of a tree and sat there most of the afternoon. I thought I'd go back there every time I could. But I never did."

Mac said, "Stand up, Jim. Let's close this door. We're coming to Wilson. No good irritating the railroad cops."

Together they pulled the door shut, and suddenly the car was dark and warm, and it throbbed like the body of a bass viol. The beat of wheels on the rail-ends grew less rapid as the freight slowed to go through the town. The three men stood up. "We get out here," the leader said. He pushed open the door a foot. His two followers swung out. He turned to Mac. "I hope you don't hold no grudge, pardner."

"No, 'course not."

"Well, so long." He swung out. "You dirty son-of-a-bitch," he yelled as he hit the ground.

Mac laughed and pulled the door nearly shut. For a few moments the train rolled slowly. And the rail-end tempo increased. Mac threw the door wide again and sat down in the sun. "There was a beauty," he said.

Jim asked, "Are you really a prize-fighter, Mac?"

"Hell no. He was the easiest kind of a sucker. He figured I was scared of him when I offered him some of my paper. You can't make a general rule of it, because sometimes it flops, but mostly a guy that tries to scare you is a guy that can be scared." He turned his heavy, good-natured face to Jim. "I don't know why it is, but every time I talk to you I either end up soap-boxing or giving a lecture."

"Well, hell, Mac, I like to listen."

"I guess that's it. We've got to get off at Weaver and catch an east-bound freight. That's about a hundred miles down. If we're lucky, we ought to get to Torgas in the middle of the night." He pulled out a sack of tobacco and rolled a cigarette, holding the paper in out of the rushing air. "Smoke, Jim?"

"No, thanks."

"You got no vices, have you. And you're not a Christer either. Don't you even go out with girls?"

"No," said Jim. "Used to be, when I got riled up I'd go to a cat-house. You wouldn't believe it, Mac, but ever since I started to grow up I been scared of girls. I guess I was scared I'd get caught."

"Too attractive, huh?"

"No, you see all the guys I used to run around with went through the mill. They used to try to make girls behind billboards and down in the lumber yard. Well, sooner or later some girl'd get knocked higher than a kite, and then—well, hell, Mac, I was scared I'd get caught like my mother and my old man—two-room flat and a wood stove. Christ knows I don't want luxury, but I don't want to get batted around the way all the kids I knew got it. Lunch pail in the morning with a piece of soggy pie and a thermos bottle of stale coffee."

Mac said, "You've picked a hell of a fine life if you don't want to get batted around. Wait till we finish this job, you'll get batted plenty."

"That's different," Jim protested. "I don't mind getting smacked on the chin. I just don't want to get nibbled to death. There's a difference."

Mac yawned. "It's not a difference that's going to keep me awake. Cat-houses aren't much fun." He got up and went back to the pile of papers, and he spread them out and lay down and went to sleep.

For a long time Jim sat in the doorway, watching the farms go by. There were big market vegetable gardens with rows of round lettuces and rows of fern-like carrots, and red beet leaves, with glistening water running between the rows. The train went by fields of alfalfa, and by great white dairy barns from which the wind brought the rich, healthy smell of manure and ammonia. And then the freight entered a pass in the hills, and the sun was cut off. Ferns and green live oaks grew on the steep sides of the right-of-way. The roaring rhythm of the train beat on Jim's senses and made him drowsy. He fought off sleep so that he might see more of the country, shook his head violently to jar himself awake; but at last he stood up, ran the door nearly closed, and retired to his own pile of papers. His sleep was a shouting, echoing black cave, and it extended into eternity.

Mac shook him several times before he could wake up. "It's nearly time to get off," Mac shouted.

Jim sat up. "Good God, have we gone a hundred miles?"

"Pretty near. Noise kind of drugs you, don't it? I can't ever stay awake in a box-car. Pull yourself together. We're going to slow down in a couple of minutes."

Jim held his dull head between his hands for a moment. "I do feel slugged," he said.

Mac threw open the door. He called, "Jump the way we're going, and land running." He leaped out, and Jim followed him.

Jim looked at the sun, almost straight overhead. In front of him he could see the clustered houses and the shade trees of a little town. The freight pulled on and left them standing.

Mac explained, "The railroad branches here. The line

we want cuts over that way toward the Torgas Valley. We won't go through town at all. Let's jump across the fields and catch the line over there."

Jim followed him over a barbed-wire fence and across a stubble field, and into a dirt road. They skirted the edge of the little town, and in half a mile came upon another railroad right-of-way.

Mac sat down on the embankment and called Jim to sit beside him. "Here's a good place. There's lots of cars moving. I don't know how long we'll have to wait." He rolled a brown cigarette. "Jim," he said. "You ought to take up smoking. It's a nice social habit. You'll have to talk to a lot of strangers in your time. I don't know any quicker way to soften a stranger down than to offer him a smoke, or even to ask him for one. And lots of guys feel insulted if they offer you a cigarette and you don't take it. You better start."

"I guess I will," said Jim. "I used to smoke with the kids. I wonder if it'd make me sick now."

"Try it. Here, I'll roll one for you."

Jim took the cigarette and lighted it. "It tastes pretty good," he said. "I'd almost forgotten what it tasted like."

"Well, even if you don't like it, it's a good thing to do in our work. It's the one little social thing guys in our condition have. Listen, there's a train coming." He stood up. "It looks like a freight, too."

The train came slowly down the track. "Well, for Christ's sake!" Mac cried. "Eighty-seven! It's our own train. They told me in town that train went on south. It must of dropped off a few cars and then come right out."

"Let's get our old car back," said Jim. "I liked that car."

As it came abreast, they hopped aboard the box-car again. Mac settled into his pile of papers. "We might just as well have stayed asleep."

Jim sat in the doorway again, while the train crept into

the round brown hills, and through two short tunnels. He could still taste the tobacco in his mouth, and it tasted good. Suddenly he dug in the pocket of his blue denim coat. "Mac," he cried.

"Yeah? What?"

"Here's a couple of chocolate bars I got last night."

Mac took one of the bars and lazily unwrapped it. "I can see you're going to be an asset in any man's revolution," he said.

In about an hour the drowsiness came upon Jim again. Reluctantly he closed the door of the car and curled up in his papers. Almost instantly he was in the black, roaring cave again, and the sound made dreams of water pouring over him. Vaguely he could see debris and broken bits of wood in the water. And the water bore him down and down into the dark place below dreaming.

He awakened when Mac shook him. "I bet you'd sleep a week if I'd let you. You've put in over twelve hours today."

Jim rubbed his eyes hard. "I feel slugged again."

"Well, get yourself together. We're coming into Torgas."

"Good God, what time is it?"

"Somewhere about midnight, I guess. Here we come; you ready to hop?"

"Sure."

"O.K. Come on."

The train pulled slowly on away from them. The station of Torgas was only a little way ahead, with its red light on and glancing along the blade of the semaphore. The brakeman was swinging a lantern back and forth. Over to the right the lonely, cold street lights of the town burned and put a pale glow in the sky. The air was cold now. A sharp, soundless wind blew.

"I'm hungry," Jim said. "Got any ideas about eating, Mac?"

"Wait till we get to a light. I think I've got a good prospect on my list." He hurried away into the darkness, and Jim trotted after him. They came immediately into the edge of the town, and on a corner, under one of the lights, Mac stopped and pulled out a sheet of paper. "We got a nice town here, Jim," he said. "Nearly fifty active sympathizers. Guys you can rely on to give you a lift. Here's the guy I want. Alfred Anderson, Townsend, between Fourth and Fifth, Al's Lunch Wagon. What do you think of that?"

"What's that paper?" Jim asked.

"Why, it's a list of all the people in town we know to be sympathizers. With this list we can get anything from knitted wristlets to a box of shotgun shells. But Al's Lunch Wagon—lunch wagons generally stay open all night, Jim. Townsend, that'll be one of the main streets. Come on, but let me work this."

They turned soon into the main street, and walked down its length until, near the end, where stores were vacant and lots occurred between buildings, they found Al's Lunch Wagon, a cozy looking little car with red stained glass in the windows, and a sliding door. Through the window they could see that two customers sat on the stools, and that a fat young man with heavy, white, bare arms hovered behind the counter.

"Pie and coffee guys," Mac said. "Let's wait till they finish."

While they loitered, a policeman approached, and eyed them. Mac said loudly, "I don't want to go home till I get a piece of pie."

Jim reacted quickly. "Come on home," he said. "I'm too sleepy to eat."

The policeman passed them. He seemed almost to sniff at them as he went by. Mac said quietly, "He thinks we're trying to get up our nerve to stick up the wagon." The policeman turned and walked back toward them.

Mac said, "Well, go home then, if you want. I'm going to get a piece of pie." He climbed the three steps and slid open the door of the lunch wagon.

The proprietor smiled at them. " 'Evening, gents," he said. "Turning on cold, ain't it?"

"Sure is," said Mac. He walked to the end of the counter farthest from the other two customers and sat down. A shadow of annoyance crossed Al's face.

"Now listen, you guys," he said. "If you got no money you can have a cup of coffee and a couple of sinkers. But don't eat up a dinner on me and then tell me to call a cop. Jesus, I'm being busted by pan-handlers."

Mac laughed shortly. "Coffee and sinkers will be just elegant, Alfred," he said.

The proprietor glanced suspiciously at him and took off his high white cook's hat, and scratched his head.

The customers drained their cups together. One of them asked, "Do you always feed bums, Al?"

"Well, Jesus, what can you do? If a guy wants a cup of coffee on a cold night, you can't let him down because he hasn't got a lousy nickel."

The customer chuckled. "Well, twenty cups of coffee is a dollar, Al. You'll fold up if you go about it that way. Coming, Will?" The two got up and paid their checks and walked out.

Al came around the corner and followed them to the door and slid it more tightly closed. Then he walked back down the counter and leaned over toward Mac. "Who are you guys?" he demanded. He had fat, comfortable white arms, bare to the elbows. He carried a damp cloth with which he wiped and wiped at the counter, with little circular movements. His manner of leaning close when he spoke made every speech seem secret.

Mac winked solemnly, like a conspirator. "We're sent down from the city on business," he said.

A red flush of excitement bloomed on Al's fat cheeks. "Oho-o. That's just what I thought when you come in. How'd you know to come to me?"

Mac explained. "You been good to our people, and we don't forget things like that."

Al beamed importantly, as though he were receiving a gift instead of being bummed for a meal. "Here, wait," he said. "You guys probably ain't ate today. I'll sling on a couple of hamburg steaks."

"That'll be swell," Mac agreed enthusiastically. "We're just about starved."

Al went to his ice-box and dug out two handfuls of ground meat. He patted them thin between his hands, painted the gas plate with a little brush and tossed down the steaks. He put chopped onions on top and around the meat. A delicious odor filled the room instantly.

"Lord," said Mac. "I'd like to crawl right over this counter and nest in that hamburger."

The meat hissed loudly and the onions began to turn brown. Al leaned over the counter again. "What you guys got on down here?"

"Well, you got a lot of nice apples," said Mac.

Al pushed himself upright and leaned against the fat buttresses of his arms. His little eyes grew very wise and secret. "Oho," he said. "O-ho-o, I get you."

"Better turn over that meat, then," said Mac.

Al flipped the steaks and pressed them down with his spatula. And he gathered in the vagrant onions and heaped them on top of the meat, and pressed them in. Very deliberate he was in his motions, as inwardly-thoughtful-looking as a ruminating cow. At last he came back and planted himself in front of Mac. "My old man's got a little orchard and a piece of land," he said. "You guys wouldn't hurt him none, would you? I been good to you."

"Sure you been good," said Mac. "The little farmers

don't suffer from us. You tell your father we won't hurt
him; and if he gives us a break, we'll see his fruit gets
picked."

"Thanks," said Al. "I'll tell him." He took up the
steaks, spooned mashed potatoes on the plates from the
steam table, made a hollow in each potato mountain and
filled the white craters with light brown gravy.

Mac and Jim ate voraciously and drank the mugs of
coffee Al set for them. And they wiped their plates with
bread and ate the bread while Al filled up their coffee
cups again. "That was swell, Al," Jim said. "I was
starved."

Mac added, "It sure was. You're a good guy, Al."

"I'd be along with you," Al explained, "if I didn't
have a business, and if my old man didn't own land. I
guess I'd get this joint wrecked if anybody ever found
out."

"They'll never find out from us, Al."

"Sure, I know that."

"Listen, Al, are there many working stiffs in yet for
the harvest?"

"Yeah, big bunch of them. Good many eat here. I set
up a pretty nice dinner for a quarter—soup, meat, two
vegetables, bread and butter, pie and two cups of coffee
for a quarter. I take a little profit and sell more."

"Good work," said Mac. "Listen, Al, did you hear any
of the stiffs talking about a leader?"

"Leader?"

"Sure, I mean some guy that kind of tells 'em where
to put their feet."

"I see what you mean," said Al. "No, I don't rightly
recall nothing about it."

"Well, where are the guys hanging out?"

Al rubbed his soft chin. "Well, there's two bunches I
know of. One's out on Palo Road, alongside the county
highway, and then there's a bunch jungled up by the

river. There's a regular old jungle down there in the willows."

"That's the stuff. How do we get there?"

Al pointed a thick finger. "You take that cross street and stay on it till you get to the edge of town, and there's the river and the bridge. Then you'll find a path through the willows, off to the left. Follow that about a quarter mile, and there you are. I don't know how many guys is there."

Mac stood up and put on his hat. "You're a good guy, Al. We'll get along now. Thanks for the feed."

Al said, "My old man's got a shed with a cot in it, if you'd like to stay out there."

"Can't do it, Al. If we're going to work, we got to get out among them."

"Well, if you want a bite now and then, come on in," said Al. "Only pick it like tonight when there's nobody here, won't you?"

"Sure, Al. We get you. Thanks again."

Mac let Jim precede him through the door and then slid it closed behind him. They walked down the steps and took the street Al had pointed out. At the corner the policeman stepped out of a doorway. "What's on your mind?" he asked harshly.

Jim jumped back at the sudden appearance, but Mac stood quietly. "Couple of workin' stiffs, mister," he said. "We figure to pick a few apples."

"What you doing on the street this time of night?"

"Hell, we just got off that freight that went through an hour ago!"

"Where you going now?"

"Thought we'd jungle up with the boys down by the river."

The policeman maintained his position in front of them. "Got any money?"

"You saw us buy a meal, didn't you? We got enough to keep out of jail on a vag charge."

The policeman stood aside then. "Well, get going, and keep off the streets at night."

"O.K., mister."

They walked quickly on. Jim said, "You sure talked to him pretty, Mac."

"Why not? That's the first lesson. Never argue with a cop, particularly at night. It'd be swell if we got thirty days for vagrancy right now, wouldn't it?"

They hugged their denim clothes against their chests and hurried along the street, and the lights grew more infrequent.

"How are you going to go about getting started?" Jim asked.

"I don't know. We've got to use everything. Look, we start out with a general plan, but the details have to be worked out with any materials we can find. We use everything we can get hold of. That's the only thing we can do. We'll just look over the situation."

Jim lengthened his stride with a drive of energy. "Well, let me do things, won't you, Mac? I don't want to be a stooge all my life."

Mac laughed. "You'll get used, all right. You'll get used till you'll wish you was back in town with an eight-hour job."

"No, I don't think I will, Mac. I never felt so good before. I'm all swelled up with a good feeling. Do you feel that way?"

"Sometimes," said Mac. "Mostly I'm too damn busy to know how I feel."

The buildings along the street were more dilapidated as they went. Welding works and used car lots and the great trash piles of auto-wrecking yards. The street lights shone on the blank, dead windows of old and neglected houses, and made shadows under shrubs that had gone to brush. The men walked quickly in the cool night air. "I think I see the bridge lights now," Jim said. "See those three lights on each side?"

"I see 'em. Didn't he say turn left?"

"Yeah, left."

It was a two-span concrete bridge over a narrow river that was reduced at this season to a sluggish little creek in the middle of a sandy bed. Jim and Mac went to the left of the bridge ramp, and near the edge of the river bed they found the opening of a trail into the willows. Mac took the lead. In a moment they were out of range of the bridge lights, and the thick willow scrub was all about them. They could see the branches against the lighter sky, and, to the right, on the edge of the river bed, a dark wall of large cottonwoods.

"I can't see this path," Mac said. "I'll just have to feel it with my feet." He moved carefully, slowly. "Hold up your arms to protect your face, Jim."

"I am. I got switched right across the mouth a minute ago." For a while they felt their way along the hard, used trail. "I smell smoke," Jim said. "It can't be far now."

Suddenly Mac stopped. "There's lights ahead. Listen, Jim, the same thing goes as back there. Let me do the talking."

"O.K."

The trail came abruptly into a large clearing, flickeringly lighted by a little bonfire. Along the farther side were three dirty white tents; and in one of them a light burned and huge black figures moved on the canvas. In the clearing itself there were perhaps fifty men, some sleeping on the ground in sausage rolls of blankets, while a number sat around the little fire in the middle of the flat cleared place. As Jim and Mac stepped clear of the willows they heard a short, sharp cry, quickly checked, which came from the lighted tent. Immediately the great shadows moved nervously on the canvas.

"Somebody's sick," Mac said softly. "We didn't hear it yet. It pays to appear to mind your own business."

They moved toward the fire, where a ring of men sat clasping their knees. "Can a guy join this club?" Mac asked, "Or does he got to be elected?"

The faces of the men were turned up at him, unshaven faces with eyes in which the firelight glowed. One of the men moved sideways to make room. "Ground's free, mister."

Mac chuckled. "Not where I come from."

A lean, lighted face across the fire spoke. "You come to a good place, fella. Everything's free here, food, liquor, automobiles, houses. Just move in and set down to a turkey dinner."

Mac squatted and motioned Jim to sit beside him. He pulled out his sack of tobacco and made a careful, excellent cigarette; then, as an afterthought, "Would any of you capitalists like a smoke?"

Several hands thrust out. The bag went from man to man. "Just get in?" the lean face asked.

"Just. Figure to pick a few apples and retire on my income."

Lean-face burst out angrily. "Know what they're payin', fella? Fifteen cents, *fifteen lousy cents!*"

"Well, what do you want?" Mac demanded. "Jesus Christ, man! You ain't got the nerve to say you want to eat? You can eat an apple while you're workin'. All them nice apples!" His tone grew hard. "S'pose we don't pick them apples?"

Lean-face cried, "We got to pick 'em. Spent every God-damned cent gettin' here."

Mac repeated softly, "All them nice apples. If we don't pick 'em, they'll rot."

"If we don't pick 'em, somebody else will."

"S'pose we don't let nobody else pick?" Mac said.

The men about the fire grew tense. "You mean—strike?" Lean-face asked.

Mac laughed. "I don't mean nothin'."

A short man who rested his chin between his knees said, "When London found out what they was payin' he damned near had a stroke." He turned to the man next to him. "You see him, Joe. Didn't he damn near have a stroke?"

"Turned green," said Joe. "Just stood there and turned green. Picked up a stick and bust it to splinters in his hands."

The bag of tobacco came back to its starting place, but there was not much left in it. Mac felt it with his fingers and then put it in his pocket. "Who's London?" he asked.

Lean-face answered him. "London's a good guy—a big guy. We travel with him. He's a big guy."

"The boss, huh?"

"Well, no, he ain't a boss, but he's a good guy. We kind of travel with him. You ought to hear him talk to a cop. He——"

The cry came from the tent again, more prolonged this time. The men turned their heads toward it, and then looked apathetically back at the fire.

"Somebody sick?" Mac asked.

"London's daughter'n-law. She's havin' a kid."

Mac said, "This ain't no place t'have a kid. They got a doctor?"

"Hell no! Where'd they get a doctor?"

"Why'n't they take her to the county hospital?"

Lean-face scoffed. "They won't have no crop tramps in the county hospital. Don't you know that? They got no room. Always full-up."

"I know it," said Mac. "I just wondered if you did."

Jim shivered and picked up a little willow stick and thrust the end into the coals until it flared into flame. Mac's hand came stealing out of the darkness and took his arm for a moment, and gripped it.

Mac asked, "They got anybody that knows anything about it?"

"Got an old woman," Lean-face said. His eyes turned suspicious under the questioning. "Say, what's it to you?"

"I had some training," Mac explained casually. "I know something about it. Thought I might help out."

"Well, go see London." Lean-face shucked off responsibility. "It ain't none of our business to answer questions about him."

Mac ignored the suspicion. "Guess I will." He stood up. "Come on, Jim. Is London in that tent with the light?"

"Yeah, that's him."

A circle of lighted faces watched Jim and Mac walk away, and then the heads swung back to the fire again. The two men picked their way across the clearing, avoiding the bundles of cloth that were sleeping men.

Mac whispered, "What a break! If I can pull it off, we're started."

"What do you mean? Mac, I didn't know you had medical training."

"A whole slough of people don't know it," said Mac. They approached the tent, where dark figures moved about on the canvas. Mac stepped close and called, "London."

Almost instantly the tent-flap bellied and a large man stepped out. His shoulders were immense. Stiff dark hair grew in a tonsure, leaving the top of the head perfectly bald. His face was corded with muscular wrinkles and his dark eyes were as fierce and red as those of a gorilla. A power of authority was about the man. It could be felt that he led men as naturally as he breathed. With one big hand he held the tent-flap closed behind him. "What you want?" he demanded.

"We just got in," Mac explained. "Some guys over by the fire says there was a girl havin' a baby."

"Well, what of it?"

"I thought I might help out as long as you got no doctor."

London opened the flap and let a streak of light fall on Mac's face. "What you think you can do?"

"I worked in hospitals," Mac said. "I done this before. It don't pay to take no chances, London."

The big man's voice dropped. "Come on in," he said. "We got an old woman here, but I think she's nuts. Come in and take a look." He held up the tent-flap for them to enter.

Inside it was crowded and very hot. A candle burned in a saucer. In the middle of the tent stood a stove made of a kerosene can, and beside it sat an old and wrinkled woman. A white-faced boy stood in one corner of the tent. Along the rear wall an old mattress was laid on the ground, and on this lay a young girl, her face pale and streaked with brown dirt, her hair matted. The eyes of all three turned to Mac and Jim. The old woman looked up for a moment and then dropped her eyes to the red-hot stove. She scratched the back of one hand with the nails of the other.

London walked over to the mattress and kneeled down beside it. The girl pulled her frightened eyes from Mac and looked at London. He said, "We got a doctor here now. You don't need to be scared no more."

Mac looked down at her and winked. Her face was stiff with fright. The boy came over from his corner and pawed Mac's shoulder. "She gonna be all right, Doc?"

"Sure, she's O.K."

Mac turned to the old woman. "You a midwife?"

She scratched the backs of her wrinkled hands and looked vacantly up at him, but she didn't answer. "I asked if you was a midwife?" he cried.

"No—but I've took one or two babies in my life."

Mac reached down and picked up one of her hands and held the lighted candle close to it. The nails were long and broken and dirty, and the hands were bluish-grey. "You've took some dead ones, then," he said. "What was you goin' to use for cloths?"

The old woman pointed to a pile of newspapers. "Lisa ain't had but two pains," she whined. "We got papers to catch the mess."

London leaned forward, his mouth slightly open with attention, his eyes searching Mac's eyes. The tonsure shone in the candle-light. He corroborated the old woman. "Lisa had two pains, just finished one."

Mac made a little gesture toward the outside with his head. He went out through the tent-flap and London and Jim followed him. "Listen," he said to London, "you seen them hands. The kid might live if he's grabbed with hands like that, but the girl don't stand a hell of a chance. You better kick that old girl out."

"You do the job then?" London demanded.

Mac was silent for a moment. "Sure I'll do it. Jim, here'll help me some; but I got to have more help, a whole hell of a lot more help."

"Well, I'll give you a hand," London said.

"That ain't enough. Will any of the guys out there give a hand?"

London laughed shortly. "You damn right they will if I tell 'em."

"Well, you tell 'em, then," Mac said. "Tell 'em now." He led the way to the little fire, around which the circle of men still sat. They looked up as the three approached.

Lean-face said, "Hello, London."

London spoke loudly. "I want you guys should listen

to Doc, here." A few other men strolled up and stood waiting. They were listless and apathetic, but they came to the voice of authority.

Mac cleared his throat. "London's got a daughter'n-law, and she's goin' to have a baby. He tried to get her in the county hospital, but they wouldn't take her. They're full-up, and besides we're a bunch of lousy crop tramps. O.K. They won't help us. We got to do it ourselves."

The men seemed to stiffen a little, to draw together. The apathy began to drop from them. They hunched closer to the fire. Mac went on, "Now I worked in hospitals, so I can help, but I need you guys to help too. Christ, we got to stand by our own people. Nobody else will."

Lean-face boosted himself up. "All right, fella," he said. "What do you want us to do?"

In the firelight Mac's face broke into a smile of pleasure and of triumph. "Swell!" he said. "You guys know how to work together. Now first we got to have water boiling. When it's boiling, we got to get white cloth into it, and boil the cloth. I don't care where you get the cloth, or how you get it." He pointed out three men. "Now you and you and you get a big fire going. And you get a couple of big kettles. There ought to be some five-gallon cans around. The rest of you gather up cloth; get anything, handkerchiefs, old shirts—anything, as long as it's white. When you get the water boiling, put the cloth in and keep it boiling for half an hour. I want a little pot of hot water as quick as I can get it." The men were beginning to get restive. Mac said, "Wait. One more thing. I want a lamp, a good one. Some of you guys get me one. If nobody'll give you one, steal it. I got to have light."

A change was in the air. The apathy was gone from the men. Sleepers were awakened and told, and added themselves to the group. A current of excitement filled the jungle, but a kind of joyful excitement. Fires were built up. Four big cans of water were put on to boil; and then cloth began to appear. Every man seemed to have something to add to the pile. One took off his undershirt and threw it into the water and then put on his shirt again. The men seemed suddenly happy. They laughed together as they broke dead cottonwood branches for the fire.

Jim stood beside Mac, watching the activity. "What do you want me to do?" he asked.

"Come in with me. You can help me in the tent." At that moment a cry came from the tent. Mac said quickly, "Bring me a can of hot water as quick as you can, Jim. Here," he held out a little bottle. "Put about four of these tablets in each of those big cans. Bring the bottle back to me when you bring the water." He hurried away toward the tent.

Jim counted the tablets into the cans, and then he scooped a large bucketful of water from one of them and followed Mac into the tent. The old woman was crouched in a corner, out of the way. She scratched her hands and peered out suspiciously while Mac dropped two of the tablets into the warm water and dipped his hands into it. "We can anyway get our hands clean," he said.

"What's the bottle?"

"Bichloride of mercury. I always take it with me. Here, you wash your hands, Jim, and then get some fresh water."

A voice outside the tent called, "Here's your lamps, Doc."

Mac went to the flap and brought them back, a round-wick Rochester lamp and a powerful gasoline lantern. "Some poor devil's going to do his milking in the dark," he said to Jim. He pumped up pressure in the gasoline lamp, and when he lighted it the mantles glared, a hard, white light, and the lantern's hiss filled the tent. The crack of breaking wood and the sound of voices came in from outside.

Mac set his lantern down beside the mattress. "Going to be all right, Lisa," he said. Gently he tried to lift the dirty quilt which covered her. London and the white-faced boy looked on. In a panic of modesty Lisa held the quilt down about her. "Come on, Lisa, I've got to get you ready," Mac said persuasively. Still she clutched at the quilt.

London stepped over. "Lisa," he said, "you do it." Her frightened eyes swung to London, and then reluctantly she let go her hold on the quilt. Mac folded it back over her breast and unbuttoned her cotton underwear. "Jim," he called, "go out and fish me a piece of cloth and get me some soap."

When Jim had brought him a steaming cloth and a thin, hard piece of soap, Mac washed the legs and thighs and stomach. He worked so gently that some of the fear left Lisa's face.

The men brought in the boiled cloths.

The pains came quicker and quicker.

It was dawn when the birth started. Once the tent shook violently. Mac looked over his shoulder. "London, your kid's fainted," he said. "Better take him out in the air." With a look of profound embarrassment London slung the frail boy over his shoulder and carried him out.

The baby's head appeared. Mac supported it with his hands, and while Lisa squealed weakly, the birth was completed. Mac cut the cord with a sterilized pocket-knife.

The sun shone on the canvas and the lantern hissed on. Jim wrung out the warm cloths and handed them to Mac when he washed the shrunken little baby. And

Jim washed and scrubbed the hands of the old woman before Mac let her take the baby. An hour later the placenta came, and Mac carefully washed Lisa again. "Now get all this mess out," he told London. "Burn all these rags."

London asked, "Even the cloths you didn't use?"

"Yep. Burn it all. It's no good." His eyes were tired. He took a last look around the tent. The old woman held the wrapped baby in her arms. Lisa's eyes were closed and she breathed quietly on her mattress. "Come on, Jim. Let's get some sleep."

In the clearing the men were sleeping again. The sun shone on the tops of the willows. Mac and Jim crawled into a little cave in the undergrowth and lay down together.

Jim said, "My eyes feel sandy. I'm tired. I never knew you worked in a hospital, Mac."

Mac crossed his hands behind his head. "I never did."

"Well, where did you learn about births?"

"I never learned till now. I never saw one before. The only thing I knew was that it was a good idea to be clean. God, I was lucky it came through all right. If anything'd happened, we'd've been sunk. That old woman knew lots more than I did. I think she knew it, too."

"You acted sure enough," Jim said.

"Well, Christ Almighty, I had to! We've got to use whatever material comes to us. That was a lucky break. We simply had to take it. 'Course it was nice to help the girl, but hell, even if it killed her—we've got to use anything." He turned on his side and pillowed his head on his arm. "I'm all in, but I feel good. With one night's work we've got the confidence of the men and the confidence of London. And more than that, we made the men work for themselves, in their own defense, as a group. That's what we're out here for anyway, to teach them to fight in a bunch. Raising wages isn't all we're after. You know all that."

"Yes," Jim said. "I knew that, but I didn't know how you were going to go about it."

"Well, there's just one rule—use whatever material you've got. We've got no machine-guns and troops. Tonight was good; the material was ready, and we were ready. London's with us. He's the natural leader. We'll teach him where to lead. Got to go awful easy, though. Leadership has to come from the men. We can teach them method, but they've got to do the job themselves. Pretty soon we'll start teaching method to London, and he can teach it to the men under him. You watch," Mac said, "the story of last night will be all over the district by tonight. We got our oar in already, and it's better than I hoped. We might go to the can later for practicing medicine without a license, but that would only tie the men closer to us."

Jim asked, "How did it happen? You didn't say much, but they started working like a clock, and they liked it. They felt fine."

"Sure they liked it. Men always like to work together. There's a hunger in men to work together. Do you know that ten men can lift nearly twelve times as big a load as one man can? It only takes a little spark to get them going. Most of the time they're suspicious, because every time someone gets 'em working in a group the profit of their work is taken away from them; but wait till they get working for themselves. Tonight the work concerned them, it was their job; and see how well they did it."

Jim said, "You didn't need all that cloth. Why did you tell London to burn it?"

"Look, Jim. Don't you see? Every man who gave part of his clothes felt that the work was his own. They all

feel responsible for that baby. It's theirs, because something from them went to it. To give back the cloth
would cut them out. There's no better way to make men
part of a movement than to have them give something to
it. I bet they all feel fine right now."

"Are we going to work today?" Jim asked.

"No, we'll let the story of last night go the rounds.
It'll be a hell of a big story by tomorrow. No, we'll go
to work later. We need sleep now. But Jesus, what a
swell set-up it is for us so far."

The willows stirred over their heads, and a few leaves
fell down on the men. Jim said, "I don't know when I
ever was so tired, but I do feel fine."

Mac opened his eyes for a moment. "You're doing
all right, kid. I think you'll make a good worker. I'm
glad you came down with me. You helped a lot last
night. Now try to shut your God-damned eyes and
mouth and get some sleep."

5

THE AFTERNOON sun glanced on the tops of the apple trees and then broke into stripes and layers of slanting light beneath the heavy branches, and threw blots of sunshine on the ground. The wide aisles between the trees stretched away until the rows seemed to meet in a visual infinity. The great orchard crawled with activity. Long ladders leaned among the branches and piles of new yellow boxes stood in the aisles. From far away came the rumble of the sorting machines and the tap of the boxers' hammers. The men, with their big buckets slung to baldrics, ran up the ladders and twisted the big green pippins free and filled the buckets until they could hold no more, and then they ran down the ladders to empty the buckets into the boxes. Between the rows came the trucks to load the picked apples and take them to the sorting and packing plant. A checker stood beside the boxes and marked with a pencil in his little book as the bucket men came up. The orchard was alive. The branches of the trees shook under the ladders. The overripes dropped with dull plops to the ground underneath the trees. Somewhere, hidden in a tree-top, a whistling virtuoso trilled.

Jim hurried down his ladder and carried his bucket to the box pile and emptied the load. The checker, a blond young man in washed white corduroys, made a mark in his book and nodded his head. "Don't dump 'em in so hard, buddy," he warned. "You'll bruise 'em."

"O.K.," said Jim. He walked back to his ladder, drumming on the bucket with his knee as he went. Up the ladder he climbed, and he hooked the wire of the bale-hook over a limb. And then in the tree he saw another man, who had stepped off the ladder and stood on a big limb. He reached high over his head for a cluster of apples. He felt the tree shudder under Jim's weight and looked down.

"Hello, kid. I didn't know this was your tree."

Jim stared up at him, a lean old man with black eyes and a sparse, chewed beard. The veins stood out heavy and blue on his hands. His legs seemed as thin and straight as sticks, too thin for the big feet with great heavy-soled shoes.

Jim said, "I don't give a damn about the tree. Aren't you too old to be climbing around like a monkey, Dad?"

The old man spat and watched the big white drop hit the ground. His bleak eyes grew fierce. "That's what you think," he said. "Lots of young punks think I'm too old. I can out-work you any day in the week, and don't you forget it, neither." He put an artificial springiness in his knees as he spoke. He reached up and picked the whole cluster of apples, twig and all, skinned the apples into his bucket and contemptuously dropped the twig on the ground.

The voice of the checker called, "Careful of those trees, over there."

The old man grinned maliciously, showing two upper and two lower yellow teeth, long and sloped outward, like a gopher's teeth. "Busy bastard, ain't he," he remarked to Jim.

"College boy," said Jim. "Every place you go you run into 'em."

The old man squatted down on his limb. "And what do they know?" he demanded. "They go to them colleges, and they don't learn a God-damn thing. That smart guy with the little book couldn't keep his ass dry in a barn." He spat again.

"They get pretty smart, all right," Jim agreed.

"Now you and me," the old man went on, "we know

—not much, maybe, but what we know we know good."

Jim was silent for a moment, and then he lanced at the old man's pride as he had heard Mac do to other men. "You don't know enough to keep out of a tree when you're seventy. I don't know enough to wear white cords and make pencil marks in a little book."

The old man snarled, "We got no pull, that's what. You got to have pull to get an easy job. We just get rode over because we got no pull."

"Well, what you going to do about it?"

The question seemed to let air out of the old man. His anger disappeared. His eyes grew puzzled and a little frightened. "Christ only knows," he said. "We just take it, that's all. We move about the country like a bunch of hogs and get beat on the ass by a college boy."

"It's not his fault," said Jim. "He's just got a job. If he's going to keep the job, he's got to do it."

The old man reached for another cluster of apples, picked them with little twisting lifts and put each one carefully into his bucket. "When I was a young man, I used to think somethin' could be done," he said, "but I'm seventy-one." His voice was tired.

A truck went by, carrying off the filled boxes. The old man continued, "I was in the north woods when the Wobblies was raising hell. I'm a top-faller, a damn good one. Maybe you noticed how I take to a tree at my age. Well, I had hopes then. 'Course the Wobblies done some good, used to be there was no crappers but a hole in the ground, and no place to take a bath. The meat used to spoil. Well, them Wobblies made 'em put in toilets and showers; but, hell, it all went to pieces." His hand went up automatically for more apples. "I joined unions," he said. "We'd elect a president and first thing we knowed, he'd be kissing the ass of the superintendent, and then he'd sell us out. We'd pay dues, and the treasurer'd run out on us. I don' know. Maybe you young squirts can figure something out. We done what we could."

"You all ready to give up?" Jim asked, glancing at him again.

The old man squatted down on his limb and held himself there with one big skinny hand. "I got feelings in my skin," he said. "You may think I'm a crazy old coot; them other things was planned; nothing come of 'em; but I got feelings in my skin."

"What kind of feelings?"

"It's hard to say, kid. You know quite a bit before water boils, it gets to heavin' around? That's the kind of feeling I got. I been with workin' stiffs all my life. There ain't a plan in this at all. It's just like that water heavin' before it boils." His eyes were dim, seeing nothing. His head rose up so that two strings of skin tautened between his chin and his throat. "Maybe there's been too much goin' hungry; maybe too many bosses've kicked hell out of the men. I dunno. I just feel it in my skin."

"Well, what is it?" Jim asked.

"It's anger," the old man cried. "That's what it is. You know when you're about to get fightin', crazy mad, you get a hot, sick, weak feelin' in your guts? Well, that's what it is. Only it ain't just in one man. It's like the whole bunch, millions and millions was one man, and he's been beat and starved, and he's gettin' that sick feelin' in his guts. The stiffs don't know what's happenin', but when the big guy gets mad, they'll all be there; and by Christ, I hate to think of it. They'll be bitin' out throats with their teeth, and clawin' off lips. It's anger, that's what it is." He swayed on his limb, and tightened his arms to steady himself. "I feel it in my skin," he said. "Ever' place I go, it's like water just before it gets to boilin'."

Jim trembled with excitement. "There's got to be a

plan," he said. "When the thing busts, there's got to be a plan all ready to direct it, so it'll do some good."

The old man seemed tired after his outburst. "When that big guy busts loose, there won't be no plan that can hold him. That big guy'll run like a mad dog, and bite anything that moves. He's been hungry too long, and he's been hurt too much; and worst thing of all, he's had his feelings hurt too much."

"But if enough men expected it and had a plan——" Jim insisted.

The old man shook his head. "I hope I'm dead before it happens. They'll be bitin' out throats with their teeth. They'll kill each other off an' after they're all wore out or dead, it'll be the same thing over again. I want to die and get shut of it. You young squirts got hopes." He lifted his full bucket down. "I got no hope. Get out of the way, I'm comin' down the ladder. We can't make no money talkin': that's for college boys."

Jim stood aside on a limb and let him down the ladder. The old man emptied his bucket and then went to another tree. Although Jim waited for him, he did not come back. The sorting belt rumbled on its rollers in the packing-house, and the hammers tapped. Along the highway the big transport trucks roared by. Jim picked his bucket full and took it to the box pile. The checker made a mark in his book.

"You're going to owe us money if you don't get off your dime," the checker said.

Jim's face went red and his shoulders dropped. "You keep to your God-damn book," he said.

"Tough guy, huh?"

Then Jim caught himself and grinned in embarrassment. "I'm tired," he apologized. "It's a new kind of work to me."

The blond checker smiled. "I know how it is," he said.

"You get pretty touchy when you're tired. Why don't you get up in a tree and have a smoke?"

"I guess I will." Jim went back to his tree. He hooked his bucket over a limb and went to picking again. He said aloud to himself, "Even me, like a mad dog. Can't do that. My old man did that." He did not work quickly, but he reduced his movements to a machine-like perfection. The sun went low, until it left the ground entirely and remained only on the tops of the trees. Far away, in the town, a whistle blew. But Jim worked steadily on. It was growing dusky when the rumble in the packing-house stopped at last and the checkers called out, "Come on in, you men. It's time to quit."

Jim climbed down the ladder, emptied his bucket and stacked it up with the others. The checker marked in the buckets and then totalled the picking. The men stood about for a few moments, rolling cigarettes, talking softly in the evening. They walked slowly away down a row, toward the county road, where the orchard bunk houses were.

Jim saw the old man ahead of him and speeded up to catch him. The thin legs moved with jointed stiffness. "It's you again," he said as Jim caught up with him.

"Thought I'd walk in with you."

"Well, who's stoppin' you?" Obviously he was pleased.

"You got any folks here?" Jim asked.

"Folks? No."

Jim said, "Well, if you're all alone, why don't you get into some charity racket and make the county take care of you?"

The old man's tone was chilled with contempt. "I'm a top-faller. Listen, punk, if you never been in the woods, that don't mean nothing to you. Damn few top-fallers ever get to be my age. I've had punks like you damn near die of heart failure just *watchin'* me work; and here

I'm climbin' a lousy apple tree. Me take charity! I done work in my life that took guts. I been ninety foot up a pole and had the butt split and snap my safety-belt. I worked with guys that got swatted to pulp with a limb. Me take charity! They'd say, 'Dan, come get your soup,' and I'd sop my bread in my soup and suck the soup out of it. By Christ, I'd jump out of an apple tree and break my neck before I'd take charity. I'm a top-faller."

They trudged along between the trees. Jim took off his hat and carried it in his hand. "You didn't get anything out of it," he said. "They just kicked you out when you got too old."

Dan's big hand found Jim's arm just above the elbow, and crushed it until it hurt. "I got things out of it while I was at it," he said. "I'd go up a pole, and I'd know that the boss and the owner of the timber and the president of the company didn't have the guts to do what I was doing. It was *me*. I'd look down on ever'thing from up there. And ever'thing looked small, and the men were little, but I was up there. I was my own size. I got things out of it, all right."

"They took all the profits from your work," Jim said. "They got rich, an' when you couldn't go up any more, they kicked you out."

"Yes," said Dan, "they did that, all right. I guess I must be gettin' pretty old, kid. I don't give a damn if they did—I just don't give a damn."

Ahead they could see the low, whitewashed building the owners set aside for the pickers—a low shed nearly fifty yards long, with a door and a little square window every ten feet. Through some of the open doors lamps and candles could be seen burning. Some men sat in the doorways and looked out at the dusk. In front of the long building stood a faucet where a clot of men and women had gathered. As the turn of each came, he cupped his hands under the stream and threw water on his face and hair and rubbed his hands together for a moment. The women carried cans and cooking pots to fill at the faucet. In and out of the dark doorways children swarmed, restless as rats. A tired, soft conversation arose from the group. Men and women were coming back, men from the orchard, women from the sorting and packing house. So built that it formed a short angle at the north end of the building stood the orchard's store, brightly lighted now. Here food and work clothes were sold on credit against the working sheets. A line of women and men stood waiting to get in, and another line came out carrying canned goods and loaves of bread.

Jim and old Dan walked up to the building. "There's the kennel," Jim said. "It wouldn't be so bad if you had a woman to cook for you."

Dan said, "Guess I'll go over to the store and get me a can of beans. These damn fools pay seventeen cents for a pound of canned beans. Why, they could get four pounds of dried beans for that, and cooked up that'd make nearly eight pounds."

Jim asked, "Why don't you do that, Dan?"

"I ain't got the time. I come in tired an' I want to eat."

"Well, what time have the others got? Women work all day, men work all day; and the owner charges three cents extra for a can of beans because the men are too damn tired to go into town for groceries."

Dan turned his bristly beard to Jim. "You sure worry at the thing, don't you, kid? Just like a puppy with a knuckle-bone. You chew and chew at it, but you don't make no marks on it, and maybe pretty soon you break a tooth."

"If enough guys got to chewing they'd split it."

"Maybe—but I lived seventy-one years with dogs and men, and mostly I seen 'em try to steal the bone from each other. I never seen two dogs help each other break a bone; but I seen 'em chew hell out of each other tryin' to steal it."

Jim said, "You make a guy feel there isn't much use."

Old Dan showed his four long, gopher teeth. "I'm seventy-one," he apologized. "You get on with your bone, and don't mind me. Maybe dogs and men ain't the same as they used to be."

As they drew nearer on the cloddy ground a figure detached itself from the crowd around the faucet and strolled out toward them. "That's my pardner," Jim said. "That's Mac. He's a swell guy."

Old Dan replied ungraciously, "Well, I don't want to talk to nobody. I don't think I'll even heat my beans."

Mac reached them. "Hello, Jim. How'd you make out?"

"Pretty good. This is Dan, Mac. He was in the north woods when the Wobblies were working up there."

"Glad to meet you." Mac put a tone of deference in his voice. "I heard about that time. There was some sabotage."

The tone pleased old Dan. "I wasn't no Wobbly," he said. "I'm a top-faller. Them Wobblies was a bunch of double-crossin' sons-of-bitches, but they done the work. Damn it, they'd burn down a sawmill as quick as they'd look at it."

The tone of respect remained in Mac's voice. "Well, if they got the work done, I guess that's all you can expect."

"They was a tough bunch," said Dan. "A man couldn't take no pleasure talkin' to 'em. They hated ever'thing. Guess I'll go over and get my beans." He turned to the right and walked away from them.

It was almost dark. Jim, looking up at the sky, saw a black V flying across. "Mac, look, what's that?"

"Wild ducks. Flying pretty early this year. Didn't you ever see ducks before?"

"I guess not," said Jim. "I guess I've read about them."

"Say, Jim, you won't mind if we just have some sardines and bread, will you? We've got things to do tonight. I don't want to take time to cook anything."

Jim had been walking loosely, tired from the new kind of work. Now his muscles tightened and his head came up. "What you got on, Mac?"

"Well, look. I worked alongside London today. That guy doesn't miss much. He came about two-thirds of the way. Now he says he thinks he can swing this bunch of stiffs. He knows a guy that kind of throws another crowd. They're on the biggest orchard of the lot, four thousand acres of apples. London's so damn mad at this wage drop, he'll do anything. His friend on the Hunter place is called Dakin. We're going over there and talk to Dakin tonight."

"You got it really moving, then?" Jim demanded.

"Looks that way." Mac went into one of the dark doorways and in a moment he emerged with a can of sardines and a loaf of bread. He laid the bread down on the doorstep and turned the key in the sardine can, rolling back the tin. "Did you sound out the men the way I told you, Jim?"

"Didn't have much chance. I talked some to old Dan, there."

Mac paused in opening the can. "What in Christ's name for? What do you want to talk to him for?"

"Well, we were up in the same tree."

"Well, why didn't you get in another tree? Listen, Jim, lots of our people waste their time. Joy would try to convert a litter of kittens. Don't waste your time on old guys like that. He's no good. You'll get yourself converted to hopelessness if you talk to old men. They've had all the kick blasted right out of 'em." He turned the can lid off and laid the open tin in front of him. "Here, put some fish on a slice of bread. London's eating his dinner right now. He'll be ready pretty soon. We'll go in his Ford."

Jim took out his pocket-knife, arranged three sardines on a slice of bread and crushed them down a little. He poured some olive oil from the can over them, and then covered them with another slice of bread. "How's the girl?" he asked.

"What girl?"

"The girl with the baby."

"Oh, she's all right. But you'd think I was God the way London talks. I told him I wasn't a doctor, but he goes right on calling me 'Doc.' London gives me credit for a lot. You know, she'll be a cute little broad when she gets some clothes and some make-up on. Make yourself another sandwich."

It was quite dark by now. Many of the doors were closed, and the dim lights within the little rooms threw square patches of light on the ground outside. Mac chewed his sandwich. "I never saw such a bunch of bags as this crowd," he said. "Only decent one in the camp is thirteen years old. I'll admit she's got an eighteen-year-old can, but I'm doing no fifty years."

Jim said, "You seem to be having trouble keeping your economics out of the bedroom."

"Who the hell wants to keep it out?" Mac demanded. He chuckled. "Every time the sun shines on my back all afternoon I get hot pants. What's wrong with that?"

The bright, hard stars were out, not many of them, but sharp and penetrating in the cold night sky. From the rooms nearby came the rise and fall of many voices talking, with now and then a single voice breaking clear.

Jim turned toward the sound. "What's going on over there, Mac?"

"Crap game. Got it started quick. I don't know what they're using for money. Shooting next week's pay, maybe. Most of 'em aren't going to have any pay when they settle up with the store. One man tonight in the store got two big jars of mincemeat. Probably eat both jars tonight and be sick tomorrow. They get awful hungry for something nice. Ever notice when you're hungry, Jim, your mind fastens on just one thing? It's always mashed potatoes with me, just slimy with melted butter. I s'pose this guy tonight had been thinking about mincemeat for months."

Along the front of the building a big man moved, and the lights from the windows flashed on him as he passed each one. "Here comes London," Mac said.

He strode up to them, swinging his shoulders. The tonsure showed white against the black rim of hair. "I finished eatin'," London said. "Let's get goin'. My Ford's around back." He turned and walked in the direction from which he had come; Mac and Jim followed him. Behind the building a topless Model T Ford touring car stood nosed in against the building. The oilcloth seats were frayed and split, so that the coil spring stuck through, and wads of horsehair hung from the holes. London got in and turned the key. The rasp of the points sounded.

"Crank 'er, Jim," said Mac.

Jim put his weight on the stiff crank. "Spark down? I don't want my head kicked off."

"She's down. Pull out the choke in front there," said London.

The gas wheezed in. Jim spun the crank. The engine choked and the crank kicked viciously backward. "Nearly got me! Keep that spark down!"

"She always kicks a little," said London. "Don't give her no more choke."

Jim spun the crank again. The engine roared. The little dim lights came on. Jim climbed into the back seat among old tubes and tire-irons and gunny sacks.

"Makes a noise, but she still goes," London shouted.

He backed around and drove out the rough dirt road through the orchard, and turned right on the concrete state highway. The car chattered and rattled over the road; the cold air whistled in through the broken windshield so that Jim crouched down behind the protection of the front seat. Town lights glowed in the sky behind them. On both sides the road was lined with big dark apple trees, and sometimes the lights of houses shone from behind them. The Ford overtook and passed great transport trucks, gasoline tank trucks, silver milk tanks, outlined with little blue lights. From a small ranch house a shepherd dog ran out, and London swerved sharply to avoid hitting him.

"He won't last long," Mac shouted.

"I hate to hit a dog," said London. "Don't mind cats. I killed three cats on the way here from Radcliffe."

The car rattled on, going about thirty miles an hour. Sometimes two of the cylinders stopped firing, so that the engine jerked along until the missing two went back to work.

When they had gone about five miles, London slowed down. "Road ought to be somewhere in here," he said. A little row of silver mail boxes showed him where to turn into the dirt road. Over the road was a wooden arch bearing the words, "Hunter Bros. Fruit Co. S Brand Apples." The car stuttered slowly along the road. Suddenly a man stepped into the road and held up his hand. London brought the Ford to a stop.

"You boys working here?" the man asked.

"No, we ain't."

"Well, we don't need any more help. We're all full up."

London said, "We just come to see some friends of ours. We're workin' on the Talbot place."

"Not bringing in liquor to sell?"

"Sure not."

The man flashed a light into the back of the car and looked at the litter of iron and old inner tubes. The light snapped off. "O.K., boys. Don't stay too long."

London pushed down the pedal. "That smart son-of-a-bitch," he growled. "There ain't no nosey cops like private cops. Busy little rat." He swung the car savagely around a turn and brought it to a stop behind a building very like the one from which they had come, a long, low, shed-like structure, partitioned into little rooms. London said, "They're workin' a hell of a big crew here. They got three bunk houses like this one." He walked to the first door and knocked. A grunt came from inside, and heavy steps. The door opened a little. A fat woman with stringy hair looked out. London said gruffly, "Where's Dakin puttin' up?"

The woman reacted instantly to the authority of his voice. "He's the third door down, mister, him and his wife and a couple of kids."

London said, "Thanks," and turned away, leaving the woman with her mouth open to go on talking. She stuck out her head and watched the three men while London knocked on the third door. She didn't go inside until Dakin's door was closed again.

"Who was it?" a man asked from behind her.

"I don't know," she said. "A big guy. He wanted Dakin."

Dakin was a thin-faced man with veiled, watchful eyes and an immobile mouth. His voice was a sharp monotone. "You old son-of-a-bitch," he said. "Come on in. I ain't seen you since we left Radcliffe." He stepped back and let them in.

London said, "This here's Doc and his friend, Dakin. Doc helped Lisa the other night. Maybe you heard about it."

Dakin put out a long, pale hand to Mac. "Sure I heard. Couple of guys working right here was there. You'd think Lisa'd dropped an elephant the way they don't talk about nothing else. This here's the missus, Doc. You might take a look at them two kids, too, they're strong."

His wife stood up, a fine, big-bosomed woman with a full face, with little red spots of rouge on her cheeks, and with a gold upper bridge that flashed in the lamp-light. "Glad to meet you boys," she said in a husky voice. "You boys like a spot of coffee or a little shot?"

Dakin's eyes warmed a trifle out of pride in her.

"Well, it was pretty cold coming over," Mac said tentatively.

The gold bridge flashed. "Just what I thought. You'll do with a snort." She set out a bottle of whisky and a jigger. "Pour your own, boys. You can't pour it no higher'n the top."

The bottle and the glass went around. Mrs. Dakin tossed hers off last. She corked the bottle and stood it in a small cupboard.

Three folding canvas chairs were in the room, and two canvas cots for the children. A big patent camp bed stood against the wall. Mac said, "You do yourself pretty nice, Mr. Dakin."

"I got a light truck," said Dakin. "I get some truckin' to do now and then, and besides I can move my stuff. The missus is quick with her hands; in good times she can make money doin' piece work." Mrs. Dakin smiled at the praise.

Suddenly London dropped his social manner. "We want to go somewheres and talk," he said.

"Well, why not here?"

"We want to talk some kind of private stuff."

Dakin turned slowly to his wife. His voice was monotonous. "You and the kids better pay a call to Mrs. Schmidt, Alla."

Her face showed her disappointment. Her lips pouted and closed over the gold. For a moment she looked questioningly at her husband, and he stared back with his cold eyes. His long white hands twitched at his sides. Suddenly Mrs. Dakin smiled widely. "You boys stay right here an' do your talkin'," she said. "I ought to been to see Mrs. Schmidt before. Henry, take your brother's hand." She put on a short jacket of rabbit's fur and pushed at her golden hair. "You boys have a good time." They heard her walk away and knock at a door down the line.

Dakin pulled up his trousers and sat down on the big bed and waved the others to the folding canvas chairs. His eyes were veiled and directionless, like the eyes of a boxer. "What's on your mind, London?"

London scratched his cheek. "How you feel about that pay cut just when we was here already?"

Dakin's tight mouth twitched. "How do you think I feel? I ain't givin' out no cheers."

London moved forward on his chair. "Got any idears what to do?"

The veiled eyes sharpened a little bit. "No. You got any idears?"

"Ever think we might organize and get some action?" London glanced quickly sideways at Mac.

Dakin saw the glance. He motioned with his head to Mac and Jim. "Radicals?" he asked.

Mac laughed explosively. "Anybody that wants a living wage is a radical."

Dakin stared at him for a moment. "I got nothing against radicals," he said. "But get this straight. I ain't doin' no time for no kind of outfit. If you belong to anythin', I don't want to know about it. I got a wife and kids and a truck. I ain't doin' no stretch because my name's on somebody's books. Now, what's on your mind, London?"

"Apples got to be picked, Dakin. S'pose we organize the men?"

Dakin's eyes showed nothing except a light grey threat. His toneless voice said, "All right. You organize the stiffs and get 'em all hopped up with a bunch of bull. They vote to call a strike. In twelve hours a train-load of scabs comes rollin' in. Then what?"

London scratched his cheek. "Then I guess we picket."

Dakin took it up. "So then they pass a supervisors' ordinance—no congregation, and they put a hundred deputies out with shot-guns."

London looked around questioningly at Mac. His eyes asked Mac to answer for him. Mac seemed to be thinking hard. He said, "We just thought we'd see what you thought about it, Mr. Dakin. Suppose there's three thousand men strikin' from a steel mill and they picket? There's a wire fence around the mill. The boss gives the wire a jolt of high voltage. They put guards at the gate. That's soft. But how many deputy sheriffs you think it'll take to guard a whole damn valley?"

Dakin's eyes lighted for a moment, and veiled. "Shot-guns," he said. "S'pose we kick hell out of the scabs, and they start shootin'? This bunch of bindle-stiffs won't stand no fire, and don't think they will. Soon's somebody sounds off with a ten-gauge, they go for the brush like rabbits. How about this picketin'?"

Jim's eyes leaped from speaker to speaker. He broke in, "Most scabs'll come off the job if you just talk to 'em."

"And how about the rest?"

"Well," said Mac, "a bunch of quick-movin' men could fix that. I'm out in the trees pickin', myself. The guys are sore as hell about this cut. And don't forget, apples got to be picked. You can't close down no orchard the way you do a steel mill."

Dakin got up and went to the box-cupboard and poured himself a short drink. He motioned to the others with the bottle, but all three shook their heads. Dakin said, "They say we got a right to strike in this country, and then they make laws against picketin'. All it amounts to is that we got a right to quit. I don't like to get mixed up in nothing like this. I got a light truck."

Jim said, "Where——," found that his throat was dry, and coughed to clear it. "Where you going when we get the apples picked, Mr. Dakin?"

"Cotton," said Dakin.

"Well, the ranches over there are bigger, even. If we take a cut here, the cotton people will cut deeper."

Mac smiled encouragement and praise. "You know damn well they will," he seconded. "They'll do it every time; cut and cut until the men finally fight."

Dakin set the whisky bottle gently down and walked to the big bed and seated himself. He look at his long white hands, kept soft with gloves. He looked at the floor between his hands. "I don't want no trouble," he said. "The missus, the kids and me got along fine so far; but damn it, you're right, we'll get a cotton cut sure as hell. Why can't they let things alone?"

Mac said, "I don't see we got anything to do but organize."

Dakin shook himself nervously. "I guess we got to. I don't want to much. What you guys want me to do?"

London said, "Dakin, you can swing this bunch, and I can swing my bunch, maybe."

Mac broke in, "You can't swing nobody that doesn't want to be swung. Dakin and London got to start talkin', that's all. Get the men talkin'. They're mad already, but they ain't talked it out. We got to get talk goin' on all the other places, too. Let 'em talk tomorrow and the next day. Then we'll call a meetin'. It'll spread quick enough, with the guys this mad."

Dakin said, "I just thought of somethin'. S'pose we go out on strike? We can't camp here. They won't let us camp on the county or the state roads. Where we goin' to go?"

"I thought of that," said Mac. "I got an idear, too. If there was a nice piece of private land, it'd be all right."

"Maybe. But you know what they done in Washington. They kicked 'em out because they said it was a danger to public health. An' then they burned down the shacks and tents."

"I know all about that, Mr. Dakin. But s'pose there was a doctor takin' care of all that? They couldn't do much then."

"You a real doctor?" Dakin said suspiciously.

"No, but I got a friend that is, and he'd prob'ly do it. I been thinkin' about it, Mr. Dakin. I've read quite a bit about strikes."

Dakin smiled frostily. "You done a hell of a lot more'n read about 'em," he said. "You know too much. I don't want to hear nothin' about you. I don't know nothin'."

London turned to Mac. "Do you honest think we can lick this bunch, Doc?"

Mac said, "Listen, London, even if we lose we can maybe kick up enough hell so they won't go cuttin' the cotton wages. It'll do that much good even if we lose."

Dakin nodded his head slowly in agreement. "Well, I'll start talkin' the first thing in the morning. You're right about the guys bein' mad; they're sore as hell, but they don't know what to do about it."

"We'll give 'em an idear," said Mac. "Try to contact the other ranches all you can, Mr. Dakin, won't you?" He stood up. "I guess we better move along." He held out his hand. "Glad I met you, Mr. Dakin."

Dakin's stiff lips parted, showing even, white false teeth. He said, "If I owned three thousand acres of apples, d' you know what I'd do? I'd get behind a bush an' when you went by, I'd blow your God-damn head off. It'd save lots of trouble. But I don't own nothing but a light truck and some camp stuff."

"Good night, Mr. Dakin. Be seein' you," said Mac.

Jim and Mac went out. They heard London talking to Dakin. "These guys are O.K. They may be reds, but they're good guys." London came out and closed the door. A door down the building a bit opened and let out a square of light. Mrs. Dakin and the two kids walked toward them. "G'night, boys," she said. "I was watchin' to see when you come out."

The Ford rattled and chuckled homeward, and pushed its nose up against the bunk house. Mac and Jim parted from London and went to their dark little room. Jim lay on the floor wrapped in a piece of carpet and a comforter. Mac leaned against the wall, smoking a cigarette. After a while he crushed out the spark. "Jim, you awake?"

"Sure."

"That was a smart thing, Jim. She was beginning to drag when you brought in that thing about that cotton. That was a smart thing."

"I want to help," Jim cried. "God, Mac, this thing is singing all over me. I don't want to sleep. I want to go right on helping."

"You better go to sleep," Mac said. "We're going to do a lot of night work."

6

THE WIND swept down the rows, next morning, swaying the branches of the trees, and the windfalls dropped on the ground with soft thuds. Frost was in the wind, and between the gusts the curious stillness of autumn. The pickers scurried at their work, coats buttoned close over their chests. When the trucks went by between the rows, a wall of dust rolled out and went sailing down the wind.

The checker at the loading station wore a sheepskin coat, and when he was not tallying, thrust hands and book and pencil into his breast pocket and moved his feet restlessly.

Jim carried his bucket to the station. "Cold enough for you?"

"Not as cold as it will be if this wind doesn't change. Freeze the balls off a brass monkey," the checker said.

A sullen-looking boy came up and dumped his bucket. His dark brows grew low to his eyes and his dark, stiff hair grew low on his forehead. His eyes were red and hot. He dumped his bucketful of apples into a box.

"Don't bruise those apples," the checker said. "Rot sets in on a bruise."

"Oh, yeah?"

"Yeah, that's what I said." The checker made a slashing mark with his pencil. "That bucket's out. Try again."

The smouldering eyes regarded him with hostility. "You sure got it comin'. An' you're goin' to get it."

The checker reddened with anger. "If you're going to get smart, you'd better pad along out and hit the road."

The boy's mouth spat venomously. "We'll get you;

one of the first." He looked knowingly at Jim. "O.K., pal?"

"You'd better get on to work," Jim said quietly. "We can't make wages if we don't work."

The boy pointed down the row. "I'm in that fourth tree, buddy," he said, and moved away.

"What's the gag?" the checker asked. "Everybody's touchy this morning."

"It's the wind, maybe," said Jim. "I guess it's the wind. Makes people nervous when the wind blows."

The checker glanced quickly at him, for his tone had been satiric. "You too?"

"Me too."

"What's in the air, Nolan? Something up?"

"What you mean, 'something'?"

"You know God-damn well what I mean."

Jim knocked his bucket lightly against his leg. He stepped aside as a truck went by, and a dust wall covered him for a moment. "Maybe the little black book keeps you ignorant," he said. "You might turn in the little book, and then see if you can find out."

"So that's it. Organizing for trouble, are you? Well, the air's full of it."

"Air's full of dust," said Jim.

"I've seen that kind of dust before, Nolan."

"Well, then you know all about it." He started to move away.

"Wait a minute, Nolan." Jim stopped and turned. "You're a good man, Nolan, a good worker. What's going on?"

"I can't hear you," said Jim. "I don't know what you're talking about."

"I'll put the black mark on you."

Jim took two fierce steps toward him. "Put down your black mark and be damned," he cried. "I never said a thing. You've built all this up because a kid got smart with you."

The checker glanced away uneasily. "I was just kidding," he said. "Listen, Nolan, they need a checker up on the north end. I thought you might do for the job. You can go to work tomorrow. It would be better pay."

Jim's eyes darkened in anger for a second, and then he smiled and stepped close to the checker again. "What do you want?" he asked softly.

"I'll tell you straight, Nolan. There's something going on. The 'super' told me to try and find out. You get the dope for me and I'll put in a word for you on that checker's job, fifty cents an hour."

Jim seemed to study. "I don't know anything," he said slowly. "I might try to find out if there was anything in it for me."

"Well, would five bucks say anything?"

"Sure would."

"O.K. You circulate around. I'll check you in on buckets so you won't lose anything today. See what you can dig up for me."

Jim said, "How do I know you won't double-cross me? Maybe I find something out and tell you. If the men ever found I told you, they'd skin me."

"Don't you worry about that, Nolan. If the 'super' can get a good man like you, he won't throw him over. There might be a steady job here for you when the picking's over, running a pump or something."

Jim thought for a moment. "I don't promise anything," he said. "I'll keep my ears open, and if I find anything, I'll let you know."

"Good boy. There's five in it, and a job."

"I'll try that tough kid," Jim said. "He seemed to know something." He walked down the row toward the fourth tree. Just as he reached it the boy came down the ladder with a full bucket.

"Hi," he said, "I'll dump these and be back."

Jim went up the ladder and sat down on a limb. The muttering of a sorting belt at the packing-plant blew clearly on the wind, and the smell of fresh cider came from the presses. From a long way off Jim could hear the hiss and bark of a switch-engine making up a train.

The sullen boy came running up the ladder like a monkey. He said angrily, "When we get down to business I'm gonna get me a nice big rock, and I'm gonna sock that bastard."

Jim used Mac's method. "A nice guy like that? What you want to hurt him for? What do you mean 'when we get down to business'?"

The boy squatted down beside him. "Ain't you heard?"

"Heard what?"

"You ain't a rat?"

"No, I won't rat."

The boy cried, "We're goin' to strike, that's what!"

"Strike? With nice jobs? What you want to strike for?"

" 'Cause we're gettin' screwed, that's why. The bunk houses is full of pants rabbits, and the company's store is takin' five per cent house-cut, and they drop the pay after we get here, that's why! And if we let 'em get by with it, we'll be worse in the cotton. We'll get screwed there, too; and you know it damn well."

"Sounds reasonable," said Jim. "Who's strikin' besides you?"

The boy squinted at him with his hot eyes. "Gettin' smart, ain't you?"

"No. I'm trying to find out something, and you aren't telling me."

"I can't tell you nothing. We can't let nothing out yet. You'll find out when it's time. We got the men all organized. We got ever'thing about ready, and we're gonna raise hell. There's gonna be a meetin' tonight for a few of us, then we'll let the rest of you guys in on it."

"Who's in back of it?" Jim asked.

"I ain't tellin'. Might spoil ever'thing if I was to tell."

"O.K.," said Jim, "if that's the way you feel about it."

"I'd tell you if I could, but I promised not to. You'll know in time. You'll go out with us, won't you?"

"I don't know," said Jim. "I won't if I don't know any more about it than I do now."

"Well, by Christ, we'll kill anybody that scabs on us; I'm tellin' you that now."

"Well, I don't ever like to get killed." Jim hung his bucket on a limb and slowly set about filling it. "What's chances of goin' to that meeting?"

"Not a chance. That's going to be only the big guys."

"You a big guy?"

"I'm on the in," said the boy.

"Well, who are these big guys?"

The sullen eyes peered suspiciously at Jim. "You ask too damn many questions. I ain't tellin' you nothin'. You act to me like a pigeon."

Jim's bucket was full. He lifted it down. "Are the guys talking it up in the trees?"

"*Are they?* Where you been all morning?"

"Working," said Jim. "Making my daily bread. It's a nice job."

The boy blazed at him. "Don't you get pushin' me around unless you'd like to step down on the ground with me."

Jim winked at him the way he'd seen Mac do. "Turn off the heat, kid. I'll be along when the stuff starts."

The boy grinned foolishly. "You catch a guy off balance," he said.

Jim carried his bucket down the row and emptied it gently into a box. "Got the time?"

The checker looked at his watch. "Eleven-thirty. Find out anything?"

"Hell, no. That kid's just shooting off his face. He thinks he's a newspaper. I'll mix around some after dinner and see."

"Well, get the dope as quick as you can. Can you drive a truck?"

"Why not?"

"We might be able to put you on a truck."

"That'd be swell." Jim walked away, down the row. The men in the trees and on the ladders were talking. He went up a heavy-laden tree where two men were.

"Hello, kid. Come on up and join the party."

"Thanks." Jim settled to picking. "Lots of talk this morning," he observed.

"Sure is. We was just doin' some. Ever'body's talkin' strike."

Jim said, "When enough guys talk strike, a strike usually come off."

The second man, high up in the tree, broke in. "I was just tellin' Jerry, I don't like it. Christ knows we ain't makin' much, but if we strike, we don't make nothin'."

"Not right now we don't," said Jerry. "But later we make more. This damn apple pickin' don't last long, but cotton pickin' lasts longer. The way I figure it out, the cotton people is watchin' this thing. If we take dirt like a bunch of lousy sheep then the cotton people will nick us deeper. That's the way I figure it out, anyway."

Jim smiled. "Sounds reasonable."

The other man said, "Well, I don't like it. I don't like no trouble if I can get out of it. Lot of men'll get hurt. I can't see no good in it at all. I never yet seen a strike raise wages for long."

Jerry said, "If the guys go out, you goin' to be a scab?"

"No, Jerry, I wouldn't do that. If the men go out, I'll go too. I won't scab, but I don't like it."

Jim asked, "They got any organization going yet?"

"Not that I heard," said Jerry. "Nobody's called a meeting up yet. We'll just sit tight; but the way I got it figured, if the guys go out, I'm goin' out too."

A wheezy whistle tooted at the packing-plant. "Noon," said Jerry. "I got some sanriches under that pile of boxes there. Want some?"

"No, thanks," said Jim. "I got to meet the guy I travel with."

He left his bucket at the checker's post and walked toward the packing-plant. Through the trees he could see a tall, whitewashed building with a loading platform along one side. The sorting belt was still now. As Jim drew near he saw men and women sitting on the platform, hanging their legs over while they ate their lunches. A group of about thirty men had collected at one end of the building. Someone in the center of the crowd was talking excitedly. Jim could hear the rise and fall of his voice, but not his words.

The wind had fallen now, so that the warmth of the sunshine got through. As Jim approached, Mac detached himself from the group and came toward him carrying two paper-wrapped parcels. "Hi, Jim," he said. "Here's lunch, French bread and some sliced ham."

"Swell. I'm hungry."

Mac observed, "More of our men go out with stomach ulcers than with firing squads. How're things out your way?"

"Buzzing," said Jim. "Buzzing to beat hell. I met a kid who knows all about it. There's going to be a meeting of the big guys tonight."

Mac laughed. "That's good. I wondered whether the men with secret knowledge had got working yet. They can do us a lot of good. Men out your way getting mad?"

"They're talking a lot, anyway. Oh, say, Mac, the checker's going to give me five bucks and a permanent job if I find out what's going on. I told him I'd keep my ears open."

"Nice work," said Mac. "Maybe you can make a little money on the side."

"Well, what do you want me to tell him?"

"Well, let's see—tell him it's just a splash, and it'll blow over. Tell him it's nothing to get excited about." He swung his head. A man had approached quietly, a heavy man dressed in dirty overalls, with a face nearly black with dirt. He came close and glanced about to see that they were alone.

"The committee sent me down," he said softly. "How're things going?"

Mac looked up at him in surprise. "What things you talkin' about, mister?"

"You know what I mean. The committee wants a report."

Mac looked helplessly at Jim. "The man's crazy," he said. "What committee's this?"

"You know what I mean—" the voice sank, "comrade."

Mac stepped stiffly forward, his face black with anger. "Where you get this 'comrade' stuff?" he growled. "If you're one of them lousy radicals, I got no use for you. Now you get on your way before I call some of the boys."

The intruder's manner changed. "Watch your step, baby," he said. "We've got the glass on you." He moved slowly away.

Mac sighed. "Well, these apple boys think quick even if they don't think awful good," he said.

"That guy a dick?" Jim asked.

"Hell, yes. A man couldn't get his face that dirty without giving nature a lift. They lined us up quick, though, didn't they? Sit down and have something to eat."

They sat in the dirt and made thick ham sandwiches.

"There goes your chance for a bribe," Mac said. He turned a serious face to Jim and quoted, " 'Watch your step, baby,' and that's straight. We can't afford to drop out now. And just remember that a lot of these guys will sell out for five bucks. Make other people talk, but keep pretty quiet yourself."

"How'd they make us, d'you s'pose?" Jim asked.

"I don't know. Some bull from town put the finger on us, I guess. Maybe I better get some help down here in case you or I go out. This thing's coming off, and it needs direction. It's a pretty good layout, too."

"Will they jail us?" Jim asked.

Mac chewed a thick crust before he answered. "First they'll try to scare us," he said. "Now listen, if any time when I'm not around somebody tells you you're going to be lynched, you just agree to anything. Don't let 'em scare you, but don't go to using Joy's tricks. Jesus, they got moving quick! Oh, well, we'll get moving tomorrow, ourselves. I sent off last night for some posters. They should be here by tomorrow morning if Dick got off his dime. There ought to be some kind of word by mail tonight."

"What do you want me to do?" Jim asked. "All I do is just listen. I want to do something."

Mac looked around at him and grinned. "I'll use you more and more," he said. "I'll use you right down to the bone. This is going to be a nice mess, from the looks of it. That crack of yours about the cotton was swell. I've heard half a dozen guys use it for their own idea this morning."

"Where we going tonight, Mac?"

"Well, you remember Al, the fellow in the lunch wagon? He said his old man had a little orchard. I thought we might go out and see Al's father."

"Is that what you meant about getting a place for the guys when they go out?"

"I'm going to try to work it, anyway," Mac said. "This thing's going to break any time now. It's like blowing up a balloon. You can't tell when it's going to bust. No two of 'em bust just the same."

"You figure the big meeting for tomorrow night?"

"Yeah, that's what I figure; but you can't ever tell. These guys are plenty steamed up. Something might set 'em off before. You can't tell. I want to be ready. If I can get that place for the guys, I'll send for Doc Burton. He's a queer kind of a duck, not a Party man, but he works all the time for the guys. He'll lay out the place and tend to the sanitation, so the Red Cross can't run us off."

Jim lay back in the dirt and put his arms under his head. "What's the big argument over by the packing-house?"

"I don't know. The men just feel like arguing, that's all. By now maybe it's Darwin versus Old Testament. They'd just as soon fight over that. When they get to feeling like this, they'll fight about anything. Be pretty careful for yourself, Jim. Some guy might slug you just because he's feeling nervous."

"I wish it would start," Jim said. "I'm anxious for it to get going. I think I can help more when it once gets going."

"Keep your pants on," said Mac.

They rested in the dirt until the wheezy whistle blew a short toot for one o'clock. As they parted, Mac said, "Come running when we quit. We've got to cover some ground tonight. Maybe Al'll give us a hand-out again."

Jim walked back to the checking station, where his bucket was. The sorting belts began rumbling in the plant. Truck motors roared as they were started. Among the trees the pickers were sullenly going back to work. A number of men were standing around the checking station when Jim got his bucket. The checker did not speak to him then; but when Jim brought in his first full bucket, the question came. "Find out anything, Nolan?"

Jim leaned over the apple box and put his apples in it by hand. "I think it's all going to blow over. Most of the guys don't seem very mad."

"Well, what makes you think that?"

Jim asked, "Did you hear what made 'em mad?"

"No, I didn't. I thought it was the cut."

"Hell, no," said Jim. "A guy over on the Hunter place got a can of fish at the Hunter store that was bad. Made him sick. Well, you know how working stiffs are; they got sore, then the feeling spread over here. But I talked to some of the guys at noon. They're getting over it."

The checker asked, "You pretty sure that's all it is?"

"Sure. How about my five bucks?"

"I'll get it for you tomorrow."

"Well, I want that five, and you said you'd see about a better job."

"I will see about it. Let you know tomorrow."

"I should've got the money first, before I told you," Jim complained.

"Don't worry, you'll get it."

Jim walked off into the orchard. Just as he started to climb a ladder, a voice called from above him, "Look out for that ladder, she's shaky."

Jim saw old Dan standing in the tree. "By God, it's the boy radical," said old Dan.

Jim climbed up carefully. The rungs were loose in the ladder. "How's things, Dan?" he asked as he hung up his bucket.

"Oh, pretty good. I ain't feeling so good. Them cold beans lay like a flatiron in me all night."

"Well, you ought to have a warm supper."

"I was just too tired to build a fire. I'm getting on. I didn't want to get up this morning. It was cold."

"You should try one of the charity rackets," said Jim.

"I don't know. All the men is talkin' strike, and there's goin' t' be trouble. I'm tired. I don't want no trouble to come now. What'll I do if the men strike?"

"Why, strike with them. Lead them." Jim tried to spur him through pride. "The men would respect an old worker like you. You could lead the pickets."

"I s'pose I could," said Dan. He wiped his nose with a big hand and flicked his fingers. "I just don't want to. It's goin' to get cold early this afternoon. I'd like a little hot soup for supper—hot as hell, with little bits of meat in it, and some hot toast to soak in it. I *love* poached eggs. When I used to come to town out of the woods, with money, sometimes I'd get me half a dozen eggs poached in milk, and let 'em soak into toast. And then I'd mash the eggs up into the toast, and I'd eat 'em. Sometimes eight eggs. I made good pay in the woods. I could just as easy of got two dozen poached eggs. I wish I had. Lots of butter, an' all sprinkled with pepper."

"Not so hard-boiled as you were yesterday, huh, Pop? Yesterday you could out-work anybody on the lot."

The light of reminiscence went out of old Dan's eyes. His scraggly chin thrust forward. "I still can out-work a bunch of lousy punks that spends their time talkin'." He reached indignantly for the apples, fumbling over his head. One big, bony hand clung to a branch.

Jim watched him with amusement. "You're just showing off, Pop."

"Think I am? Well, try an' keep up with me, then."

"What's the use of you an' me racing, and then the orchard owner's the only one that makes anything?"

Old Dan piled apples into his bucket. "You punks got something to learn yet. There's more to work than you ever knew. Like a bunch of horses—you want more hay! Whining around for more hay. Want all the hay there is! You make a good man sick, that's what you do, whining around." His bucket was over-full. When he lifted it clear of the hook, five or six fat apples rolled out and bounced on the limbs and struck the ground under the tree. "Get out o' my way, punk," Dan cried. "Go on, get out o' the way o' that ladder."

"O.K., Pop, but take your time. You won't get a thing for rushing." Jim stepped clear of the ladder-top and climbed out on a limb. He hung his bucket and reached for an apple. Behind him he heard a splintering crash and a sullen thump. He looked around. Old Dan lay on his back on the ground under the tree. His open eyes looked stunned. His face was blue pale under the white stubble. Two rungs were stripped out of the ladder.

Jim cried, "That was a fall! Hurt yourself, Pop?"

The old man lay still. His eyes were full of a perplexed question. His mouth writhed, and he licked his lips.

Jim shinnied down the tree and knelt beside him. "Where are you hurt, Pop?"

Dan gasped, "I don't know. I can't move. I think I've bust my hip. It don't hurt none, yet."

Men were running toward them. Jim could see men dropping from the trees all around and running toward them. The checker trotted over from his pile of boxes. The men crowded close. "Where's he hurt?"

"How'd it happen?"

"Did he bust his leg?"

"He's too old to be up a tree."

The ring of men was thrust inward by more arriving. Jim heard the checker cry, "Let me through here." The faces were dull and sullen and quiet.

Jim shouted, "Stand back, can't you. Don't crowd in." The men shifted their feet. A little growl came from the back row. A voice shouted, "Look at that ladder."

All heads went up with one movement, and all eyes looked to where the old loose rungs had splintered and torn out. Someone said, "That's what they make us work on. Look at it!"

Jim could hear the thudding of feet as more men ran up in groups. He stood up and tried to push the ring apart. "Get back, you bastards. You'll smother him."

Old Dan had closed his eyes. His face was still and white with shock. On the outskirts of the mob the men began to shout, "Look at the ladder! That's what they make us work on!" The growl of the men, and the growl of their anger arose. Their eyes were fierce. In a moment their vague unrest and anger centered and focused.

The checker still cried, "Let me through there."

Suddenly a voice shrill with hysteria shouted, "You get out of here, you son-of-a-bitch." There was a scuffle.

"Look out, Joe. Hold Joe. Don't let him. Grab his feet."

"Now, mister, scram, and go fast."

Jim stood up. "You guys clear away. We got to get this poor fellow out of here." The men seemed to awaken from a sleep. The inner ring pushed violently outward. "Get a couple of sticks. We can make a stretcher out of a pair of coats. There, put the sticks through the arms. Now, button up the fronts." Jim said, "Easy now, with him. I think his hip's busted." He looked down at Dan's quiet, white face. "I guess he's fainted. Now, easy."

They lifted Dan on to the coat stretcher. "You two guys carry him," Jim said. "Some of you clear a way."

At least a hundred men had collected by this time. The men with the stretcher stepped out. Newcomers stood looking at the broken ladder. Over and over the words, "Look what they give us to use."

Jim turned to a man who stood stupidly staring up into the tree. "What happened to the checker?"

"Huh? Oh, Joe Teague slugged him. Tried to kick his

brains out. The guys held Joe. Joe went to pieces."

"Damn good thing he didn't kill him," Jim said.

The band of men moved along behind the stretcher, and more were running in from all over the orchard. As they drew near the packing-plant the rumble of the sorting belt stopped. Men and women crowded out of the loading doors. A quiet had settled on the growing mob. The men walked stiffly, as men do at a funeral.

Mac came tearing around the corner of the packing-plant. He saw Jim and ran to him. "What is it? Come over here away from the mob." The crowd of ominous, quiet people moved on after the stretcher. Newcomers were told in low tones, "The ladder. An old ladder." The body of the mob went ahead of Mac and Jim.

"Now what happened? Tell me quick. We've got to move while they're hot."

"It was old Dan. He got smart about how strong he was. Broke a couple of rungs out of a ladder and fell on his back. He thought he broke his hip."

Mac said, "Well, it's happened. I kind of expected it. It doesn't take much when the guys feel this way. They'll grab on anything. The old buzzard was worth something after all."

"Worth something?" Jim asked.

"Sure. He tipped the thing off. We can use him now." They walked quickly after the mob of men. The dust, raised by many feet, filled the air with a slow-blowing brown cloud. From the direction of the town the switch-engine crashed monotonously making up a train. On the outskirts of the mob women ran about, but the men were silent, trudging on after the stretcher, toward the bunk houses.

"Hurry up, Jim," Mac cried. "We've got to rush."

"Where we going?"

"We've got to find London first, and tell him how to

work; then we've got to go in and send a telegram; and I want to go and see Al's old man, right away. Look, there's London over there.

"Hi, London." Mac broke into a run, and Jim ran behind him. "It's busted out, London," Mac said breathlessly. "That old guy, Dan, fell out of a tree. It's wide open, now."

"Well, that's what we want, ain't it?" said London. He took off his hat and scratched his tonsure.

"The hell it is," Mac broke in. "These guys'll go nuts if we don't take charge. Look, there goes your long lean buddy. Call him over."

London cupped his hands. "Sam," he yelled.

Jim saw that it was the same man who had sat by the campfire in the jungle. Mac said, "Listen, London, and you, Sam. I'm going to tell you a lot of stuff quick, 'cause I've got to get along. These guys are just as likely to pop in a few minutes. You go over, Sam, and tell 'em they ought to hold a meeting. And then you nominate London, here, for chairman. They'll put him in all right. They'll do almost anything. That's all you got to do, Sam." Mac picked up a handful of dirt and rubbed it between his palms. His feet stirred and kicked at the ground. "Now listen, London, soon's you're chairman, you tell 'em we got to have order. You give 'em a list of guys, about ten, and tell 'em to vote for those guys as a committee to figure things out. Got that?"

"Sure. I get you."

"Now look—here's the way to do it. If you want 'em to vote for something, you say, 'Do you want to do it?' and if you want to vote down somethin', just say, 'You don't want to do this, do you?' and they'll vote no. Make 'em vote on everythin', *everythin'*, see? They're all ready for it."

They looked toward the crowd at the bunk house.

The men were still quiet, shifting about, never standing very long in a place, moving their arms; their faces were as relaxed as those of sleeping men.

London demanded, "Where you guys going now?"

"We're going to see about that place for the crowd to stay when the thing busts open, that little farm. Oh, one other thing, you pick out a bunch of the craziest of these guys and send 'em over to the other ranches to talk. Get the men that are doin' the most talkin'. You all set now?"

"All set," said London.

"Well, let us use your Ford, will you? We got to cover ground."

"Sure, take it, if you can run it; it's got tricks."

Mac turned to Sam. "All right, get over there. Just stand up on somethin' and yell, 'Boys, we ought to hold a meetin',' and then yell, 'I move London for chairman.' Get going, Sam. Come on, Jim."

Sam trotted off toward the bunk houses, and London followed more slowly. Mac and Jim circled the buildings and went to the ancient Ford touring car. "Get in, Jim. You drive the jalopy." A roar of voices came from the other side of the bunk house. Jim turned the key and retarded the spark lever. The coils buzzed like little rattlesnakes. Mac spun the crank and primed, and spun again. A second roar from the mob came over the house. Mac threw his shoulder into the work. The engine caught and its noise drowned the shouting of the men. Mac leaped into the car, yelling, "Well, I guess London's our new chairman. Push 'er along."

Jim backed around and drove out to the highway. The road was deserted. The green, heavy-laden trees threw their shadows' weight sideways under the declining sun. The car rolled along, its pistons battering in the cylinders. "First to a telegraph office, and then to the post office," Mac shouted.

They rolled into the town. Jim drove to the main street and parked in front of a Western Union office. "Post office is just a block up, see?" he said.

"Well, listen, Jim, while I send the wire, you go up and ask for mail for William Dowdy."

In a few moments Jim came back with three letters. Mac was already sitting in the car. He ripped the letters open and read them. "Hot-damn, listen. This one's from Dick. He says Joy broke jail; they don't know where he is. He was bein' taken for a hearing and he smacked a cop and beat it. I just wired for more help, and for Doc Burton to take over the sanitation. Wait, I'll crack 'er up. Let's move along to Al's lunch wagon."

When Jim drew up in front of the lunch wagon, he could see Al through the windows, leaning over his deserted counter, staring out at the sidewalk. Al recognized them as they got out. He raised a fat arm at them.

Mac pushed open the sliding door. "Hi, Al. How's business?"

Al's eyes were bright with interest. "Been just fine," he said. "Whole flock of guys from the orchards come in last night."

"I been tellin' 'em what a swell steak you put out," said Mac.

"Nice of you. Like a bite yourself?"

"Sure," said Mac. "We could even pay for it. Imagine us guys payin' for anything."

"Aw, this is just your cut," said Al. "Kind of a commission for sending the guys in town." He opened his ice-box and patted out two hamburger steaks and slapped them down on the stove-top; and he arranged a wreath of chopped onions about each one. "How's things coming out your way?" he asked.

Mac leaned confidentially over the counter. "Listen, Al. I know you're a guy I can trust. We got you on the books. You been swell to us."

Al blushed with pleasure at the praise. "Well, I'd be out with you guys if I didn't have a business to keep up. A man sees the way conditions is, and injustice, and things—and if he's got any brains he comes to it."

"Sure," said Mac hurriedly. "A guy with brains don't have to be taught. He sees things for himself."

Al turned away to hide his pleasure. He flipped the steaks and pressed them down with his spatula and gathered up the wilting onions and forced them into the meat. He scraped the grease into the little trough on the side of the stove-top. When he had forced his face back to a proper gravity, he turned around again. "Sure you guys can trust me," he said. "You ought to know it. What you got on?" He filled two cups with coffee and slid them along the counter.

Mac tapped delicately on the counter with a knife-blade. "There may be bulls askin' about me and Jim."

"Sure. I don't know nothin' about you," said Al.

"That's right. Now here's the dope, Al. This valley's about to bust wide open. Already has over on the place where we been working. The others'll probably crack tonight."

Al said softly, "You know, the way the guys was talkin' in here, I thought it wasn't far off. What d'you want me to do?"

"Better take up that meat." Al held two plates fan-wise in one hand, put a steak on each, mashed potatoes, carrots and turnips, loaded the plates.

"Gravy, gents?"

"Smear it," said Mac.

Al ladled gravy over the whole pile of food and set the plates before them. "Now go on," he said.

Mac filled his mouth. His speech was muffled and spaced with chewing. "You said your old man had a little ranch."

"He has. Want to hide out there?"

"No." Mac pointed his fork at Al. "There won't be an apple picked in this valley."

"Well, say—mister——"

"Wait. Listen. Any plow land on your old man's place?"

"Yeah, about five acres. Had it in hay. Hay's all out now."

"Here it is," said Mac. "We're goin' to have a thousand or two men with no place to go. They'll kick 'em off the ranches and won't let 'em on the road. Now if they could camp on that five acres, they'd be safe."

Al's face sagged with fear and doubt. "Aw, no, mister. I don't think my old man'd do it."

Mac broke in, "He'd get his apples picked, picked quick, and picked for nothing. Price'll be high with the rest of 'em shut off."

"Well, wouldn't the town guys raise hell with him afterwards?"

"Who?" Mac asked.

"Why, the Legion, and guys like that. They'd sneak out and beat him up."

"No, I don't think they would. He's got a right to have men on his place. I'll have a doctor lay out the camp and see it's kept clean, and your old man'll get his crop picked for nothing."

Al shook his head. "I don't know."

"Well, we can easy find out," said Mac. "Let's go talk to your old man."

"I got to keep this place open. I can't go away."

Jim suddenly saw his neglected food and began to eat. Mac's squinted eyes never left Al's face. He sat and chewed and looked. Al began to get nervous. "You think I'm scared," he began.

"I don't think anything before I see it," said Mac. "I

just wondered why a guy can't close up his own joint for an hour, if he wants to."

"Well, the guys that eat early'll be here in an hour."

"You could get back in an hour."

Al fidgeted. "I don't think my old man'll do it. He's got to look out for himself, don't he?"

"Well, he ain't been jumped yet. How do you know what'll happen?" A chill was creeping into Mac's voice, a vague hostility.

Al picked up a rag and mopped around on the counter. His nervous eyes came to Mac's and darted away and came back. At last he stepped close. "I'll do it," he said. "I'll just pin a little card to the door. I don't think my old man'll do it, but I'll take you out there."

Mac smiled broadly. "Good guy. We won't forget it. Next time I see any stiff with a quarter, I'll send him in to get one of your steaks."

"I give a nice dinner for the money," said Al. He took off his tall cook's hat and rolled down his shirt sleeves, and turned the gas off under the cooking plate.

Mac finished his food. "That was good."

Jim had to bolt his dinner not to be late.

"I got a little car in the lot behind here," said Al. "Maybe you guys could just follow me; then I don't get into no trouble and I'm still some good to you."

Mac drained his cup. "That's right, Al. Don't you get into no bad company."

"You know what I mean."

"Sure, I know. Come on, Jim, let's go."

Al wrote a sign and pinned it inside the door, facing out through the glass. He struggled his chubby arms into his coat and held the door open for Mac and Jim.

Mac cranked the Ford and jumped in, and Jim idled the motor until Al came bumping out of the lot in an old Dodge roadster. Jim followed him down the street to the east, across the concrete bridge over the river and out into the pleasant country. The sun was nearly down by now, red and warm with autumn dust. The massed apple trees along the road were grey with dust.

Mac turned in the seat and looked down the rows as they passed. "I don't see anybody working," he cried to Jim. "I wonder if he took hold already. There's boxes, but nobody working."

The paved road gave way to a dirt road. The Ford leaped and shuddered on the rough road. About a mile further Al's dust-cloud swung off into a yard. Jim followed and came to a stop beside the Dodge. A white tank-house rose into the air, and on its top a windmill thrashed and glittered in the sun, and the pump bonged with a deep, throaty voice. It was a pleasant place. The apple trees grew in close to a small white ranch house. Tame mallards nuzzled the mud in the overflow under the tank. In a wire-bounded kennel against a big barn two rubbery English pointers stood against the screen and yearned out at the men with little yelps. The house itself was surrounded by a low picket fence, behind which geraniums grew big and red, and a Virginia creeper, dropping its red leaves, hung over the porch. Big square Plymouth Rock chickens strolled about, cawing contentedly and cocking their heads at the newcomers.

Al got out of the car. "Look a' them dogs," he said. "Best pointers in the Valley. My old man loves them better'n me."

Mac asked, "Where's the five acres, Al?"

"Down that way, behind the trees, on the other road."

"Good. Let's find your old man. You say he likes his dogs?"

Al laughed shortly. "Just make a pass at one o' them dogs an' see. He'll eat you."

Jim stared at the house, and at the newly whitewashed barn. "This is nice," he said. "Makes a man want to live in a place like this."

Al shook his head. "Takes an awful lot of work to keep it up. My old man works from dawn till after dark, and then he don't keep up with the work."

Mac insisted, "Where is your old man? Let's find him."

"Look," Al said. "That's him coming in from the orchard."

Mac glanced up for a moment, and then he moved back to the kennel. The squirming pointers flung themselves at the wire, moaning with love. Mac stuck his fingers through the mesh and rubbed their muzzles.

Jim said, "Do you like dogs, Mac?"

Mac retorted irritably, "I like anything."

Al's father came walking up. He was totally unlike Al, small and quick as a terrier. The energy seemed to pour out of some inner reservoir into his arms and legs, and into his fingers so that all of him was on the move all of the time. His white hair was coarse, and his eyebrows and mustache bristled. His brown eyes flitted about as restlessly as bees. Because his fingers had nothing else to do while he walked, they snapped at his sides with little rhythmic reports. When he spoke, his words were like the rest of him, quick, nervous, sharp. "What's the matter with your business?" he demanded of Al.

Al went heavily on the defensive. "Well, you see—I thought——"

"You wanted to get off the ranch, wanted to go into town, start a business, town boy, wanted to lounge around. Didn't like to whitewash, never did. What's the matter with your business?" His eyes hovered on each of the men, on their shoes and on their faces.

Mac still looked into the kennel and rubbed the dogs'

noses. Al explained, "Well, you see, I brang these guys out, they wanted to see you."

The old man eliminated Al. "Well, they're here. You can get back to your business now."

Al looked at his little father with the hurt eyes of a dog about to be bathed, and then reluctantly he climbed into his car and drove disconsolately away.

Mac said, "I haven't seen such pointers in a long time."

Al's father stepped up beside him. "Man, you never seen such pointers in your life." A warmth was established.

"Do you shoot over 'em much?"

"Every season. And I get birds, too. Lots of fools use setters. Setter's a net dog, nobody nets birds any more. Pointer's a real gun dog."

"I like the looks of that one with the liver saddle."

"Sure, he's good. But he can't hold up to that sweet little bitch. Name's Mary, gentle as Jesus in the pen, but she's jumping hell in the field. Never seen a dog could cover the ground the way she can."

Mac gave the noses a rub. "I see they got holes into the barn. You let 'em run in the barn?"

"No, their beds are tight against the wall. Warmer in there."

"If the bitch ever whelps, I'd like to speak a pup."

The old man snorted. "She'd have to whelp ever'day in the year to supply the people that wants her pups."

Mac turned slowly from the pen and looked into the brown eyes. "My name's McLeod," he said, and held out his hand.

"Anderson's mine. What you want?"

"I want to talk straight to you."

The sun was gone now, and the chickens had disappeared from the yard. The evening chill settled down among the trees. "Selling something, Mr. McLeod? I don't want none."

"Sure, we're selling something, but it's a new product."

His tone seemed to reassure Anderson. "Why'n't you come into the kitchen and have a cup of coffee?"

"I don't mind," said Mac.

The kitchen was like the rest of the place, painted, scrubbed, swept. The nickel trimmings on the stove shone so that it seemed wet.

"You live here alone, Mr. Anderson?"

"My boy Al comes out and sleeps. He's a pretty good boy." From a paper bag the old man took out a handful of carefully cut pine splinters and laid them in the stove, and on top he placed a few little scraps of pitchwood, and on top of those, three round pieces of seasoned apple wood. It was so well and deftly done that the fire flared up when he applied a match. The stove cricked, and a burst of heat came from it. He put on a coffee-pot and measured ground coffee into it. From a bag he took two egg shells and dropped them into the pot.

Mac and Jim sat at a kitchen table covered with new yellow oilcloth. Anderson finished his work at the stove. He came over, sat primly down, put his two hands on the table; they lay still, even as good dogs do when they want to be off. "Now, what is it, McLeod?"

A look of perplexity lay on Mac's muscular face. "Mr. Anderson," he said hesitatingly, "I haven't got a hell of a lot of cards. I ought to play 'em hard and get the value out of 'em. But I don't seem to want to. I think I'll lay 'em down. If they take the pot, O.K. If they don't, there's no more deal."

"Well, lay 'em then, McLeod."

"It's like this. By tomorrow a couple of thousand men will be on strike, and the apple picking will stop."

Anderson's hands seemed to sniff, to stiffen, and then to lie still again.

Mac went on, "The reason for the strike is this pay-cut. Now the owners'll run in scabs, and there'll be trouble. But there's a bunch of men going out, enough to picket the Valley. D'you get the picture?"

"Part of it; but I don't know what you're driving at."

"Well, here's the rest. Damn soon there'll be a supervisors' ordinance against gathering on a road or on any public property. The owners'll kick the strikers off their land for trespassing."

"Well, I'm an owner. What do you want of me?"

"Al says you've got five acres of plow land." Anderson's hands were still and tense as dogs at point. "Your five acres are private proterty. You can have men on it."

Anderson said cautiously, "You're selling something; you don't say what it is."

"If the Torgas Valley apples don't go on the market, the price'll go up, won't it?"

"Sure it will."

"Well, you'll get your crop picked free."

Anderson relaxed slightly in his chair. The coffee-pot began to breathe gently on the stove. "Men like that'd litter the land up," he said.

"No, they won't. There's a committee to keep order. There won't even be any liquor allowed. A doctor's coming down to look out for the sanitation. We'll lay out a nice neat camp, in streets."

Anderson drew a quick breath. "Look here, young fellow, I own this place. I got to get along with my neighbors. They'd raise hell with me if I did a thing like that."

"You say you own this place?" Mac said. "Is it clear? Is there any paper on it?"

"Well, no, it ain't clear."

"And who are your neighbors?" Mac asked quickly. "I'll tell you who they are: Hunter, Gillray, Martin. Who holds your paper? Torgas Finance Company. Who owns Torgas Finance Company? Hunter, Gillray, Martin. Have they been squeezing you? You know God damn well they have. How long you going to last? Maybe one year; and then Torgas Finance takes your place. Is that straight? Now suppose you got a crop out with no labor charges; suppose you sold it on a rising market? Could you clear out your paper?"

Anderson's eyes were bright and beady. Two little spots of anger were on his cheeks. His hands crept under the edge of the table and hid. For a moment he seemed not to breathe. At last he said softly, "You didn't lay 'em down, fellow, you played 'em. If I could get clear—if I could get a knife in——"

"We'll give you two regiments of men to get your knife in."

"Yeah, but my neighbors'd run me out."

"Oh, no they won't. If they touch you or your place we won't leave a barn standing in the Valley."

Anderson's lean old jaw set hard. "What you getting out of it?"

Mac grinned. "I could tell you the other stuff straight. I don't know whether you'd believe the answer to that one or not. Me an' Jim here get a sock in the puss now and then. We get sixty days for vagrancy pretty often."

"You're one of those reds?"

"You win; we're reds, as you call them."

"And what do you figure to do with your strike?"

"Don't get us wrong, Mr. Anderson. We didn't start it. Gillray, Martin and Hunter started it. They told you what to pay the men, didn't they?"

"Well, the Growers' Association did. Torgas Finance Company runs that."

"O.K. We didn't start it. But once it's started, we want to help it win. We want to keep the men from running to hell, teach 'em to work together. You come in with us, and you'll never have labor trouble as long as you live."

Anderson complained, "I don't know whether I can trust a red."

"You never tried; but you've tried trusting Torgas Finance."

Anderson smiled coldly. His hands came up on the table, and played together like puppies. "It'll probably break me, and put me on the road. Christ knows I'm headed for it anyway. Might as well have some fun. I'd give a hell of a lot to stick Chris Hunter." The coffee boiled over and fizzed fiercely on the stove, and the smell of burning coffee filled the air. The electric light glistened on Anderson's white eyebrows, and on his stiff hair. He lifted the coffee-pot and wiped the stove carefully with a newspaper. "I'll pour you out some coffee, Mr. Red."

But Mac sprang to his feet. "Thanks, but we've got to get along. We'll see you get a square deal out of this. Right now we got a million things to do. Be seeing you tomorrow." They left the old man standing holding the coffee-pot in his hand. Mac forced a trot across the yard. He muttered, "Jesus, that was ticklish. I was scared I'd slip any minute. What a tough old baby he is. I knew a hunting man'd be tough."

"I like him," said Jim.

"Don't you go liking people, Jim. We can't waste time liking people."

"Where'd you get that dope on him about the Finance Company, Mac?"

"Came in the mail tonight. But thank God for those dogs! Jump in, Jim. I'll turn her over."

They rattled through the clear night. The little flaring headlamps flickered dizzily along the road. Jim looked up at the sky for a moment. "Lord, I'm excited. Look at the stars, Mac. Millions of 'em."

"You look at the road," Mac growled. "Listen, Jim,

I just happened to think. That guy this noon means they've got us spotted. From now on you be careful, and don't go away from the crowd very far. If you want to go someplace, see you take about a dozen men with you."

"You mean they'll try to get us?"

"You're damn right! They'll figure they can stop the ruckus with us out of it."

"Well, when're you going to give me something to do, Mac? I'm just following you around like a little dog."

"You're learning plenty, kid. When there's some use for you, I'll get it out, don't you worry. You can take out a flock of pickets in a day or so. Turn off to the left, Jim. We won't be wanting to go through town much from now on."

Jim bumped the car along rutty side-roads. It was an hour before he came finally to the ranch and turned into the dark road among the apple trees. He throttled down the Ford until it was barely able to fire. The headlights jerked and shivered. Without warning a blinding light cut out through the darkness and fell on the men's faces. At the same moment two men, muffled in overcoats, stepped into the road ahead. Jim ground the Ford to a stop.

A voice behind the light called, "These are the guys." One of the overcoated men lounged around the car and leaned on the door. The motor idled unevenly. Because of the light beam, the man leaning on the door was almost invisible. He said, "We want you two out of the Torgas Valley by daylight tomorrow, get it? Out."

Mac's foot crept over and pressed Jim's leg. His voice became a sweet whine. "Wha's the matter 'th us, mister? We never done nothing."

The man answered angrily, "Lay off, buddy. We know who you are, and what you are. We want you *out*."

Mac whined, "If you're the law, we're citizens. We got a right to stand trial. I pay taxes back home."

"Well, go home and pay 'em. This isn't the law: this is a citizens' committee. If you think you God-damned reds can come in here and raise hell, you're crazy. You get out of here in your tin can or you'll go out in a box. Get it?"

Jim felt Mac's foot creep under his legs and find the gear pedal of the Ford. Jim tapped the foot with his toe to show he understood. The old engine staggered around and around. Sometimes one cylinder missed fire, sometimes two. Mac said, "You got us wrong, mister. We're just workin' stiffs. We don't want no trouble."

"I said '*out*.'"

"Well, leave us get our stuff."

"Listen, you're turning right around and getting out."

Mac cried, "You're yellow, that's what you are. You put twenty men hiding along the road. You're yellow as hell."

"Who's yellow? There's just three of us. But if you're not out of the Valley by morning, there'll be fifty."

"*Step on it, Jim!*"

The engine roared. The Ford bucked ahead like a horse. The man on the side spun off into the darkness, and the man in front jumped for his life. The rattling car leaped over the road with a noise of falling andirons.

Mac looked over his shoulder. "The flashlight's gone," he shouted.

Jim ran the car behind the long building. They jumped out and sprinted around the end of the bunk house.

The space in front of the doorways was dense with men standing in groups, talking in low tones. On the doorsteps the women sat, hugging their skirts down around their knees. A droning, monotonous hum of talk came from the groups. At least five hundred men were there, men from other ranches. The tough kid Jim had spoken to stalked near. "Didn't believe me, huh? Well, how's this look to you?"

Mac asked him, "Seen London?"

"Sure I seen him. We elected him chairman. He's in his room now with the committee. Thought I was nuts, didn't you?" he said to Jim. "I told you I was on the in."

Mac and Jim edged their way among the crowded men and into the hum of voices. London's door was closed, and his window was closed. A press of men stood on tiptoe and looked through the glass into the lighted room. Mac started up the steps. Two men threw themselves in his way. "What the hell do you want?"

"We want to see London."

"Yeah? Does London want to see you?"

"Ask him, why don't you?"

"What's your name?"

"Tell London Doc and Jim want to see him."

"You're the guy that helped the girl have a kid?"

"Sure."

"Well, I'll ask." The man opened the door and stepped inside. A second later he emerged and held the door open. "Go right on in, boys, London's waitin' for you."

London's room had been hurriedly made into an office by bringing in boxes for seats. London sat on his bed, his tonsured head forward. A committee of seven men stood, sat on boxes, smoked cigarettes. They turned their heads when Jim and Mac entered. London looked glad. "Hello, Doc. Hello, Jim. Glad to see you. Heard the news?"

Mac flopped down on a box. "Heard nothing," he said. "Me and Jim been covering ground. What happened?"

"Well, it seems to be all right. Dakin's crowd went out. There's a guy named Burke, chairman on the Gillray place. There's a meetin' of everybody called for to-morrow."

"Fine," said Mac. "Workin' out fine. But we can't do much till we get an executive committee and a general chairman."

London asked, "How'd you come out on that thing you went for? I didn't tell the boys, case it didn't come off."

"Got it." Mac turned to the seven men. "Listen," he said. "A guy's loaned us five acres for the guys to camp on. It's private property, so nobody but the health people can kick us off. We got a doctor coming down to take care of that." The committeemen sat up straight, grinning with enthusiasm. Mac continued, "Now I've promised this farmer that the men'd pick his crop for nothing. It won't take 'em long. There's plenty of water. It's a good central location, too."

One of the men stood up excitedly. "Can I go tell the guys outside, London?"

"Sure, go ahead. Where is this place, Doc? We can have our big meetin' there tomorrow."

"It's Anderson's orchard, a little way out of town." Three of the committeemen broke for the door, to tell the news. Outside there was first a silence, and then a roll of voices, not shouting, but talking excitedly; and the roll spread out and grew louder, until the air was full of it.

Jim asked: "What happened to old Dan?"

London raised his head. "They wanted to take him to a hospital. He wouldn't do no good in a hospital. We got a doctor to set his hip. He's down the row a little. Couple of good women takin' care of the poor old bum. He's havin' a fine time. Couldn't get 'im out of here now. He just gives everybody hell, women and all."

Mac asked, "Have you heard from the owners yet?"

"Yeah, 'super' came in. Asked if we was goin' back to work. We says 'no.' He says, 'Get the hell off the place by morning.' Says he'll have a trainload of stiffs in here by mornin'."

"He won't," Mac interrupted. "He can't get 'em in before day after tomorrow. It takes some time to hand-pick a bunch of scabs. And day after tomorrow we'll be ready for 'em. Say, London, some guys that call 'em-selves a committee tried to run me and Jim out of the Valley. Better pass the word to the guys not to go out alone. Tell 'em if they want to go any place take some friends along for company."

London nodded at one of his committeemen. "Pass the word, Sam." Sam went out. Again the roll of voices spreading out and rumbling, like a wave over round stones. This time the tone was deep and angry.

Mac slowly rolled a brown cigarette. "I'm tired," he said. "We got so much to do. I guess we can do it to-morrow."

"Go to bed," said London. "You been goin' like a fool."

"Yep, I been goin', all right. Seems kind of hard when you're tired. They got guns. We can't have no guns. They got money. They can buy our boys. Five bucks looks like a hell of a lot of jack to these poor half-starved bastards. Be pretty sure before you tell anythin', London. After all, you can't blame the guys much if they sell out. We got to be clever and mean and quick." His voice had grown sad. "If we don't win, we got to start all over again. It's too bad. We could win so easy, if the guys would only stick together. We could just kick Billy Hell out of the owners. No guns, no money. We got to do it with our hands and our teeth." His head jerked up. London was grinning in sympathy, embarrassed, as men are when one of their number opens his heart.

Mac's heavy face flushed with shame. "I'm tired. You guys carry it while me and Jim get some sleep. Oh, London, in the mail tomorrow there'll be a package for Alex Little. It's handbills. Ought to be in by eight o'clock. Send some of the guys down to get it, will you? And see the handbills get around. They ought to do some good. Come on, Jim. Let's sleep."

They lay in their room in the dark. Outside the men sat and waited, and the murmur of their voices penetrated the walls and seemed to penetrate the world. Away, in town, a switch-engine crashed back and forth making up a train. The night milk trucks rumbled over the highway beside the orchard. Then oddly, sweetly, someone played a few tunes on a harmonica, and the murmur of voices stopped and the men listened. It was quiet outside, except for the harmonica, so quiet that Jim heard a rooster crowing before he went to sleep.

7

THE DAY was coming in grey and cold when Jim started awake at voices outside the door. He heard a man say, "They're in here, probably asleep yet." The door opened. Mac sat up.

A familiar voice said, "You here, Mac?"

"Dick! How the hell'd you get here this early?"

"Came down with Doc Burton."

"Doc here too?"

"Sure, he's right outside the door."

Mac scratched a match and lighted a candle in a broken saucer. Dick turned to Jim. "Hello, kid. How you makin' it?"

"Fine. What you all dressed up for, Dick? Pants pressed, clean shirt?"

Dick smiled self-consciously. "Somebody in this dump's got to look respectable."

Mac said, "Dick'll be infesting every pink parlor in Torgas. Listen, Dick, I got a list of sympathizers right here. We want money, of course; but we want tents, pieces of canvas, beds. Remember that—tents. Here's your list. There's lots of names on it. Make the contacts, and we'll send cars for the stuff. Lot of the boys 've got cars."

"O.K., Mac. How's she going?"

"Going like a bat out of hell. We got to work quick to keep up." He tied his shoe. "Where's Doc? Why don't you call him in? Come on in, Doc."

A young man with golden hair stepped into the room. His face was almost girlish in its delicacy, and his large eyes had a soft, sad look like those of a bloodhound. He carried his medical bag and a brief case in one hand.

"How are you, Mac? Dick got your wire and picked me up."

"I'm sure glad you got here quick, Doc. We need you right away. This is Jim Nolan."

Jim stood up, stamping his heels into his shoes. "Glad to know you, Doc."

Mac said, "Better start, Dick. You can bum breakfast at Al's Lunch Wagon, on Townsend. Don't hit 'im up for anything else but breakfast. We already got a ranch off his old man. Shove along, Dick, and remember: tents, canvas, money—and anything else you can get."

"O.K., Mac. All the names on this list good?"

"I don't know. Try 'em. You want me to drive 'em up to you?"

"Go to hell," said Dick. He went out the door and closed it behind him. The candle and the dawn fought each other so that together they seemed to make less light than either would have made alone. The room was cold.

Dr. Burton said, "There wasn't much information in your wire. What's the job?"

"Wait a minute, Doc. Look out the window and see if you can see any coffee cooking outside."

"Well, there's a little fire outside and a pot on it, or rather a can."

Mac said, "Well, wait a minute." He went outside, and in a moment returned carrying a tin can of steaming, unpleasant-smelling coffee.

"Jesus, that looks hot," said Jim.

"And lousy," Mac added. "All right, Doc. This is the best set-up I've seen for a long time. I want to work out some ideas. I don't want this ruckus to get out of hand." He gulped some of the coffee. "Sit down on that box. We've got five acres of private property. You'll have all the help you need. Can you lay out a camp, a perfect camp, all straight lines? Dig toilets, take care of sanitation, garbage disposal? Try to figure out some way to take baths? And fill the air so God-damn full of carbolic or chloride of lime that it smells healthy? Make the whole district smell clean—can you do that?"

"Yes. I can do it. Give me enough help and I can." The sad eyes grew sadder. "Give me five gallons of crude carbolic and I'll perfume the country for miles."

"Good. Now, we're moving the men today. You look 'em over as quick as you can. See there's no contagion in any of 'em, will you? The health authorities are going to do plenty of snooping. If they can catch us off base, they'll bounce us. They let us live like pigs in the jungle, but just the minute we start a strike, they get awful concerned about the public health."

"All right, all right."

Mac looked confused. "I busted right into a song, didn't I? Well, you know what's needed. Let's go see London now."

Three men sat on the steps of London's room. They got up and moved aside for Mac. Inside, London was lying down, dozing. He rose up on his elbow. "Chroust! Is it morning?"

"It's Christmas," said Mac. "Mr. London, this here's Doc Burton, Director of Public Health. He wants some men. How many you want, Doc?"

"Well, how many men are we going to handle?"

"Oh—between a thousand and fifteen hundred."

"Better give me fifteen or twenty men, then."

London called, "Hi, out there." One of the sentinels opened the door and looked in. "Try find Sam, will you?"

"Sure."

London said, "We called a meetin' for ten o'clock this mornin'. Great big meetin', I mean. I sent word to the other camps about this Anderson place. They'll start movin' in pretty soon."

The door opened and Sam entered, his lean face sharp with curiosity.

"Sam, this here's Doc Burton. He wants you for his right-hand. Go outside and tell the guys you want volunteers to help the Doc. Get twenty good men."

"O.K., London. When you want 'em?"

Burton said, "Right now. We'll go right over and lay out the camp. I can pile eight or nine in my old car. Get somebody with a car to take the rest."

Sam glanced from London to Burton, and back to London to verify the authority. London nodded his big head. "That's straight, Sam. Anything Doc says."

Burton stood up to go with him. "I'd like to help pick the men."

"Wait," Mac said. "You're all clear in town, aren't you, Doc?"

"What do you mean 'clear'?"

"I mean, is there anything they could hang a malpractice charge on you for?"

"Not that I know of. 'Course they can do anything if they want to bad enough."

"Sure," said Mac. "I know; but it might take 'em some time. 'Bye, Doc. See you later."

When Burton and Sam were gone, Mac turned to London. "He's a good guy. Looks like a pansy with his pretty face, but he's hard-boiled enough. And he's thorough as croton oil. Got anything to eat, London?"

"Loaf of bread and some cheese."

"Well, what are we waitin' for? Jim and me forgot to eat last night."

Jim said, "I woke up in the night and remembered."

London brought a bag from the corner and laid out a loaf of bread and a slab of cheese. There was a stirring outside. The hum of voices that had been still for several hours broke out again. Doors opened and slammed. Men hacked their throats clear of mucus and spat and blew their noses. The clear day had come, and the sun was red through the windows.

Mac, talking around a mouthful of cheese, said, "London, what do you think of Dakin for general chairman of the strike committee and boss-in-chief?"

London looked a little disappointed. "Dakin's a good guy," he said. "I've knowed Dakin for a long time."

Mac went into London's disappointment and dug it out. "I'll be straight with you, London. You'd be a hell of a good chairman, except you'd get mad. Now Dakin don't look like a guy that would ever get mad. If the boss of this mess ever gets mad, we're sunk."

The attempt was successful. London agreed, "I get sore as hell. I get so damn mad it makes me sick. You're straight about Dakin, too; he's a gamblin' kind of a man. Never opens up his eyes wide; never lets his voice get loose. The worse things gets, the quieter Dakin gets."

Mac said, "Then when the meetin' comes off, you throw your weight to Dakin, will you?"

"Sure."

"I don't know about this guy Burke, but I think with our guys and Dakin's guys we could soft-pedal him if he gets rank. We better start the guys movin' pretty soon; it's quite a ways over there."

London asked, "When you think the scabs'll start comin'?"

"Not before tomorrow. I don't think the bosses around here think we mean it yet. They can't get in any scabs before tomorrow."

"What we goin' to do when they land?"

"Well," said Mac. "We'll meet the train an' give 'em the keys of the city. I ought to have a wire before they start from town. Some of the boys'll kind of be checkin' up on the employment agencies." He lifted his head and looked toward the door. The hum of voices outside had been casual and monotonous, and now it stopped altogether. Suddenly, through the silence, there came a cat-call, and then other voices broke into shouts. There was an argument outside.

London stepped over to the door and opened it. The three sentinels stood side by side before the door, and in front of them stood the orchard superintendent in mole-skin trousers and field boots. On either side of him stood a man wearing a deputy sheriff's badge, and in each of his hands were shot-guns.

The superintendent looked over the heads of the guardians. "I want to talk to you, London."

"You sure come with an olive-branch," said London.

"Well, let me come in. Maybe we can work something out." London looked at Mac, and Mac nodded. The great crowd of men was silent, listening. The 'super' stepped forward, with his deputies beside him. The guards maintained their position. One of them said, "Let him leave his bulls outside, chief."

"That's a good idear," said London. "You don't need no buckshot to talk with."

The 'super' glanced nervously about at the silent, threatening men. "What proof have I that you'll play straight?" he demanded.

"Just about as much as I have that you will."

The 'super' made his decision. "Stay outside and keep order," he said.

Now the guardians stepped aside, letting the one man enter, and then resumed their position. The deputies were nervous. They stood fingering their guns and look-ing fiercely about them.

London closed the door. "I don't know why you couldn't say it outside, where the guys could hear."

The 'super' saw Mac and Jim. He looked angrily at London. "Put those men out."

"Uh-uh," said London.

"Now look here, London, you don't know what you're

doing. I'm offering you the chance to go back to work if you kick those men out."

"What for?" London asked. "They're good guys."

"They're reds. They're getting a lot of good men into trouble. They don't give a *damn* about you men if they can start trouble. Get rid of 'em and you can go back to work."

London said, "S'pose we kick 'em out? Do we get the money we're strikin' for? Do we get what we would of got before the cut?"

"No; but you can go back to work with no more trouble. The owners will overlook everything that's happened."

"Well, what good was the strike, then?"

The 'super' lowered his voice. "I'll tell you what I'm prepared to offer. You get the men back to work and you'll get a steady job here as assistant superintendent at five dollars a day."

"And how about these guys, these friends of mine?"

"Fifty dollars apiece if they get out of the Valley."

Jim looked at the heavy, brooding face of London. Mac was grinning meanly. London went on, "I like to see both sides. S'pose me an' my friends here don't take it, what then?"

"Then we kick you off this place in half an hour. Then we blacklist the whole damn bunch of you. You can't go any place; you can't get a job any place. We'll have five hundred deputy sheriffs if we need 'em. That's the other side. We'll see you can't get a job this side of hell. What's more, we'll jug your pals here, and see they get the limit."

London said, "You can't bag 'em if they've got money."

The 'super' stepped closer, pressing his advantage. "Don't be a fool, London. You know as well as I do what the vagrancy laws are. You know vagrancy's anything the judge doesn't want you to do. And if you *don't* know it, the judge here's named Hunter. Come on, now, London. Bring the men back to work. It's a steady job for you, five dollars a day."

London's eyes fell away. He looked at Mac, asking mutely for instructions. Mac let the silence hang.

"Well, come on, London. How about it? Your red pals here can't help you, and you know it damn well."

Jim, on the outskirts, was shivering. His eyes were wide and quiet. Mac watched London and saw what the 'super' did not see, the shoulders gradually settling and widening, the big, muscled neck dropping down between the shoulders, the arms hooking slowly up, the eyes taking on a dangerous gleam, a flush stealing up the neck and out on the cheeks.

Suddenly Mac cried sharply, "London!" London jerked, and then relaxed a little. Mac said quietly, "I know a way out, London. While this gent is here, let's hold a meetin' of all the men. Let's tell the guys what we've been offered to sell 'em out. We'll take a vote on whether you get that five dollar job and—then—we'll try to keep the guys from lynchin' this gent here."

The 'super' turned red with anger. "This is the last offer," he cried. "Take this, or get out."

"We was just about to get out," Mac said.

"You'll get out of the Torgas Valley. We'll run you out."

"Oh, no, you won't. We got a piece of private property we can stay on. The owner invited us."

"That's a lie!"

"Listen, mister," Mac said, "we're goin' to have a little trouble gettin' you and your bodyguard out of here as it is. Don't make it no worse."

"Well, where do you think you're going to stay?"

Mac sat down on a box. His voice grew cold. "Listen, mister, we're goin' to camp on the Anderson place.

Now the first thing you babies are goin' to think of is gettin' us off. That's O.K. We'll take our chance. The second thing you weasels are goin' to do is try to get back at Anderson. Now I'm tellin' you this, if any of your boys touch that property or hurt Anderson, if you hurt one single fruit tree, a thousand guys'll start out an' every one of 'em'll have a box of matches. *Get it, mister?* Take it as a threat if you want to: you touch Anderson's ranch and by Christ we'll burn every fucking house and barn on every ranch in the Valley!" Tears of fury were in Mac's eyes. His chest shuddered as though he were about to cry.

The 'super' snapped his head around to London. "You see the kind of men you're mixed up with, London? You know how many years you can get for arson?"

London choked. "You better scram on, Mister. I'm goin' to kill you if you don't. You better go now. Make him go now, Mac," he cried. "For Christ's sake, make him *go!*"

The 'super' backed away from the heavy, weaving body of London and reached behind him to find the doorknob. "Threat of murder," he said thickly. The door was open behind him.

"You got no witness to a threat," Mac said.

Outside the deputies tried to see in between the stiff bodies of the guardians. "You're fools, all of you," the 'super' said. "If I need 'em, I'll have a dozen witnesses to anything I want. You've had my last word."

The guardians stepped aside for the 'super.' The deputies ranged up beside him. Not a sound came from the bunched men. A lane opened up for the three and they strode out through it. The silent men followed them with their eyes, and the eyes were puzzled and angry. The three marched stiffly to a big roadster that stood at one end of the building. They climbed in and drove away. And then the crowd looked slowly back at the

open door of London's room. London stood leaning
against the doorjamb, looking weak and sick.

Mac stepped into the doorway and put his arm around
London's shoulders. They were two feet above the heads
of the quiet men. Mac cried, "Listen, you guys. We
didn't want to tell you before they got away; we was
afraid you'd stomp 'em to death. That mug come here to
try to get London to sell you out. London was goin' to
get a steady job, an' you guys was goin' to get screwed."

A growl started, a snarling growl. Mac held up his
hand. "No need to get mad, wait a minute, now. Jus'
remember it later; they tried to buy London—an' they
couldn't. Now shut up for a minute. We got to get out o'
here. We got a ranch to stay on. There's goin' to be
order, too. That's the only way we can win this. We all
got to take orders. Now the guys that got cars take all the
women an' kids an' the truck that can't be carried. The
rest'll have to walk. Now be nice. Don't break nothing—
yet. An' stay together. While you're gettin' your stuff
picked up, London wants to see his committee."

The moment he stopped talking a turbulence broke
out. Shouting and laughing, the men eddied. They
seemed filled with a terrible joy, a bloody, lustful joy.
Their laughter was heavy. Into the rooms they swarmed,
and carried out their things and piled them on the
ground—pots and kettles, blankets, bundles of clothing.
The women rolled out push-carts for the children. Six of
the committeemen forced and shouldered their way
through the press, and entered London's room.

The sun was clear of the trees now, and the air was
warmed by it. Behind the buildings battered old cars began to start with bursts of noise. There were sounds of
hammering as possessions were boxed. The place swam
with activity, with the commotion of endless trips back
and forth, of opinions shouted, of judgments made and
overruled.

London let his committee in and shut the door to keep out the noise. The men were silent, dignified, grave and important. They sat on boxes and clasped their knees and bent portentous looks at the walls.

Mac said, "London, d'you mind if I talk to them?"

"Sure, go ahead."

"I don't mean to hog the show, gents," Mac continued. "I had some experience. I been through this before. Maybe I can show you where the thing breaks down, and maybe we can steer clear of some of the things that conk us."

One of the men said, "Go ahead, fella. We'll listen."

"O.K. We got plenty of fire now. That's the trouble with workin' stiffs, though. One minute they're steamed up like a keg of beer, and the next, they're cold as a whore's heart. We got to cut down the steam and warm up the cold. Now I want to make a suggestion. You guys can think it over, an' then you can maybe get the whole bunch to vote on it. Most strikes break down because they got no discipline. Suppose we divide the men in squads, let each squad elect a leader, and then he's responsible for his squad. We can work 'em in groups, then."

One of the men said, "Lot of these guys was in the army. They di'n't like it none."

"Sure they didn't. They was fightin' some other guy's war. They had officers shoved down their throats. If they elect their officers and fight their own war, it'd be different."

"Most o' these guys don't like *no* officers."

"Well, they got to have 'em. We'll get the pants kicked off us if we got no discipline. If the squad don't like the leader, let 'em vote 'im into the ranks an' elect another leader. That ought to satisfy 'em. Then we ought to have officers over hundreds, an' one chief high-tail boss. Just give it a thought, gents. There's goin' to be a big meetin' in about two hours. We got to have a plan ready."

London scratched his tonsure. "Sounds O.K. to me. I'll talk it over with Dakin soon's I see him."

"All right," said Mac. "Let's get movin'. Jim, you stay close to me."

"Give *me* some work," Jim said.

"No, you stay close. I may need you."

8

big breeze in about two weeks. We got to have 'em ready."

Tom shook his fingers. "So'll me,"

"I'll be over with them and take 'em."

"All right," said Al. "I'll be ready. Jim, you say...

THE FIVE acres of plow land on the Anderson place were surrounded on three sides by big, dark apple trees; and on the fourth it was bounded by the narrow, dusty county road. The men had arrived in droves, laughing and shouting to one another, and they had found preparations made for them. Stakes were driven into the soft ground defining the streets for the camp. There were five streets running parallel to the county road, and opposite the end of each street a deep hole was dug in the ground as a toilet.

Before the work of building the camp started, they held their general meeting with some order; elected Dakin chairman and assented to his committee. They agreed with enthusiasm to the suggestion of the squads.

Hardly had they begun to assemble when five motor-cycle police rode up and parked their motors in the county road. They leaned against the machines and watched the work. Tents were pitched, and shelters laid out. The sad-eyed Dr. Burton was everywhere, ordering the building of the camp. At least a hundred old automobiles lined the road, drawn up like caissons in an artillery park, all facing out toward the road. There were ancient Fords, ravaged in their upholstery; Chevrolets and Dodges with rusty noses, paintless, with loose fenders or no fenders at all. There were worn-out Hudsons that made a noise like machine-guns when they were starting. They stood like aged soldiers at a reunion. At one end of the line of cars stood Dakin's Chevrolet truck, clean and new and shiny. Alone of all the cars it was in good condition; and Dakin, as he walked about the camp, surrounded by members of his committee, rarely got out of sight of his truck. As he talked or listened his cold, secret eyes went again and again to his shining green truck.

When the grey old tents were pitched Burton insisted that the canvas be scrubbed with soap and water. Dakin's truck brought barrels of water from Anderson's tank. The women washed the tents with old brooms.

Anderson walked out and watched with worried eyes while his five acres were transformed into a camp. By noon it was ready; and nine hundred men went to work in the orchard, picking apples into their cooking kettles, into their hats, into gunny sacks. There were not nearly ladders enough. The men climbed up the trunks into the trees. By dark the crop was picked, the lines of boxes filled, the boxes trucked to Anderson's barn and stored.

Dick had worked quickly. He sent a boy to ask for men and a truck to meet him in town, and the truck came back loaded with tents of all kinds—umbrella tents of pale brown canvas, pup-tents, low and peaked, big troop tents with room in them for ten men. And the truck brought two sacks of rolled oats and sacks of flour, cases of canned goods, sacks of potatoes and onions and a slaughtered cow.

The new tents went up along the streets. Dr. Burton superintended the cooking arrangements. Trucks went out to the city dump and brought back three rusty, discarded stoves. Pieces of tin covered the gaping tops. Cooks were assigned, washtubs filled with water, the cow cut up and potatoes and onions set to cooking in tremendous stews. Buckets of beans were boiled. In the dusk, when the picking was over, the men came in and found tubs of stew waiting for them. They sat on the ground and ate from basins and cups and tin cans.

As darkness fell, the motorcycle police were relieved by five deputy sheriffs armed with rifles. For a time they marched up and down the road in military manner, but finally they sat in the ditch and watched the men. There were few lights in the camp. Here and there a tent was lighted with a lantern. The flares of little fires threw shadows. At one end of the first street, so pitched that it was directly behind his shining green truck, stood Dakin's tent—a large, patented affair with a canvas wall in the middle, making two rooms. His folding table and chairs were set up. A ground cloth lay on the floor, and from the center pole a hissing gasoline lantern hung. Dakin lived in style and traveled in luxury. He had no vices; every cent he or his wife made went to his living, to his truck, to providing new equipment for his camp.

When it was dark, London and Mac and Jim strolled to the tent and went in. With Dakin in the tent sat Burke, a lowering, sullen Irishman, and two short Italian men who looked very much alike. Mrs. Dakin had retired to the other side of the partition. Under the white light of the gasoline lamp Dakin's pink scalp showed through his blond hair. His secret eyes moved restlessly about. "Hello, boys, find some place to sit."

London chose a chair, the only one left. Mac and Jim squatted on the ground; Mac brought out his Durham bag and made a cigarette. "Things seem to be goin' O.K.," he observed.

Dakin's eyes flicked to him, and then away. "Yeah, they seem to be all right."

"They got those cops here quick," said Burke. "I'd like to take a poke at a few of 'em."

Dakin reproved him calmly. "Let cops alone till you can't no more. They ain't hurtin' a thing."

Mac asked, "How the squads shapin'?"

"All right. They all elected their chiefs. Some of 'em kicked out the chief and elected new ones already. Say, that Doc Burton is a swell guy."

"Yeah," Mac said. "He's O.K. Wonder where he's at? You better have one of the squads watch out for him. When we get started, they'll try to get him out of here. If they can get him out, they can clear us out. 'Danger to public health,' they call it."

Dakin turned to Burke. "Fix that up now, will you, Burke? Tell a good bunch to keep care o' Doc. The guys like him." Burke got up and went out of the tent.

London said, "Tell 'im what you told me, Mac."

"Well, the guys think this is a kind of a picnic, Dakin. Tomorrow morning the picnic's over. The fun begins."

"Scabs?"

"Yep, a train-load. I got a kid in town. He goes to the telegraph office for me. Got a wire tonight. A freight train-load of scabs is startin' out from the city today. Ought to be in some time in the mornin'."

"Well," said Dakin. "Guess we better meet that train an' have a talk with the new guys. Might do some good, before they all get scattered."

"That's what I thought," said Mac. "I've saw the time when a whole slough of scabs come over if you just told 'em how things was."

"We'll tell 'em, all right."

"Listen," said Mac. "The cops'll try to head us off. Couldn't we let the guys kind of sneak off through the trees just before daylight, and leave them cops holding the bag here?"

For a second Dakin's cold eyes twinkled. "Think that'd work, you guys?" They laughed delightedly. Dakin went on, "Well, go out an' tell the men about it."

Mac said, "Wait a minute, Dakin. If you tell the guys tonight, it won't be no secret."

"What do you mean?"

"Well, you don't think we ain't got stools in the camp, do you? I bet there's at least five under cover, besides the guys that'd spill anything and hope to get a buck out of it. Hell, it's always that way. Don't tell 'em nothing till you're ready to start."

"Don't trust the guys, huh?"

"Well, if you want to take the chance, go ahead. I bet you find the cops comin' right along with us."

Dakin asked, "What do you guys think?"

"I guess he's right," said one of the little Italian men.

"O.K. Now we got to leave a bunch to take care of the camp."

"At least a hundred," Mac agreed. "If we leave the camp, they'll burn 'er, sure as hell."

"The boys sure got Anderson's crop down quick."

"Yeah," said Dakin. "There's two or three hundred of 'em out in the orchard next door right now. Anderson's goin' to have a bigger crop than he thought."

"I hope they don't cause trouble yet," Mac said. "There'll be plenty later on."

"How many scabs comin'? Did you find out?"

"Somewheres between four and five hundred tomorrow. Be more later, I guess. Be sure an' tell the guys to take plenty of rocks in their pockets."

"I'll tell 'em."

Burke came back in. He said, "The Doc's goin' to sleep in one of them big army tents. There'll be ten guys sleepin' in the same tent with him."

"Where's Doc at now?" Mac asked.

"He's dug up a couple of ringworms on a guy. He's fixin' 'im over by the stoves."

At that moment a chorus of yells broke out in the camp, and then a high, angry voice shouting. The six men ran out of the tent. The noise came from a group of men standing in front of the camp street that faced the road. Dakin pushed his way in among the men. "What th' hell's the matter here?"

The angry voice answered, "I'll tell you. Your men started throwin' rocks. I'm tellin' you now if there's any more rocks we're goin' to start shootin', an' we don't care who we hit."

Mac turned to Jim, standing beside him. He said softly, "I wish they would start shooting. This bunch of mugs is going to pieces, maybe, if something dirty doesn't happen pretty soon. They're feeling too good. They'll start fighting themselves."

London walked fiercely into the crowd of men. "You guys get back," he cried. "You got enough to do without no kid tricks. Go on, now, get back where you belong." The authority of the man drove them sullenly back, but they dispersed reluctantly.

The deputy shouted, "You keep those guys in order or we'll do it with Winchesters."

Dakin said coldly, "You can pull in your neck and go back to sleep."

Mac muttered to Jim, "Those cops are scared as hell. That makes 'em dangerous. Just like rattlesnakes when they're scared: they'll shoot at anything."

The crowd had moved away now and the men were scattering to their tents. Mac said, "Let's go have a look at Doc, Jim. Come on over by the stoves." They found Dr. Burton sitting on a box, bandaging a man's arm. A kerosene lantern shed a thin yellow light on his work and illumined a small circle on the ground. He stuck down the bandage with adhesive.

"There you are," he said. "Next time don't let it get so sore. You'll lose an arm some day, if you do."

The man said, "Thanks, Doc," and went away, rolling down his sleeve.

"Hello, Mac. Hello, Jim. I guess I'm finished."

"Was that the ringworm?"

"No, just a little cut, and a nice infection started. They won't learn to take care of cuts."

Mac said, "If Doc could only find a case of small-pox

now and set up a quarantine ward, he'd be perfectly happy. What're you going to do now, Doc?"

The sad brown eyes looked tiredly up at Mac. "Well, I think I'm all through. I ought to go and see whether the squad disinfected the toilets the way I told them."

"They smell disinfected," Mac said. "Why don't you get some sleep, Doc? You didn't have any last night."

"Well, I'm tired, but I don't feel sleepy. For the last hour I've thought when I was through I might walk out into the orchard and sit down against a tree and rest."

"Mind company?"

"No. I'd like to have you." Burton stood up. "Wait till I wash my hands." He scrubbed his hands in a pan of warm water and covered them with green soap and rinsed them. "Let's stroll, then," he said.

The three walked slowly away from the tent streets and toward the dark orchard. Their feet crunched softly on the crisp little clods of the plowed ground.

"Mac," Burton said wearily. "You're a mystery to me. You imitate any speech you're taking part in. When you're with London and Dakin you talk the way they do. You're an actor."

"No," said Mac. "I'm not an actor at all. Speech has a kind of a feel about it. I get the feel, and it comes out, perfectly naturally. I don't try to do it. I don't think I could help doing it. You know, Doc, men are suspicious of a man who doesn't talk their way. You can insult a man pretty badly by using a word he doesn't understand. Maybe he won't say anything, but he'll hate you for it. It's not the same thing in your case, Doc. You're supposed to be different. They wouldn't trust you if you weren't."

They entered the arches under the trees, and the leaf clusters and the limbs were dark against the sky. The little murmuring noise of the camp was lost. A barn-owl, screeching overhead with a ripping sound, startled the men.

"That's an owl, Jim," Mac explained. "He's hunting mice." And then to Burton, "Jim's never been in the country much. The things we know are new to him. Let's sit down here."

Mac and the doctor sat on the ground and leaned against the big trunk of an old apple tree. Jim sat in front of them, folding his legs before him. The night was still. Above, the black leaves hung motionless in the quiet air.

Mac spoke softly, for the night seemed to be listening. "You're a mystery to me, too, Doc."

"Me? A mystery?"

"Yes, you. You're not a Party man, but you work with us all the time; you never get anything for it. I don't know whether you believe in what we're doing or not, you never say, you just work. I've been out with you before, and I'm not sure you believe in the cause at all."

Dr. Burton laughed softly. "It would be hard to say. I could tell you some of the things I think; you might not like them. I'm pretty sure you wouldn't like them."

"Well, let's hear them, anyway."

"Well, you say I don't believe in the cause. That's like not believing in the moon. There've been communes before, and there will be again. But you people have an idea that if you can *establish* the thing, the job'll be done. Nothing stops, Mac. If you were able to put an idea into effect tomorrow, it would start changing right away. Establish a commune, and the same gradual flux will continue."

"Then you don't think the cause is good?"

Burton sighed. "You see? We're going to pile up on that old rock again. That's why I don't like to talk very often. Listen to me, Mac. My senses aren't above reproach, but they're all I have. I want to see the whole picture—as nearly as I can. I don't want to put on the blinders of 'good' and 'bad,' and limit my vision. If I used the term 'good' on a thing I'd lose my license to inspect it, because there might be bad in it. Don't you see? I want to be able to look at the whole thing."

Mac broke in heatedly, "How about social injustice? The profit system? You have to say they're bad."

Dr. Burton threw back his head and looked at the sky. "Mac," he said. "Look at the physiological injustice, the injustice of tetanus, the injustice of syphilis, the gangster methods of amoebic dysentery—that's my field."

"Revolution and communism will cure social injustice."

"Yes, and disinfection and prophylaxis will prevent the others."

"It's different, though; men are doing one, and germs are doing the other."

"I can't see much difference, Mac."

"Well, damn it, Doc, there's lockjaw every place. You can find syphilis in Park Avenue. Why do you hang around with us if you aren't for us?"

"I want to *see*," Burton said. "When you cut your finger, and streptococci get in the wound, there's a swelling and a soreness. That swelling is the fight your body puts up, the pain is the battle. You can't tell which one is going to win, but the wound is the first battleground. If the cells lose the first fight the streptococci invade, and the fight goes on up the arm. Mac, these little strikes are like the infection. Something has got into the men; a little fever had started and the lymphatic glands are shooting in reinforcements. I want to see, so I go to the seat of the wound."

"You figure the strike is a wound?"

"Yes. Group-men are always getting some kind of infection. This seems to be a bad one. I want to *see*, Mac. I want to watch these group-men, for they seem to me to be a new individual, not at all like single men. A man in a group isn't himself at all, he's a cell in an organism that isn't like him any more than the cells in your body are like you. I want to watch the group, and see what it's like. People have said, 'mobs are crazy, you can't tell what they'll do.' Why don't people look at mobs not as men, but as mobs? A mob nearly always seems to act reasonably, for a mob."

"Well, what's this got to do with the cause?"

"It might be like this, Mac: When group-man wants to move, he makes a standard. 'God wills that we recapture the Holy Land'; or he says, 'We fight to make the world safe for democracy'; or he says, 'We will wipe out social injustice with communism.' But the group doesn't care about the Holy Land, or Democracy, or Communism. Maybe the group simply wants to move, to fight, and uses these words simply to reassure the brains of individual men. I say it *might* be like that, Mac."

"Not with the cause, it isn't," Mac cried.

"Maybe not, it's just the way I think of things."

Mac said, "The trouble with you, Doc, is you're too God-damn far left to be a communist. You go too far with collectivization. How do you account for people like me, directing things, moving things? That puts your group-man out."

"You might be an effect as well as a cause, Mac. You might be an expression of group-man, a cell endowed with a special function, like an eye cell, drawing your force from group-man, and at the same time directing him, like an eye. Your eye both takes orders from and gives orders to your brain."

"This isn't practical," Mac said disgustedly. "What's all this kind of talk got to do with hungry men, with lay-offs and unemployment?"

"It might have a great deal to do with them. It isn't a very long time since tetanus and lockjaw were not connected. There are still primitives in the world who don't know children are the result of intercourse. Yes, it might be worth while to know more about group-man, to know his nature, his ends, his desires. They're not the same as ours. The pleasure we get in scratching an itch causes death to a great number of cells. Maybe group-man gets pleasure when individual men are wiped out in a war. I simply want to see as much as I can, Mac, with the means I have."

Mac stood up and brushed the seat of his pants. "If you see too darn much, you don't get anything done."

Burton stood up too, chuckling softly. "Maybe some day—oh, let it go. I shouldn't have talked so much. But it does clarify a thought to get it spoken, even if no one listens."

They started back over the crisp clods toward the sleeping camp. "We can't look up at anything, Doc," Mac said. "We've got to whip a bunch of scabs in the morning."

"Deus vult," said Burton. "Did you see those pointers of Anderson's? Beautiful dogs; they give me a sensual pleasure, almost sexual."

A light still burned in Dakin's tent. The camp slept. Only a few coals of fire still burned in the streets. The silent line of old cars stood against the road, and in the road itself a clump of sparks waxed and waned, cigarettes of the watchful deputies.

"D'you hear that, Jim? That'll show you what Burton is. Here's a couple of fine dogs, good hunting dogs, but they're not dogs to Doc, they're feelings. They're dogs, to me. And these guys sleeping here are men, with stomachs; but they're not men to Doc, they're a kind of a collective Colossus. If he wasn't a doctor, we couldn't have 'im around. We need his skill, but his brain just gets us into a mess."

Burton laughed apologetically. "I don't know why I go on talking, then. You practical men always lead practical men with stomachs. And something always gets out of hand. Your men get out of hand, they don't follow the rules of common sense, and you practical men either deny that it is so, or refuse to think about it. And when someone wonders what it is that makes a man with a stomach something more than your rule allows, why you howl, 'Dreamer, mystic, metaphysician.' I don't know why I talk about it to a practical man. In all history there are no men who have come to such wild-eyed confusion and bewilderment as practical men leading men with stomachs."

"We've a job to do," Mac insisted. "We've got no time to mess around with high-falutin ideas."

"Yes, and so you start your work not knowing your medium. And your ignorance trips you up every time."

They were close to the tents now. "If you talked to other people that way," Mac said, "we'd have to kick you out."

A dark figure arose suddenly from the ground. "Who is it?" a voice demanded; and then, "Oh, hello. I didn't know who it was coming in."

"Dakin set out guards?" Mac asked.

"Yeah."

"He's a good man. I knew he was a good man, cool-headed man."

They stopped by a big, peaked troop tent. "Guess I'll turn in," Doc said. "Here's where my bodyguard sleeps."

"Good idea," Mac agreed. "You'll probably have some bandaging to do tomorrow."

When Doc had disappeared inside the tent, Mac turned to Jim. "No reason why you shouldn't get some sleep too."

"What are you going to do, Mac?"

"Me? Oh, I thought I'd take a look around, see if everything's all right."

"I want to go with you. I just follow you around."

"Sh-h, don't talk so loud." Mac walked slowly toward the line of cars. "You do help me, Jim. It may be sloppy as an old woman, but you keep me from being scared."

"I don't do anything but pad around after you," said Jim.

"I know. I guess I'm getting soft. I'm scared something might happen to you. I shouldn't have brought you down, Jim. I'm getting to depend on you."

"Well, what're we going to do now, Mac?"

"I wish you'd go to bed. I'm going to try to have a talk with those cops in the road."

"What for?"

"Listen, Jim, you didn't get bothered by what Doc said, did you?"

"No. I didn't listen."

"Well, it's a bunch of bunk; but here's something that isn't bunk. You win a strike two ways, because the men put up a steady fight, and because public sentiment comes over to your side. Now most of this valley belongs to a few guys. That means the rest of the people don't own much of anything. The few owners either have to pay 'em or lie to 'em. Those cops out in the road are special deputies, just working stiffs with a star and a gun and a two-weeks' job. I thought I'd try and sound 'em out; try and find out how they feel about the strike. I guess how they feel is how the bosses told 'em to feel. But I might get a line on 'em, anyway."

"Well, how about it if they arrest you? Remember what that man said in the road last night."

"They're just deputies, Jim. They won't recognize me the way a regular cop would."

"Well, I want to go with you."

"O.K., but if anything looks funny, you cut for the camp and yell like hell."

In a tent behind them a man started shouting in his sleep. A soft chorus of voices awakened him and stopped his dreaming. Mac and Jim wedged their way silently between two cars and approached a little group of glowing cigarettes. The sparks died down and shifted as they approached.

Mac called, "Hey, you guys, can we come out there?"

From the group a voice, "How many of you?"

"Two."

"Come on, then." As they drew near, a flashlight glanced out and touched their faces for a second, and then went off. The deputies stood up. "What do you want?" their spokesman demanded.

Mac replied, "We just couldn't sleep; thought we'd come out and talk."

The man laughed. "We been having lots of company tonight."

In the dark Mac pulled out his Bull Durham bag. "Any of you guys want to smoke?"

"We got smokes. What is it you want?"

"Well, I'll tell you. A lot of the guys want to know how you fellows feel about the strike. They sent us out to ask. They know you're just working men, the same as them. They want to know if you maybe won't help your own kind of guys."

Silence met his words. Mac looked uneasily around.

A voice said softly, "All right, you chickens. Get 'em up. Let out a squawk and we plug you."

"Say, what the hell is this? What's the idea?"

"Get behind 'em, Jack, and you, Ed, get your guns

in their backs. If they move, let 'em have it. Now, march!"

The rifles pushed into their backs and punched them along through the darkness. The leader's voice said, "Thought you was God-damn smart, didn't you? You didn't know those day-cops pointed you two guys out." They marched across the road, and in among the trees on the other side. "Thought you was darn smart, getting the men out of here before daylight; thought you'd leave us holding the sack. Hell, we knew that gag ten minutes after you decided it."

"Who told you, mister?"

"Don't you wish you knew?" Their feet pounded along. The rifles jabbed into their backs.

"You takin' us to jail, mister?"

"Jail, hell, we're takin' you God-damn reds to the Vigilance Committee. If you're lucky they'll beat the crap out of you and dump you over the county line; if you ain't lucky, they'll string you up to a tree. We got no use for radicals in this valley."

"But you guys are cops, you got to take us to jail."

"That's what *you* think. There's a nice little house a little ways from here. That's where we're taking you."

Under the orchard trees even the little light from the stars was shut off. "Now be quiet, you guys."

Jim cried, "Go, Mac!" and at the same instant he dropped. His guard toppled over him. Jim rolled around the trunk of a tree, stood up and bolted. At the second row he climbed up into an apple tree, far up, among the leaves. He heard a scuffle and a grunt of pain. The flashlight darted about and then fell to the ground and aimlessly lighted a rotten apple. There came a rip of cloth, and then steady pounding of footsteps. A hand reached down and picked up the flashlight and switched it off. Muffled, arguing voices came from the place of the scuffle.

Jim eased himself gently out of the tree, panting with apprehension every time the leaves quivered. He moved quietly along, came to the road and crossed it. At the line of cars a guard stopped him. "This is the second time tonight, kid. Whyn't you go to bed?"

Jim said, "Listen, did Mac come through?"

"Yeah, goin' like a bat out of hell. He's in Dakin's tent."

Jim hurried on, lifted the brown tent-flap and went in. Dakin and Mac and Burke were there. Mac was talking excitedly. He stopped on a word and stared as Jim came in. "Jesus, I'm glad," he said, "We was just goin' to send out a party to try and get you. What a damn fool I was! What a damn fool! You know, Dakin, they was marchin' us along, had guns right in our backs. I didn't think they'd shoot, but they might of. Jim, what in hell did you do?"

"I just dropped, and the guy fell over me, and his gun dug in the dirt. We used to do that trick in the school yard."

Mac laughed uneasily. "Soon's the guns wasn't touching us, I guess they was afraid they'd kill each other. I jumped sideways and kicked my guy in the stomach."

Burke was standing behind Mac. Jim saw Mac wink at Dakin. The cold eyes almost disappeared behind pale-lashed lids. Dakin said, "Burke, you'd better make the rounds, and see if the guards are all awake."

Burke hesitated. "I think they're O.K."

"Well, you better see, anyway. We don't want no more raids. What they got in their hands, Burke?"

"They got nice clubs."

"Well, go take a look around."

Burke went out of the tent. Mac stepped close to Dakin. "Tent walls is thin," he said quietly. "I'd like to talk to you alone. Want to take a little walk?"

Dakin nodded his head with two jerks. The three of

them strolled out into the darkness, going in the direction Dr. Burton had taken earlier. A guard looked them
over as they passed.

Mac said, "Somebody's double-crossin' us already. Them
deputies knew we was goin' to shove off before daylight."

Dakin asked coldly, "D'you think it's Burke? He
wasn't there, even."

"I don't know who it was. Anybody hanging around
could of heard through the tent."

"Well, what are we goin' to do about it? You seem to
know all about this stuff." The cold voice went on, "I
got an idea you reds ain't goin' to do us no good. A guy
come in tonight and says if we kick you out, maybe the
bosses'll talk business."

"And you think they will? They cut the wages before
we showed up, don't forget that. Hell, you'd think we
started this strike, and you know damn well we didn't.
We're just helpin' it to go straight instead of shootin' its
wad."

Dakin's monotone cut him off. "What you gettin' out
of this?"

Mac retorted hotly, "We ain't gettin' nothin'."

"How do I know that?"

"You don't know it unless you believe it. They ain't
no way to prove it."

Dakin's voice became a little warmer. "I don't know
that I'd trust you guys if that was so. If a man's gettin'
somethin' you know he's only goin' to do one or two
things, he's goin' to take orders, or he's goin' to double-
cross. But if a guy ain't gettin' nothin', you can't tell
what he'll do."

"All right," Mac said irritably. "Let's lay off that junk.
When the guys want to kick us out, let 'em take a vote
on us. And let us argue our case. But there ain't no
good of us fighting each other."

"Well, what we goin' to do, then? No good sneakin' the guys out tomorrow mornin' if the cops know we're goin' to do it."

"Sure not. Let's just march along the road and take our chances. When we see the scabs, and see how they act, we'll know whether we got to fight or talk."

Dakin stopped and moved his foot sideways against the dirt. "What do you want me out here for?"

"'I just wanted to tell you we're bein' double-crossed. If you get somethin' you don't want the cops to know, don't tell nobody."

"All right, I got that. Long as everybody's goin' to know, we might as well let 'em know. I'm goin' to bed. You guys see if you can keep out of a mess till morning."

Mac and Jim shared a little pup-tent with no floor cloth. They crawled into the little cave and curled up in their old comforters. Mac whispered, "I think Dakin's straight, but he isn't taking orders."

"You don't think he'll try to get us out of here, do you, Mac?"

"He might. I don't think he will. By tomorrow night enough guys will be bruised up and mad so they'll be meat for us. Jesus, Jim, we can't let this thing peter out. It's too good."

"Mac?"

"Yeah?"

"Why don't the cops just come and take us out of here, you and me?"

"Scared to. They're scared the men might go haywire. It might be like when old Dan fell off the ladder. Cops know pretty well when they've got to leave the stiffs alone. We better go to sleep."

"I just want to ask, Mac, how'd you get loose over in the orchard? You had a battle, didn't you?"

"Sure, but it was so dark they couldn't see who they were socking. I knew I could sock anybody."

Jim lay quiet for a while. "Were you scared, Mac, when they had the guns in our backs?"

"Damn right. I've been up against vigilantes before; so's poor old Joy. Ten or fifteen of 'em gang up on you and beat you to a pulp. Oh, they're brave guys, all right. Mostly they wear masks. Damn right I was scared, weren't you?"

"Sure, I guess so. At first I was. And then they started marching us, and I got cold all over. I could see just what would happen if I dropped. I really saw that guy fall over me, saw it before it happened. I was mostly scared they'd plug you."

Mac said, "It's a funny thing, Jim, how the worse danger you get in, the less it scares you. Once the fuss started, I wasn't scared. I still don't like the way that gun felt."

Jim looked out through the tent opening. The night seemed grey in contrast with the blackness inside the tent. Footsteps went by, crushing the little clods. "D'you think we'll win this strike, Mac?"

"We ought to go to sleep; but you know, Jim, I wouldn't have told you this before tonight: No, I don't think we have a chance to win it. This valley's *organized*. They'll start shooting, and they'll get away with it. We haven't a chance. I figure these guys here'll probably start deserting as soon as much trouble starts. But you don't want to worry about that, Jim. The thing will carry on and on. It'll spread, and some day—it'll work. Some day we'll win. We've got to believe that." He raised up on one elbow. "If we didn't believe that, we wouldn't be here. Doc was right about infection, but that infection is invested capital. We've *got* to believe we can throw it off, before it gets into our hearts and kills us. You never change, Jim. You're always here. You give me strength."

Jim said, "Harry told me right at first what to expect. Everybody hates us, Mac."

"That's the hardest part," Mac agreed. "Everybody hates us; our own side and the enemy. And if we won, Jim, if we put it over, our own side would kill us. I wonder why we do it. Oh, go to sleep!"

9

BEFORE THE night had broken at all the voice of awakening men sounded through the camp. There were axe-strokes on wood, and the rattling of the rusty stoves. In a few moments the sweet smell of burning pine and apple wood filled the camp. The cooks' detail was busy. Near the roaring stoves the buckets of coffee were set. The wash boilers of beans began to warm. Out of the tents the people crept, and went to stand near the stoves where they crowded so closely that the cooks had no room to work.

Dakin's truck drove off to Anderson's house and came back with three barrels of water. The word passed, "Dakin wants to see the squad leaders. He wants to talk to 'em right away." The leaders walked importantly toward Dakin's tent.

Now the line of orchard top grew sharp against the eastern sky and the parked cars were greyly visible. The buckets of coffee began to boil, and a rank, nourishing smell came from the bean kettles. The cooks ladled out beans into anything the people brought, pans, jars, cans and tin plates. Many sat on the ground, and with their pocket-knives carved little wooden paddles with which to eat their beans. The coffee was black and bitter, but men and women who had been silent and uncomfortable were warmed by it so that they began to talk, to laugh, to call greetings to one another. The daylight came over the trees and the ground turned greyish-blue. Three great bands of geese flew over, high in the light.

Meanwhile Dakin, flanked by Burke and London, stood in front of his tent. Before Dakin the squad leaders stood and waited, and Mac and Jim stood among them, for Mac had explained to Jim, "We've got to go pretty slow for a while. We don't want the guys to throw us out now."

Dakin had put on a short denim jacket and a tweed cap. His pale eyes darted about over the faces of the men. He said, "I'm goin' to tell you guys what's on, and then you can pull of it if you want to. I don't want nobody to come that don't want to come. There's a train-load of scabs comin' in. We figure to go in town an' try to stop 'em. We'll talk to 'em some, and then we might have to fight 'em. How's that sound to you?"

A murmur of assent arose.

"All right, then. We'll march in. Keep your guys in hand. Keep 'em quiet, and on the side of the road." He grinned coldly. "If any of 'em want to pick up a few rocks an' shove 'em in their pockets, I can't see no harm in that."

The men laughed appreciatively.

"O.K. If you got that, go talk to your men. I want to get all the kicks in before we start. I'm goin' to leave about a hundred guys to look after the camp. Go get some breakfast."

The men broke and hurried back to the stoves. Mac and Jim moved up to where the leaders stood. London was saying, "I wouldn't trust 'em to put up much of a scrap. They don't look none too mean to me."

"Too early in the morning," Mac assured him. "They ain't had their coffee yet. Guys are different before they've ate."

Dakin demanded, "You guys goin' along?"

"Damn right," said Mac. "But look, Dakin, we got men out gettin' food and supplies together. Fix it so some cars can go in for the stuff when they send the word."

"O.K. We'll need it by tonight, too. Them beans'll be all gone. It takes a hell of a lot to feed a bunch like this."

Burke said, "I'm for startin' a mix soon's the scabs get off the train. Scare hell out of 'em."

"Better talk first," Mac said. "I seen half a train-load of scabs go over to the strike if they was talked to first. You jump on 'em and you'll scare some, and make some mad."

Dakin watched him suspiciously while he talked. "Well, let's be movin'," he said. "I got to pick the guys to stay. Doc and his men can clean up the camp. I'm goin' in my truck; London an' Burke can ride with me. We better leave these damn old cans here."

The sun was just coming up when the long, ragged column started out. The squad leaders kept their men to one side of the road. Jim heard a man say, "Don't bother with clods. Wait till we get to the railroad right-of-way. There's nice granite rocks in the roadbed."

Singing broke out, the tuneless, uneven singing of un-trained men. Dakin's green Chevrolet truck led off, idling in low gear. The column of men followed it, and the crowd left in camp with the women howled good-byes after them.

They had hardly started when ten motorcycle police-men rode up and spaced themselves along the line of march. When they had gone half a mile along the road a big open car, jammed with men, dashed to the head of the column and parked across the road. All of the men carried rifles in their hands, and all wore deputies' badges. The driver stood up on the seat. "You men are going to keep order, and don't forget it," he shouted. "You can march as long as you don't block traffic, but you're not going to interfere with anybody. Get that?" He sat down, moved his car in front of Dakin's truck and led the whole march.

Jim and Mac marched fifty feet behind Dakin's truck. Mac said, "They got a reception committee for us. Ain't that kind of 'em?" The men about him tittered. Mac continued, "They say 'you got a right to strike, but you can't picket,' an' they know a strike won't work without picketin'." There was no laughter this time. The men growled, but there was little anger in the tone. Mac glanced nervously at Jim. "I don't like it," he said softly. "This bunch of bums isn't keyed up. I hope to Christ something happens to make 'em mad before long. This's going to fizzle out if something don't happen."

The straggling parade moved into town and took to the sidewalks. The men were quiet now, and most of them looked shamefaced. As they came into the town, householders watched through the windows, and children stood on the lawns and looked at them until the parents dragged them into the houses and shut the doors. Very few citizens moved about in the streets. The motorcycles of the police idled along so slowly that the riders had to put out their feet and touch the ground occasionally to keep upright. Led by the sheriff's car, the procession moved along back streets until it came at last to the railroad yard. The men stopped along the edge of the right-of-way, for the line was guarded by twenty men armed with shot-guns and tear gas bombs.

Dakin parked his truck at the curb. The men silently spread out and faced the line of special policemen. Dakin and London walked up and down the dense front, giving instructions. The men must not start any trouble with the cops if they could help it. There was to be talk first, and that was all.

On the right-of-way two long lines of refrigerator cars stood idle. Jim said, aside, to Mac, "Maybe they'll stop the freight way up the track and unload the guys. Then we wouldn't get a chance at them."

Mac shook his head. "Later they might, but now I think they want a show-down. They figure they can scare us off. Jesus, I wish the train'd come in. Waiting raises hell with guys like ours. They get scared when they have to wait around."

A number of the men were sitting down on the curb by now. A buzz of quiet talk came from the close-pressed line. They were hemmed in, railroad guards on one side, motorcycle police and deputy sheriffs on the other. The men looked nervous and self-conscious. The sheriff's deputies carried their rifles in two hands, held across their stomachs.

"The cops are scared, too," Mac said.

London reassured a group of men. "They ain't a goin' to do no shootin'," he said. "They can't afford to do no shootin'."

Someone shouted, "She's in the block!" Far along the track the block arm of the semaphore was up. A line of smoke showed above the trees, and the tracks rumbled under approaching wheels. Now the men stood up from the curb and craned their necks up the track.

London bellowed, "Hold the guys in, now."

They could see the black engine and the freight cars moving slowly in; and in the doorways of the cars they could see the legs of men. The engine crashed slowly in, puffing out bursts of steam from under its wheels. It drew into a siding and its brakes set. The cars jarred together, the engine stood wheezing and panting.

Across the street from the right-of-way stood a line of dilapidated stores and restaurants with furnished rooms in their upper storeys. Mac glanced over his shoulder. The windows of the rooms were full of men's heads looking out. Mac said, "I don't like the looks of those guys."

"Why not?" Jim asked.

"I don't know. There ought to be some women there. There aren't any women at all."

In the doorways of the box-cars strike-breakers sat, and

standing behind them were others. They stared uneasily. They made no move to get out on to the ground.

Then London stepped out in front, stepped so close to a guard that the shot-gun muzzle turned and pointed at his stomach, and the guard moved back a pace. The engine panted rhythmically, like a great, tired animal. London cupped his hands around his mouth. His deep voice roared, "Come on over, you guys. Don't fight against us. Don't help the cops." His voice was cut off by a shriek of steam. A jet of white leaped from the side of the engine, drowning London's voice, blotting out every sound but its own swishing scream. The line of strikers moved restively, bellied out in the middle, toward the guards. The shot-gun muzzles turned and swept the ranks. The guards' faces tightened, but their threat had stopped the line. The steam shrieked on, and its white plume rose up and broke into little pieces.

In the doorway of one of the box-cars a commotion started, a kind of a boiling of the men. A man squirmed through the seated scabs and dropped to the ground.

Mac shouted in Jim's ear, "My God! It's Joy!"

The misshapen, gnome-like figure faced the doorway, and the men. The arms waved jerkily. Still the steam screeched. The men in the doorway dropped to the ground and stood in front of the frantic, jerking Joy. He turned and waved his arm toward the strikers. His beaten face was contorted. Five or six of the men fell in behind him, and the whole group moved toward the line of strikers. The guards turned sideways, nervously trying to watch both sides at once.

And then—above the steam—three sharp, cracking sounds. Mac looked back at the stores. Heads and rifles were withdrawn quickly from the room windows and the windows dropped.

Joy had stopped, his eyes wide. His mouth flew open and a jet of blood rolled down his chin, and down his shirt. His eyes ranged wildly over the crowd of men. He fell on his face and clawed outward with his fingers. The guards stared unbelievingly at the squirming figure on the ground. Suddenly the steam stopped; and the quietness fell on the men like a wave of sound. The line of strikers stood still, with strange, dreaming faces. Joy lifted himself up with his arms, like a lizard, and then dropped again. A little thick river of blood ran down on the crushed rock of the roadbed.

A strange, heavy movement started among the men. London moved forward woodenly, and the men moved forward. They were stiff. The guards aimed with their guns, but the line moved on, unheeding, unseeing. The guards stepped swiftly sideways to get out of the way, for the box-car doors were belching silent men who moved slowly in. The ends of the long line curled and circled slowly around the center of the dead man, like sheep about a nucleus.

Jim clung shivering to Mac's arm. Mac turned and muttered. "He's done the first real, useful thing in his life. Poor Joy. He's done it. He'd be so glad. Look at the cops, Jim. Let go my arm. Don't lose your nerve. Look at the cops!"

The guards were frightened; riots they could stop, fighting they could stop; but this slow, silent movement of men with the wide eyes of sleep-walkers terrified them. They held to their places, but the sheriff started his car. The motorcycle police moved imperceptibly toward their parked machines.

The strike-breakers were out of the cars by now. Some of them crept between the box-cars or under the wheels and hurried away on the other side, but most of them moved up and packed tightly about the place where Joy lay.

Mac saw Dakin standing on the outskirts of the mob, his little pale eyes for once looking straight ahead and not moving. Mac walked over to him. "We better get him in your truck and take him out to the camp."

Dakin turned slowly. "We can't touch him," he said. "The cops'll have to take him."

Mac said sharply, "Why didn't the cops catch those guys in the windows? Look at the cops, they're scared to death. We've got to take him, I tell you. We've got to use him to step our guys up, to keep 'em together. This'll stick 'em together, this'll make 'em fight."

Dakin grimaced. "You're a cold-blooded bastard. Don't you think of nothing but 'strike'?"

Jim broke in, "Dakin, that little guy got shot trying to help us. D'you want to stop him now from doing it?"

Dakin's eyes moved slowly from Mac to Jim, and then to Mac again. He said, "What do you know about what he was doin'? Couldn't hear nothing but that damn steam."

"We know him," Mac said. "He was a pal of ours."

Dakin's eyes were filled with dislike. "Pal of yours, and you won't let him rest now. You want to use him. You're a pair of cold-blooded bastards."

Mac cried, "What do you know about it? Joy didn't want no rest. Joy wanted to work, and he didn't know how." His voice rose hysterically. "And now he's got a chance to work, and you don't want to let 'im."

A number of the men had turned toward the voices, turned with a dull curiosity. Dakin peered at Mac for a moment longer. "Come on," he said. They pushed and jabbed their way into the tight mass of men, who gave way reluctantly.

Mac shouted, "Come on, you guys, let us in. We got to get this poor fellow out o' there." The men opened a narrow pathway, pushing violently backward to make it.

London joined them, and helped to force a way in. Joy was quite dead. When they had cleared a little space around him, London turned him over and started to wipe the bloody dirt from Joy's mouth. There was a foxy look in the open eyes; the mouth smiled terribly.

Mac said, "Don't do that, London. Leave it that way, just the way it is."

London lifted the little man in his arms. Joy looked very small against London's big chest. A path opened for them easily this time. London marched along, and the men arranged themselves into a crude column, and followed.

Beside Dakin's bright green truck the sheriff stood, surrounded by his deputies. London stopped, and the following men stopped. "I want that body," the sheriff said.

"No. You can't have it."

"You men shot a strike-breaker. We'll bring the charge. I want that body for the coroner."

London's eyes glowed redly. He said simply, "Mister, you know the guys that killed this little man; you know who did it. You got laws and you don't keep 'em." The mob was silent, listening.

"I tell you, I want that body."

London said plaintively, "Can't you see, mister? If you guys don't get the hell out of here, can't you see you're goin' get *killed?* Can't you see *that*, mister? Don't you *know* when you can't go no further?"

From the mob there came a rustle of released breath. The sheriff said, "I'm not through with you," but he backed away, and his deputies backed away. The mob growled, so softly that it sounded like a moan. London set Joy over the tailboard of the truck, and he climbed in and lifted the body forward, until it leaned against the back of the cab.

Dakin started his motor and backed around and rolled along the street, and the dull, menacing mob fell in behind. They made no noise. They walked with heavy, padding footsteps.

No motorcycle police lined the road. The streets and

the roads were deserted on their line of march. Mac and Jim walked a little to one side of the truck. "Was it vigilantes, Mac?"

"Yep. But they overdid it this time. Everything went wrong for them. That steam—if our guys could've heard the shooting better, they'd probably have run away. But the steam was too loud. It was over too soon; our guys didn't have a chance to get scared. No, they made a mistake."

They trudged slowly along, beside the column of marching men. "Mac, who in hell are these vigilantes, anyway? What kind of guys are they?"

"Why, they're the dirtiest guys in any town. They're the same ones that burned the houses of old German people during the war. They're the same ones that lynch Negroes. They like to be cruel. They like to hurt people, and they always give it a nice name, patriotism or protecting the constitution. But they're just the old nigger torturers working. The owners use 'em, tell 'em we have to protect the people against reds. Y'see that lets 'em burn houses and torture the beat people with no danger. And that's all they want to do, anyway. They've got no guts; they'll only shoot from cover, or gang a man when they're ten to one. I guess they're about the worst scum in the world." His eyes sought the body of Joy, in the truck. He said, "During the war there was a little fat German tailor in my town, and a bunch of these patriotic bastards, about fifty of 'em, started his house on fire, and beat him to a pulp. They're great guys, these vigilantes. Not long ago they shot tracer bullets through a kerosene tank and started a fire in a bunk house. They didn't have the guts to do it with a match."

The column marched on through the country, raising a great dust. The men were coming slowly out of their dream. They talked together in low voices. Their feet scuffed heavily against the ground. "Poor Joy," Jim said. "He was a good little fellow. He'd been beaten so much. He reminded me of my old man, always mad."

Mac reproved him. "Don't feel sorry for Joy. If he could know what he did, he'd be cocky. Joy always wanted to lead people, and now he's going to do it, even if he's in a box."

"How about the scabs, Mac? We got a bunch of them with us."

"Sure, a bunch came over, but a lot of 'em beat it. Some of our guys beat it, too. We got just about the same number we started with. Didn't you see 'em crawling under the cars and running away?" Mac said, "Look at these guys. They're waking up. It's just as though they got a shot of gas for a while. That's the most dangerous kind of men."

"The cops knew it, too," said Jim.

"Damn right they did. When a mob don't make a noise, when it comes on with dead pans, that's the time for a cop to get out of the way."

They were nearing the Anderson place. Jim asked, "What do we do now, Mac?"

"Well, we hold the funeral, and we start picketing. It'll settle down now. They'll run in scabs with trucks."

"You still think we'll get beat, Mac?"

"I don't know. They got this valley organized. God, how they've got it organized. It's not so hard to do when a few men control everything, land, courts, banks. They can cut off loans, and they can railroad a man to jail, and they can always bribe plenty."

Dakin's truck pulled to the end of the line of cars and backed into place. The camp guards came streaming out, and the column of returning men deployed among them. Groups collected to hear the story, over and over. Dr. Burton trotted over to Dakin's truck. London stood up heavily. His wide blue shirt-front was streaked with

Joy's blood. Burton took one look at Joy. "Killed him, eh?"

"Got him," said London.

Burton said, "Bring him to my tent. I'll look him over." From behind the tents a hoarse, bubbling scream broke out. All of the men turned, frozen at the sound. Burton said, "Oh, they're killing a pig. One of the cars brought back a live pig. Bring this body to my tent."

London bent over wearily and lifted Joy in his arms again. A crowd of men followed him, and stood clustered about the big troop tent. Mac and Jim followed Dr. Burton inside the tent. They watched silently while he unbuttoned the stiff, bloody shirt and disclosed a wound in the chest. "Well, that's it. That'd do it."

"Recognize him, Doc?"

Burton looked closely at the distorted face. "I've seen him before."

"Sure you have. It's Joy. You've set damn near every bone in his body."

"Well, he's through this time. Tough little man. You'll have to send his body to town. The coroner'll have to have it."

London said, "If we do that, they'll bury him, hide him."

Mac said, "We can send some guys in to see that he gets back here. Let 'em picket the morgue till they get the body back. Those damn vigilantes made a mistake; an' they know it by now."

Dakin lifted the flap and stepped into the big tent. "They're fryin' pork," he said. "They sure cut up that pig quick."

Mac said, "Dakin, can you have the guys build a kind of a platform? We'll want some place for the coffin to set. Y'ought to have a place to talk from, too."

"Want to make a show of it, do you?"

"You're damn right! You got me kinda wrong, Dakin.

What we got to fight with? Rocks, sticks. Even Indians
had bows an' arrows. But let us get one little gun to protect ourselves, an' they call out the troops to stop the
revolution. We got damn few things to fight with. We
got to use what we can. This little guy was my friend.
Y'can take it from me he'd want to get used any way we
can use him. We *got* to use him." He paused. "Dakin,
can't you see? We'll get a hell of a lot of people on our
side if we put on a public funeral. We got to get public
opinion."

London was nodding his head slowly up and down.
"The guy's right, Dakin."

"O.K., if you want it too, London. I s'pose somebody's got to make a speech, but I ain't goin' to do it."

"Well, I will if I have to," London cried. "I seen the
little guy start over to us. I seen him get it. I'll make the
speech if you won't."

"Sounds like Cock Robin," Burton said.

"Huh?"

"Nothing. I was just talking. Better get the body taken
in now, and turn it over to the coroner."

London said, "I'm going to send a flock of my own
guys to stay with him."

Jim's voice came from outside the tent. "Oh, Mac,
come on out. Anderson wants to see you."

Mac walked quickly outside. Anderson was standing
with Jim. He looked tired and old. "You just played
hell," he began fiercely.

"What's the matter, Mr. Anderson?"

"Said you'd protect us, didn't you?"

"Sure I did. The guys here'll take care of you. What's
the matter?"

"I'll tell you what's the matter. Bunch of men burned
up Al's lunch wagon last night. They jumped on Al an'
broke his arm an' six ribs. They burned his lunch wagon
right down."

"Jesus!" Mac said. "I didn't think they'd do that."

"You didn't think, but they did it just the same."

"Where's Al now, Mr. Anderson?"

"He's over to the house. I had to bring him out from the hospital."

"I'll get the doctor. We'll go over and see him."

"Eighteen hundred dollars!" the old man cried. "He got some of it together, and I loaned him some, and then along you come. Now he hasn't got a thing."

"I'm awful sorry," Mac said.

"Sure, you're sorry. That don't unburn Al's wagon. That don't mend his arm and his ribs. And what you doing to protect me? They'll burn my house next."

"We'll put a guard around your house."

"Guards, hell. What good's a bunch of bums? I wish I never let you on the place. You'll ruin me." His voice had risen to a high squeak. His old eyes were watering. "You just played hell, that's what you did. That's what we get for mixing up with a bunch of damn radicals."

Mac tried to soothe him. "Let's go over and see Al," he suggested. "Al's a swell guy. I want to see him."

"Well, he's all busted up. They kicked 'im in the head, too."

Mac edged him slowly away, for the men were beginning to move in, toward the shrill voice. "What you blaming us for?" he said. "We didn't do it. It was those nice neighbors of yours."

"Yes, but it wouldn't have happened if we didn't get mixed up with you."

Mac turned angrily on him. "Listen, mister, we know you got a sock in the teeth; little guys like you and me get it all the time. We're tryin' to make it so guys like you won't get it."

"That wagon cost eighteen hundred dollars. Why, man, I can't go in town without the kids throw rocks at me. You ruined us, that's what you did."

Mac asked, "How's Al feel about it?"

"I think Al's red as hell himself. Only people he's sore at are the men that did it."

"Al's got a good head," Mac said. "Al sees the whole thing. You would of been out on your can anyway. Now, if you get bounced, you got a big bunch of men in back of you. These men aren't going to forget what you're doing for 'em. And we'll put a guard around your house tonight. I'll have the doctor come over pretty soon and look at Al."

The old man turned tiredly, and walked away.

Smoke from the rusty stoves hung low over the camp. The men had begun to move in toward the smell of frying pork. Mac looked after the retreating figure of Anderson. "How's it feel to be a Party man now, Jim? It's swell when you read about it—romantic. Ladies like to get up and squawk about the 'boss class' and the 'downtrodden working man.' It's a heavy weight, Jim. That poor guy. The lunch wagon looks bigger than the world to him. I feel responsible for that. Hell," Mac continued. "I thought I brought you out here to teach you, to give you confidence; and here I spend my time belly-aching. I thought I was going to bolster you up, and instead— oh, what the hell! It's awful hard to keep your eyes on the big issue. Why the devil don't you say something?"

"You don't give me a chance."

"I guess I don't. Say something now! All I can think of is that poor little Joy shot up. He didn't have much sense, but he wasn't afraid of anything."

"He was a nice little guy," Jim said.

" 'Member what he said? Nobody was going to make him stop calling sons-of-bitches 'sons-of-bitches.' I wish I didn't get this lost feeling sometimes, Jim."

"A little fried pork might help."

"By God, that's right. I didn't have much this morning. Let's go over."

A long delivery wagon drove up the road and stopped in front of the line of cars. From the seat a fussy little man stepped down and walked into the camp. "Who's in charge here?" he demanded of Mac.

"Dakin. He's over in that big tent."

"Well, I'm the coroner. I want that corpse."

"Where's your bodyguard?" Mac asked.

The little man puffed at him. "What do I want with a bodyguard? I'm the coroner. Where's that corpse?"

"In the big tent over there. It's all ready for you."

"Well, why didn't you say so?" He went puffing away like a small engine.

Mac sighed. "Thank God we don't have many like him to fight," he said. "That little guy's got guts. Came out all alone. He's kind of like Joy, himself." They walked on toward the stoves. Two men passed, carrying the body of Joy between them, and the coroner walked fussily along behind.

Men were walking away from the stoves with pieces of greasy fried pork in their hands. They wiped their lips with their sleeves. The tops of the stoves were covered with little slabs of hissing meat. "God, that smells good," said Mac. "Let's get some. I'm hungry as hell." The cooks handed out ill-cut, half-cooked pieces of pork to them, and they strolled away, gnawing at the soft meat. "Only eat the outside," Mac said. "Doc shouldn't let the men eat raw pork. They'll all be sick."

"They got too hungry to wait," said Jim.

10

A N A P A T H Y had fallen on the men. They sat staring in front of them. They seemed not to have the energy to talk, and among them the bedraggled, discontented women sat. They were listless and stale. They gnawed thoughtfully at their meat, and when it was finished, wiped their hands on their clothes. The air was full of their apathy, and full of their discontent.

Mac, walking through the camp with Jim, grew discontented, too. "They ought to be doing something," Mac complained. "I don't care what it is. We can't let 'em sit around like this. Our strike'll go right out from under us. Christ, what's the matter with 'em? They had a man killed this morning; that ought to keep 'em going. Now it's just after noon, and they're slumped already. We got to get them working at something. Look at their eyes, Jim."

"They're not looking at anything—they're just staring."

"Yeah, they're thinking of themselves. Every man there is thinkin' how hurt he is, or how much money he made during the war. Just like Anderson. They're falling apart."

"Well, let's do something. Let's make them move. What is there to do?"

"I don't know. If we could make 'em dig a hole, it'd be as good as anything else. If we can just get 'em all pushing on something, or lifting something, or all walking in one direction—doesn't matter a hell of a lot. They'll start fighting each other if we don't move 'em. They'll begin to get mean, pretty soon."

London, hurrying past, caught the last words. "Who's goin' to get mean?"

Mac turned around. "Hello, London. We been talkin' about these here guys. They're all fallin' to pieces."

"I know it. I been around with these stiffs long enough to tell."

"Well, I just said they'd start fightin', if we didn't put 'em to work."

"They already did. That bunch we left in camp this morning had a fuss. One of the guys tried to make another guy's woman. An' the first guy come in an' stuck him with a pair of scissors. Doc fixed him up. He like to bled to death, I guess."

"You see, Jim? I told you. Listen, London, Dakin's sore at me. He don't want to listen to nothing I tell him, but he'll listen to you. We got to move these guys before they get into trouble. Make 'em march in a circle— make 'em dig a hole and then fill it up. It don't make no difference."

"I know it. Well, how about picketin'?"

"Swell, but I don't think there's much work goin' on yet."

"What do we care, if it moves the guys off their ass."

"You got a head, London. See if you can get Dakin to send 'em out, about fifty in a bunch, out in different directions. Let 'em keep to the roads, and if they see any apple pickin', let 'em break it up."

"Sure I will," London said, and he turned and walked toward Dakin's brown tent.

Jim began, "Mac, you said I could go out with the pickets."

"Well, I'd rather have you with me."

"I want to get into it, Mac."

"O.K., go with one of the bunches, then. But stick close to them, Jim. They got your number here. You know that. Don't let 'em pick you off."

They saw Dakin and London come out of the tent. London talked rapidly. Mac said, "You know, I think we made a mistake about putting Dakin in. He's too tied up with his truck, and his tent, and his kids. He's too careful. London'ud have been the best man. London hasn't got anything to lose. I wonder if we could get the guys to kick Dakin out and put London in. I think the guys like London better. Dakin's got too much property. Did you see that folding stove of his? He don't even eat with the guys. Maybe we better start working and see if we can't get London in. I thought Dakin was cool, but he's too damn cool. We need somebody that can work the guys up a little."

Jim said, "Come on, Dakin's making up the pickets now."

Jim joined a picket group of about fifty men. They moved off along the road in a direction away from town. Almost as soon as they started the apathy dropped away. The straggling band walked quickly along.

The lean-faced Sam was in charge of it, and he instructed the men as he walked along. "Pick up rocks," he said. "Get a lot of good rocks in your pocket. And keep lookin' down the rows."

For a distance the orchards were deserted. The men began to sing tunelessly,

> "It was Christmas on the Island,
> All the convicts they were there——"

They scuffed their feet in time. Across the intersecting road they marched, and a cloud of grey dust followed them. "Like France," a man said. "If it was all mud, it's just like France."

"Hell, you wasn't in France."

"I was so. I was five months in France."

"You don't walk like no soldier."

"I don't want to walk like no soldier. I walked like a soldier enough. I got schrap' in me, that's what I got."

"Where's them scabs?"

"Looks like we got 'em tied up. I don't see nobody workin'. We got this strike tied up already."

Sam said, "Sure, you got it won, fella. Just set on your can and won it, didn't you? Don't be a damn fool."

"Well, we sure scared hell out of the cops this mornin'. You don't see no cops around, do you?"

Sam said, "You'll see plenty before you get out of this, fella. You're just like all the stiffs in the world. You're king of hell, now. In a minute you'll start belly-achin', an' the *next* thing, you'll sneak out." An angry chorus broke on him.

"You think so, smart guy? Well, just show us somethin' to do."

"You got no call to be talkin' like that. What the hell'd you ever do?"

Sam spat in the road. "I'll tell you what I done. I was in 'Frisco on Bloody Thursday. I smacked a cop right off a horse. I was one of the guys that went in and got them night sticks from a carpenter's shop that the cops was gettin' made. Got one of 'em right now, for a souvenir."

"Tha's a damn lie. You ain't no longshoreman; you're a lousy fruit tramp."

"Sure I'm a fruit tramp. Know why? 'Cause I'm blacklisted with every shippin' company in the whole damn country, that's why." He spoke with pride. A silence met his assertion. He went on, "I seen more trouble than you can-heat bindle-stiffs ever seen." His contempt subjugated them. "Now keep your eyes down them rows, and cut out all this talk." They marched along a while.

"Look. There's boxes."

"Where?"

"Way to hell an' gone down that row."

Jim looked in the pointed direction. "There's guys down there," he cried.

A man said, "Come on, longshoreman, let's see you go."

Sam stood still in the road. "You guys takin' orders?" he demanded.

"Sure, we'll take 'em if they're any damn good."

"All right, then. Keep in hand. I don't want no rush at first, and then you guys runnin' like hell when anythin' busts. Come on, stick together."

They turned off the road and crossed a deep irrigation ditch, and they marched down the row between the big trees. As they approached the pile of boxes men began to drop out of the trees and to gather in a nervous group.

A checker stood by the box pile. As the pickets approached he took a double-barreled shot-gun from a box and advanced toward them a few steps. "Do you men want to go to work?" he shouted.

A chorus of derisive yells answered him. One man put his forefingers in his mouth and whistled piercingly.

"You get off this land," the checker said. "You've got no right on this land at all."

The strikers marched slowly on. The checker backed up to the box pile, where his pickers shifted nervously, and watched with frightened faces.

Sam said, over his shoulder, "All right. You guys stop here." He stepped forward alone a few paces. "Listen, you workers," he said. "Come over to our side. Don't go knifin' us guys in the back. Come on and join up with us."

The checker answered, "You take those men off this land or I'll have the whole bunch of you run in."

The derisive yell began again, and the shrill whistling.

Sam turned angrily. "Shut up, you crazy bastards. Lay off the music."

The pickers looked about for a retreat. The checker

reassured them. "Don't let him scare you, men. You've got a right to work if you want to."

Sam called again, "Listen, guys, we're givin' you this chance to come along with us."

"Don't let him bully you," the checker cried. His voice was rising. "They can't tell a man what he's got to do."

The pickers stood still. "You comin'?" Sam demanded. They didn't answer. Sam began to move slowly toward them.

The checker stepped forward. "There's buckshot in this gun. I'll shoot you if you don't get off."

Sam spoke softly as he moved. "You ain't shootin' nobody, fella. You might get one of us, and the rest'd slaughter you." His voice was low and passionless. His men moved along, ten feet behind him. He stopped, directly in front of the checker. The quivering gun pointed at his chest. "We just want to talk," he said, and with one movement he stooped and dived, like a football tackle, and clipped the feet from under the checker. The gun exploded, and dug a pit in the ground. Sam spun over and drove his knees between the legs of the checker. Then he jumped up, leaving the man, writhing and crying hoarsely, on the ground. For a second both the pickers and the strikers had stood still. Too late the pickers turned to run. Men swarmed on them, cursing in their throats. The pickers fought for a moment, and then went down.

Jim stood a little apart; he saw a picker wriggle free and start to run. He picked up a heavy clod and hurled it at the man, struck him in the small of the back, and brought him down. The group surrounded the fallen man, feet working, kicking and stamping; and the picker screamed from the ground. Jim looked coldly at the checker. His face was white with agony and wet with the perspiration of pain.

Sam broke free and leaped at the kicking, stamping

men. "Lay off, God-damn you, lay off," he yelled at them; and still they kicked, growling in their throats. Their lips were wet with saliva. Sam picked up an apple box from the pile and smashed it over a head. "Don't kill 'em," he shouted. "Don't kill 'em."

The fury departed as quickly as it had come. They stood away from the victims. They panted heavily. Jim looked without emotion at the ten moaning men on the ground, their faces kicked shapeless. Here a lip was torn away, exposing bloody teeth and gums; one man cried like a child because his arm was bent sharply backward, broken at the elbow. Now that the fury was past, the strikers were sick, poisoned by the flow from their own anger glands. They were weak; one man held his head between his hands as though it ached terribly.

Suddenly a man went spinning around and around, croaking. A rifle-crack sounded from down the row. Five men came running along, stopping to fire now and then. The strikers broke and ran, dodging among the trees to be out of the line of fire.

Jim ran with them. He was crying to himself, "Can't stand fire. We can't stand fire." The tears blinded him. He felt a heavy blow on the shoulder and stumbled a little. The group reached the road and plunged on, looking back over their shoulders.

Sam was behind them, running beside Jim. "O.K.," he shouted. "They stopped." Still some of the men ran on in a blind panic, ran on and disappeared at the road intersection. Sam caught the rest. "Settle down," he shouted. "Settle down. Nobody's chasin' you." They came to a stop. They stood weakly at the side of the road. "How many'd they get?" Sam demanded.

The men looked at one another. Jim said, "I only saw one guy hit."

"O.K. He'll be all right, maybe. Got him in the chest."

He looked more closely at Jim. "What's the matter with you, kid? You're bleedin'."

"Where?"

"All down your back."

"I ran into a limb, I guess."

"Limb, hell." Sam pulled the blue denim coat down from Jim's shoulder. "You got bored with a high-power. Can you move your arm?"

"Sure. It just feels numb."

"I guess it didn't get a bone. Shoulder muscle. Must of been a steel-jacket. You ain't even bleedin much. Come on, guys, let's get back. There's goin' to be cops thick as maggots around here."

They hurried along the road. Sam said, "If you get feelin' weak, I'll help you, kid."

"I'm all right. We couldn't take it, Sam."

Sam said bitterly, "We done noble when we was five to one; we made messes of them scabs."

Jim asked, "Did we kill any of 'em?"

"I don't think so. Some of 'em ain't ever goin' be the same again."

Jim said, "Jesus, it was pretty awful, wasn't it. Did you see that guy with his lip torn?"

"Hell, they'll sew his lip back on. We got to do it, kid. We just got to. If they won't come over, we just got to scare 'em."

"Oh, I know it," said Jim. "I'm not worrying about 'em."

Far ahead they heard a siren. Sam cried, "Jump for the ditch, you guys. Lie down in the ditch. Here comes the cops." He saw that they were all flat in a deep irrigation ditch along the road. The motorcycles roared by, and crossed the intersection, and an ambulance clanged after them. The men did not raise their heads until the motors had disappeared across the intersection. Sam jumped up. "Come on, now. We got to beat it fast."

They dog-trotted along the road. The sun was going down by now, and the road was in a blue evening shadow. A heavy cloud sailed like a ship toward the sun, and its dark edge reddened as it drew near. The men jumped for the ditch again when the ambulance came back. The motorcycles went by more slowly this time, the policemen looking down the rows as they went, but they did not search the ditch.

As the evening fell the pickets came back to the camp. Jim's legs were wobbling under him. His shoulder stung deeply, for the nerves were awakening after being stunned by the high-powered bullet. The men dispersed into camp.

Mac walked over toward Jim, and when he saw how white Jim was, he broke into a trot. "What's the matter with you, Jim? Did you get hurt?"

"No, not much. Sam says I'm shot in the shoulder. I can't see it. It doesn't hurt much."

Mac's face turned red. "By God, I knew I shouldn't let you go."

"Why not? I'm no pansy."

"Maybe you aren't one, but you'll be pushing 'em up pretty soon, if I don't watch you. Come on, let Doc look at you. He was right here a minute ago. There he goes. Hi, Doc!" They took Jim into a white tent. "This one just came in. Doc's going to use it for a hospital," said Mac.

The autumn darkness was falling quickly, and the evening was hastened by the big black cloud, which spread out over the western sky. Mac held a lantern while Burton pulled Jim's shirt free of his shoulder. He washed the wound carefully, with hot, sterile water. "Lucky boy," he said. "A lead slug would have smashed your shoulder to pieces. You've got a little auger-hole through the muscle. It'll be stiff for a while. Bullet went right on through." His deft hands cleansed the wound with a probe, applied a dressing and taped it on. "You'll be all right," he said. "Take it easy for a couple of days. Mac, I'm going over to see Al Anderson later. Want to come?"

"Sure, I'll be with you. I want to get Jim a cup of coffee." He shoved a tin can of black, ugly coffee in Jim's hand. "Come on, sit down," he said. He shoved a box out and sat Jim down on it, and reclined on the ground beside him. "What happened, Jim?"

"We went in after some scabs. Mac, our guys just kicked hell out of 'em. Kicked 'em in the heads."

Mac said softly, "I know, Jim. It's terrible, but it's the only thing to do if they won't come over. We've got to do it. It's not nice to see a sheep killed, either, but we've got to have mutton. What happened then?"

"Well, five men came running and shooting. Our guys ran like rabbits. They couldn't take it."

"Well, why should they, Jim, with nothing to fight with but their bare hands?"

"I hardly knew it when I got hit. One of our guys went down. I don't know whether he was killed or not."

"Nice party," Mac said. "The other crowds brought in about thirty scabs. They didn't have any trouble; just called 'em out, and they came along." He reached up and touched Jim's leg for a moment. "How's the shoulder feel now?"

"Hurts a little, not much."

"Oh say, Jim. Looks like we're goin' to have a new boss."

"Kicked Dakin out, you mean?"

"No, but he's out, all right. Dick sent word he had a load of blankets. Well, Dakin took six men and went in with his shiny truck. One of the six guys got away and came back and told how it was. They got their load and started back. A little way this side of town they ran over a bunch of nails, stopped to change a tire. Well, then a dozen men with guns jumped out and held them up.

Well, six of them stand the guys up while they wreck Dakin's truck, smash the crank-case and set it on fire. Dakin stands there with a gun on him. He turns white, and then he turns blue. Then he lets out a howl like a coyote and starts for 'em. They shoot him in the leg, but that don't stop him. When he can't run any more, he crawls for 'em, slavering around the mouth like a mad dog—just nuts, he just went *nuts!* I guess he loved that truck better'n anything in the world. The guy that came back said it was just awful, the way he crawled for 'em. Tried to bite 'em. He was snarling—like a mad dog. Well, then, some traffic cops come along, and the vigilante boys fade. The cops pick Dakin up and take him in. The guy that came in and told about it was up a gum tree watching. He says Dakin bit a cop on the hand, and they had to stick a screw-driver back in his teeth to pry 'im loose. And that's the guy I said wouldn't lose his temper. He's in the can now. I guess the guys'll elect London in his place."

Jim said, "Well, he sure looked cool enough to me. I'm glad I didn't lay a finger on his truck."

Mac heaped a little pile of dirt on the floor with his hand, and moulded it round, and patted a little flat top on it. "I'm kind of worried, Jim. Dick hasn't sent any food today. We haven't heard anything from him except those blankets. They're cooking up all the rest of the beans with pork bones, but that's all there is, except some mush. That's all there is for tomorrow."

"Do you suppose they knocked Dick off?"

Mac patted his mound flatter. "Dick's clever as a weasel. I don't think they could catch him. I don't know what's the matter. We've got to get food in. The minute the guys get hungry, they're through, I'm afraid."

"Maybe he didn't collect anything. He sent that pig this morning."

"Sure, and the pig's in the beans now. Dick knows how much it takes to feed these guys. Dick must have organized the sympathizers by now."

Jim asked, "How do the guys feel now?"

"Oh, they're better. They got a shot of life, this afternoon. I know it's quick, but we got to have that funeral tomorrow. That ought to steam 'em up for a while." He looked out the tent entrance. "God, look at that cloud!" He stepped outside and looked overhead. The sky was nearly dark with the thick black cloud. A skirmishing wind sprang up, blowing the dust along, blowing the smoke from the fires, flapping the canvases, whisking the apple trees that surrounded the camp. "That looks like a rain cloud," Mac said. "Lord, I hope it doesn't rain. It'll drown this bunch like rats."

Jim said, "You worry too much about what might happen, Mac. All the time you're worrying. These guys are used to the open. A little rain won't hurt 'em. You fidget all the time."

Mac sat down on the floor again, "Maybe that's right, Jim. I get so scared the strike'll crack, maybe I imagine things. I've been in so many strikes that got busted, Jim."

"Yeah, but what do you care if it's busted? It solidifies the unrest, you said so yourself."

"Sure, I know. I s'pose it wouldn't matter if the strike broke right now. The guys won't ever forget how Joy got killed; and they won't ever forget about Dakin's truck."

"You're getting just like an old woman, Mac."

"Well, it's my strike—I mean, I feel like it's mine. I don't want to see it go under now."

"Well, it won't, Mac."

"Huh? What do you know about it?"

"Well, I was thinkin' this morning. Ever read much history, Mac?"

"A little, in school. Why?"

"Well, you remember how the Greeks won the battle of Salamis?"

"Maybe I knew. I don't remember."

"Well, here's the Greeks with some ships, all boxed in a harbor. They want to run away to beat hell. And here's a whole slough of Persian ships out in front. Well, the Greek admiral knows his guys are going to run away, so he sends word to the enemy to box 'em in tight. Next morning the Greeks see they can't run away; they've got to fight to get away, and they win. They beat hell out of the Persian fleet." Jim fell silent.

Men began moving past, toward the stoves. Mac patted the ground hard with his open hand. "I see what you mean, Jim," he said. "We don't need it now, but if we do, by God, it's an idea. Jim," he said plaintively. "I bring you out here to teach you things, and right away you start teaching me things."

"Nuts," said Jim.

"O.K., then, nuts. I wonder how men know when food's ready. Kind of mind reading, I guess. Or maybe they've got that same kind of a sense that vultures have. Look, there they go. Come on, Jim. Let's eat."

11

THEY HAD beans, swimming in pork fat to eat. Mac and Jim brought their cans from the tent and stood in line until some of the mess was dumped into each of their cans. They walked away. Jim took a little wooden paddle from his pocket and tasted the beans. "Mac," he said, "I can't eat it."

"Used to better things, huh? You've got to eat it." He tasted his own, and immediately dumped the can on the ground. "Don't eat it, Jim. It'll make you sick, beans and grease! The guys'll raise hell about this."

They looked at the men sitting in front of the tents, trying to eat their food. The storm cloud spread over the sky and swallowed the new stars. Mac said, "Somebody'll try to kill the cooks, I guess. Let's go over to London's tent."

"I don't see Dakin's tent, Mac."

"No, Mrs. Dakin took it down. She went into town and took it along with her. Funny guy, Dakin; he'll have money before he's through. Let's find London."

They walked down the line to the grey tent of London. A light shone through the canvas. Mac raised the flap. Inside, London sat on a box, holding an open can of sardines in his hand. The dark girl, Lisa, crouched on the floor mattress nursing the baby. She drew a piece of blanket about the baby and the exposed breast as the men entered. She smiled quickly at them, and then looked down at the baby again.

"Just in time for dinner!" Mac said.

London looked embarrassed. "I had a little stuff left over."

"You tasted that mess out there?"

"Yeah."

"Well, I hope the other guys got some stuff left over. We got to do better than that, or them guys'll run out on us."

"Food kind of stopped comin' in," said London. "I got another can of sardines. You guys like to have it?"

"Damn right." Mac took the proffered can greedily, and twisted the key to open it. "Get out your knife, Jim. We'll split this."

"How's your arm?" London asked.

"Getting stiff," said Jim.

Outside the tent a voice said, "That's the place, that one with the light." The flap raised and Dick entered. His hair was combed neatly. He held a grey cap in his hand. His grey suit was clean, but unpressed. Only his dusty, unpolished shoes showed that he had been walking through the country. He stood in the tent entrance, looking about. "Hi, Mac. Hello, Jim," and to the girl, "Hi ya, baby?" Her eyes brightened. A spot of red came into her cheeks. She drew the piece of blanket coquettishly down around her shoulders.

Mac waved his hand. "This here's London—this here's Dick." Dick made a half salute. "H'ya?" he said. "Look, Mac, these babies in town have been taking lessons."

"What do you mean? What you doin' out here anyways?"

Dick took a newspaper from his outside pocket and handed it over. Mac opened it and London and Jim looked over his shoulder. "Come out before noon," said Dick.

Mac exclaimed, "Son-of-a-bitch!" The paper carried a headline, "Supervisors vote to feed strikers. At a public meeting last night the Board of Supervisors voted unanimously to feed the men now striking against the apple growers."

"They sure took lessons," Mac said. "Did it start workin', yet, Dick?"

"Hell, yes."

London broke in, "I don't see no reason to kick. If they want to send out ham and eggs, it's O.K. by me."

"Sure," Mac said sarcastically, "*if* they want to. This paper don't tell about the other meeting right afterwards when they repealed the vote."

"What's the gag?" London demanded. "What the hell's it all about?"

"Listen, London," Mac said. "This here's an old one, but it works. Here's Dick got the sympathizers lined up. We got food and blankets and money comin'. Well, then *this* comes out. Dick goes the round. The sympathizers say, 'What the hell? The county's feeding 'em.' 'Th' hell it is,' says Dick. And the guy says, 'I seen it in the paper. It says they're sendin' food to you. What you gettin' out of this?' That's how it works, London, Did you see any county food come in today?"

"No——"

"Well, Dick couldn't get a rise either. Now you know. They figure to starve us out. And by God they can do it, too, if we don't get help." He turned to Dick. "You was goin' good."

"Sure," Dick agreed. "It was a push-over. Take me some time to work it all up again. I want a paper from this guy here saying you aren't getting any food. I want it signed by the strike chairman."

"O.K.," said London.

"Lots of sympathizers in Torgas," Dick went on. " 'Course the joint's organized by the Growers' Association, so the whole bunch is underground like a flock o' gophers. But the stuff is there, if I can get to it."

"You were doin' swell till this busted," Mac said.

"Sure I was. I had some trouble with one old dame. She wanted to help the cause somethin' terrible."

Mac laughed. "I never knew no maiden modesty to keep you out of the feed bag. S'pose she *did* want to give her all to the cause?"

Dick shuddered. "Her all was sixteen axe-handles acrost," he said.

"Well, we'll get your paper for you, and then I want you to get the hell out of here. They ain't got you spotted yet, have they?"

"I don't know," said Dick. "I kind of think they have. I wrote in for Bob Schwartz to come down. I got a feeling I'm going to get vagged pretty soon. Bob can take over then."

London rooted in a box and brought out a tablet of paper and a pencil. Mac took them from him and wrote out the statement. "You write nice," London said admiringly.

"Huh? Oh, sure. Can I sign it for you, London?"

"Sure. Go ahead."

"Hell," said Dick. "I could of done that myself." He took the paper and folded it carefully. "Oh, say, Mac. I heard about one of the guys gettin' bumped."

"Didn't you know, Dick? It was Joy."

"Th' hell!"

"Sure, he come down with a bunch of scabs. He was tryin' to bring 'em over when he got it."

"Poor bastard."

"Got him quick. He didn't suffer more'n a minute."

Dick sighed. "Well, it was in the books for Joy. He was sure to get it sooner or later. Going to have a funeral?"

"Tomorrow."

"All the guys goin' to march in it?"

Mac looked at London. "Sure they are," he said. "Maybe we can drag public sympathy our way."

"Well, Joy would like that," Dick said. "Nothing he'd like better. To bad he can't see it. Well, so long, I got to go." He turned to leave the tent. Lisa raised her eyes. " 'Bye, baby. See you sometime," said Dick. The spots of color came into her cheeks again. Her lips parted a little and, when the tent flaps dropped behind Dick, her eyes remained there for some time.

Mac said, "Jesus, they got an organization here. Dick's a good man. If he can't get stuff to eat, it ain't to be got."

Jim asked, "How about that platform for the speech?"

Mac turned to London, "Yeah, did you get at it, London?"

"The guys'll put it up tomorrow mornin'. Couldn't get nothing but some old fence posts to make it. Have to be just a little one."

"Don't matter," Mac said, "just as long as it's high enough so every guy here can see Joy, that's enough."

A worried look came on London's face. "What t'hell am I goin' to say to the guys? You said I ought to make a speech."

"You'll get steamed up enough," said Mac. "Tell 'em this little guy died for 'em. And if he could do that they can at least fight for themselves."

"I never made no speeches much," London complained.

"Well, don't make a speech. Just talk to the guys. You done that often enough. Just tell 'em. That's better'n a speech, anyway."

"Oh. Like that. O.K."

Mac turned to the girl. "How's the kid?"

She blushed and pulled the blanket closer over her shoulders. Her lashes shadowed her cheeks. "Pretty good," she whispered. "He don't cry none."

The tent-flap jerked open and the doctor entered, his quick, brusque movements at variance with the sad, dog-like eyes. "I'm going over to see young Anderson, Mac," he said. "Want to come?"

"Sure I do, Doc." And to London, "Did you send the guys over to guard Anderson's place?"

"Yeah. They didn't want to go none, but I sent' em."

"All right. Let's go, Doc. Come on, Jim, if you can make it."

"I feel all right," said Jim.

Burton looked steadily at him. "You should be in bed."

Mac chuckled. "I'm scared to leave him. He raises hell when I leave him alone for a minute. See you later, London."

Outside the darkness was thick. The big cloud had spread until it covered the sky, and all the stars were gone. A muffled quietness lay on the camp. Those men who sat around a few little fires spoke softly. The air was still and warm and damp. Doc and Mac and Jim picked their way carefully out of the camp and into the blackness that surrounded it. "I'm afraid it's going to rain," Mac said. "We'll have one hell of a time with the guys when they get wet. It's worse than gun-fire for taking the hearts out of men. Most of those tents leak, I guess."

"Of course they do," said Burton.

They reached the line of the orchard and walked down between the rows of trees. And it was so dark that they put their hands out in front of them.

"How do you like your strike now?" Doc asked.

"Not so good. They've got this valley organized like Italy. Food supply's cut off now. We're sunk if we can't get some food. And if it rains good and hard tonight the men'll be sneaking out on us. They just won't take it, I tell you. It's a funny thing, Doc. You don't believe in the cause, and you'll probably be the last man to stick. I don't get you at all."

"I don't get myself," Doc said softly. "I don't believe in the cause, but I believe in men."

"What do you mean?"

"I don't know. I guess I just believe they're men, and

not animals. Maybe if I went into a kennel and the dogs were hungry and sick and dirty, and maybe if I could help those dogs, I would. Wouldn't be their fault they were that way. You couldn't say, 'Those dogs are that way because they haven't any ambition. They don't save their bones. Dogs always are that way.' No, you'd try to clean them up and feed them. I guess that's the way it is with me. I have some skill in helping men, and when I see some who need help, I just do it. I don't think about it much. If a painter saw a piece of canvas, and he had colors, well, he'd want to paint on it. He wouldn't figure why he wanted to."

"Sure, I get you. In one way it seems cold-blooded, standing aside and looking down on men like that, and never getting yourself mixed up with them; but another way, Doc, it seems fine as the devil, and clean."

"Oh, Mac, I'm about out of disinfectant. You'll get no more fine smell if I don't get some more carbolic."

"I'll see what I can do," said Mac.

A hundred yards away a yellow light was shining. "Isn't that Anderson's house?" Jim asked.

"I guess it is. We ought to pick up a guard pretty soon." They walked on toward the light, and they were not challenged. They came to the gate of the house-yard without being challenged. Mac said, "God-damn it, where *are* the guys London sent over? Go on in, Doc, I'm going to see if I can find 'em." Burton walked up the path and into the lighted kitchen. Mac and Jim went toward the barn, and inside the barn they found the men, lying down in the low bed of hay smoking cigarettes. A kerosene lamp hung on a hook on the wall and threw a yellow light on the line of empty stalls and on the great pile of boxed apples—Anderson's crop, waiting to be moved.

Mac spluttered with anger, but he quickly controlled himself, and when he spoke his voice was soft and friendly. "Listen, you guys," he argued. "This isn't any joke. We got the word the damn vigilantes is going to try something on Anderson to get back at him for lettin' us stay on his place. S'pose he never let us stay? They'd be kickin' us all over hell by now. Anderson's a nice guy. We hadn't ought to let nobody hurt him."

"There ain't nobody around," one of the men protested. "Jesus, mister, we can't hang around all night. We was out picketin' all afternoon."

"Go on, then," Mac cried angrily. "Let 'em raid this place. Then Anderson'll kick us off. Then where in hell would we be?"

"We could jungle up, down by the river, mister."

"You *think* you could. They'd run you over the county line so quick your ass'd smoke, and you know it!"

One of the men got slowly to his feet. "The guy's right," he said. "We better drag it out of here. My old woman's in the camp. I don't want to have her get in no trouble."

"Well, put out a line," Mac suggested. "Don't let nobody through. You know what they done to Anderson's boy—burned his lunch wagon, kicked hell out of Al."

"Al put out a nice stew," said one of the men. They stood up tiredly. When they were all out of the barn Mac blew out the lantern. "Vigilantes like to shoot at a light," he explained. "They take big chances like that. We better have Anderson pull down his curtains, too."

The guards filed off into the darkness. Jim asked, "You think they'll keep watch now, Mac?" he asked.

"I wish I thought so. I think they'll be back in that barn in about ten minutes. In the army they can shoot a guy if he goes to sleep. We can't do a thing but talk. God, I get sick of this helplessness! If we could only use guns! If we could only use punishment to keep discipline!" The sound of the guards' footsteps died away in the darkness. Mac said, "I'll rouse 'em out once more before we go back." They walked up on the kitchen porch and knocked on the door. Barking and growling dogs answered them. They could hear the dogs leaping around inside the house, and Anderson quieting them. The door opened a crack. "It's us, Mr. Anderson."

"Come on in," he said sullenly.

The pointers weaved about, whipping their thin, hard tails and whining with pleasure. Mac leaned over and patted each one and pulled the leathers. "You ought to leave the dogs outside, Mr. Anderson, to watch the place," he said. "It's so dark the guards can't see any thing. But the dogs could smell anybody coming through."

Al lay on a cot by the stove. He looked pale and weak. He seemed to have grown thin, for the flesh on his jowls was loose. He lay flat on his back, and one arm was strapped down in front of him. Doc sat in a chair beside the cot.

"Hello, Al," Mac said quietly. "How's she go, boy?"

The eyes brightened. "O.K.," said Al. "It hurts quite a lot. Doc says it'll keep me down some time." Mac leaned over the cot and picked up Al's good hand. "Not too hard," Al said quickly. "There's busted ribs on that side."

Anderson stood by; his eyes were burning. "Now you see," he said. "You see what comes of it. Lunch wagon burned, Al hurt, now you see."

"Oh, for Christ's sake, Dad," Al said weakly. "Don't start that again. They call you Mac, don't they?"

"Right."

"Well, look, Mac. D'you think I could get into the Party?"

"You mean you want to go in active work?"

"Yeah. Think I could get in?"

"I think so—" Mac said slowly. "I'll give you an application card. What you want to come in for, Al?"

The heavy face twisted in a grimace. Al swung his

head back and forth. "I been thinkin'," he said. "Ever since they beat me up I been thinkin'. I can't get those guys outa my head—my little wagon all burned up, an' them jumpin' on me with their feet; and two cops down on the corner watchin', and not doin' a thing! I can't get that outa my head."

"And so you want to join up with us, huh, Al?"

"I want to be against 'em," Al cried. "I want to be fightin' 'em all my life. I want to be on the other side."

"They'll just beat you up worse, Al. I'm tellin' you straight. They'll knock hell out of you."

"Well, I won't care then, because I'll be fightin' 'em, see? But there I was, just runnin' a little lunch wagon, an' givin' bums a handout now an' then—" His voice choked and tears squeezed out of his eyes.

Dr. Burton touched him gently on the cheek. "Don't talk any more, Al."

"I'll see you get an application card," Mac said. And he continued, "By God, it's funny. Guy after guy gets knocked into our side by a cop's night stick. Every time they maul hell out of a bunch of men, we get a flock of applications. Why, there's a Red Squad cop in Los Angeles that sends us more members than a dozen of our organizers. An' the damn fools haven't got sense enough to realize it. O.K., Al. You'll get your application. I don't know whether it'll go through, but it will if I can push it through." He patted Al's good arm. "I hope it goes through. You're a good guy, Al. Don't blame me for your wagon."

"I don't, Mac. I know who to blame."

Burton said, "Take it easy, Al. Just rest; you need it."

Anderson had been fidgeting about the room. The dogs circled him endlessly, putting up their liver-colored noses and sniffing, waving their stiff tails like little whips. "Well, I hope you're satisfied," he said helplessly. "You break up everything I've got. You even take Al away. I hope you take good joy of it."

Jim broke in, "Don't worry, Mr. Anderson. There's guards around your house. You're the only man in the Valley that has his apples picked."

Mac asked, "When are you going to move your apples?"

"Day after tomorrow."

"Well, do you want some guards for the trucks?"

"I don't know," Anderson said uneasily.

"I guess we better put guards on the trucks," said Mac, "just in case anybody tried to dump your crop. We'll get going now. Good night, Mr. Anderson. 'Night, Al. In one way I'm glad it happened."

Al smiled. " 'Night, you guys. Don't forget that card, Mac."

"I won't. Better pull your curtains down, Mr. Anderson. I don't think they'll shoot through your windows, but they might; they've done it before, other places."

The door closed instantly behind them. The lighted spot on the ground, from the window, shrank to darkness as the curtain was pulled down. Mac felt his way to the gate, and when they were out, shut it after them. "Wait here a minute," he said. "I'm going to look at those guards again." He stepped away into the darkness.

Jim stood beside the doctor. "Better take good care of that shoulder," Burton advised. "It might cause you some trouble later."

"I don't care about it, Doc. It seems good to have it."

"Yes, I thought it might be like that."

"Like what?"

"I mean you've got something in your eyes, Jim, something religious. I've seen it in you boys before."

Jim flared, "Well, it isn't religious. I've got no use for religion."

"No, I guess you haven't. Don't let me bother you, Jim. Don't let me confuse you with terms. You're living the good life, whatever you want to call it."

"I'm happy," said Jim. "And happy for the first time. I'm full-up."

"I know. Don't let it die. It's the vision of Heaven."

"I don't believe in Heaven," Jim said. "I don't believe in religion."

"All right, I won't argue any more. I don't envy you as much as I might, Jim, because sometimes I love men as much as you do, maybe not in just the same way."

"Do you get that, Doc? Like that—like troops and troops marching into you? And you closing around them?"

"Yes, something like that. Particularly when they've done something stupid, when a man's made a mistake, and died for it. Yes, I get it, Jim—pretty often."

They heard Mac's voice, "Where are you guys? It's so damn dark."

"Over here." They joined him and all three moved along into the orchard, under the black trees.

"The guards weren't in the barn," said Mac. "They were out on watch. Maybe they're going to stick it."

Far down the road they heard the mutter of a truck coming toward them. "I feel sorry for Anderson," Burton said quietly. "Everything he respects, everything he's afraid of is turning against him. I wonder what he'll do. They'll drive him out of here, of course."

Mac said harshly, "We can't help it, Doc. He happens to be the one that's sacrificed for the men. Somebody has to break if the whole bunch is going to get out of the slaughter-house. We can't think about the hurts of one man. It's necessary, Doc."

"I wasn't questioning your motives, nor your ends. I was just sorry for the poor old man. His self-respect is down. That's a bitter thing to him, don't you think so, Mac?"

"I can't take time to think about the feelings of one man." Mac said sharply. "I'm too busy with big bunches of men."

"It was different with the little fellow who was shot," Doc went on musingly. "He liked what he did. He wouldn't have had it any other way."

"Doc, you're breakin' my heart," Mac said irritably. "Don't you get lost in a lot of sentimental foolishness. There's an end to be gained; it's a real end, hasn't anything to do with people losing respect. It's people getting bread into their guts. It's *real*, not any of your high-falutin ideas. How's the old guy with the broken hip?"

"All right, then, change the subject. The old man's getting mean as a scorpion. Right at first he got a lot of attention, he got pretty proud for a while; and now he's mad because the men don't come and listen to him talk."

"I'll go in and see him in the morning," said Jim. "He was a kind of a nice old fellow."

Mac cried, "Listen! Didn't that truck stop?"

"I think it did. Sounded as though it stopped at the camp."

"I wonder what the hell. Come on, let's hurry. Look out for trees." They had gone only a little distance when the truck roared, its gears clashed, and it moved away again. Its sound softened into the distance until it merged with the quiet. "I hope nothing's wrong," said Mac.

They trotted out of the orchard and crossed the cleared space. The light still burned in London's tent, and a group of men moved about near it. Mac dashed up, threw up the tent-flap and went inside. On the ground lay a long, rough pine box. London sat on a box and stared morosely up at the newcomers. The girl seemed to cower down on her mattress, while London's dark-haired, pale son sat beside her and stroked her hair. London motioned to the box with his thumb. "What the hell 'm I goin' to do with it?" he asked. "It's scared this here girl half to death. I can't keep it in here."

"Joy?" Mac asked.

"Yeah. They just brang him."

Mac pulled his lip and studied the coffin. "We could put it outside, I guess. Or we can let your kids sleep in the hospital tent tonight and leave it here, that is, unless it scares you, London."

"It don't mean nothing to me," London protested. "It's just another stiff. I seen plenty in my time."

"Well, let's leave it here, then. Jim an' me'll stay here with it. The guy was a friend of ours." Behind him the doctor chuckled softly. Mac reddened and swung around. "S'pose you do win, Doc? What of it? I knew the little guy."

"I didn't say anything," Burton said.

London spoke softly to the girl, and to the dark boy, and in a moment they went out of the tent, she holding the shoulder blanket tight about herself and the baby.

Mac sat down on one end of the oblong box and rubbed the wood with his forefinger. The coarse pine grains wriggled like little rivers over the wood. Jim stood behind Mac and stared over his shoulder. London moved nervously about the tent, and his eyes avoided the coffin. Mac said, "Nice piece o' goods the county puts out."

"What you want for nothing?" London demanded.

"Well," Mac replied, "I don't want nothing for myself but a bonfire, just a fire to get rid of me, so I won't lie around." He stood up and felt in his jeans pocket and brought out a big knife. One of the blades had a screwdriver end. He fitted it to a screw in the coffin-lid and twisted.

London cried, "What do you want to open it for? That won't do no good. Leave him be."

"I want to see him," said Mac.

"What for? He's dead—he's a lump of dirt."

The doctor said softly, "Sometimes I think you realists are the most sentimental people in the world."

Mac snorted and laid the screw carefully on the ground. "If you think this is sentiment, you're nuts, Doc. I want to see if it'd be a good idea for the guys to look at him tomorrow. We got to shoot some juice into 'em some way. They're dyin' on their feet."

Burton said, "Fun with dead bodies, huh?"

Jim insisted earnestly, "We've got to use every means, Doc. We've got to use every weapon."

Mac looked up at him appreciatively. "That's the idea. That's the way it is. If Joy can do some work after he's dead, then he's got to do it. There's no such things as personal feelings in this crowd. Can't be. And there's no such things as good taste, don't you forget it."

London stood still, listening and nodding his big head slowly up and down. "You guys got it right," he agreed. "Look at Dakin. He let his damn truck make him mad. I heard he comes up for trial tomorrow—for assault."

Mac quickly turned out the screws and laid them in a line on the ground. The lid was stuck. He kicked it loose with his heel.

Joy looked flat and small and painfully clean. He had on a clean blue shirt, and his oil-soiled blue jeans. The arms were folded stiffly across the stomach. "All he got was a shot of formaldehyde," Mac said. A stubble was growing on Joy's cheeks, looking very dark against the grey, waxy skin. His face was composed and rested. The gnawing bitterness was gone from it.

"He looks quiet," Jim remarked.

"Yes," said Mac. "That's the trouble. It won't do no good to show him. He looks so comfortable all the guys'll want to get right in with him." The doctor moved close and looked down at the coffin for a moment, and then he walked to a box and sat down. His big, plaintive eyes fastened on Mac's face. Mac still stared at Joy. "He was such a good little guy," he said. "He didn't want nothing for himself. Y'see, he wasn't very bright. But some way he got it into his head something was wrong. He didn't see why food had to be dumped and left to rot when people were starving. Poor little fool, he could never understand that. And he got the notion he might help to stop it. I wonder how much he helped? It's awful hard to say. Maybe not at all—maybe a lot. You can't tell." Mac's voice had become unsteady. The doctor's eyes stayed on his face, and the doctor's mouth was smiling a curious, half-sardonic, half-kindly smile.

Jim interposed, "Joy wasn't afraid of anything."

Mac picked up the coffin-lid and set it in place again. "I don't know why we say 'poor little guy.' He wasn't poor. He was greater than himself. He didn't know it —didn't care. But there was a kind of ectsasy in him all the time, even when they beat him. And Jim says it— he wasn't afraid." Mac picked up a screw, and stuck it through the hole and turned it down with his knife.

London said, "That sounds like a speech. Maybe you better give the speech. I don't know nothin' about talkin'. That was a pretty speech. It sounded nice."

Mac looked up guiltily and searched London for sarcasm, and found none. "That wasn't a speech," he said quietly. "I guess it could be, but it wasn't. It's like tellin' the guy he hasn't been wasted."

"Why don't you make the speech tomorrow? You can talk."

"Hell, no. You're the boss. The guys'd be sore if I sounded off. They expect you to do it."

"Well, what do I got to say?"

Mac drove the screws in, one after another. "Tell 'em

the usual stuff. Tell 'em Joy died for 'em. Tell 'em he was tryin' to help 'em, and the best they can do for him is to help 'emselves by stickin' together, see?"

"Yeah, I get it."

Mac stood up and regarded the grained wood of the lid. "I hope somebody tries to stop us," he said. "I hope some of them damn vigilantes gets in our way. God, I hope they try to stop us paradin' through town."

"Yeah, I see," said London.

Jim's eyes glowed. He repeated, "I hope so."

"The guys'll want to fight," Mac continued. "They'll be all sore inside. They'll want to bust something. Them vigilantes ain't got much sense; I hope they're crazy enough to start something tomorrow."

Burton stood up wearily from his box and walked up to Mac. He touched him lightly on the shoulder. "Mac," he said, "you're the craziest mess of cruelty and hausfrau sentimentality, of clear vision and rose-colored glasses I ever saw. I don't know how you manage to be all of them at once."

"Nuts," said Mac.

The doctor yawned. "All right. We'll leave it at nuts. I'm going to bed. You know where to find me if you want me, only I hope you won't want me."

Mac looked quickly at the tent ceiling. Fat, lazy drops were falling on the canvas. One—two—three, and then a dozen, patting the tent with a soft drumming. Mac sighed. "I hoped it wouldn't. Now by morning the guys'll be drowned rats. They won't have no more spirit than a guinea pig."

"I'm still going to bed," the doctor said. He went out and dropped the flaps behind him.

Mac sat down heavily on the coffin. The drumming grew quicker. Outside, the men began calling to one another, and their voices were blurred by the rain. "I don't suppose there's a tent in the camp that don't leak," said

Mac. "Jesus, why can't we get a break without getting it cancelled out? Why do we always have to take it in the neck—always?"

Jim sat gingerly down on the long box beside him. "Don't worry about it, Mac. Sometimes, when a guy gets miserable enough, he'll fight all the harder. That's the way it was with me, Mac, when my mother was dying, and she wouldn't even speak to me. I just got so miserable I'd've taken any chance. Don't you worry about it."

Mac turned on him. "Catching me up again, are you? I'll get mad if you show me up too often. Go lie down on the girl's mattress there. You've got a bad arm. It must hurt by now."

"It burns some, all right."

"Well, lie down there. See if you can't get some sleep." Jim started to protest, and then he went to the mattress on the ground and stretched out on it. The wound throbbed down his arm and across his chest. He heard the rain increase until it swept on the canvas, like a broom. He heard the big drops falling inside the tent, and then, when a place leaked in the center of the tent, he heard the heavy drops splash on the coffin box.

Mac still sat beside it, holding his head in his arms. And London's eyes, like the sleepless eyes of a lynx, stared and stared at the lamp. The camp was quiet again, and the rain fell steadily, out of a windless sky. It was not very long before Jim fell into a burning sleep. The rain poured down hour after hour. On the tent-pole the lamplight yellowed and dropped to the wick. A blue flame sputtered for a while, and then went out.

12

To Jim it seemed that he awakened out of a box. One whole side of him was encased in painful stiffness. He opened his eyes and looked about the tent. A grey and listless dawn had come. The coffin still lay in its place, but Mac and London were gone. He heard the pounding that must have awakened him, hammers on wood. For a time he lay quietly looking about the tent, but at last he tried to sit up. The box of pain held him. He rolled over and climbed up to his knees, and then stood up, drooping his hurt shoulder to protect it from tension.

The flap swung up and Mac entered. His blue denim jacket glistened with moisture. "Hi, Jim. You got some sleep, didn't you. How's the arm?"

"Stiff," he said. "Is it still raining?"

"Dirty drizzle. Doc's coming to look at your shoulder in a minute. Lord, it's wet outside! Soon's the guys walk around a little bit, it'll be all slop."

"What's the pounding?"

"Well, we've been building the stand for Joy. Even dug up an old flag to go over him." He held up a small dingy package of cloth, and unrolled it, a threadbare and stained American flag. He spread it carefully on the coffin top. "No," he said. "I think that's wrong. I think the field should be over the left breast, like this?"

"It's a lousy dirty flag," Jim said.

"I know, but it'll get over big. Doc ought to be along any minute now."

"I'm hungry as hell," said Jim.

"Who isn't? We're going to have rolled oats, straight, for breakfast, no sugar or no milk—just oats."

"Even that sounds good to me. You don't sound so low this morning, Mac."

"Me? Well, the guys aren't knocked out as much as I thought they would be. The women 're raising hell, but the guys are in pretty good shape, considering."

Burton hustled in. "How's it feel, Jim?"

"Pretty sore."

"Well, sit down over here. I'll put on a clean bandage." Jim sat on a box and braced himself against expected pain, but the doctor worked deftly, removed the old wrapping and applied a new one without hurting him. "Old Dan's upset," he said. "He's afraid he isn't going to get to go to the funeral. He says he started this strike, now everybody's forgetting him."

Mac asked, "Do you think we could put him on a truck and take him along, Doc? It'd be swell publicity if we could."

"You could, Mac, but it'd hurt him like the devil; and it might cause shock complications. He's an old man. Hold still, Jim. I'm nearly through. No, I'll tell you what we'd better do. We'll tell him we're going to take him, and then when we start to lift him, I think he'll beg off. His pride's just hurt. He thinks Joy stole the show from him." He patted the finished bandage. "There you are, Jim. How do you feel now?"

Jim moved his shoulder cautiously. "Better. Sure, that's lots better."

Mac said, "Why don't you go and see the old guy, Jim, after you eat. He's a friend of yours."

"I guess I will."

Burton explained, "He's a little bit off, Jim. Don't worry him. All this excitement has gone to his head a little bit."

Jim said, "Sure, I'll lead him along." He stood up. "Say, that feels lots better."

"Let's get some mush," said Mac. "We want to start this funeral in time so it'll tie up the noon traffic in town, if we can."

Doc snorted. "Always a friend to man. God, you're a scorpion, Mac! If I were bossing the other side I'd take you out and shoot you."

"Well, they'll do that some day, I guess," Mac replied. "They've done everything else to me."

They filed out of the tent. Outside the air was filled with tiny drops of falling water, a grey, misty drizzle. The orchard trees were dim behind a curtain of grey gauze. Jim looked down the line of sodden tents. The streets between the lines were already whipped to slushy mud by the feet of moving people, and the people moved constantly for there was no dry place to sit down. Lines of men waited their turns at the toilets at the ends of the streets.

Burton and Mac and Jim walked toward the stoves. Thick blue smoke from wet wood poured from the chimneys. On the stove-tops the wash-boilers of mush bubbled, and the cooks stirred with long sticks. Jim felt the mist penetrating down his neck. He pulled his jacket closer and buttoned the top button. "I need a bath," he said.

"Well, take a sponge bath. That's the only kind we have. Here, I brought your food can."

They stepped to the end of the line of men waiting by the stove. The cooks filled the containers with mush as the line filed by. Jim gathered some of it on his eating stick and blew it cool. "It tastes good," he said, "I'm half-starved, I guess."

"Well, you ought to be, if you aren't. London's over supervising the platform. Come on, let's go over." They slushed through the mud, stepping clear of the tracks when any untrampled ground showed. In back of the stoves the new platform stood, a little deck, constructed of old fence-posts and culvert planks. It was raised about four feet above the ground level. London was just nailing on a hand-rail. "Hello," he said. "How was breakfast?"

"Roast dirt would taste swell this morning," said Mac. "This is the last, ain't it?"

"Yep. They ain't no more when that's gone."

"Maybe Dick'll have better luck today," Jim suggested. "Why don't you let me go out and rustle food, Mac? I'm not doing anything."

Mac said, "You're stayin' here. Look, London, this guy's marked; they try to get him twice already, and here he wants to go out and walk the streets alone."

"Don't be a damn fool," said London. "We're goin' to put you on the truck with the coffin. You can't walk none with that hurt. You ride on the truck."

"What th' hell?" Jim began.

London scowled at him. "Don't get smart with me," he said. "I'm the boss here. When you get to be boss, you tell me. I'm tellin' you, now."

Jim's eyes flared rebelliously. He looked quickly at Mac and saw that he was grinning and waiting. "O.K.," said Jim. "I'll do what you say."

Mac said, "Here's something you can do, Jim. See if you think it's all right, London. S'pose Jim just circulates and talks to the guys? Just finds out how they feel? We ought to know how far we can go. I think the guys'd talk to Jim."

"What do you want to know?" London asked.

"Well, we ought to know how they feel about the strike now."

"Sounds all right to me," said London.

Mac turned to Jim. "Go and see old Dan," he said. "And then just get to talkin' to a lot of the guys, a few at a time. Don't try and sell 'em nothing. Just 'yes' 'em until you find out how they feel. Can you do that, Jim?"

"Sure. Where do they keep old Dan?"

"Look. See down that second row, that tent that's whiter'n the rest? That's Doc's hospital tent. I guess old Dan'll be in there."

"I'll look in on him," said Jim. He scraped up the last of his mush on his paddle and ate it. At one of the water barrels he dipped water to wash the eating can, and, on passing his pup-tent threw the can inside. There was a little movement in the tent. Jim dropped on his knees and crawled inside. Lisa was there. She had been nursing the baby. She covered her breast hastily.

"Hello," said Jim.

She blushed and said faintly, "Hello."

"I thought you were going to sleep in the hospital tent."

"There was guys there," she said.

"I hope you didn't get wet here last night."

She pulled the shoulder blanket neatly down. "No, there wasn't no leak."

"What you scared of?" Jim asked. "I won't hurt you. I helped you once, Mac and I did."

"I know. That's why."

"What are you talking about?"

Her head almost disappeared under the blanket. "You seen me—without no clothes on," she said faintly.

Jim started to laugh, and then caught himself. "That doesn't mean anything," he said. "You shouldn't feel bad about that. We had to help you."

"I know." Her eyes rose up for a moment. "Makes me feel funny."

"Forget it," said Jim. "How's the baby?"

"All right."

"Nursing it all right?"

"Yeah." Then her face turned very red. She blurted, "I like to nurse."

" 'Course you do."

"I like to—because it—feels good." She hid her face. "I hadn't ought to told you."

"Why not?"

"I don't know, but I hadn't ought to of. It ain't—decent, do you think? You won't tell nobody?"

" 'Course not." Jim looked away from her and out the low doorway. The mist drifted casually down. Big drops slid down the tent slope like beads on a string. He continued to stare out of the tent, knowing instinctively that the girl wanted to look at him, and that she couldn't until he looked away.

Her glance went over his face, a dark profile against the light. She saw the lumpy, bandaged shoulder. "What's the matter 'th your arm?" she demanded.

He turned back and this time her eyes held. "I got shot yesterday."

"Oh. Does it hurt?"

"Little bit."

"Just shot? Just up an' shot by a guy?"

"Fight with some scabs. One of the owners potted me with a rifle."

"You was fightin'? You?"

"Sure."

Her eyes stayed wide. She looked fascinatedly at his face. "You don't have no gun, do you?"

"No."

She sighed. "Who was that fella come in the tent last night?"

"Young fellow? That was Dick. He's a friend of mine."

"He looks like a nice fella," she said.

Jim smiled. "Sure, he's O.K."

"Kinda fresh, though," she said. "Joey, that's my

hubby, he didn't like it none. I thought he was a nice fella."

Jim got to his knees and prepared to crawl out of the tent. "Had any breakfast?"

"Joey's out gettin' me some." Her eyes were bolder now. "You goin' to the funeral?"

"Sure."

"I can't go. Joey says I can't."

"It's too wet and nasty." Jim crawled out. " 'Bye, kid. Take care o' yourself."

" 'B-bye." She paused. "Don't tell nobody, will you?"

He looked back into the tent. "Don't tell 'em what? Oh, about the baby. No, I won't."

"Y'see," she explained, "you seen me that way, so I told you. I don't know why."

"I don't either. 'Bye, kid." He straightened up and walked away. Few men were moving about in the mist. Most of the strikers had taken their mush and gone back to the tents. The smoke from the stoves swirled low to the ground. A little wind blew the drizzle in a slow, drifting angle. As Jim went by London's tent, he looked in and saw a dozen men standing about the coffin, all looking down at it. Jim started to go in, but he caught himself and walked to the white hospital tent down the row. There was a curious, efficient neatness inside the tent, a few medical supplies, bandage, bottles of iodine, a large jar of salts, a doctor's bag, all arranged with precision on a big box.

Old Dan lay propped in a cot, and on the ground stood a wide-necked bottle for a urinal, and an old-fashioned chamber for a bed-pan. Old Dan's beard had grown longer and fiercer, and his cheeks were more sunken. His eyes glinted fiercely at Jim. "So," he said. "You finally come. You damn squirts get what you want, and then run out on a man."

"How you feeling, Dan?" Jim asked placatingly.

"Who cares? That doctor's a nice man; he's the only nice one in this bunch of lice."

Jim pulled up an apple box and sat down. "Don't be mad, Dan. Look, I got it myself; got shot in the shoulder."

"Served you damn well right," Dan said darkly. "You punks can't take care o' yourselves. Damn wonder you 'ain't all dead fallin' over your feet." Jim was silent. "Leave me lyin' here," Dan cried. "Think I don't remember nothing. Up that apple tree all you could talk was strike, strike. And who starts the strike? You? Hell, no. I start it! Think I don't know. I start it when I bust my hip. An' then you leave me here alone."

"We know it, Dan. All of us know it."

"Then why don't I get no say? Treat me like a Goddamn baby." He gesticulated furiously, and then winced. "Goin' to leave me here an' the whole bunch go on a funeral! Nobody cares about me!"

Jim interposed, "That's not so, Dan. We're going to put you on a truck and take you right along, right at the head of the procession."

Dan's mouth dropped open, exposing his four long squirrel-teeth. His hands settled slowly to the bed. "Honest?" he said. "On a truck?"

"That's what the chief said. He said you were the real leader, and you had to go."

Dan looked very stern. His mouth became dignified and military. "He damn well ought to. He knows." He stared down at his hands. His eyes grew soft and childlike. "I'll lead 'em," he said gently. "All the hundreds o' years that's what the workin' stiffs needed, a leader. I'll lead 'em through to the light. All they got to do is just what I say. I'll say, 'You guys do this,' an' they'll do it. An' I'll say, 'You lazy bastards get over there!' an' by Christ, they'll git, 'cause I won't have no lazy bastards.

When I speak, they got to jump, right now." And then he smiled with affection. "The poor damn rats," he said. "They never had nobody to tell 'em what to do. They never had no real leader."

"That's right," Jim agreed.

"Well, you'll see some changes now," Dan exclaimed. "You tell 'em I said so. Tell 'em I'm workin' out a plan. I'll be up and around in a couple of days. Tell 'em just to have patience till I get out an' lead 'em."

"Sure I'll tell 'em," said Jim.

Dr. Burton came into the tent. " 'Morning, Dan. Hello, Jim. Dan, where's the man I told to take care of you?"

"He went out," Dan said plaintively. "Went out to get me some breakfast. He never come back."

"Want the pot, Dan?"

"No."

"Did he give you the enema?"

"No."

"Have to get you another nurse, Dan."

"Say, Doc, this young punk here says I'm goin' to the funeral on a truck."

"That's right, Dan. You can go if you want."

Dan settled back, smiling. "It's about time somebody paid some attention," he said with satisfaction.

Jim stood up from his box. "See you later, Dan." Burton went out with him. Jim asked, "Is he going nuts, Doc?"

"No. He's an old man. He's had a shock. His bones don't knit very easily."

"He talks crazy, though."

"Well, the man I told to take care of him didn't do it. He needs an enema. Constipation makes a man light-headed sometimes; but he's just an old man, Jim. You made him pretty happy. Better go in and see him often."

"Do you think he'll go to the funeral?"

"No. It'd hurt him, banging around in a truck. We'll

have to get around it some way. How is your arm feeling?"

"I forgot all about it."

"Fine. Try not to get cold in it. It could be nasty, if you don't take care of it. See you later. The men won't shovel dirt in the toilets. We're out of disinfectant. Simply have to get some disinfectant—anything." He hurried away, mutteringly softly to himself as he went.

Jim looked about for someone to talk to. Those men who were in sight walked quickly through the drizzle from one tent to another. The slush in the streets was deep and black by now. One of the big brown squad tents stood nearby. Hearing voices inside, Jim went in. In the dim brown light he saw a dozen men squatting on their blankets. The talk died as he entered. The men looked up at him and waited. He reached in his pocket and brought out the bag of tobacco Mac had given him. "Hi," he said. The men still waited. Jim went on, "I've got a sore arm. Will one of you guys roll me a cigarette?"

A man siting in front of him held out a hand, took the bag and quickly made the cigarette. Jim took it and waved it to indicate the other men. "Pass it around. God knows they ain't much in this camp." The bag went from hand to hand. A stout little man with a short mustache said, "Sit down, kid, here, on my bed. Ain't you the guy that got shot yesterday?"

Jim laughed. "I'm one of 'em. I'm not the dead one. I'm the one that got away."

They laughed appreciatively. A man with a lantern-jaw and shiny cheek-bones broke up the laughter. "What they goin' to bury the little guy today for?"

"Why not?" Jim asked.

"Yeah, but ever'body waits three days."

The stout little man blew a jet of smoke. "When you're dead, you're dead."

Lantern-jaw said somberly, "S'pose he ain't dead. S'pose he's just in a kind of a state? S'pose we bury him alive. I think we ought to wait three days, like ever'body else."

A smooth, sarcastic voice answered. Jim looked at a tall man with a white, unlined forehead. "No, he isn't sleeping," the man said. "You can be very sure of that. If you knew what an undertaker does, you'd be sure he isn't in any 'state'."

Lantern-jaw said, "He might just be. I don't see no reason to take a chance."

White-forehead scoffed. "Well, if he can sleep with his veins full of embalming fluid, he's a God-damn sound sleeper."

"Is that what they do?"

"Yes it is. I knew a man who worked for an undertaker. He told me things you wouldn't believe."

"I rather not hear 'em," said Lantern-jaw. "Don't do no good to talk like that."

The stout man asked, "Who was the little guy? I seen him try to get the scabs over, an' then I seen 'im start over, an' then, whang! Down he goes."

Jim held his unlighted cigarette to his lips for a moment. "I knew him. He was a nice little guy. He was a kind of a labor leader."

White-forehead said, "There seems to be a bounty on labor leaders. They don't last long. Look at that rattle-snake, Sam. Says he's a longshoreman. I bet he's dead inside of six months."

A dark boy asked, "How about London? Think they'll get him like they got Dakin?"

Lantern-jaw: "No, by God. London can take care of himself. London's got a head on him."

White-forehead: "If London has a head on him, why in hell are we sitting around here? This strike's screwy.

Somebody's making money out of it. When it gets tough somebody'll sell out and leave the rest of us to take it on the chin."

A broad, muscular man got to his knees and crouched there like an animal. His lips snarled away from his teeth and his eyes blazed with a red light. "That's enough from you, wise guy," he said. "I've knew London for a long time. If you're gettin' around to sayin' London's fixin' to sell out, me an' you's goin' round and round, right now! I don't know nothin' about this here strike. I'm doin' it 'cause London says it's O.K. But you lay off the smart cracks."

White-forehead looked coldly at him. "You're pretty hard, aren't you?"

"Hard enough to beat the ass off you anyway, mister."

"Lay off," Jim broke in. "What do we want to get fighting for? If you guys want to fight, there's going to be plenty of it for everybody."

The square man grunted and sat back on his blankets. "Nobody's sayin' nothin' behind London's back when I'm there," he said.

The little stout man looked at Jim. "How'd you get shot, kid?"

"Running," said Jim. "I got winged running."

"I heard a guy say you all beat hell out of some scabs."

"That's right."

White-forehead said, "They say there are scabs coming in in trucks. And they say every scab has tear gas bombs in his pocket."

"That's a lie," Jim said quickly. "They always start lies like that to scare the guys off."

White-forehead went on, "I heard that the bosses sent word to London that they won't deal as long as there's reds in camp."

The broad, muscular man came to life again. "Well,

who's the reds? You talk more like a red than anybody I seen."

White-forehead continued, "Well, I think that doctor's a red. What's a doctor want out here? He doesn't get any pay. Well, who's paying him? He's getting his; don't worry about that." He looked wise. "Maybe he's getting it from Moscow."

Jim spat on the ground. His face was pale. He said quietly, "You're the God-damned meanest son-of-a-bitch I ever saw! You make everybody out the kind of a rat you are."

The square man got to his knees again. "The kid's right," he said. "He can't kick hell out of you, but I can. And by Christ I will if you don't keep that toilet seat of yours shut."

White-forehead got up slowly and went to the entrance. He turned back. "All right, you fellows, but you watch. Pretty soon London'll tell you to settle the strike. An' then he'll get a new car, or a steady job. You just watch."

The square man leaped to his knees again, but White-forehead dodged out of the tent.

Jim asked, "Who is that guy? Does he sleep in here?"

"Hell, no. He just come in a little while ago."

"Well, did any of you guys ever see him before?"

They shook their heads. "Not me."

"I never."

Jim cried, "By Christ! Then they sent him in."

The fat man asked, "Who sent him?"

"The owners did. He's sent in here to talk like that an' get you guys suspecting London. Don't you see? It splits the camp up. Couple you guys better see he gets run out of camp."

The square man climbed to his feet. "I'll do it myself," he said. "They's nothin' I'd admire better." He went out of the tent.

Jim said, "You got to watch out. Guys like that'll give you the idea the strike's just about through. Don't listen to lies."

The fat man gazed out of the tent. "It ain't a lie that the food's all gone," he said. "It ain't a lie that boiled cow food ain't much of a breakfast. It don't take no spies to spread that."

"We got to stick," Jim cried. "We simply got to stick. If we lose this, we're sunk; and not only us, either. Every other working stiff in the country gets a little of it."

The fat man nodded. "It all fits together," he agreed. "There ain't nothing separate. Guys think they want to get something soft for themselves, but they can't without everybody gets it."

A middle-aged man who had been lying down toward the rear of the tent sat up. "You know the trouble with workin' men?" he asked. "Well, I'll tell you. They do too God-damn much talkin'. If they did more sluggin' an' less arguin', they'd get some place." He stopped. The men in the tent listened. From outside there came the sound of a little bustling, the mutter of footsteps, the murmur of voices, the sound of people, penetrating as an odor, and soft. The men in the tent sat still and listened. The sound of people grew a little louder. Footsteps were slushing in the mud. A group walked past the tent.

Jim stood up and walked to the entrance just as a head was thrust in. "They're goin' to bring out the coffin. Come on, you guys." Jim stepped out between the tent-flaps. The mist still fell, blowing sideways, drifting like tiny, light snowflakes. Here and there the loose canvas of a tent moved soddenly in the wind. Jim looked down the street. The news had traveled. Out of the tents men and women came. They moved slowly in together and converged on the platform. And as their group became more and more compact, the sound of their many voices blended into one voice, and the sound of their footsteps became a great restlessness. Jim looked at the faces. There was a blindness in the eyes. The heads were tipped back as though they sniffed for something. They drew in about the platform and crowded close.

Out of London's tent six men came, bearing the box. There were no handles on the coffin. Each pair of men locked hands underneath, and bore the burden on their forearms. They hesitated jerkily, trying to get in step, and having established the swinging rhythm, moved slowly through the slush toward the platform. Their heads were bare, and the drops of moisture stood out on their hair like grey dust. The little wind raised a corner of the soiled flag, and dropped it, and raised it again. In front of the casket a lane opened through the people, and the bearers moved on, their faces stiff with ceremonial solemnity, necks straight, chins down. The people on the edge of the lane stared at the box. They grew quiet during the movement of its passage, and when it was by whispered nervously to one another. A few men surreptitiously crossed themselves. The bearers reached the platform. The leading pair laid the end on the planks, and the others pushed the box forward until it rested safely.

Jim hurried to London's tent. London and Mac were there. "Jesus, I wish you'd do the talkin', I can't talk."

"No. You'll do fine. 'Member what I told you. Try to get 'em answering you. Once you get responses started, you've got 'em. Regular old camp-meeting stuff; but it sure works on a crowd."

London looked frightened. "You do it, Mac. Honest to God I can't. I didn't even know the guy."

Mac looked disgusted. "Well, you get up there and make a try. If you fall down, I'll be there to pick it up."

London buttoned the collar of his blue shirt and turned up the flaps against his throat. He buttoned his old black serge coat over his stomach and patted it down.

His hand went up to the tonsured hair and brushed it down, back and sides; and then he seemed to shake himself down to a tight, heavy solemnity. The lean-faced Sam came in and stood beside him. London stepped out of the tent, great with authority. Mac and Jim and Sam fell in behind him, but London walked alone, down the muddy street, and his little procession followed him. The heads of the people turned as he approached. The tissue of soft speech stopped. A new aisle opened to allow the leader to pass, and the heads turned with him as he passed.

London climbed up on the platform. He was alone, over the heads of the people. The faces pointed up at him, the eyes expressionless as glass. For a moment London looked down at the pine coffin, and then his shoulders squared. He seemed reluctant to break the breathing silence. His voice was remote and dignified. "I come up here to make some kind of speech," he said. "And I don't know no speeches." He paused and looked out over the upturned faces. "This little guy got killed yesterday. You all seen it. He was comin' over to our side, an' somebody plugged him. He wasn't doin' no harm to nobody." Again he stopped, and his face grew puzzled. "Well, what can a guy say? We're goin' to bury him. He's one of our own guys, an' he got shot. What can I say? We're goin' to march out and bury him—all of us. Because he was one of us. He was kind of like all of us. What happened to him is like to happen to any guy here." He stopped, and his mouth stayed open. "I—I don't know no speeches," he said uneasily. "There's a guy here that knowed this little fellow. I'm goin' to let him talk." His head turned slowly to where Mac stood. "Come on up, Mac. Tell 'em about the little guy."

Mac broke out of his stiffness and almost threw himself on the platform. His shoulders weaved like a boxer's. "Sure I'll tell 'em," he cried passionately. "The guy's name was Joy. He was a radical. Get it? A radical. He wanted guys like you to have enough to eat and a place to sleep where you wouldn't get wet. He didn't want nothing for himself. He was a radical!" Mac cried. "D'ye see what he was? A dirty bastard, a danger to the government. I don't know if you saw his face, all beat to rags. The cops done that because he was a radical. His hands were broke, an' his jaw was broke. One time he got that jaw broke in a picket line. They put him in the can. Then a doctor come an' looked at him. 'I won't treat a God-damned red,' the doctor says. So Joy lies there with a busted jaw. He was dangerous—he wanted guys like you to get enough to eat." His voice was growing softer and softer, and his eyes watched expertly, saw faces becoming tense, trying to catch the words of his softening tone, saw the people leaning forward. "I knew him." Suddenly he shouted, "What are you going to do about it? Dump him in a mud-hole, cover him with slush. Forget him."

A woman in the crowd began to sob hysterically. "He was fightin' for you," Mac shouted. "You goin' to forget it?"

A man in the crowd yelled, "No, by Christ!"

Mac hammered on, "Goin' to let him get killed, while you lie down and take it?"

A chorus this time, "No-o-o!"

Mac's voice dropped into a sing-song. "Goin' to dump him in the mud?"

"No-oo." The bodies swayed a little bit.

"He fought for you. Are you going to forget him?"

"No-o-o."

"We're going to march through town. You going to let any damn cops stop us?"

The heavy roar, "No-oo." The crowd swayed in the rhythm. They poised for the next response.

Mac broke the rhythm, and the break jarred them.

He said quietly, "This little guy is the spirit of all of us. We won't pray for him. He don't need prayers. And we don't need prayers. We need clubs!"

Hungrily the crowd tried to restore the rhythm. "Clubs," they said. "Clubs." And then they waited in silence.

"O.K.," Mac said shortly. "We're going to throw the dirty radical in the mud, but he's going to stay with us, too. God help anybody that tries to stop us." Suddenly he got down from the platform, leaving the crowd hungry and irritated. Eyes looked wondering into other eyes.

London climbed down from the platform. He said to the bearers, "Put him in Albert Johnson's truck. We'll get goin' in a few minutes now." He followed Mac, who was working his way out of the crowd.

Dr. Burton fell in beside Mac when he was clear of the bunched people. "You surely know how to work them, Mac," he said quietly. "No preacher ever brought people to the mourners' bench quicker. Why didn't you keep it up awhile? You'd've had them talking in tongues and holy-rolling in a minute."

Mac said irritably, "Quit sniping at me, Doc. I've got a job to do, and I've got to use every means to do it."

"But where did you learn it, Mac?"

"Learn what?"

"All those tricks."

Mac said tiredly, "Don't try to see so much, Doc. I wanted them mad. Well, they're mad. What do you care how it's done?"

"I know how it's done," said Burton. "I just wondered how you learned. By the way, old Dan's satisfied not to go. He decided when we lifted him."

London and Jim caught up with them. Mac said, "You better leave a big guard here, London."

"O.K. I'll tell Sam to stay and keep about a hundred. That sure was a nice speech, Mac."

"I didn't have no time to figure it out ahead. We better get movin' before these guys cool off. Once they get goin' they'll be O.K. But we don't want 'em just to stand around and cool off."

They turned and looked back. Through the crowd the bearers came swinging, carrying the box on their forearms. The clot of people broke up and straggled behind. The light mist fell. To the west a rent in the cloud showed a patch of pale blue sky, and a high, soundless wind tore the clouds apart as they watched.

"It might be a nice day yet," Mac said. He turned to Jim. "I nearly forgot about you. How do you feel?"

"All right."

"Well, I don't think you better walk all that distance. You ride on the truck."

"No. I'll walk. The guys wouldn't like it if I rode."

"I thought of that," said Mac. "We'll have the pallbearers ride too. That'll make it all right. We all set, London?"

"All set."

13

THE COFFIN rested on the flat bed of an old Dodge truck. On each side of it the bearers sat, hanging their legs over. And Jim rode hanging his feet over the rear. The motor throbbed and coughed, Albert Johnson drove out of the park and stopped in the road until the line formed, about eight men to a file. Then he dropped into low gear and moved slowly along the road, and the long line of men shuffled after him. The hundred guards stood in the camp and watched the parade move away.

At first the men tried to keep step, saying, "Hep, hep," but they tired of it soon. Their feet scuffed and dragged on the gravel road. A little hum of talk came from them, but each man was constrained to speak softly, in honor to the coffin. At the concrete state highway the speed cops were waiting, a dozen of them on motorcycles. Their captain, in a roadster, shouted, "We're not interfering with you men. We always conduct parades."

The feet sounded sharply on the concrete. The ranks straggled along in disorder. Only when they reached the outskirts of the town did the men straighten up. In the yards and on the sidewalks the people stood and watched the procession go by. Many took off their hats to the casket. But Mac's wish was denied. At each corner of the line of march the police stood, re-routing the traffic, turning it aside, and opening the way for the funeral. As they entered the business district of Torgas the sun broke through and glittered on the wet streets. The damp clothes of the marching men steamed under the sudden warmth. Now the sidewalks were dense with curious people, staring at the coffin; and the marchers straightened up. The squads drew close together. The men fell into step, while their faces took on expressions of importance. No one interfered, and the road was kept clear of vehicles.

Behind the truck, they marched through the town, through the thinning town again, and out into the country, toward the county cemetery. About a mile out they came to it, weed-grown and small. Over the new graves were little galvanized posts, stamped with names and dates. At the back of the lot a pile of new, wet dirt was heaped. The truck stopped at the gate. The bearers climbed down and took the casket on their forearms again. In the road the traffic cops rested their machines and stood waiting.

Albert Johnson took two lengths of tow-rope from under his seat and followed the bearers. The crowd broke ranks and followed. Jim jumped down from the truck and started to join the crowd, but Mac caught him. "Let them do it now; the main thing was the march. We'll wait here."

A young man with red hair strolled through the cemetery gate and approached. "Know a guy they call Mac?" he asked.

"They call me Mac."

"Well, do you know a guy they call Dick?"

"Sure."

"Yeah? What's his other name?"

"Halsing. What's the matter with him?"

"Nothing, but he sent you this note."

Mac opened the folded paper and read it. "Hot damn," he said. "Look, Jim!"

Jim took the note. It said:

"The lady wins. She has got a ranch, R.F.D. Box 221, Gallinas Road. Send out a truck there right away.

They have got two cows, old, and one bull calf and ten sks. lima beans. Send some guys to kill the cows.

Dick.

P.S. I nearly got picked up last night.
P.P.S. Only twelve axe-handles."

Mac was laughing. "Oh, Jesus! Oh, Christ! Two cows and a calf and beans. That gives us time. Jim, run over and find London. Tell him to come here as quick as he can."

Jim plunged off, and walked through the crowd. In a moment he came back, with London hurrying beside him. Mac cried, "Did he tell you, London? Did he?"

"He says you got food."

"Hell yes. Two cows and a calf. Ten sacks of beans! Why, the guys can go right out in this truck now."

From the crowded side of the cemetery came the beating of mud thrown down on the pine casket. "Y'see," Mac said. "The guys'll feel fine when they get their stomachs full of meat and beans."

London said, "I could do with a piece of meat myself."

"Look, London, I'll go on the truck. Give me about ten men to guard it. Jim, you can come with me." He hesitated. "Where we going to get wood? We're about out of wood. Look, London, let every guy pick up a piece or two of wood, fence picket, piece of culvert, anything. Tell 'em what it's for. When you get back, dig a hole and start a fire in it. You'll find enough junk in those damned old cars to piece out a screen. Get your fire going." He turned back to the red-haired young man. "Where is this Gallinas Road?"

" 'Bout a mile from here. You can drop me off on the way."

London said, "I'll get Albert Johnson and some men." He hurried over and disappeared in the crowd.

Mac still laughed softly to himself. "What a break!" he said. "New lease on life. Oh, Dick's a great guy. He's a great guy."

Jim, looking at the crowd, saw it stir to life, it swirled. An excited commotion overcame it. The mob eddied, broke and started back to the truck. London, in the lead, was pointing out men with his finger. The crowd surrounded the truck, laughing, shouting. Albert Johnson put his muddy ropes under the seat and climbed in. Mac got in beside him, and helped Jim in. "Keep the guys together, London," he shouted. "Don't let 'em straggle." The ten chosen men leaped on the bed of the truck.

And then the crowd played. They held the tailboard until the wheels churned. They made mud-balls and threw them at the men sitting on the truck. Outside, in the road, the police stood quietly and waited.

Albert Johnson jerked his clutch in and tore loose from the grip of the crowd. The motor panted heavily as he struck the road. Two of the cops kicked over their motors and fell in beside the truck. Mac turned and looked out through the rear window of the cab at the crowd. They came boiling out of the cemetery in a wave. They broke on the road, hurrying along, filling the road, while the cops vainly tried to keep a passage clear for automobiles. The jubilant men mocked them and pushed them and surged around them, laughing like children. The truck, with its escorts, turned a corner and moved quickly away.

Albert watched his speedometer warily. "I guess these babies'd like to pick me up for speeding."

"Damn right," said Mac. He turned to Jim. "Keep your head down if we pass anybody, Jim." And then to Albert, "If anybody tries to stop us, drive right over 'em. Remember what happened to Dakin's truck."

Albert nodded and dropped his speed to forty. "Nobody ain't goin' to stop me," he said. "I've drove a truck all my life when I could get it."

They did not go through the town, but cut around one end of it, crossed a wooden bridge over the river and turned into Gallinas Road. Albert slowed up to let the red-haired youth drop off. He waved his hand airily as they drove away. The road lay between the interminable apple trees. They drove three miles to the foothills before the orchards began to fall off, giving place to stubble fields. Jim watched the galvanized postboxes at the side of the road. "There's two-eighteen," he said. "Not very far now."

One of the cops turned back and went toward the town, but the other hung on.

"There it is," Jim said. "That big white gate there."

Albert headed in, and stopped while one of the men jumped down and opened the gate. The cop cut off his motor and leaned it against its stand.

"Private property," Mac called to him.

"I'll stick around, buddy," he said. "I'll just stick around."

A hundred yards ahead a little white house stood under a huge, spreading pepper tree, and behind it a big white barn reared. A stocky ranchman with a straw-colored mustache slouched out of the house and stood waiting for them. Albert pulled up. Mac said, "Hello, mister. The lady told us to come for some stuff."

"Yah," said the man. "She told me. Two old milk cow, little bully calf."

"Well, can we slaughter 'em here, mister?"

"Yah. You do it yourself. Clean up after. Don't make mess."

"Where are they, mister?"

"I got them in barn. You don't kill them there. Makes mess in the barn."

"Sure, mister. Pull around by the barn, Albert."

When the truck was stopped, Mac walked around it. "Any of you guys ever slaughter a cow?"

Jim broke in, "My old man was a slaughterhouse man. I can show 'em. My arm's too sore to hit 'em myself."

"O.K.," said Mac.

The farmer had walked around the house toward them. Jim asked, "You got a sledge-hammer?"

He pointed a thumb at a little shed that sloped off the barn.

"And a knife?"

"Yah. I got goot knife. You give him back." He walked away toward the house.

Jim turned toward the men. "Couple of you guys go into the barn and bring out the calf first. He's probably the liveliest."

The farmer hurried back carrying a short-handled, heavy-headed hammer in one hand and a knife in the other. Jim took the knife from him and looked at it. The blade was ground away until it was slender and bright, and the point was needle-like. He felt the edge with his thumb. "Sharp," the farmer said. "He's always sharp." He took the knife back, wiped it on his sleeves and reflected the light from it. "Cherman steel. Goot steel."

Four men came running out of the barn with a red yearling bull calf between them. They clung to a rope around its neck and steered it by butting it with their shoulders. They dug their heels into the ground to stop it, and held it, plunging, between them.

"Over here," the farmer said. "Here the blood could go into the ground."

Mac said, "We ought to save the blood. It's good strong food. If only we had something to carry it in."

"My old man used to drink it," said Jim. "I can't drink it: makes me sick. Here, Mac, you take the hammer. Now, you hit him right here on the head, good and hard." He handed the knife to Albert Johnson. "Look.

See where my hand is? Now that's the place to stick him, just as soon as Mac hits him. There's a big artery there. Get it open."

"How's a guy to know?"

"You'll know, all right. It'll shoot blood like a half-inch pipe. Stand back out of the way, you guys."

Two men on the sides held the plunging calf. Mac slugged it to its knees. Albert drove in the knife and cut the artery open and jumped back from the spurting blood. The calf leaped, and then settled slowly down. Its chin rested flat on the ground, and its legs folded up. The thick, carmine blood pool spread out on the wet ground.

"It's a damn shame we can't save it," Mac said. "If we only had a little keg we could."

Jim cried, "O.K. Bring out another. Bring her over here." The men had been curious at the first slaughter, but when the two old cows were killed, they did not press in so close to see. When all the animals were down and the blood oozed slowly from their throats, Albert wiped the sticky knife on a piece of sack and handed it back to the farmer. He backed his truck to the animals and the men lifted the limp, heavy creatures up on the bed, and let the heads hang loosely over so that they might bleed on the ground. Last, they piled the ten sacks of lima beans on the front of the truck bed and took their places on the sacks.

Mac turned to the farmer. "Thanks, mister."

"Not my place," he said. "Not my cow. I farm shares."

"Well, thanks for the loan of your knife." Mac helped Jim a little as he got into the truck and moved over against Albert Johnson. The shirt sleeve on Albert's right arm was red to the shoulder with blood. Albert started his slow, chugging motor and moved carefully over the rough road. At the gate the traffic cop waited for them, and when they got out on the country road he followed a little way behind.

The men on the sacks started to sing.

"Soup, soup, give us some soup—
We don't want nothing but just some soup."

The cop grinned at them. One of the men chanted at him,

"Whoops my dear, whoops my dear,
Even the chief of police is queer."

In the cab, Mac leaned forward and spoke across Jim. "Albert, we want to dodge the town. We got to get this stuff to the camp. See if you can sort of edge around it, will you, even if it's longer?"

Albert nodded morosely.

The sun shone now, but it was high, and there was no warmth in it. Jim said, "This ought to make the guys feel fine."

Albert nodded again. "Let 'em get their guts full of meat, and they'll go to sleep."

Mac laughed. "I'm surprised at you, Albert. Haven't you got no idears about the nobility of labor?"

"I got nothing," Albert said. "No idears, no money, no nothing."

"Nothing to lose but your chains," Jim put in softly.

"Bull," said Albert, "nothing to lose but my hair."

"You got this truck," Mac said. "How'd we get this stuff back without a truck?"

"This truck's got me," Albert complained. "The God-damned truck's just about two-bitted me to death." He looked sadly ahead. His lips scarcely moved when he talked. "When I'm workin' and I get three dollars to the good and I get set to look me up a floozy, somethin' on this buggy busts and costs three dollars. Never fails. God damn truck's worse'n a wife."

Jim said earnestly, "In any good system, you'd have a good truck."

"Yeah? In any good system I'd have a floozy. I ain't Dakin. If Dakin's truck could of cooked, he wouldn't of wanted nothing else."

Mac said to Jim, "You're talkin' to a man that knows what he wants, and it ain't an automobile."

"That's the idear," said Albert. "I guess it was stickin' them cows done it. I felt all right before."

They were back in the endless orchards now, and the leaves were dark and the earth was dark with the rain. In the ditches beside the road a little muddy storm water ran. The traffic cop rode behind them as Albert turned from road to road, making an angular circuit of the town. They could see among the trees the houses where the owners or the resident share-croppers lived.

Mac said, "If it didn't make our guys so miserable, I wish the rain'd go on. It isn't doin' those apples no good."

"It isn't doin' my blankets no good, neither," Albert said sullenly.

The men on the back were singing in chorus,

"Oh, we sing, we sing, we sing
    Of Lydia Pinkham
    And her gift to the human race——"

Albert turned a corner and came into the road to Anderson's place. "Nice work," said Mac. "You didn't go near the town. It would of been hell if we'd got held up and lost our load."

Jim said, "Look at the smoke, Mac. They've got a fire going, all right." The blue smoke rolled among the trees, hardly rising above their tops.

"Better drive along the camp, near the trees," Mac advised. "They're going to have to cut up these animals, and there's nothing to hang them on but the apple trees."

Men were standing in the road, watching for them. As the truck moved along the men on the bean sacks stood up and took off their hats and bowed. Albert dropped into low gear and crawled through the crowd of men to the end of the camp, near the apple trees.

London, with Sam behind him, came pushing through the shouting mill of hysterical men and women.

Mac cried, "String 'em up. And listen, London, tell the cooks to cut the meat thin, so it'll cook quick. These guys are hungry."

London's eyes were as bright as those of the men around him. "Jesus, could I eat," he said. "We'd about give you up."

The cooks came through the crowd. The animals were hung to the lower branches of the trees, entrails scooped out, skins ripped off. Mac cried, "London, don't let 'em waste anything. Save all the bones and heads and feet for soup." A pan of hacked pieces of meat went to the pit, and the crowd followed, leaving the butchers more room to work. Mac stood on the running-board, overlooking the scene, but Jim still sat in the cab, straddling the gear-shift lever. Mac turned anxiously to him. "What's the matter, Jim? You feel all right?"

"Sure, I'm O.K. My shoulder's awful stiff, though. I darn near can't move it."

"I guess you're cold. We'll see if Doc can't loosen you up a little." He helped Jim down from the truck and supported him by the elbow as they walked across toward the meat pit. A smell of cooking meat hung over the whole camp, and the meat dripped fat on the coals so that fierce little flames leaped up and devoured each drop. The men crowded so densely about the pit that the cooks, who went about turning the meat with long

pointed sticks, had to push their way through the throng.
Mac guided Jim toward London's tent. "I'm going to ask
Doc to come over. You sit down in there. I'll bring you
some meat when it's done."

It was dusky inside the tent. What little light got
through the grey canvas was grey. When Jim's eyes
grew accustomed to the light, he saw Lisa sitting on her
mattress holding the baby under her shoulder blanket.
She looked at him with dark, questionless eyes. Jim said,
"Hello. How you getting along?"

"All right."

"Well, can I sit down on your mattress? I feel a little
weak."

She gathered her legs under her and moved aside. Jim
sat down beside her. "What's that good smell?" she asked.

"Meat. We're going to have lots of meat."

"I like meat," she said. "I could just about live on
meat." London's dark, slender son came through the tent-
flaps. He stopped and stared at the two of them. "He's
hurt," Lisa said quickly. "He ain't doin' nothing. He's
hurt in the shoulder."

The boy said, "Oh," softly. "I wasn't thinkin' he was."
He said to Jim, "She always thinks I'm lookin' at her that
way, and I ain't." He said sententiously, "I always think,
if you can't trust a girl, it don't do no good to try to
watch her. A tramp is a tramp. Lisa ain't no tramp. I got
no call to treat her like a tramp." He stopped. "They got
meat out there, lots of meat. They got limey beans, too.
Not for now, though."

Lisa said, "I like them, too."

The boy went on, "The guys don't want to wait till
the meat's done. They want to eat it all pink inside. It'll
make 'em sick if they ain't careful."

The tent-flaps whipped open, admitting Dr. Burton.
In his hands he carried a pot of steaming water. "This

looks like the holy family," he said. "Mac told me you were stiffening up."

"I'm pretty sore," said Jim.

Doc looked down at the girl. "Do you think you could put that baby down long enough to hold some hot cloths on his shoulder?"

"Me?"

"Yes. I'm busy. Get his coat off and keep hot water on the stiff place. Don't get it in the wound if you can help."

"D'you think I could?"

"Well, why not? He did things for you. Come on, get his coat off and strip down his shirt. I'm busy. I'll put on a new bandage when you finish." He went out.

The girl said, "D'you want me to?"

"Sure. Why not? You can."

She handed the baby to Joey, helped Jim off with his blue denim jacket and slipped his shirt down. "Don't you wear no un'erclo's?"

"No."

She fell silent then, and put the hot cloths on the shoulder muscle until the sore stiffness relaxed. Her fingers pressed the cloth down and moved about, pressing and pressing, gently, while her young husband looked on. In a little while Dr. Burton returned, and Mac came with him, carrying a big piece of black meat on a stick.

"Feel better now?"

"Better. Much better. She did it fine."

The girl backed away, her eyes dropped with self-consciousness. Burton quickly put on a new bandage and Mac handed over the big piece of meat. "I salted it out there," he said. "Doc thinks you better not run around any more today."

Burton nodded. "You might catch cold and go into a fever," he said. "Then you couldn't do anything."

Jim filled his mouth with tough meat and chewed. "Guys like the meat?" he asked.

"Cocky'r'n hell. They think they run the world now. They're going out and clean up on somebody. I knew it would happen."

"Are they going out to picket today?"

Mac thought a moment. "You're not, anyhow. You're going to sit here and keep warm."

Joey handed the baby to his wife. "Is they plenty meat, mister?"

"Sure."

"Well, I'm goin' to get some for Lisa and I."

"Well, go ahead. Listen, Jim. Don't go moaning around. There's not going to be much going on. It's along in the afternoon now. London's going to send out some guys in cars to see how many scabs are working. They'll see how many and where, an' then, tomorrow morning, we'll start doing something about it. We can feed the guys for a coupla days now. Clouds are going. We'll have clear, cold weather for a change."

Jim asked, "Did you hear anything about scabs?"

"No, not much. Some of the guys say that scabs are coming in in trucks with guards on them, but you can't believe anything in a camp like this. Damnedest place in the world for rumors."

"The guys are awful quiet now."

"Sure. Why not? They've got their mouths full. Tomorrow we've got to start raising hell. I guess we can't strike long, so we've got to strike hard."

The sound of a motor came up the road and stopped. Outside the tent there was a sudden swell of voices, and then quiet again. Sam stuck his head into the tent. "London here?" he demanded.

"No. What's the matter?"

"There's a dressed-up son-of-a-bitch in a shiny car wants to see the boss."

"What about?"

"I don't know. Says he wants to see the chief of the strikers."

Mac said, "London's over by the pit. Tell him to come over. The guy probably wants to talk things over."

"O.K. I'll tell him."

In a moment London came into the tent, and the stranger followed him, a chunky, comfortable-looking man dressed in a grey business suit. His cheeks were pink and shaven, his hair nearly white. Wrinkles of good nature radiated from the corners of his eyes. On his mouth an open, friendly smile appeared every time he spoke. To London he said, "Are you the chairman of the camp?"

"Yeah," said London suspiciously. "I'm the elected boss."

Sam came in and took his place just behind London, his face dark and sullen. Mac squatted down on his haunches and balanced himself with his fingers. The newcomer smiled. His teeth were white and even. "My name's Bolter," he said simply. "I own a big orchard. I'm the new president of the Fruit Growers' Association of this valley."

"So what?" said London. "Got a good job for me if I'll sell out?"

The smile did not leave Bolter's face, but his clean, pink hands closed gently at his sides. "Let's try to get a better start than that," he begged. "I told you I was the *new* president. That means there's a change in policy. I don't believe in doing things the way they were being done." While he spoke Mac looked not at Bolter, but at London.

Some of the anger left London's face. "What you got to say?" he asked. "Spill it out."

Bolter looked around for something to sit on, and saw nothing. He said, "I never could see how two men could get anything done by growling at each other. I've always had an idea that no matter how mad men were, if they could only get together with a table between them, something good would come out of it."

London snickered. "We ain't got a table."

"You know what I mean," Bolter continued. "Everybody in the Association said you men wouldn't listen to reason, but I told them I know American working men. Give American working men something reasonable to listen to, and they'll listen."

Sam spat out, "Well, we're listenin', ain't we? Go on an' give us somethin' reasonable."

Bolter's white teeth flashed. He looked around appreciatively. "There, you see? That's what I told them. I said, 'Let me lay our cards down on the table, and then let them lay theirs down, and see if we can't make a hand.' American working men aren't animals."

Mac muttered, "You ought to run for Congress."

"I beg your pardon?"

"I was talkin' to this here guy," said Mac. London's face had grown hard again.

Bolter went on, "That's what I'm here for, to lay our cards on the table. I told you I own an orchard, but don't think because of that I haven't your interests at heart. All of us know we can't make money unless the working man is happy." He paused, waiting for some kind of answer. None came. "Well, here's the way I figure it; you're losing money and we're losing money because we're sitting growling at each other. We want you to come back to work. Then you'll get your wages, and we'll get our apples picked. That way we'll both be happy. Will you come back to work? No questions, no grudges, just two people who figured things out over the table?"

London said, "Sure we'll go back to work, mister. Ain't we American working men? Just give us the raise we want and kick out the scabs and we'll be up in those old trees tomorrow morning."

Bolter smiled around at them, one at a time, until his smile had rested on each face. "Well, I think you ought to have a raise," he said. "And I told everybody I thought so. Well, I'm not a very good business man. The rest of the Association explained it all to me. With the price of apples what it is, we're paying the top price we can. If we pay any more, we lose money."

Mac grinned. "I guess we ain't American workin' men after all," he said. "None of this sounds reasonable to me. So far it's sounded like a sock full of crap."

Jim said, "The reason they can't pay the raise is because that'd mean we win the strike; and if we did that, a lot of other poor devils'd go on strike. Isn't that it, mister?"

Bolter's smile remained. "I thought from the first you deserved a raise, but I didn't have any power. I still believe it, and I'm the president of the Association. Now I've told the Association what I'm going to do. Some of 'em don't like it, but I insisted you men have to have a raise. I'm going to offer you twenty cents, and no questions and no grudges. And we'll expect you back at work tomorrow morning."

London looked around at Sam. He laughed at Sam's scowling face, and slapped the lean man on the shoulder. "Mr. Bolter," he said, "like Mac says, I guess we ain't American workin' men. You wanted cards laid down, and then you laid yours down backs up. Here's ours, and by Christ, she's a full house. Your God-damn apples got to be picked and we ain't pickin' 'em without our raise. Nor neither is nobody else pickin' 'em. What do you think of that, Mister Bolter?"

At last the smile had faded from Bolter's face. He said gravely, "The American nation has become great because everybody pitched in and helped. American labor is the best labor in the world, and the highest paid."

London broke in angrily, "S'pose a Chink does get half a cent a day, if he can eat on it? What the hell do we care how much we get, if we got to go hungry?"

Bolter put on his smile again. "I have a home and children," he said. "I've worked hard. You think I'm different from you. I want you to look on me as a working man, too. I've worked for everything I've got. Now we've heard that radicals are working among you. I don't believe it. I don't believe American men, with American ideals, will listen to radicals. All of us are in the same boat. Times are hard. We're all trying to get along, and we've got to help each other."

Suddenly Sam yelled, "Oh, for Christ's sake, lay off. If you got somethin' to say, say it; only cut out this God-damn speech."

Bolter looked very sad. "Will you accept half?"

"No," said London. "You wouldn't offer no half unless you was pressed."

"How do you know the men wouldn't accept, if you put it to a vote?"

"Listen, mister," London said, "them guys is so full of piss and vinegar they'll skin you if you show that slick suit outside. We're strikin' for our raise. We're picketin' your God-damn orchards, and we're kickin' hell out of any scabs you run in. Now come on through with your 'or else.' Turn your damn cards over. What you think you're goin' to do if we don't go back?"

"Turn the vigilantes loose," said Mac.

Bolter said hurriedly, "We don't know anything about any vigilantes. But if the outraged citizens band together to keep the peace, that's their affair. The Association knows nothing about that." He smiled again. "Can't you men see that if you attack our homes and our children we have to protect them? Wouldn't you protect your own children?"

"What the hell do you think we're doin'?" London cried. "We're trying to protect 'em from starving. We're usin' the only way a workin' stiff's got. Don't you go talkin' about no children, or we'll show you something."

"We only want to settle this thing peacefully," said Bolter. "American citizens demand order, and I assure you men we're going to have order if we have to petition the governor for troops."

Sam's mouth was wet. He shouted, "And you get order by shootin' our men from windows, you yellow bastard. And in 'Frisco you got order by ridin' down women. An' the newspapers says, 'This mornin' a striker was killed when he threw himself on a bayonet.' *Threw himself!*"

London wrapped his arm about the furious man and forced him slowly away from Bolter. "Lay off, Sam. Stop it, now. Just quiet yourself."

"Th' hell with you," Sam cried. "Stand there and take the lousy crap that big baloney hands you!"

London stiffened suddenly. His big fist lashed out and cracked into Sam's face, and Sam went down. London stood looking at him. Mac laughed hysterically. "A striker just threw himself into a fist," he said.

Sam sat up on the ground. "O.K., London. You win. I won't make no more fuss, but you wasn't in 'Frisco on Bloody Thursday."

Bolter stood where he was. "I hoped you would listen to reason," he said. "We have information that you're being influenced by radicals, sent here by red organizations. They are misleading you, telling you lies. They only want to stir up trouble. They're professional trouble-makers, paid to cause strikes."

Mac stood up from his haunches. "Well, the dirty

rats," he said. "Misleadin' American workin' men, are they? Prob'ly gettin' paid by Russia, don't you think, Mr. Bolter?"

The man looked back at him for a long time, and the healthy red was gone from his cheeks. "You're going to make us fight, I guess," he said. "I'm sorry. I wanted peace. We know who the radicals are, and we'll have to take action against them." He turned imploringly to London. "Don't let them mislead you. Come back to work. We only want peace."

London was scowling. "I had enough o' this," he said. "You want peace. Well, what we done? Marched in two parades. An' what you done? Shot three of our men, burned a truck and a lunch wagon and shut off our food supply. I'm sick o' your God-damned lies, mister. I'll see you get out without Sam gets his hands on you, but don't send nobody else again till you're ready to talk straight."

Bolter shook his head sadly. "We don't want to fight you men," he said. "We want you to come back to work. But if we do have to fight, we have weapons. The health authorities are pretty upset about this camp. And the government doesn't like uninspected meat moving in this county. The citizens are pretty tired of all this riot. And of course we may have to call troops, if we need them."

Mac got up and went to the tent-flaps and looked out. Already the evening was coming. The camp was quiet, for the men stood watching London's tent. All the faces, white in the gathering evening, were turned in toward the tent. Mac yelled, "All right, boys. We ain't goin' to sell you out." He turned back into the tent. "Light the lamp, London. I want to tell this friend of man a few things."

London set a match to the tin lantern and hung it on the tent-pole, where it cast a pale, steady light. Mac took up a position in front of Bolter, and his muscled face broke into a derisive grin. "All right, Sonny Boy," he said. "You been talkin' big, but I know you been wettin' your pants the whole time. I admit you can do all the things you say you can, but look what happens after. Your health service burned the tents in Washington. And that was one of the reasons that Hoover lost the labor vote. You called out guardsmen in 'Frisco, and damn near the whole city went over to the strikers. Y' had to have the cops stop food from comin' in to turn public opinion against the strike. I'm not talkin' right an' wrong now, mister. I'm tellin' you what happens." Mac stepped back a pace. "Where do you think we're gettin' food and blankets an' medicine an' money? You know damn well where we're gettin' 'em. Your valley's lousy with sympathizers. Your 'outraged citizens' are a little bit outraged at you babies, and you know it. And you know, if you get too tough, the unions'll go out. Truck drivers and restaurant men and field hands, everybody. And just because you do know it, you try to throw a bluff. Well, it don't work. This camp's cleaner'n the lousy bunk houses you keep for us on your ranches. You come here to try to scare us, an' it don't work."

Bolter was very pale. He turned away from Mac and faced London. "I've tried to make peace," he said. "Do you know that this man was sent out by red headquarters to start this strike? Watch out that when he goes to jail you don't go too. We have a right to protect our property, and we'll do it. I've tried to deal man to man with you, and you won't deal. From now on the roads are closed. An ordinance will go through tonight forbidding any parading on the county roads, or any gathering. The sheriff will deputize a thousand men, if he needs them."

London glanced quickly at Mac, and Mac winked at him. London said, "Jesus, mister, I hope we can get you out of here safe. When the guys out there hear what you just said, why they'll want to take you to pieces."

Bolter's jaw tightened and his eyelids drooped. He straightened his shoulders. "Don't get the idea you can scare me," he said. "I'll protect my home and my children with my life if I have to. And if you lay a hand on me we'll wipe out your strike before morning."

London's arms doubled, and he stepped forward, but Mac jumped in his way. "The guy's right, London. He don't scare. Plenty do, but he don't." He turned around. "Mister Bolter, we'll see you get out of the camp. We understand each other now. We know what to expect from you. And we know how careful you have to be when you use force. Don't forget the thousands of people that are sending us food and money. They'll do other things, if they have to. We been good, Mr. Bolter, but if you start any funny business, we'll show you a riot you'll remember."

Bolter said coldly, "That seems to be all. I'm sorry, but I'll have to report that you won't meet us halfway."

"Halfway?" Mac cried. "There ain't any halfway to nowhere." His voice dropped to softness. "London, you get on one side of him, and Sam on the other, and see that he gets away all right. Then I guess you'd better tell the guys what he said. But don't let 'em get out of hand. Tell 'em to tighten up the squads for trouble."

They surrounded Bolter and took him through the press of silent men, saw him into his coupe and watched him drive away down the road. When he was gone London raised his voice. "If you guys want to come over to the stand, I'll get up on it and tell you what the son-of-a-bitch said, and what we answered him back." He flailed his way through, and the men followed, excitedly. The cooks left the stoves where they were boiling beans and chunks of beef. The women crawled like rodents from the tents and followed. When London climbed up on the stand it was ringed closely with men, standing in the dusk looking up at him.

During the talk with Bolter Doc Burton had effaced himself, had been so quiet that he seemed to have disappeared, but when the group went out, leaving only Jim and Lisa sitting on the mattress, he came out of his corner and sat down on the edge of the mattress beside them. His face was worried. "It's going to be a mean one," he said.

"That's what we want, Doc," Jim told him. "The worse it is, the more effect it'll have."

Burton looked at him with sad eyes. "You see a way through," he said. "I wish I did. It all seems meaningless to me, brutal and meaningless."

"It has to go on," Jim insisted. "It can only stop when the men rule themselves and get the profits of their labor."

"Seems simple enough," Burton sighed. "I wish I thought it was so simple." He turned smiling to the girl. "What's your solution, Lisa?"

She started. "Huh?"

"I mean, what would you like to have to make you happy."

She looked self-consciously down at the baby. "I like to have a cow," she said. "I like to have butter an' cheese like you can make."

"Want to exploit a cow?"

"Huh?"

"I'm being silly. Did you ever have a cow, Lisa?"

"When I was a little kid we had one," she said. "Went out an' drunk it warm. Old man used to milk it into a cup-like, to drink. Tasted warm. That's what I like. Bet it would be good for the baby." Burton turned slowly away from her. She insisted, "Cow used to eat grass, an' sometimes hay. Not ever'body can milk 'em, neither. They kick."

Burton asked, "Did you ever have a cow, Jim?"

"No."

Burton said, "I never thought of cows as counter-revolutionary animals."

Jim asked, "What are you talking about, Doc, anyway?"

"Nothing. I'm kind of unhappy, I guess. I was in the army in the war. Just out of school. They'd bring in one of our men with his chest shot away, and they'd bring in a big-eyed German with his legs splintered off. I worked on 'em just as though they were wood. But sometimes, after it was all over, when I wasn't working, it made me unhappy, like this. It made me lonely."

Jim said, "Y'ought to think only of the end, Doc. Out of all this struggle a good thing is going to grow. That makes it worthwhile."

"Jim, I wish I knew it. But in my little experience the end is never very different in its nature from the means. Damn it, Jim, you can only build a violent thing with violence."

"I don't believe that," Jim said. "All great things have violent beginnings."

"There aren't any beginnings," Burton said. "Nor any ends. It seems to me that man has engaged in a blind and fearful struggle out of a past he can't remember, into a future he can't foresee nor understand. And man has met and defeated every obstacle, every enemy except one. He cannot win over himself. How mankind hates itself."

Jim said, "We don't hate ourselves, we hate the invested capital that keeps us down."

"The other side is made of men, Jim, men like you. Man hates himself. Psychologists say a man's self-love is balanced neatly with self-hate. Mankind must be the same. We fight ourselves and we can only win by killing every man. I'm lonely, Jim. I have nothing to hate. What are you going to get out of it, Jim?"

Jim looked startled. "You mean me?" He pointed a finger at his breast.

"Yes, you. What will you get out of all the mess?"

"I don't know; I don't care."

"Well, suppose blood-poisoning sets in in that shoulder, or you die of lockjaw and the strike gets broken? What then?"

"It doesn't matter," Jim insisted. "I used to think like you, Doc, but it doesn't matter at all."

"How do you get that way?" Burton asked. "What's the process?"

"I don't know. I used to be lonely, and I'm not any more. If I go out now it won't matter. The thing won't stop. I'm just a little part of it. It will grow and grow. This pain in the shoulder is kind of pleasant to me; and I bet before he died Joy was glad for a moment. Just in that moment I bet he was glad."

They heard a rough, monotonous voice outside, and then a few shouts, and then the angry crowd-roar, a bellow like an animal in fury. "London's telling them," said Jim. "They're mad. Jesus, how a mad crowd can fill the air with madness. You don't understand it, Doc. My old man used to fight alone. When he got licked, he was licked. I remember how lonely it was. But I'm not lonely any more, and I can't be licked, because I'm more than myself."

"Pure religious ecstasy. I can understand that. Partakers of the blood of the Lamb."

"Religion, hell!" Jim cried. "This is men, not God. This is something you know."

"Well, can't a group of men be God, Jim?"

Jim wrenched himself around. "You make too damn many words, Doc. You build a trap of words and then you fall into it. You can't catch me. Your words don't mean anything to me. I know what I'm doing. Argument doesn't have any effect on me."

"Steady down," Burton said soothingly. "Don't get so excited. I wasn't arguing, I was asking for information. All of you people get angry when you're asked a question."

As the dusk turned into night the lantern seemed to grow brighter, to find deeper corners of the tent with its yellow light. Mac came in quietly, as though he crept away from the noise and shouting outside. "They're wild," he said. "They're hungry again. Boiled meat and beans tonight. I knew they'd get cocky on that meat. They'd like to go out and burn houses right now."

"How does the sky look?" Burton asked. "Any more rain in it?"

"Clear and stars. It'll be good weather."

"Well, I want to talk to you, Mac. I'm low in supplies. I need disinfectant. Yes, and I could use some salvarsan. If any kind of epidemic should break out, we'd be out of luck."

"I know," Mac said. "I sent word to town how it was. Some of the boys are out trying to get money. They're trying to get money to bail Dakin out now. I'd just as soon he stayed in jail."

Burton stood up from his seat on the mattress. "You can tell London what to do, can't you. Dakin wouldn't take everything."

Mac studied him. "What's the matter, Doc? Don't you feel well?"

"What do you mean?"

"I mean your temper's going. You're tired. What is it, Doc?"

Burton put his hands in his pockets. "I don't know; I'm lonely, I guess. I'm awfully lonely. I'm working all alone, towards nothing. There's some compensation for you people. I only hear heartbeats through a stethoscope. You hear them in the air." Suddenly he leaned over and put his hand under Lisa's chin and raised her head up and looked into her shrinking eyes. Her hand came slowly up and pulled gently at his wrist. He let go and put his hand back in his pocket.

Mac said, "I wish I knew some woman you could go to, Doc, but I don't. I'm new around here. Dick could steer you, in town. He prob'ly has twenty lined up by now. But you might get caught and jailed, Doc; and if you weren't taking care of us, they'd bounce us off this land in a minute."

Burton said, "Sometimes you understand too much, Mac. Sometimes—nothing. I guess I'll go along and see Al Anderson. I haven't been there all day."

"O.K., Doc, if it'll make you feel any better. I'll keep Jim under cover tonight."

Doc looked down at Lisa once more, and then he went out.

The shouting had settled to talk by now, low talk. It made the night alive outside the tent.

"Doc doesn't eat," Mac complained. "Nobody's seen him sleep. I suppose he'll break, sooner or later, but he never has before. He needs a woman bad; someone that would like him for a night; you know, really like him. He needs to feel someone—with his skin. So do I. Lisa, you're a lucky little twirp, you just had a kid. You'd have me in your hair."

"Huh?"

"I say: How's the baby?"

"All right."

Mac nodded gravely at Jim. "I like a girl who doesn't talk too much."

Jim asked, "What went on out there? I'm sick of staying in already."

"Why, London told what Sonny Boy said, and asked for a vote of confidence. He sure as hell got it, too. He's out there now, talking to the squad leaders about tomorrow."

"What about tomorrow?"

"Well, Sonny Boy was telling the truth about that ordinance. By tomorrow it'll be against the law for the boys to march along the county road. I don't think they'll remember about trucks. So, instead of standing around orchards, we're going to send out flying squads in the cars. We can raid one bunch of scabs and get out, and raid another. It ought to work."

"Where we going to get gasoline?"

"Well, we'll take it out of all the cars and put it in the ones we use. That should last tomorrow. The next day we may have to try something else. Maybe we can hit hard enough tomorrow so we can rest up the next day, until they get in a new load of scabs."

Jim asked, "I can go tomorrow, can't I?"

Mac cried, "What good would you be? The guys that go have to be fighters. You just take up room with that bum arm. Use your head."

London pushed open the flaps and came in. His face was flushed with pleasure. "Them guys is sure steamed up," he said. "Jesus, they're belly-for-back to kick Torgas for a growler."

"Don't give 'em no headway," Mac advised. "They got their guts full of chow. If they go loose, we ain't never goin' to catch up with them."

London pulled up a box and sat down on it. "The chow's about ready, the guy says. I want to ast you, Mac, ever'body says you're a red. Them two guys that come to talk both said it. Seemed to know all about you."

"Yeah?"

"Tell me straight, Mac. Is you an' Jim reds?"

"What do you think?"

London's eyes flashed angrily, but he controlled himself. "Don't get mean, Mac. I don't take it nice if the guys on the other side know more about you'n I do. What the hell do I know? You come into my camp and done us a good turn. I never ast you no questions—never did. I wouldn't ast you any now, on'y I got to know what to expect."

Mac looked puzzled. He glanced at Jim. "O.K.?"

"O.K. by me."

"Listen, London," Mac began. "A guy can get to like you awful well. Sam'll kick the ass off any guy that looks crooked at you."

"I got good friends," said London.

"Well, that's why. I feel the same way. S'pose I was a red, what then?"

London said, "You're a friend of mine."

"O.K., then, I'm a red. There ain't a hell of a secret about it. They say I started this strike. Now get me straight. I would of started it if I could, but I didn't have to. It started itself."

London eyed him cautiously, as though his mind slowly circled Mac's mind. "What do you get out of it?" he asked.

"Money, you mean? Not a damn thing."

"Then what do you do it for?"

"Well, it's hard to say—you know how you feel about Sam an' all the guys that travel with you? Well, I feel that way about all the workin' stiffs in the country."

"Guys you don't even know?"

"Yes, guys I don't even know. Jim here's just the same, just the same."

"Sounds crazy as hell," said London. "Sounds like a gag. An' you don't get no money?"

"You don't see no Rolls-Royces around, do you?"

"But how about after?"

"After what?"

"Maybe after this is over you'll collect."

"There ain't no after," Mac said. "When this one's done, we'll be in another one."

London squinted at him, as though he tried to read his

thoughts. "I believe it," he said slowly. "You ain't give me no bum steers yet."

Mac reached over and struck him sharply on the shoulders. "I'd of told you before, if you asked me."

London said, "I got nothing against reds. Y'always hear how they're sons-of-bitches. Sam's kind of rattle-snake and whip-tempered, but he ain't no son-of-a-bitch. Let's go over an' get some food."

Mac stood up. "I'll bring you and Lisa some, Jim."

London said, from the doorway, "Moon's comin' up nice. I didn't know it was full moon."

"It isn't. Where do you see it?"

"Look, see over there? Looks like moonrise."

Mac said, "That ain't east—Oh, Jesus! It's Anderson's. *London,*" he shouted. "They've set fire to Anderson's! Get the guys. Come on, God damn it! Where are those guards? Get the guys quick!" He ran away toward the red, gathering light behind the trees.

Jim jumped up from the mattress. He didn't feel his wounded arm as he ran along, fifty yards behind Mac. He heard London's voice roaring, and then the drumming of many feet on the wet ground. He reached the trees and speeded up. The red light mushroomed out behind the trees. It was more than a glow now. A lance of flame cleared the tree-tops. Above the sound of steps there was a vicious crackling. From ahead came shrill cries and a muffled howling. The trees threw shadows away from the light. The end of the orchard row was blocked with fire, and in front of it black figures moved about. Jim could see Mac pounding ahead of him, and he could hear the increasing, breathy roar of the flames. He sprinted, caught up with Mac, and ran beside him. "It's the barn," he gasped. "Were the apples out yet?"

"Jim! Damn it, you shouldn't come. No, the apples are in the barn. Where the hell were the guards? Can't trust anybody." They neared the end of the row, and the hot air struck their faces. All the barn walls were sheathed in fire, and the strong flames leaped from the roof. The guards stood by Anderson's little house, quiet, watching the light, while Anderson danced jerkily in front of them.

Mac stopped running. "No go. We can't do a thing. They must of used gasoline."

London plunged past them, and his face was murderous. He drew up in front of the guards and shouted, "You God-damn rats! Where in hell were you?"

One of the men raised his voice above the fire. "You sent a guy to tell us you wanted us. We was halfway to the camp when we seen it start."

London's fury drained out of him. His big fists undoubled. He turned helplessly to where Mac and Jim stood, their eyes glaring in the light. Anderson capered close to them in his jerky, wild dance. He came close to Mac and stood in front of him and pushed his chin up into Mac's face. "You dirty son-of-a-bitch!" His voice broke, and he turned, crying, back toward the tower of flame. Mac put his arm around Anderson's waist, but the old man flung it off. Out of the fire came the sharp, sweet odor of burning apples.

Mac looked weak and sad. To London he said, "God, I wish it hadn't happened. Poor old man, it's all his crop." A thought stopped him. "Christ Almighty! Did you leave anybody to look after the camp?"

"No. I never thought."

Mac whirled. "Come on, a flock of you. Maybe they're drawin' us. Some of you stay here so the house won't get burnt too." He sprinted back, the way he had come. His long black shadow leaped ahead of him. Jim tried to keep up with him, but a sick weakness set in. Mac drew away from him, and the men passed him, until he was alone, behind them, stumbling along giddily over the uneven earth. No flames broke from the camp ahead. Jim settled down to walk along the vague aisle between the rows. He heard the crash of the falling barn, and did not even turn to look. When he was halfway back, his legs buckled with weakness, and he sat down heavily on the ground. The sky was bright with fire over his head, and behind the low, rosy light the icy stars hung.

Mac, retracing his steps, found him there. "What's the matter, Jim?"

"Nothing. My legs got weak. I'm just resting. Is the camp all right?"

"Sure. They didn't get to it. There's a man hurt. Fell down, I think he busted his ankle. We've got to find Doc. What a damn fool easy trick that was! One of their guys tells the guards to get out while the rest splash gasoline around and throw in a match. Jesus, it was quick! Now we'll get *hell* from Anderson. Get kicked off the place tomorrow, I guess."

"Where'll we go then, Mac?"

"Say! You're all in. Here, give me your arm. I'll help you back. Did you see Doc at the fire?"

"No."

"Well, he said he was going over to see Al. I didn't see him come back. Come on, climb to your feet. I've got to get you bedded down."

Already the light was dying. At the end of the row lay a pile of fire, but the flames no longer leaped up in long streamers. "Hold on to me, now. Anderson was nearly crazy, wasn't he? Thank God they didn't get his house."

London, with Sam behind him, caught up. "How's the camp?"

"O.K. They didn't get it."

"Well, what's the matter with the kid?"

"Just weak from his wound. Give 'im a lift on that side." Together they half-carried Jim down the row and across the open space to London's tent. They set him down on the mattress. Mac asked, "Did you see the Doc over there? A guy's bust his ankle."

"No. I never seen him."

"Well, I wonder where he is?"

Sam entered the tent silently. His lean face was ridged with tight muscles. He walked stiffly over and stood in front of Mac, "That afternoon, when that guy says what he'd do——"

"What guy?"

"That first guy that come, an' you told him."

"I told him what?"

"Told 'im what we'd do."

Mac started and looked at London. "I don't know, Sam. It might switch public sympathy. We should be getting it now. We don't want to lose it."

Sam's voice was thick with hatred. "You can't let 'em get away with it. You can't let the yellow bastards burn us out."

London said, "Come out of it, Sam. What do you want?"

"I want to take a couple guys—an' play with matches." Mac and London watched him carefully. "I'm goin'," Sam said. "I don' give a damn. I'm goin'. There's a guy name Hunter. He's got a big white house. I'm takin' a can of gasoline."

Mac grinned. "Take a look at this guy, London. Ever see him before? Know who he is?"

London caught it. "No, can't say I do. Who is he?"

"Search me. Was he ever in camp?"

"No, by God! Maybe he's just a guy with a grudge. We get all kind of things pinned on us."

Mac swung back on Sam. "If you get caught, you got to take it."

"I'll take it," Sam said sullenly. "I ain't sharin' no

time. I ain't takin' nobody with me, neither. I changed my mind."

"We don't know you. You just got a grudge."

"I hate the guy 'cause he robbed me," said Sam.

Mac stepped close to him and gripped his arm. "Burn the bastard into the ground," he said viciously. "Burn every stick in the house. I'd like to go with you. Jesus, I would!"

"Stick here," said Sam. "This ain't your fight. This guy robbed me—an' I'm a firebug. I always like to play with matches."

London said, "So long, Sam. Drop in some time."

Sam slipped quietly out of the tent and disappeared. London and Mac looked for a moment at the gently swaying tent-flap. London said, "I got a feelin' he ain't comin' back. Funny how you can get to like a mean man like that. Always got his chin stuck out, lookin' for trouble."

Jim had sat quietly on the mattress. His face was troubled. Through the tent walls the glow of the fire was still faintly visible, and now the shriek of sirens sounded, coming nearer and nearer, lonely and fierce in the night.

Mac said bitterly, "They gave it a good long time to get started before the trucks came out. Hell, we never did get anything to eat. Come on, London. I'll get some for you, Jim."

Jim sat waiting for them to come back. Lisa, beside him, was secretly nursing the baby under the blanket again. "Don't you ever move around?" Jim asked.

"Huh?"

"You just sit still. All these things go on around you, and you pay no attention. You don't even hear."

"I wisht it was over," she replied. "I wisht we lived in a house with a floor, an' a toilet close by. I don't like this fightin'."

"It's got to be done," Jim said. "It will be over some-time, but maybe not in our lives."

Mac came in carrying two steaming food cans. "Well, the fire trucks got there before it was all out, anyway. Here, Jim, I put the beef in with the beans. You take this one, Lisa."

Jim said, "Mac, you shouldn't've let Sam go."

"Why the hell shouldn't I?"

"Because you didn't feel right about it, Mac. You let your own personal hatred get in."

"Well, Jesus! Think of poor old Anderson, losing his barn and all his crop."

"Sure, I know. Maybe it's a good idea to burn Hunter's house. You got hot about it, though."

"Yeah? An' I guess you're goin' to be reportin' me, maybe. I bring you out to let you get some experience, an' you turn into a God-damn school teacher. Who th' hell do you think you are, anyway? I was doin' this job when you were slobberin' your bib."

"Now wait a minute, Mac. I can't do anything to help but use my head. Everything's going on, and I sit here with a sore shoulder. I just don't want you to get mad, Mac. You can't think if you get mad."

Mac glared sullenly at him. "You're lucky I don't knock your can off, not because you're wrong, but be-cause you're right. You get sick of a guy that's always right." Suddenly he grinned. "It's done, Jim. Let's forget it. You're turning into a proper son-of-a-bitch. Every-body's going to hate you, but you'll be a good Party man. I know I get mad; I can't help it. I'm worried as hell, Jim. Everything's going wrong. Where you s'pose Doc is?"

"No sign of him yet? Remember what he said when he went out?"

"Said he was going to see Al."

"Yes, but before that, how lonely he was. He sounded

screwy, like a guy that's worked too hard. Maybe he went off his nut. He never did believe in the cause, maybe he's scrammed."

Mac shook his head. "I've been around with Doc plenty. That's one thing he didn't do. Doc never ran out on anybody. I'm worried, Jim. Doc was headed for Anderson's. S'pose he took those raiders for our guards, an' they caught him? They'd sure as hell catch him if they could."

"Maybe he'll be back later."

"Well, I'll tell you. If the health office gets out an order against us tomorrow, we can be damn sure that Doc was snatched. Poor devil! I don't know what to do about the man with the busted ankle. One of the guys set it, but he probably set it wrong. Oh, well, maybe Doc's just wanderin' around in the orchard. It's my fault for letting him start over there alone, all my fault. London's doing everything he can. I forget things. I'm getting a weight on me, Jim. Anderson's barn's right on top of me."

"You're forgetting the whole picture," Jim said.

Mac sighed. "I thought I was a tough baby, but you're a hell of a lot tougher. I hope I don't get to hate you. You better sleep in the hospital tent, Jim. There's an extra cot, and I don't want you sleeping on the ground until you feel better. Why don't you eat?"

Jim looked down at the can. "Forgot it, and I'm hungry, too." He picked up a piece of boiled beef out of the beans and gnawed it. "You better get some yourself," he said.

"Yeah, I'm going now."

After he had gone, Jim quickly ate the beans, the big oval, golden beans. He speared three of them at a time on a sharpened stick, and when they were gone tilted the can and drank the juice. "Tastes good, doesn't it," he said to Lisa.

"Yeah. I always like limey beans. Don't need nothing but salt. Salt pork's better."

"The men are quiet, awfully quiet."

"They got their mouths full," said the girl. "Always talkin', except their mouths' full. Always talkin'. If they got to fight, why don' they fight an' get it over, 'stead o' talkin'?"

"This is a strike," Jim said defensively.

"Even you talk all the time," she said. "Talk don't turn no wheel."

"Sometimes it gets steam up to turn 'em, Lisa."

London came in, and stood picking his teeth with a sharpened match. The bald spot in his tonsure shone dully in the lamplight. "I been watchin' all over the country," he said. "Ain't seen no fire yet. Mebbe they caught Sam."

"He was a clever guy," said Jim. "The other day he knocked over a checker, and the checker had a gun, too."

"Oh, he's smart all right. Smart like a snake. Sam's a rattlesnake, only he don't never rattle. He went out alone, didn't take nobody with him."

"All the better. If he gets caught, he's just a nut. If three guys got caught, it'd be a plot, see?"

"I hope he don't get caught, Jim. He's a nice guy, I like him."

"Yeah, I know."

Mac came back in with his can of food. "Jesus, I'm hungry. I didn't know it till I got the first bite. Have enough to eat, Jim?"

"Sure. Why don't the men build fires to sit by? They did last night."

"They got no wood," said London. "I made 'em put all the wood over by the stoves."

"Well, what makes 'em so quiet? You can hardly hear a thing," Jim said. "It's all quiet."

Mac mused, "It's damn funny about a bunch of men,

how they act. You can't tell. I always thought if a guy watched close enough he might get to know what they're goin' to do. They get steamed up, an' then, all of a sudden, they're scared as hell. I think this whole damn camp is scared. Word's got out that Doc's been snatched. An' they're scared to be without 'im. They go an' take a look at the guy with the busted ankle, an' then they walk away. An' then, pretty soon, they go an' take a look at 'im again. He's all covered with sweat, he hurts so bad." Mac gnawed at a beef bone, tearing the white gristle with his teeth.

Jim asked, "D'you suppose anybody knows?"

"Knows what?"

"How a bunch o' guys'll act."

"Maybe London knows. He's been bossin' men all his life. How about it, London?"

London shook his head. "No," he said. "I've saw a bunch of guys run like rabbits when a truck backfired. Other times, seems like nothin' can scare 'em. Y'can kind of feel what's goin' to happen before it starts, though."

"I know," said Mac. "The air gets full of it. I saw a nigger lynched one time. They took him about a quarter of a mile to a railroad overpass. On th' way out that crowd killed a little dog, stoned it to death. Ever'body just picked up rocks. The air was just full of killin'. Then they wasn't satisfied to hang the nigger. They had to burn 'im an' shoot 'im, too."

"Well, I ain't lettin' nothin' like that get started in this camp," London said.

Mac advised, "Well, if it does start, you better stand out of the way. Listen, there's a sound."

There was a tramp of feet outside the tent, almost a military rhythm. "London in there?"

"Yeah. What do you want?"

"We got a guy out here."

"What kind of a guy?" A man came in, carrying a

Winchester carbine. London said, "Ain't you one of the guys I left to guard that house?"

"Yes. Only three of us came over. We saw this fellow moving around, and we kind of got around him and caught him."

"Well, who is it?"

"I don't know. He had this gun. The guys wanted to beat hell out of him, but I says we better bring him here, so we done it. We got him outside, tied up."

London looked at Mac, and Mac nodded toward Lisa. London said, "You better get out, Lisa."

She got slowly to her feet. "Where I'm goin' to go?"

"I don't know. Where's Joey?"

"Talkin' to a guy," said Lisa. "This guy wrote to a school that's goin' to get him to be a postman. Joey, he wants to be a postman too, so he's talkin' to this guy about it."

"Well, you go an' find some woman an' set with her."

Lisa shrugged up the baby on her hip and went out of the tent. London took the rifle from the man and threw down the lever. A loaded shell flipped out. "Thirty-thirty," said London. "Bring the guy in."

"O.K. Bring him in." Two guards pushed the prisoner through the flaps. He stumbled and recovered his balance. His elbows were bound together behind him with a belt, and his wrists were wrapped together with baling wire. He was very young. His body was thin and his shoulders narrow. He was dressed in corduroy trousers, a blue shirt and a short leather jacket. His light blue eyes were fixed with terror.

"Hell," said London. "It's a kid."

"Kid with a thirty-thirty," Mac added. "Can I talk to him, London?"

"Sure. Go ahead."

Mac stepped in front of the captive. "What are you doin' out there?"

The boy swallowed painfully. "I wasn't doing a thing." His voice was a whisper.

"Who sent you?"

"Nobody."

Mac struck him in the face with his open hand. The head jerked sideways, and an angry red spot formed on the white, beardless cheek. "Who sent you?"

"Nobody." The open hand struck again, harder. The boy lurched, tried to recover and fell on his shoulder.

Mac reached down and pulled him to his feet again. "Who sent you?"

The boy was crying. Tears rolled down his nose, into his bleeding mouth. "The fellows at school said we ought to."

"High school?"

"Yes. An' the men in the street said somebody ought to."

"How many of you came out?"

"Six of us."

"Where did the rest go?"

"I don't know, mister. Honest, I lost 'em."

Mac's voice was monotonous. "Who burned the barn?"

"I don't know." This time Mac struck with a closed fist. The blow flung the slight body against the tent-pole. Mac jerked him up again. The boy's eye was closed and cut.

"Be careful about that 'don't know' business. Who burned the barn?"

The boy could not speak; his sobs choked him. "Don't hit me, mister. Some fellows at the pool room said it would be a good thing. They said Anderson was a radical."

"All right, now. Did you kids see anything of our doctor?"

The boy looked at him helplessly. "Don't hit me, mister. I don't know. We didn't see anybody."

"What were you going to do with the gun?"

"Sh—sh-shoot through the tents an' try to scare you."

Mac smiled coldly. He turned to London. "Got any ideas what to do with him?"

"Oh, hell," said London. "He's just a kid."

"Yes, a kid with a thirty-thirty. Can I still have him, London?"

"What you want to do with him?"

"I want to send him back to high school so no more kids with rifles will come out."

Jim sat on the mattress and watched. Mac said, "Jim, you gave me hell about losing my head a little while ago. I'm not losing it now."

"It's O.K. if you're cold," said Jim.

"I'm a sharpshooter," Mac said. "You feeling sorry for the kid, Jim?"

"No, he's not a kid, he's an example."

"That's what I thought. Now listen, kid. We can throw you out to the guys there, but they'll probably kill you. Or we can work you over in here."

The one open eye glared with fear.

"O.K. with you, London?"

"Don't hurt him too much."

"I want a billboard," said Mac, "not a corpse. All right, kid. I guess you're for it." The boy tried to retreat. He bent down, trying to cower. Mac took him firmly by the shoulder. His right fist worked in quick, short hammer-blows, one after another. The nose cracked flat, the other eye closed, and the dark bruises formed on the cheeks. The boy jerked about wildly to escape the short, precise strokes. Suddenly the torture stopped. "Untie him," Mac said. He wiped his bloody fist on the boy's leather jacket. "It didn't hurt much," he said. "You'll show up pretty in high school. Now shut up your bawling. Tell the kids in town what's waitin' for 'em."

"Shall I wash his face?" London asked.

"Hell, no! I do a surgeon's job, and you want to spoil it. You think I liked it?"

"I don't know," said London.

The prisoner's hands were free now. He sobbed softly. Mac said, "Listen to me, kid. You aren't hurt bad. Your nose is busted, but that's all. If anybody here but me did it, you'd of been hurt bad. Now you tell your little play-mates that the next one gets his leg broke, and the next one after that gets both his legs broke. Get me——? I said, did you get me?"

"Yes."

"O.K. Take him down the road and turn him loose." The guards took the boy under the arms and helped him out of the tent. Mac said, "London, maybe you better put out patrols to see if there's any more kiddies with cannons."

"I'll do it," said London. He had kept his eyes on Mac the whole time, watching him with horror. "Jesus, you're a cruel bastard, Mac. I can unda'stand a guy gettin' mad an' doin' it, but you wasn't mad."

"I know," Mac said wearily. "That's the hardest part." He stood still, smiling his cold smile, until London went out of the tent; and then he walked to the mattress and sat down and clutched his knees. All over his body the muscles shuddered. His face was pale and grey. Jim put his good hand over and took him by the wrist. Mac said wearily, "I couldn't of done it if you weren't here, Jim. Oh, Jesus, you're hard-boiled. You just looked. You didn't give a damn."

Jim tightened his grip on Mac's wrist. "Don't worry about it," he said quietly. "It wasn't a scared kid, it was a danger to the cause. It had to be done, and you did it right. No hate, no feeling, just a job. Don't worry."

"If I could only of let his hands go, so he could take a pop at me once in a while, or cover up a little."

"Don't think of it," Jim said. "It's just a little part of the whole thing. Sympathy is as bad as fear. That was like a doctor's work. It was an operation, that's all. I'd done it for you if I wasn't bunged up. S'pose the guys outside had him?"

"I know," Mac agreed. "They'd butchered him. I hope they don't catch anybody else; I couldn't do it again."

"You'd have to do it again," said Jim.

Mac looked at him with something of fear in his eyes. "You're getting beyond me, Jim. I'm getting scared of you. I've seen men like you before. I'm scared of 'em. Jesus, Jim, I can see you changing every day. I know you're right. Cold thought to fight madness, I know all that. God Almighty, Jim, it's not human. I'm scared of you."

Jim said softly, "I wanted you to use me. You wouldn't because you got to like me too well." He stood up and walked to a box and sat down on it. "That was wrong. Then I got hurt. And sitting here waiting, I got to know my power. I'm stronger than you, Mac. I'm stronger than anything in the world, because I'm going in a straight line. You and all the rest have to think of women and tobacco and liquor and keeping warm and fed." His eyes were as cold as wet river stones. "I wanted to be used. Now I'll use you, Mac. I'll use myself and you. I tell you, I feel there's strength in me."

"You're nuts," said Mac. "How's your arm feel? Any swelling? Maybe the poison got into your system."

"Don't think it, Mac," Jim said quietly. "I'm not crazy. This is real. It has been growing and growing. Now it's all here. Go out and tell London I want to see him. Tell him to come in here. I'll try not to make him mad, but he's got to take orders."

Mac said, "Jim, maybe you're not crazy. I don't know. But you've got to remember London is the chairman of this strike, elected. He's bossed men all his life. You start telling him what to do, and he'll throw you to the lions." He looked uneasily at Jim.

"Better go and tell him," said Jim.

"Now listen——"

"Mac, you want to obey. You better do it."

They heard a low wail, and then the rising scream of a siren, and then another and another, rising and falling, far away. "It's Sam," Mac cried. "He's set his fire."

Jim scrambled up. Mac said, "You better stay there. You're too weak, Jim."

Jim laughed mirthlessly. "You're going to find out how weak I am." He walked to the entrance and went out, and Mac followed him.

To the north the starred sky was black over the trees. In the direction of Torgas the city lights threw a pale glow into the sky. To the left of the town, over the high rampart of trees, the new fire put a dome of red light over itself. Now the sirens screamed together, and now one was up while another sunk its voice to a growl. "They don't waste any time now," Mac said.

The men came tumbling out of the tents and stood looking at the rising fire. The flames broke over the trees, and the dome of light spread and climbed. "A good start," Mac said. "If they put it out now, the house'll be ruined anyway. They can't use anything but chemicals out that far."

London hurried over to them. "He done it!" London cried. "Christ, he's a mean guy. I knew he'd do it. He wasn't scared of nothing."

Jim said calmly, "We can use him, if he comes back."

"Use him?" London asked.

"Yes, a man who could give a fire that good a start could do other things. It's burning fine. London, come into the tent. We've got to figure some things out."

Mac broke in, "What he means, London——"

"I'll tell him what I mean. Come into the tent, London." Jim led the way inside and seated himself on a box.

"What's the idear?" London demanded. "What's this you're talkin' about?"

Jim said, "This thing is being lost because there's no authority. Anderson's barn was burned because we couldn't trust the guards to obey orders. Doc got snatched because his bodyguard wouldn't stick with him."

"Sure. An' what we goin' to do about it?"

"We're going to create authority," said Jim. "We're going to give orders that stick. The men elected you, didn't they? Now they've got to take it whether they like it or not."

Mac cried, "For Christ's sake, Jim! It won't work. They'll just fade out. They'll be in the next county in no time."

"We'll police 'em, Mac. Where's that rifle?"

"Over there. What do you want with it?"

"That's authority," said Jim. "I'm damn sick of this circle-running. I'm going to straighten it out."

London stepped up to him. "Say, what the hell is this 'I'm goin' to straighten things out'? You're goin' to jump in the lake."

Jim sat still. His young face was carven, his eyes motionless; his mouth smiled a little at the corners. He looked steadily and confidently at London. "Sit down, London, and put on your shirt," he said gently.

London looked uneasily at Mac. "Is this guy gone screwy?"

Mac missed his eyes. "I don't know."

"Might as well sit down," said Jim. "You will sooner or later."

"Sure, I'll sit down."

"O.K. Now you can kick me out of the camp if you

want to. They'll make room for me in jail. Or you can let me stay. But if I stay, I'm going to put this over, and I can do it."

London sighed. "I'm sick of it. Nothin' but trouble. I'd give you the job in a minute, even if you ain't nothing but a kid. I'm the boss."

"That's why," Jim broke in. "I'll put out the orders through you. Don't get me wrong, London; it isn't authority I want, it's action. All I want is to put over the strike."

London asked helplessly, "What d'you think, Mac? What's this kid puttin' over?"

"I don't know. I thought it might be poison from that shot, but he seems to talk sense," Mac laughed, and his laugh dropped heavily into silence.

"The whole thing sounds kind of Bolshevik," London said.

"What do you care what it sounds like, if it works?" Jim replied. "You ready to listen?"

"I don't know. Oh, sure, shoot."

"All right, tomorrow morning we're going to smack those scabs. I want you to pick the best fighters. Give the men clubs. I want two cars to go together, always in pairs. The cops'll probably patrol the roads, and put up barricades. Now we can't let 'em stop us. If they put up barricades, let the first car knock 'em off the road, and the second pick up the men from the wreck and go on through. Understand? Anything we start goes through. If we don't succeed, we're farther back than when we started."

"I'm goin' to have a hell of a time with the guys if you give orders," London said.

"I don't want to give orders. I don't want to show off. The guys won't know. I'll tell you, and you tell them. Now the first thing is to send out some men to see how that fire's getting on. We're going to get a dose of trouble tomorrow. I wish Sam hadn't set it; but it's done now. We've got to have this camp plenty guarded tonight, too. There's going to be reprisals, and don't forget it. Put out two lines of guards and have them keep in touch. Then I want a police committee of five to beat hell out of any guy that goes to sleep or sneaks away. Get me five tough ones."

London shook his head. "I don't know if I ought to smack you down or let you go ahead. The whole thing's so damn much trouble."

"Well, put out guards while you think it over. I'm afraid we're going to have plenty of trouble before morning."

"O.K., kid. I'll give it a try."

After he had gone out, Mac still stood beside the box where Jim sat. "How's your arm feel, Jim?" he asked.

"I can't feel it at all. Must be about well."

"I don't know what's happened to you," Mac went on. "I could feel it happen."

Jim said, "It's something that grows out of a fight like this. Suddenly you feel the great forces at work that create little troubles like this strike of ours. And the sight of those forces does something to you, picks you up and makes you act. I guess that's where authority comes from." He raised his eyes.

Mac cried, "What makes your eyes jump like that?"

"A little dizzy," Jim said, and he fainted and fell off the box.

Mac dragged him to the mattress and brought a box for his feet. In the camp there was a low murmur of voices, constant and varying and changing tone like the voice of a little stream. Men passed back and forth in front of the tent. The sirens raised their voices again, but this time there was no excitement in them, for the trucks were going home. Mac unbuttoned Jim's shirt. He brought a bucket of water that stood in a corner of the tent, and splashed water on Jim's head and throat.

Jim opened his eyes and looked up into Mac's face. "I'm dizzy," he said plaintively. "I wish Doc would come back and give me something. Do you think he'll come back, Mac?"

"I don't know. How do you feel now?"

"Just dizzy. I guess I've shot my wad until I rest."

"Sure. You ought to go to sleep. I'm going out and try to rustle some of the soup that meat was cooked in. That'll be good for you. You just lie still until I bring it."

When he was gone, Jim looked, frowning, at the top of the tent. He said aloud, "I wonder if it passed off. I don't think it did, but maybe." And then his eyes closed, and he went to sleep.

When Mac came in with the soup, he set it on the ground. He took the box from under Jim's legs and then sat down on the edge of the mattress and watched the drawn, sleeping face.

The face was never still. The lips crept back until the teeth were exposed, until the teeth were dry; and then the lips drew down and covered them. The cheeks around the eyes twitched nervously. Once, as though striving against weight, Jim's lips opened to speak and worked on a word, but only a growling mumble was said. Mac pulled the old coverlets over Jim's body.

Suddenly the lamp flame was sucked down, the wick and darkness crept in toward the center of the tent. Mac jumped up and found a spout-can of kerosene. He unscrewed the lantern cap and filled the reservoir. Slowly the flame grew up again, and its edges spread out like a butterfly's wings.

Outside, the slow footsteps of patrolling men went by. In the distance there could be heard the grumble of the great night cargo trucks on the highway. Mac took down the lantern from the tent-pole and carried it to the mattress and set it on the ground. From his hip pocket he brought out a packet of folded papers and a mussy stamped envelope and a broken piece of pencil. With the paper on his knee he wrote slowly, in large, round letters:

Dear Harry:

Christ sake get some help down here. Doc Burton was snatched last night. I think he was. Doc was not a man to run out on us, but he is gone. This valley is organized like Italy. The vigilantes are raising hell. We need food and medicine and money. Dick is doing fine, only if we don't get some outside help I am afraid we are sunk. I never ran into a place that was so God damn organized. About three men control the situation. For all I know Dick may be in the can now.

Jim is sure coming through. He makes me look like a pin. Tomorrow I expect that we will get kicked out of this place. The V's. burned the owner's barn, and he is awfully sore. With Doc Burton gone, the county health officers will bounce us. So try to think of something. They are after Jim's and my scalp all the time. There ought to be somebody down here in case they get us.

I am howling for help, Harry. The sympathizers are scared, but that's not the worst.

He picked up a new piece of paper.

The men are touchy. You know how they get. Tomorrow morning they might go down and burn the city hall, or they might bolt for the mountains and hide for six months. So for Christ's sake, Harry, tell everybody we have to have help. If they run us out of here, we'll have trouble finding a spot. We are going to picket in trucks. We can't find out much that's going on.

Well, so long. Jack will hand this to you. And for the love of God try to get some help here.

Mac

He read the letter over, crossed a neglected t, folded the paper and put it in the dirty envelope. This he addressed to John H. Weaver, *esq*.

Outside he heard a challenge. "Who is it?"

"London."

"O.K."

London came into the tent. He looked at Mac, and at the sleeping Jim. "Well, I got the guards out like he said."

"That's good. He's all in. I wish Doc was here. I'm scared of that shoulder. He says it don't hurt, but he's a fool for punishment." Mac turned the lantern back to the tent-pole and hung it on its nail.

London sat down on a box. "What got into him?" he asked softly. "One minute he's a blabber-mouth kid, and the next minute, by Christ, he just boots me out and takes over."

Mac's eyes were proud. "I don't know. I've saw guys get out of theirself before, but not like that. Jesus, you *had* to do what he said. At first I thought he was off his nut. I still don't know if he was. Where's the girl, London?"

"I bedded her and my kid down in an empty tent."

Mac looked up sharply. "Where did you get an empty tent?"

"Some of the guys scrammed, I guess, in the dark."

"Maybe it's only the guards."

"No," London said. "I figured on them. I guess some of the guys run off."

Mac rubbed his eyes hard with his knuckles. "I thought it was about time. Some of 'em just can't take it. Listen, London, I got to sneak in an' try to get a letter in the mailbox. I want to take a look around, too."

"Whyn't you let me send one of the guys?"

"Well, this letter's got to get there. I better go my-self. I been watched before. They won't catch me."

London regarded his thick hands. "Is—is it a *red* let-ter?" he asked.

"Well, I guess so. I'm trying to get some help, so this strike won't flop."

London spoke constrainedly. "Mac—like I said, you always hear about reds is a bunch of son-of-bitches. I guess that ain't true, is it, Mac?"

Mac chuckled softly. "Depends on how you look at it. If you was to own thirty thousand acres of land and a million dollars, they'd be a bunch of sons-of-bitches. But if you're just London, a workin' stiff, why they're a bunch of guys that want to help you live like a man, and not like a pig, see? 'Course you get your news from the papers, an' the papers is owned by the guys with land and money, so we're sons-of-bitches, see? Then you come acrost us, an' we ain't. You got to make up your own mind which it is."

"Well, could a guy like I work in with you guys? I been doin' kind o' like that, lookin' out for the guys that travel with me."

"Damn right," said Mac eagerly. "You're damn right. You got leadership, London. You're a workin' stiff, but you're a leader, too."

London said simply, "Guys always done what I told 'em. All my life they done it."

Mac lowered his voice. He moved close and put his hand on London's knee. "Listen," he said. "I guess we're goin' to lose this strike. But we raised enough hell so maybe there won't be a strike in the cotton. Now the papers say we're just causing trouble. But we're getting the stiffs used to working together; getting bigger and bigger bunches working together all the time, see? It doesn't make any difference if we lose. Here's nearly a thousand men who've learned how to strike. When we get a whole slough of men working together, maybe— maybe Torgas Valley, most of it, won't be owned by three men. Maybe a guy can get an apple for himself without going to jail for it, see? Maybe they won't dump apples in the river to keep up the price. When guys like you and me need a apple to keep our God-damn bowels open, see? You've got to look at the whole thing, London, not just this little strike."

London was staring painfully at Mac's mouth, as though he tried to see the words as they came out. "That's kind of reva—revolution, ain't it?"

"Sure it is. It's a revolution against hunger and cold. The three guys that own this valley are going to raise hell to keep that land, and to keep dumping the apples to raise the price. A guy that thinks food ought to be eaten is a God-damned red. D'you see that?"

London's eyes were wide and dreaming. "I heard a lot of radical guys talkin'," he said. "Never paid much attention. They always got mad. I ain't got no faith in a mad guy. I never seen it the way you say it before, never."

"Well, keep on seeing it, London. It'll make you feel different. They say we play dirty, work underground. Did you ever think, London? We've got no guns. If anything happens to us, it don't get in the newspapers. But if anything happens to the other side, Jesus, they smear it in ink. We've got no money, and no weapons, so we've got to use our heads, London. See that? It's like a man with a club fighting a squad with machine-guns. The only way he can do it is to sneak up and smack the gunners from behind. Maybe that isn't fair, but hell, London, this isn't any athletic contest. There aren't any rules a hungry man has to follow."

"I never seen it," London said slowly. "Nobody never took time out to tell me. I like to see some of the guys that talk nice an' quiet. Always, when I hear them, they're mad. 'God damn the cops,' they say. 'T'hell with the government.' They're goin' to burn down the government buildings. I don't like that, all them nice buildings. Nobody never told me about that other."

"They didn't use their heads, then," said Mac.

"Mac, you said you guessed we'd lose this strike. What makes you think like that?"

Mac considered. "No—" he said, as though to himself, "You wouldn't pull out now. I'll tell you why, London. Power in this valley is in very few hands. The guy that came out yesterday was trying to get us to quit. But now they know we won't quit. The only thing left is to drive us out or to kill us off. We could stand 'em off a while if we had food and a doctor, and if Anderson would back us up. But Anderson's sore. They'll kick us out if they have to use cannons. Once they get a court order, they'll kick us right out. Then where are we going to go? Can't jungle up, because there'll be ordinances. They'll split us up, an' beat us that way. Our guys aren't any too strong as it is. I'm afraid we can't get any more stuff to eat."

London said, "Whyn't we just tell the guys to beat it, an' the whole bunch of us get out?"

"Don't talk so loud. You'll wake up the kid. Here's why. They can scare our guys, but we can throw a scare into them, too. We'll take one last shot at them. We'll hang on as long as we can. If they kill some of us the news'll get around even if the papers don't print it. Other guys'll get sore. And we've got an enemy, see? Guys work together nice when they've got an enemy. That barn was burned down by our own kind of men, but they've been reading the papers, see? We've got to get 'em over on our side as quick as we can." He took out a slim, limp bag of tobacco. "I've been saving this. I want a smoke. You smoke, London?"

"No. I chew when I can get it."

Mac rolled himself a slender cigarette in the brown paper. He raised the lantern chimney to light the cigarette. "You ought to get in a nap, London. Christ knows what's going to happen tonight. I've *got* to go in town and find a mailbox."

"You might get caught."

"No, I won't. I'll go in through the orchards. I won't even get seen." He stared past London, at the back of the tent. London swung around. The tent wall bellied up from the bottom, and Sam wriggled in, and stood up. He was muddy, and his clothes were torn. A long cut extended down his lean cheek. His lips were drawn back with fatigue, and his eyes were sunken.

"I on'y got a minute," he said softly. "Jesus, what a job! You got a lot of guards out. I didn't want nobody to see me. Somebody'd double-cross us sure."

"You done it nice," Mac said. "We seen the fire."

"Sure. Damn near the whole house gone. But that ain't it." He looked nervously at Jim, sleeping on the mattress. "I—got caught."

"Th' hell!"

"Yeah, they grabbed me and got a look at me."

"You oughtn't to be here," London said severely.

"I know. I wanted to tell you, though. You ain't never seen me or heard of me. I had to—I kicked his brains out. I got to go now. If they get me again, I don't want nothing, see? I'm nuts, see? I'm screwy. I talk about God told me to do it, see? I wanted to tell you. Don't take no risk for me. I don't want it."

London went over to him and took his hand. "You're

a good guy, Sam. They don't make 'em no better. I'll see you sometime."

Mac had his eye on the tent-flap. He said very quietly, over his shoulder, "If you get to town, forty-two Center Avenue. Say Mabel sent you. It's only a meal. Don't go more than once."

"O.K., Mac. G'bye." He was on his knees, with his head out, looking into the dark. In a second he squirmed out, and canvas dropped back into place.

London sighed. "I hope he makes it, Mac. He's a good guy. They don't make 'em no better."

Mac said, "Don't give it a thought. Somebody'll kill him sometime, like that little guy, Joy. He was sure to get popped off. Me an' Jim'll go that way, sooner or later. It's almost sure, but it doesn't make any difference."

London's mouth was open. "Jesus, what a hell of a way to look at it. Don't you guys get no pleasure?"

"Damn right," said Mac. "More than most people do. It's an important job. You get a hell of a drive out of something that has some meaning to it, and don't you forget it. The thing that takes the heart out of a man is work that doesn't lead any place. Ours is slow, but it's all going in one direction. Christ, I stand here shooting off my face. I've got to go."

"Don't let 'em get you, Mac."

"I won't, but listen, London, there's nothing those guys would like better than to rub me and Jim out. I can take care of myself. Will you stay right here and not let anything happen to Jim? Will you?"

"Sure I will. I'll set right here."

"No, lie down on part of the mattress and get some sleep. But don't let 'em get the kid. We need him, he's valuable."

"O.K."

"So long," said Mac. "I'll get back as soon as I can.

I'd like to find out what's going on. Maybe I can get a paper."

"So long."

Mac went silently out of the doorway. London heard him speak to a guard, and then, farther off, to another. Even after he was gone, London listened to the sounds of the night. It was quiet outside, but there was no feeling of sleep. The footsteps of the prowling guards came and went, and their voices sounded in short greetings when they met. The roosters crowed, one near, and far away the deep voice of an old, wise cock—train bell and spurt of steam and pounding of a starting engine. London sat down on the mattress, beside Jim, one folded leg flat, and the other standing up and clasped between his hands. He bowed his head over his knee and rested his chin, and his eyes questioned Jim and probed him.

Jim moved restlessly. One arm flung out and dropped again. He said, "Oh—and—water." He breathed heavily. "Tar over everything." His eyes opened and blinked quickly, sightlessly. London unclasped his hands as though to touch Jim, but he didn't touch him. The eyes closed and were quiet. A great transport truck rumbled into hearing. London heard a muffled cry outside the tent, some distance away. "Hey," he cried softly.

One of the patrol came up. "What's the matter, boss?"

"Well, who's doin' the yellin'?"

"That? Didn't you hear that before? That's the old guy with the busted hip. He's crazy. They're holdin' him down. Fightin' like a cat, an' bitin'. They got a rag in his mouth."

"Ain't you Jake Pedroni? Sure you are. Look, Jake, I heard Doc say if the old guy didn't get soap and water up him to keep him cleared out, he'd get like that. I got to stay here. You go over and get it done, will you, Jake?"

"Sure, boss."

"O.K. Get along. It ain't doin' his hip no good to fight. How's the guy with the busted ankle?"

"Oh, him. Somebody give 'im a slug of whiskey. He's O.K."

"Call me if anything happens, Jake."

"All right, I will."

London went back to the mattress and lay down beside Jim. Far away, the engine pounded, faster and faster in the night. The old tough rooster crowed first, and the young one answered. London felt heavy sleep creeping into his brain, but he rose up on his elbow and looked at Jim once more before he let the sleep wash over him.

14

THE DARK was just beginning to thin when Mac looked into the tent. On the central post the lantern still burned. London and Jim were sleeping, side by side. Mac stepped in, and as he did London jerked upright and peered about. "Who is it?"

"Me," said Mac. "Just got in. How's the kid?"

"I been asleep," said London. He yawned and scratched the round bald spot on his head.

Mac stepped over and looked down at Jim. The tired lines were gone out of the boy's face, and the nervous muscles were relaxed. "He looks fine. He got a good rest."

London stood up. "What time is it?"

"I don't know. It's just starting to get light."

"The guys building the fires yet?"

"I saw somebody moving around over there. I smelled wood smoke. It might be Anderson's barn smouldering."

"I didn't leave the kid a minute," said London.

"Good for you."

"When you goin' to get some sleep?"

"Oh, Christ knows. I don't feel it much yet. I got some last night, or rather the night before, it was. Seems a week ago. We just buried Joy yesterday, just yesterday."

London yawned again. "I guess it's beef and beans this morning. God, I'd like a cup of coffee!"

"Well, let's go in and get coffee and ham and eggs in town."

"Oh, go to hell. I'm goin' to get them cooks movin'." He stumbled sleepily outside.

Mac pulled a box under the light and took a rolled newspaper out of his pocket. As he opened it, Jim said, "I've been awake, Mac. Where have you been?"

"Had to go mail a letter. I picked a paper off a lawn. We'll see what's going on."

"Mac, did I make a horse's ass of myself last night?"

"Hell, no, Jim. You made it stick. You had us eating out of your hand."

"It just came over me. I never felt that way before."

"How do you feel this morning?"

"Fine. But not like that. I could of lifted a cow last night."

"Well, you sure lifted us around. That's a good gag about the two trucks, too. The owner of the car that has to bust the barricade may not like it much. Now let's see what's going on in town. Oh—oh, headlines for the scrap-book! Listen, Jim:

STRIKERS BURN HOUSES—KILL MEN!

Last night at ten o'clock fire destroyed the suburban home of William Hunter. Police say the men now on strike from the apple orchards are responsible. A suspect, captured, assaulted his captor and escaped. The injured man, Olaf Bingham, special deputy, is not expected to live.

Now let's see, farther down:—

Earlier in the evening strikers, either through carelessness or malice, burned the barn on the Anderson farm. Mr. Anderson had previously given the men permission to camp on his land.

It's a long story, Jim. You can read it if you want to." He turned the page. "Oh boy, oh boy. Listen to this editorial:

We believe the time has come to take action. When transient laborers tie up the Valley's most important industry, when fruit tramps, led and inspired by paid foreign agitators (That's us, Jim), carry on a campaign of violence and burning, bringing Red Russia into peaceful America, when our highways are no longer safe for American citizens, nor their homes safe from firebrands, we believe the time for action has come!

This county takes care of its own people, but these strikers do not belong here. They flout the laws, and destroy life and property. They are living on the fat of the land, supplied by secret sympathizers. This paper does not, and has never believed in violence; but it does believe that when law is not sufficient to cope with these malcontents and murderers, an aroused citizenry must take a hand. The incendiary deserves no mercy. We must drive out these paid trouble-makers. This paper recommends that citizens inquire into the sources of luxuries these men have been given. It is reported that three prime steers were slaughtered in their camp yesterday."

Mac smashed the paper down on the ground. "And that last means that tonight a flock of pool-room Americans will start slinging rocks through the windows of poor devils who said they wished times might get better."

Jim was sitting up. "Jesus Christ, Mac! Do we have to take all the blame?"

"Every damn bit."

"How about that guy they say was murdered."

"Well, Sam did it. They caught him. He had to get away. The guy had a gun; all Sam had was his feet."

Jim lay back again. "Yeah," he said. "I saw him use

his feet the other day. But God, it sounds bad. Sounds awful!"

"Sure. That editor used some dollar-an'-a-half words, all right. 'Paid foreign agitators.' Me, born in Minneapolis! An' granpaw fought in the Battle of Bull Run. He always said he thought it was a bull-fight instead of a battle he was goin' to till they started shootin' at him. An' you're about as foreign as the Hoover administration. Oh, hell, Jim. That's the way it always is. But—" he brought out the last of his tobacco—"it's closing in, Jim. Sam shouldn't of set that fire."

"You told him to go ahead."

"I know, I was mad about the barn."

"Well, what do we do now?"

"Just go ahead, just go ahead. We start those cars out at the scabs. We keep it up as long as we can fight, and then we get away, if we can. Are you scared, Jim?"

"N-no-o."

"It's closing in on us, Jim. I can feel it, closing in." He got up from his box and walked to the mattress and sat down. "Maybe it's because I need sleep. On the way out from town just now it seemed to me there was a bunch of guys waiting for me in the shadow under every tree. I got so scared, I'd of run if a mouse moved."

"You're all tired," Jim said gently. "Maybe I could of been some use around here, if I hadn't got myself hurt. I just lie around, and get in the way."

Mac said, "The hell you do. Every time I get low you steam me up, and, baby, I need steam this morning. My guts are just water! I'd take a drink if I could get it."

"You'll be all right when you get something to eat."

Mac said, "I wrote to Harry Nilson; told him we had to have help and supplies. But I'm afraid it's too late." He stared strangely at Jim. "Listen, Jim, I found Dick last night. Now you listen close. Remember the night we came in?"

"Sure."

"Well, you remember when we turned left at that bridge and went to the jungle?"

"Yeah."

"Well, listen close. If hell should pop and we get separated, you get to that bridge and go underneath, clear up under the arch, on the side away from town. You'll find a pile of dead willows there. Lift 'em aside. There's a deep cave underneath. Get inside, and pull the willows over the hole. You can go in about fifteen feet, see? Now Dick's putting blankets in there, an' canned goods. If they dynamite us, you go there an' wait for me a couple o' days. If I don't come, you'll know something's happened to me. You get back to town. Travel at night till you're clear of this county. They've got nothing on us that'll get us more than six months unless they pad up a murder charge about that guy last night. I don't think they will, because it'd be too much publicity. I.L.D.'d come through and break that upstairs shooting of Joy. Now will you remember, Jim? Go there and wait for a couple of days. I don't think they'll root you out of there."

Jim asked, "What do you know, Mac? You're keeping something back."

"I don't know a thing," Mac said. "I've just got a feeling this joint's closing in on us—just a feeling. A lot of the guys took it on the lam last night, mostly the guys with women and kids. London's O.K. He'll be a Party member pretty soon. But right now I wouldn't trust the rest of these guys with a road-apple at a banquet. They're so God-damn jumpy they might knife us themselves."

"You're jumpy yourself, Mac. Calm down." Jim got to his knees and stood carefully up, his head cocked as though he listened for pain. Mac watched him in alarm. "It's swell," said Jim. "Shoulder's a little bit heavy, but

I feel swell. Not even light-headed. I ought to get around some today."

"That bandage ought to be changed," said Mac.

"Oh, yeah, say, did Doc come back?"

"No, I guess they got him. What a nice guy he was."

"Was?"

"No. I hope not. Maybe they'd only beat hell out of him. But so many of our guys just disappear and never show up again."

"You're a fine, happy influence," said Jim.

"I know. If I wasn't sure you could take it, I'd shut up. Makes me feel better to get it off my chest. I want a cup of coffee so bad I could bust into tears. Just think of all the coffee we used to have in town. Three cups if we wanted. All we wanted."

Jim said sternly, "Maybe a little bit of that might be good for you. You better pull up now. You'll get feeling sorry for yourself."

Mac tightened his loose face. "O.K., kid. I'm all right now. You want to go outside? Can you walk all right?"

"Sure I can."

"Well, blow out that lantern. We'll go see about some beef and beans."

The shade screeched when Jim raised it. The dawn grey leapt into the tent, grey like a wash of ink. Jim lifted the tent-flaps and tied them back. "Let's air this place out," he said. "It's getting strong. The whole damn bunch of us could do with a bath."

Mac agreed. "I'll try to get a bucket of warm water, and we'll sponge off after we eat."

The dawn had come into the sky. The trees were still black against the light east, and a colony of crows, flapping eastward, were etched heavily against it. Under the trees a dusk still held, and the earth was dark, as though the light had to be sucked in slowly. Now that they could see, the guards had given up their pacing.

They stood in tired groups, hands in pockets, coats turned up and buttoned over their throats. And they talked in the soft monotone of men who only talk to stay awake.

Mac and Jim approached a group of them on their way to the stove. "Anything happen last night?" Mac asked.

Talk stopped. The men looked at him with weary, blood-shot eyes. "Not a thing, buddy. Frank was just sayin'—sayin' he had a feelin' there was people movin' around all night. I had that feelin' too, just creepin' around; but we didn't hear nothing. We went around two together."

Mac laughed, and his voice seemed to penetrate deep into the air. "I was in the army," he said, "trained in Texas. By Christ, when I'd go on guard duty I could hear Germans all around me, could hear 'em whispering in German." The men chuckled softly, without amusement.

One said, "London told us we could sleep today. Soon's I get somethin' in my stomach, I'm goin' to roll in."

"Me too. Roll right in. I got gravel in my skin, like a hop-head. Ever seen a hop-head when he's got bugs in his skin? Make you laugh to watch him."

Mac asked, "Whyn't you come over to the stoves an' warm up?"

"Well, we was just talkin' about doin' that."

Jim said, "I'm going down to the can, Mac. See you over at the stove." He walked down the line of tents, and each tent was a little cave of darkness. Snores came from some, and in the entrances of others men lay on their stomachs and looked out at the morning, and their eyes were full of the inwardness of sleep. As he walked along, some men came into the air and hunched their shoulders and drew down their necks against the cold.

He heard an irritable, sleepy voice of a woman detailing how she felt. "I want to get out o' this dump. What good we doin' here? An' I got a lump in my stomach big's your fist. It's a cancer, that's what it is. Card-reader tol' me two years ago I'd get a cancer if I din' watch out. Said I was the cancer type. Sleepin' on the ground, eatin' garbage." An inaudible grumble answered.

As Jim passed another tent, a tousled head stuck out. "Come on in quick, kid. He's gone."

"Can't," said Jim.

Two tents down a man kneeling on his blankets said, "Got the time, buddy?"

"No. Must be after six, I guess, though."

"I heard her give you the come-on. God damn lucky you didn' go. She's caused more trouble in this camp'n the scabs. They ought to run her out. Gets ever'body fightin'. They got a fire goin' over there?"

"Yes," said Jim. He passed out from between the row of tents. Fifteen yards away, in the open, stood the square canvas screen. Inside there was a two-by-four supported at each end, over a hole. There was room on board for three men. Jim picked up a box of chloride of lime and shook it, but it was empty. One man sat hunched up on the board. "Sompin' ought to be done about it," he said. "Where in hell is 'at doctor? He ain't done nothing about it since yesterday."

"Maybe we could shovel in a little dirt," said Jim. "That'd help."

"It ain't my business. That doctor ought to do sompin' about it. The guys are liable t'get sick."

Jim's voice was angry. "Guys like you that won't do anything damn well deserve to get sick." He kicked dirt into the hole with the side of his foot.

"You're a smart punk, ain't you?" the man said. "Wait till you been around a little and got dry behind the ears, 'n'en maybe you'll know sompin'."

"I know enough right now to know you're a lazy bastard."

"You wait till I get my pants up; I'll show you who's a lazy bastard." But he made no move.

Jim looked down at the ground. "I can't take you on. I'm shot in the shoulder."

"Sure, an' when you know you're safe from a sportin' man, you miscall a man. You lousy punks got sompin' comin' to you."

Jim controlled his voice. "I didn't mean to miscall you, mister. I wouldn't fight you. We got all the fighting to do we can take care of, without fighting each other."

"Well, now, that's better," said the man. "I'll he'p you kick some dirt in when I get through. What's goin' on today? You know?"

Jim began, "We're——" and then he remembered. "Damn' if I know. I guess London'll tell us when he gets ready."

"London ain't done nothing yet," said the man. "Hey, don't sit so near the middle. You're liable to break that two-by-four. Get over near the edge. London ain't done nothing. Just walks around lookin' big. Know what a guy told me? London's got cases an' cases of can' goods in his tent—ever'thing. Corn-beef, an' sardines, an' can' peaches. He won't eat what us poor stiffs got to eat, not him. He's too God-damned good."

"And that's a God-damn lie," said Jim.

"Got smart again, have you? There's plenty guys seen them can' goods. How do you know it's a lie?"

"Because I've been in that tent. He let me sleep in there last night because I was hurt. There's an old mattress and two empty boxes in that tent, and not another damn thing."

"Well, a whole slough o' guys says there's can' peaches an' sardines in there. Some of the boys was goin' to bust in an' get some last night."

Jim laughed hopelessly. "Oh, Jesus, what a bunch of swine! You get a good man, and you start picking him to pieces."

"There you go, miscalling guys again. Wait'll you get well an' somebody's goin' to slap that smart puss right off you."

Jim got up from the plank and buttoned his jeans and went outside. The short stove-pipes of the cook stoves puffed grey smoke into the air, still, straight columns that went up fifty feet before they mushroomed at the top and spread out evenly. The eastern sky was yellow now, and the sky overhead had turned eggshell-blue. From the tents men came rapidly. The awakening silence of the camp was replaced with the rustling footsteps, the voices, the movement of people.

A dark-haired woman stood in front of a tent, her head thrown back; and her throat was white. She combed her hair with long, beautiful sweeps of her arm. When Jim walked by she smiled wisely and said, "Good morning," and the combing didn't pause. Jim stopped. "No," she said. "Only good morning."

"You make me feel good," he said. For a moment he looked at the long white throat and the sharply defined jaws. "Good morning again," he said, and he saw her lips form to a line of deep and delicious understanding. And when he passed along, and the tousled head darted out and the husky voice whispered, "Come on in, quick, he's gone now," Jim only glanced, and went quickly on without responding.

Men were gathering about the old stoves, stretching their hands to the warmth, waiting patiently until the beef and beans in the big wash-boilers should be hot. Jim stepped to a water-barrel and dipped some water into a tin basin. He threw the cold water into his face, and into his hair, and he rubbed his hands together without soap. He let the water cling in drops to his face.

Mac saw him and walked over, holding out a food can. "I rinsed it out," he said. "What's the matter, Jim? You look tickled to death."

"I saw a woman——"

"You couldn't. Didn't have time."

"I just *saw* her," said Jim. "She was combing her hair. It's a funny thing—sometimes a person gets into an ordinary position, and it seems wonderful, it just stays in your mind all your life."

"If I saw a decent-looking woman, I'd go nuts," said Mac.

Jim looked down into the empty can. "She had her head back. She was combing her hair—she had a funny kind of a smile on her face. You know, Mac, my mother was a Catholic. She didn't go to church Sunday because my old man hated churches as bad as we do. But in the middle of the week, sometimes, she'd go into the church when my old man was working. When I was a little kid she took me in sometimes, too. The smile on that woman —that's why I'm telling you this—— Well, there was a Mary in there, and she had the same kind of smile, wise and cool and sure. One time I asked my mother why she smiled like that. My mother said, 'She can smile because she's in Heaven.' I think she was jealous, a little." His voice tumbled on, "And one time I was there, looking at that Mary, and I saw a ring of little stars in the air, over her head, going around and around, like little birds. Really saw them, I mean. It's not funny, Mac. This isn't religion—it's kind of what the books I've read call wish-fulfillment, I guess. I saw them, all right. They made me feel happy, too. My old man would have been sore if he knew. He never took any position that lasted. Everything was wasted in him."

Mac said, "You're going to be a great talker some time, Jim. You got a kind of a persuasive tone. Jesus, just now you made me think it'd be nice to sit in church. Nice! That's good talking. If you can talk guys over to our side, you'll be good." He took a little clean tin can that hung on a nail on the side of the water-barrel, and he filled the can and drank from it. "Let's go over and see if the slum is hot."

The men were forming in a line, and as they passed the stoves, the cooks ladled lima beans and lumps of boiled beef into the cans. Mac and Jim got on the end of the line and eventually passed the boilers. "Is that all the food?" Mac asked a cook.

"There's beans and beef enough for one more meal. We're out of salt, though. We need more salt."

They drifted along, eating as they went. A lance of sunlight shot over the trees and fell on the ground of the clearing, fell on the tents and made them seem less dingy. At the line of old cars London was talking to a group of men. "Let's see what's doing," Mac suggested. They walked toward the road, where the old cars stood. A light rust was settling on radiators, and some of the worn tires were down, and all of the cars had the appearance of having stood there a long while.

London saluted with a wave of his hand. "Hello, Mac. H'ya, Jim?"

"Fine," said Jim.

"Me and these guys is lookin' over the heaps. Tryin' to see which ones to send out. There ain't none of 'em worth a hoot in hell."

"How many'd you figure to send out?"

" 'Bout five couples. Two together, so if anything went wrong with one the other'd pick our guys up and go on." He pointed down the line. "That old Hudson's all right. There's five four-cylinder Dodges, and them old babies will go to hell on their bellies after you knock the wheels off. My model T's all right—runs, anyway. Let's see, we don't want no closed cars; y'can't heave a rock out of a closed car. Here's a shovel-nose. Think she'll run?"

A man stepped up. "Damn right she'll run. I brung her straight through Louisiana in winter. She never even warmed up, even comin' over the mountains."

They walked down the row, picking out prospects in the line of wrecks. "These guys is squad leaders," London explained. "I'm goin' give one of 'em charge of each bus, an' let 'em pick their own guys, five or six apiece. Guys they can trust, good fighters, see?"

"Sounds swell," said Mac. "I don't see how anybody's goin' to stop 'em."

One of the men turned on him. "And they *ain't* nobody goin' to stop us, neither," he said.

"Feelin' pretty tough, huh?"

"Just give us a show, an' see."

Mac said, "We'll walk around a little bit, London."

"Oh, wait a minute, the guys come back from Anderson's a little while ago. They say Anderson cussed 'em all night. An' this mornin' he started in town, still cussin'."

"Well, I thought he would. How about Al?"

"Al?"

"Yeah, Anderson's boy, the one that got smacked."

"Well, the guys went in an' seen him. He wanted to come over here, but they didn't want to move him. Couple guys stayed with him."

London stepped close and lowered his voice so the other men could not hear. "Where do you think Anderson's goin', Mac?"

"I guess he's goin' in town to put in a complaint and get us kicked off. He'll probably claim we burned his barn now. He's so scared he'll do anything to get in good with the other side."

"Uh-huh. Think we ought to fight here?"

"I'll tell you how I think it'll be," said Mac. "I think first they might send out a few guys to try to scare us off. We'll stand up to 'em. After that, they'll come out with a mob. We'll see how our guys feel. If they're sore and mean, we'll fight. But if they look yellow, we'll clear out, if we can." He tapped London on the shoulder. "If that happens, you and me and Jim have to go quick and far. That mob's going to want a chicken to kill, and they won't care much who it is."

London called to the men, "Drain the gas out of all the tanks, and put it in them cars we picked out. Start up the motors 'n' see if they're all right, but don't waste no gas." He turned back. "I'll walk along. I want to talk this out. What you think about our guys? Them babies over by the heaps'll fight. How about the others?"

Mac said, "If I could tell in advance what a bunch of guys'd do, I'd be president. Some things I do know, though. A smell of blood seems to steam 'em up. Let 'em kill somethin', even a cat, an' they'll want to go right on killin'. If there's a fight, an' our guys get first blood, they'll put up a hell of a battle. But if we lose a man first, I wouldn't be surprised to see them hit for the trees."

"I know," London agreed. "Take one guy that you know ever'thing about him, an' take ten more the same, an' you can't tell what in hell they'll do. What you think of doin'? Just waitin' to see?"

"That's it," said Mac. "When you're used to mobs, you can tell, just a little bit ahead of time. You can feel it in the air. But remember, if our guys crack, get under somethin', an' stay there. Listen, under the Torgas River bridge there's a dug-out covered with dead willows. It's got food and blankets in it. That's the place to hit for. A mob don't stay crazy long. When you get in town, go to forty-two Center Avenue and say I sent you."

"I wish they was some way to get the kid and Lisa out. I don't want 'em to get hurt."

Jim broke in on them. "You guys talk like it was sure to happen. Nothing's happened yet, maybe nothing will. Maybe Anderson only went in to stay with somebody."

"I know it sounds like I'm calamity-howling," Mac said apologetically. "Maybe it won't happen. But London's a valuable guy. We need him. I don't like to get these stiffs killed off; they're good guys. But we need London. This whole strike's worth it if London comes over."

London looked pleased. "You been in plenty strikes, Mac. Always do they go this way?"

"Hell, no. This place is organized, I tell you. None of the other workers came out on strike with us. The owners cut us off out here with nothing to eat. If this bunch of raiders gets stopped today, we'll catch it good. You weren't planning to go out, were you, London?"

"Sure. I ain't been in a fight yet."

"I don't think you'd better go," Mac advised. "We're goin' to need you here. They'll try to root us out to-day. If you aren't here the guys might get scared and beat it. You're still the boss, London. The boss's got to stick in the center of the biggest group till the last minute. Let's get those cars on the move, shall we? There's plenty of scabs out, and they'll be working by now."

London turned and hurried back to the cars. "Come on, you guys. Step on it. Let's get rollin'."

The squad leaders trotted to the tents and picked their men, men armed with rocks and pieces of wood, and here and there a knife. The whole crowd moved out of the edge of the road, talking loudly and giving advice.

"Give 'em hell, Joe."

"Knock their can off."

The motors started and struggled against their age. The chosen men climbed in and took their places. London held up both hands to stop the noise. He shouted, "Three pairs go that way, and two this way." The gears dropped in. The cars crawled across the ditch and lined up in the road. Raiders stood up and waved their hats furiously, and shook their fists and made murderous cuts in the air with their clubs. The cars moved away slowly, in two directions, and the mob left in the camp shrieked after them.

When they had gone, the shouting stopped suddenly. The men stood, wondering and uneasy. They looked down the road and saw the cars jog out of sight. Mac and Jim and London walked back into the camp side by side.

"I hope to Christ they do some damage," Mac said. "If everything happens to us and nothing to anybody else, we aren't goin' to last much longer. Come on, Jim. Let's take a look at the old guy Dan. An' then maybe we can gets some guys together and go over and see Al. I promised Al something. He'll need some encouragement."

London said, "I'm goin' to see about gettin' some water. The barrel's low."

Jim led the way to the hospital tent. The flaps were tied back to let in the morning sunshine. In a pool of sun old Dan lay. His face was transparent white and waxen, and heavy black veins puffed out on his cheeks. "How you feeling, Dan?" Jim asked.

The old man mumbled weakly.

"What's that you say?" Mac bent over to hear.

Dan's lips worked carefully this time. "I ain't had nothing to eat."

Jim cried, "You poor devil. I'll get you something." He stepped out of the door. "Mac," he shouted, "they're coming back."

From the direction of the town four cars drew up and stopped in the road. London came running and flung himself through the crowd. "What th' hell's the matter?"

The driver of the first car smiled foolishly. The

crowd fell completely silent. "We couldn't get through," the driver said, and he smiled again. "There's a barricade across the road."

"I thought I told you to crash it if it was there."

"You don't unda'stan'," the driver said dully. "They was two cars ahead of us. We come to the barricade. There's about twenty guys with guns behind it." He swallowed nervously. "A guy with a star on to him gets up on top an' he says, 'It's unlawful to picket in this county. Get back.' So that old Hudson tries to go around, an' it tips over in a ditch, an' the guys spill out. So, like you said, the guys run an' get in the shovel-nose." The men in the other seats nodded solemnly at his words.

"Go on." London's voice was subdued.

"So then the shovel-nose starts to try to knock over the barricade. So then those guys start the tear gas an' shoot the tires off the shovel-nose. Then our guys start coughin', an' there's so much gas you can't see. So then those guys got on gas masks, an' they come in, an' they got 'bout a thousan' handcuffs." He smiled again. "So we come back. We couldn't do nothing. We didn' even have a decent rock to throw. They grabbed all the guys in the shovel-nose. Hell, I never seen so much gas." He looked up. "There's the other bunch comin'," he said hopelessly. "I guess they got the road blocked at both ends."

A curious, long sigh escaped from the crowd. Some of the men turned and walked slowly back toward the tents, walked glidingly, with their heads down, as though they were in deep thought.

London turned to Mac, and his face was perplexed. Mac said, "Do you suppose we could get the cars across the orchard, and out that way? They can't have all the roads blocked."

London shook his head. "Too wet. A car'd squat

down in the mud before we could get it ten feet."

Mac leaped on the running-board of one of the cars. "Listen, you guys," he cried "There's one way we can get through. Let's the whole bunch of us go down there and knock those barricades off the road. They can't block us in, God damn it!" He paused for a response, a quickening. But the men looked away from him, each waiting for another to speak.

At last a man said, "We got nothing to fight with, mister. We can't fight guns an' gas with our han's. Give us guns, an' we'll fight."

Mac's speech turned into fury. "You let 'em shoot our guys, an' burn the buildings of our friends, an' you won't fight. Now they got you trapped, an' still you won't fight. Why even a God-damn rat'll fight when he's in a trap."

The hopelessness hung in the air like a gas itself. The same man repeated, "Mister, we can't fight guns and gas with our han's."

Mac's voice broke with rage. "Will any six of you yellow bastards fight *me* with your hands? *Will you?*" His mouth worked helplessly. "Try to help you—try to get something for you——" he shrieked.

London reached up and pulled him firmly off the running-board. Mac's eyes were mad. He tried to jerk free. "I'll kill the yellow bastards myself," he cried.

Jim stepped over and took his other arm. "Mac," he said. "Mac, for Christ's sake, you don't know what you're saying." Between them, Jim and London turned him and led him through the crowd, and the men looked shamefacedly at the ground. They told each other softly, "But we can't fight guns and gas with our hands."

The raiders climbed stiffly down from their cars and joined the crowd, and left the automobiles standing in the road.

Mac was limp now. He allowed himself to be led into

London's tent, and settled down on the mattress. Jim soaked a rag in the water bucket and tried to wash his face, but Mac took the cloth from him and did it for himself. "I'm all right now," he said quietly. "I'm no good. The Party ought to get rid of me. I lose my head."

"You're dead for sleep," said Jim.

"Oh, I know. But it isn't that. They won't help themselves. Sometimes I've seen men just like these go through a machine-gun nest with their hands. And here today they won't fight a few green deputy-sheriffs. Just scared to death." He said, "Jim, I'm as bad as they are. I'm supposed to use my head. When I got up on that running-board, I was going to try to steam them up. An' then the God-damn sheep made me mad. I didn't have any right to get mad. They ought to kick me out of the Party."

London said in sympathy, "I got pretty damn mad myself."

Mac looked at each of his fingers carefully. "Makes me want to run away," he said ruefully. "I'd like to crawl down in a haystack and go to sleep, and to hell with the whole damn bunch of them."

Jim said, "Just as soon as you get rested up, you'll feel strong again. Lie down and get some sleep, Mac. We'll call you if we need you, won't we, London?"

"Sure," said London. "You just stretch out. There ain't nothing you can do now. I'm goin' to go out an' talk to them squad leaders. Maybe we could take a few good guys an' sneak up on the barricades."

"I'm scared they've got us now," Mac said. "They took the heart out of the guys before they could get going." He lay down on the mattress. "What they need is blood," he muttered. "A mob's got to kill something. Oh, Christ, I guess I've bungled everything right from the start." He closed his eyes, then suddenly opened them again. "Listen, they'll pay us a visit pretty soon, the sheriff or somebody. Be sure and wake me up. Don't let 'em get away with anything. Be sure and call me." He stretched like a cat and clasped his hands over his head. His breathing became regular.

The sun threw shadows of the tent-ropes on the canvas, and in the open entrance a piece of sunlight lay on the foot-beaten earth. Jim and London walked quietly outside. "Poor guy," London said. "He needs it. I never seen a guy so far gone for sleep. I heard how the cops keep a guy awake till he goes crazy."

"He'll be different when he wakes up," said Jim. "Lord, I said I'd take something to old Dan. An' then those cars came up. I better do it now."

"I'll go see how Lisa's getting along. Maybe she better go an' take care of the old duck."

Jim walked to the stove and ladled some beans into a can and carried them to the hospital tent. The idle men, standing about, had collected into little groups. Jim looked into the hospital tent. The triangular sunny place had shortened and fallen off the cot. Old Dan's eyes were closed, and his breathing was slow and light. A curious musty, rancid odor filled the tent, the breath from a congested and slowly dying body. Jim leaned over the cot. "Dan, I brought you something to eat."

Dan opened his eyes slowly. "I don't want none. I ain't got the strength to chew."

"You have to eat, Dan. Have to eat to get strong. Look, I'll put a pillow under your head, and I'll feed you."

"Don't want to get strong." His voice was languorous. "Just want to lay here. I been a top-faller." His eyes closed again. "You'd go up the stick, way up, way up, an' you could see all the little trees, second, third growth timber down below. Then you fix your safety belt." He sighed deeply, and his mouth went on whispering. A shadow fell in the spot of sunlight. Jim looked up.

Lisa stood in the door of the tent, and her baby was

under the shoulder blanket. "I got enough to do, takin' care of the baby. He says I got to come an' take care of a old man, too."

Jim said, "Sh-h." He stood from the cot so she could see Dan's sunken face.

She crept in and sat down on the extra cot. "Oh, I di'n' know. What you want me to do?"

"Nothing. Just stay with him."

She said, "I don't like 'em like that. I can smell 'em. I know that smell." She shifted nervously, covered the baby's round face to protect it from the smell.

"Shh-h," Jim said. "Maybe he's going to be all right."

"Not with that smell. I know that smell. Part of 'im's dead already."

"Poor devil!" Jim said.

Something in the words caught at her. Her eyes grew wet with tears. "I'll stay. I seen it before. It don't hurt nobody."

Jim sat down beside her. "I like to be near you," he said softly.

"Don't you come none of that."

"No, I won't. I just wondered why it was warm beside you."

"I ain't cold."

He turned his face away. "I'm going to talk to you, Lisa. You won't understand, and it won't matter, not a bit. Everything's crumbling down and washing away. But this is just a little bit of the whole thing. This isn't anything, Lisa. You and I aren't much in the whole thing. See, Lisa? I'm telling it to myself, but I understand it better with you listening. You don't know what I'm talking about, do you, Lisa?"

He saw a blush creep up the side of her neck. "I jus' had a baby," she said. "Besides, I ain't that kind." She lifted her shamed eyes. "Don't talk that way. Don't get that tone on you," she begged. "You know I ain't that kind." He reached out his hand to pat her, but she shrank away from him. "No."

He stood up. "Be nice to the old guy. See? There's water and a spoon on the table. Give him a little, now and then." He raised his head tensely to listen to a stir of voices in the camp, a gradually increasing stir. And then, over the bass of voices, a haranguing voice sounded, a voice that rose and fell angrily. "I've got to go," Jim said. "Take care of him." He hurried out of the tent.

By the stoves he saw men collecting around some central object, all faces inward. The angry voice came from the center. As Jim watched, the crowd moved sideways toward the naked little stand that had been built for Joy's body. The mob touched the stand and flowed around it, but out of the group one man shot up and took his position in the stand. Jim ran over. He could see, now. It was the sullen, scowling Burke. His arms gesticulated. His voice bellowed over the heads of the crowd. Jim saw London hurrying in from the road.

Burke grasped the hand-rail. "There he is now," he shouted. "Look at 'im. That's the guy that's spoiled ever'thing. What the hell's he done? Set in his tent an' et canned peaches while we got wet and lived on garbage a pig wouldn' touch."

London's mouth was open with astonishment. "What's goin' on here?" he cried.

Burke leaned forward over the rail. "I'll tell you what's goin' on. Us guys decided we wanted a real leader. We decided we want a guy that won't sell out for a load o' canned goods."

London's face paled, and his shoulders dropped. With a roar he charged the unresisting crowd, flung men aside, burrowed through the mass of men. He came to the stand and grasped the hand-rail. As he pulled himself up, Burke kicked at his head, missed, struck the shoulder and tore one hand loose from the rail. London roared again. He was under the rail and on his feet. Burke struck at his face, and missed. And then, with the terrible smooth speed of a heavy man, London lanced with his left hand and, as Burke ducked, the great right fist caught him on the side of the jaw, lifted him clear, and dropped him. His head hung over the edge of the platform, broken jaw torn sideways, shattered teeth hanging loosely between his lips. A thin stream of blood flowed from his mouth, beside his nose and eye, and disappeared into his hair.

London stood, panting, over him, looking down. He raised his head slowly. "Does any more sons-of-bitches think I double-crossed 'em?"

The men nearest Burke's hanging head stared, fascinated. From the other sides of the stand the people began to mill, to press in, standing on tiptoes for a look. Their eyes were bright and angry. A man said, "Bust his jaw clean off. That's blood out o' his brain." Another shouted hysterically, "Killed 'um. Busted his head off."

Women swam through the crowd and looked woodenly at the hanging head. A heavy, sobbing gasp went up from the mob. The eyes flared. All the shoulders were dropped, and the arms bowed dangerously. London still stood panting, but his face was perplexed. He looked down at his fist, at the split and bleeding knuckles. Then he looked out over the crowd for help, and he saw Jim standing on the outskirts. Jim shook his clasped hands together over his head. And then he pointed to the road, where the cars stood, and down the road, and to the cars again, and down the road again. London looked back at the snarling mob. The perplexity left his face and he scowled.

"All right, you guys," he yelled. "Why ain't I done nothing? Because you ain't helped me. But by Christ, now you're ready! Nothin' can stop you now." A long, throaty animal howl went up. London held up his hands. "Who'll follow now, and knock hell out o' that barricade?" The crowd was changing rapidly. The eyes of the men and women were entranced. The bodies weaved slowly, in unison. No more lone cries came from lone men. They moved together, looked alike. The roar was one voice, coming from many throats.

"Some of you bring cars," London shouted. "Come on, the rest of you. Come on, we'll see. Come, come on." He vaulted down from the stand and fought his way through to the head of the mob. Quickly the cars were started. The crowd poured into the road, and it was no longer loose and listless. It had become a quick, silent and deadly efficient machine. It swung down the road at a dog-trot, controlled and directed. And behind it the cars moved slowly along.

Jim had watched the start. He commanded himself aloud, "Don't get caught. Don't get caught. Don't let it catch you. Use your head."

Most of the women were running with the departing men, but a few who remained behind looked strangely at Jim, for his eyes, too, were entranced as he stared down the road after the terrible mechanism. When it had disappeared he sighed shudderingly and turned away. His hand went up to the hurt shoulder and pressed it, to make a steadying pain. He walked slowly to London's tent, went in silently, and sat down on a box.

Mac looked at him under lowered eyelids. Only a shiny slit showed that he was awake. "How long've I been sleeping, Jim?"

"Just a little while. I don't think it's even noon yet, near noon."

"I dreamed a lot, but I'm rested. I think I'll get up now."

"Better get some more sleep if you can."

"What's the use? I'm rested now." He opened his eyes wide. "Lost the sandy feeling. You sleep hard when you're that tired. I dreamed commotion."

"Better go to sleep again."

"No." He sat up and stretched. "Anything happen while I was asleep? It's awful quiet out there."

"Plenty happened," Jim said. "Burke tried to kick London out, and London smashed him—nearly killed him, and—Christ! I forgot Burke." He ran to the door, and around the back to the tent, and looked toward the stand. Then he went into the tent again. "Somebody took him in," he said.

Mac was up now, and excited. "Tell me."

"Well, when the crowd saw the blood they went nuts, and London started 'em down to break the barricade."

Mac cried, "Didn't I tell you? They need blood. That works. That's what I told you. Well then—what?"

"They're down there now. God, Mac, you ought to of seen them. It was like all of them disappeared, and it was just one big—animal, going down the road. Just all one animal. I nearly was there. I wanted to go, and then I thought, 'You can't. You've got to use your head.'"

"Right!" said Mac. "People think a mob is wasteful, but I've seen plenty; and I tell you, a mob with something it wants to do is just about as efficient as trained soldiers, but tricky. They'll knock that barricade, but then what? They'll want to do something else before they cool off." And he went on, "That's right, what you said. It *is* a big animal. It's different from the men in it. And it's stronger than all the men put together. It doesn't want the same things men want—it's like Doc said—and we don't know what it'll do."

"It'll get that barricade," said Jim.

"That's not what I mean. The *animal* don't want the barricade. I don't know what it wants. Trouble is, guys that study people always think it's men, and it isn't men.

It's a different kind of animal. It's as different from men as dogs are. Jim, it's swell when we can use it, but we don't know enough. When it gets started it might do anything." His face was alive and excited, and slightly fearful.

Jim said, "Listen, I think I hear——" He ran to the entrance. "Coming back," he cried. "It's different now. It's spread out now, not the same."

Mac stood beside him. The road was full of the returning men. London broke out ahead and trotted heavily toward them. And when he came near enough he yelled, "Get back in the tent. Get back in the tent."

"What's he mean?" Jim asked. But Mac pushed him inside the tent, untied the strings and dropped the flaps.

"He knows," Mac said. "Just keep quiet and let him handle it. No matter what happens, don't go out there."

They heard the rain of footsteps on the ground, and shouting voices. Then they saw London's squat black shadow on the canvas and heard him yell, "Now you guys cool off."

"We'll show 'im who's yellow bastards!"

London cried, "You're sore because we told you off. Now you go an' get a drink an' cool down. You just done fine, but you ain't a'gonna get my friend. He's your friend, too. I tell you he's been workin' for you till he's dead tired."

Mac and Jim, in the tent, could feel the thrust change, break up, lose itself in a hundred cries. "We know, London."

"Sure, but he called us yellow."

Mac's breath came out, heavily. "That was close, Jim. Jesus, that was close." London's square shadow still stood on the tent wall, but the many excited voices drifted and lost their impact.

London stretched the subject. "If any of you guys think I got canned peaches, you can come in and look."

"Hell, no, London. We never thought that."

"It was that son-of-a-bitch Burke."

"He's been workin' against you, London. I heard him."

"Well, you guys clear out, then. I got work to do."
The shadow stayed still on the tent until the voices had
dwindled until no crowd faced the tent. London lifted
the flap and stepped tiredly inside.

"Thanks," said Mac. "You don't know how close it
was any better than I do. You handled 'em, London. Oh,
you handled 'em."

London said, "I was scared. You won't think no worse
of me, Mac, for that. On the way back I caught myself
wantin' to come an' kill you myself." He grinned. "I
don't know why."

"Nobody does," said Mac. "But that's the way it is.
Tell us what happened down the road."

"We ironed 'em out," said London. "We just rolled
over 'em like they wasn't there. They give us the gas,
an' some of the guys coughed an' cried, but, hell, them
green cops didn't stand a chance. Some of 'em got away
—I guess most of 'em did. But the rest of 'em got kicked
to pieces like cheese. God, the guys was sore."

"Any shooting?"

"No. Too quick for 'em. They shot over us, thought
we'd stop, I guess. But we come right on. Some cops like
to shoot guys, but most of 'em don't, I guess. An' then
we just rolled 'em out, an' tore down the barricade."

"Well, did the cars get out?"

"Hell, yes, eight of 'em went through, loaded with
guys cuttin' hell loose."

"Kill any of the cops?" Mac demanded.

"Huh? Kill 'em? I don't know. I didn't look. Maybe
we did. We might of. I bet machine-guns wouldn't of
stopped us."

"That's swell," said Mac. "If we could turn on the

heat like that when we wanted it, and turn it off when we were through, we'd have our God-damn revolution tomorrow, and all over tomorrow night. The guys got over it pretty quick."

"It was all that runnin' that did it," London said. "Damn near a mile. Time they got back, they was clear winded. I feel sick myself. I ain't used to runnin'."

"I know," said Mac. "It's not the running, so much, though. A thing like that gets you all messed up inside. I bet a lot of the guys are losing their breakfast right now."

London seemed suddenly to see Jim. He went over and banged him a clap on the back. "You pulled it, Jim. I was standin' up there after I cold-cocked Burke; I didn't know what the hell to do. An' them guys in the circle didn't know what to do, neither. They was all ready to get me, or anybody. An' I look out, and I seen you pointin', an' I know what to do with 'em."

Jim's face was alight with pleasure. "I'm not much use, with my bum shoulder. I was thinking what Mac said about a little blood setting the guys off. You remember saying that, Mac?"

"Sure I remember. But I'm not sure I would of thought of it out there. I don't know how you do it, Jim. Everbody loses their head except you. I heard about your old man; he wasn't a genius, all he knew was fight. I don't know where you learned to use your bean and keep clear."

"I've got to be some use," Jim said. "My father was like you say, but my mother was so cool she'd make you shiver."

London flexed his hand at his side, and then he looked in astonishment at his crushed knuckles. "Holy Christ! Look at that!"

"You sure smashed 'em," said Mac.

"I smashed 'em on that son-of-a-bitch Burke. How is he, Jim? Felt like I knocked his head clear off when I socked 'im."

Jim said, "I don't know how he is. Somebody took 'im off the stand."

"Guess I better see," said London. "Funny I never felt that hand till now."

"When you get mixed up with the animal, you never feel anything," said Mac.

"What animal?"

"Oh, it's just a kind of a joke. Be a good idea if you look at Burke. And see how the guys feel. They'll feel pretty rocky by now, I think."

London said, "I don't trust 'em no more. I can't tell what they'll do no more. I'm glad I wasn't back of that barricade."

Mac said, "Well, I'm glad you was in front of this tent. Jim an' me might be hangin' up on an apple tree by now."

"There was a minute there——" said London. He gathered the tent-flaps and tied them back. The sun did not enter the tent, it had passed its meridian. Mac and Jim watched London walk away, and then they faced each other again. Mac flopped down on the mattress. Jim looked at him until Mac said, "You accusing me of something?"

"No, I was just wondering—seems to me now we've won a fight an' got our guys through we're more in danger of losing than ever. We came out here to do something, Mac. Have we messed up everything?"

Mac said sharply, "You think we're too important, and this little bang-up is too important. If the thing blew up right now it'd be worth it. A lot of the guys've been believing this crap about the noble American workingman, an' the partnership of capital and labor. A lot of 'em are straight now. They know how much capital thinks of 'em, and how quick capital would poison 'em like a bunch of ants. An' by Christ, we showed 'em two things—what they are, an' what they've got to do. And this last little ruckus showed 'em they could do it. Remember what the 'Frisco strike did to Sam? Well, all these guys'll get to be a little like Sam."

"But do you think they've got brains enough to see it?"

"Not brains, Jim. It don't take brains. After it's all over the thing'll go on working down inside of 'em. They'll know it without thinking it out."

"Well, what do you think's going to happen now?"

Mac rubbed his front teeth with a finger. "I guess they'll just have to steam-roller us out of here, Jim. Might be this afternoon, might be tonight."

"Well, what do you think; had we better just fade, or put up a fight?"

"Fight, if we can make the guys do it," said Mac. "If they sneak off, they get a bad feeling out of it, but if they fight and get licked, well, they still fought; and it's worth doing."

Jim settled down on one knee. "Look, if they come through with guns they're going to kill a lot of our guys."

Mac's eyes grew slitted and cold. "We keep switching sides, Jim. Suppose they do kill some of our men? That helps our side. For every man they kill ten new ones come over to us. The news goes creeping around the country and men all over hear it and get mad. Guys that are just half-warm get hot, see? But if we sneak off and the word gets around, and men say, 'They didn't even put up a fight,' why all the working stiffs will be unsure of themselves. If we fight, an' the news gets around, other men in the same position'll fight too."

Jim put down the other knee and squatted on his heels. "I wanted to get the thing straight. But will the guys fight?"

"I don't know. Right now they won't. They're pretty sick. Maybe later. Maybe if we could throw 'em another chicken like Burke they would. Burke stepped on the third rail just in time, just when we needed him. Maybe somebody else'll spill a little blood for the cause."

Jim said, "Mac, if blood's all we need, I could pull off this bandage and start the hole bleeding."

"You're kind of funny, Jim," Mac said kindly. "You're so God-damn serious."

"I don't see anything funny."

"No. Remember the lady that was buying a dog? She asks, 'Are you sure he's a bloodhound?' The owner says, 'Sure he is. Bleed for the lady, Oscar.' "

Jim smiled thinly. Mac went on, "No, Jim, you're more use to the cause than a hundred of these guys."

"Well, a little loss of blood won't hurt me."

Mac stroked his lower lip nervously. "Jim," he said. "Did you ever see four or five dogs all fighting?"

"No."

"Well, if one of those dogs gets hurt or goes down, all the rest'll turn on him and kill him."

"So what?"

"So—men do that sometimes, too. I don't know why. It's kind of like Doc says to me one time, 'Men hate something in themselves.' "

"Doc was a nice guy, but he didn't get anywhere with his high-falutin ideas. His ideas didn't go anywhere, just around in a circle."

"All the same, I wish he was here. Your shoulder feel all right?"

"Sure. I'm not using it any more than I can help."

Mac got up. "Come on, let's look at it. Take off that coat." Jim worked the coat off. Mac pulled the plaster loose and carefully raised the bandage. "Looks pretty good. It's a little bit angry. I'll throw away a couple of layers of this gauze. I'll be glad when we get in town. You can get it taken care of. Now I'll put this clean part back." He pressed the plaster down in place and held it firmly until the body heat made it take hold.

"Maybe we'll find Doc in town," said Jim. "He talked awful funny just before he disappeared. Maybe he got disgusted, or scared, and beat it."

"Here, I'll help you with your coat. You can forget that. If Doc was goin' to get disgusted, he'd of got years ago. An' I've seen him under fire. He don't get scared."

London came in and stood quietly in the doorway. He looked serious and frightened. "I didn't kill 'im, but damn near. His jaw's busted terrible. I'm scared he'll die if he don't get a doctor."

"Well, we can ship him to town, but I don't think they'd take very good care of him in there."

London went on, "That woman of his is raisin' hell. Says she's goin' to have the whole bunch of us up for murder. Says the whole strike was just to get Burke."

Mac said, "It'd almost be worth it, at that. I never liked the bastard. I always thought he was the stoolpigeon. How do the guys feel?"

"They're just sittin' around, like you said. Look sick, like a bunch of kids that broke into a candy store."

"Sure," said Mac. "They used up the juice that should of lasted 'em about a week. We better get some food into 'em if we can. Maybe they'll sleep it off then. You're sure right, London. We need a doctor. How's the guy that hurt his ankle?"

"Well, he's raisin' merry hell too. Says it ain't set right, an' it hurts. An' he won't never be able to walk no more. All this howlin' around ain't helpin' the way the guys feel none."

"Yeah, an' there's Al," said Mac. "I wonder how Al is?

We ought to go over an' see him. Think the guys you told to stay there stayed?"

London shrugged. "I don't know."

"Well, could we get half a dozen guys to go over with us?"

London said, "I don't think you'll get none of these guys to go no place. They just want to set there an' look at their feet."

"Well, by Christ, I'll go alone, then. Al's a good guy."

"I'll go with you, Mac," Jim broke in.

"No. You stay here."

London said, "I don't think there's nobody to bother you."

Mac begged, "Jim, I wish you'd stay. S'pose they got both of us? There'd be nobody here to go on. Stay here, Jim."

"I'm going. I've sat around here and nursed myself long enough. Why don't you stay and let me go?"

"All right, kid," Mac said resignedly. "We'll just be careful, and keep our eyes open. Try to keep the guys alive till we get back, London. Try to get a little of that beef and beans into 'em. They're sick of it, but it's food. We ought to be hearing something about those cars pretty soon."

London grunted, "I guess I'll just open me up a can of them peaches, an' some sardines. The guys said I had a flock of 'em, piled right up to the roof. I'll have some ready for you when you get back."

THEY WALKED out into the clear yellow sunshine. The camp looked bedraggled and grey in the clean light. A litter had accumulated since Burton was gone, bits of paper, strings, overalls hung on the guy-ropes of the tents. Mac and Jim walked out of the camp and across the surrounding field, to the edge of the orchard. At the line of trees Mac stopped. His eyes moved slowly across the horizontal fields of vision. "Look close, Jim," he advised. "It's probably a damn fool thing to go over alone. I know it isn't good sense." He studied the orchard. The long, sun-spotted aisles were silent. There was no movement. "It's so quiet. Makes me suspicious. It's too quiet." He reached to a limb and took down a small, misshapen apple the pickers had left. "God, that tastes good. I'd forgot about apples. Always forget what's so easy."

"I don't see anybody moving," said Jim. "Not a soul."

"Well look, we'll edge down in line with the trees. Anybody looking down a row won't see us, then." They stepped slowly in under the big apple trees. Their eyes moved restlessly about. They walked through shadows of branches and leaves, and the sun struck them with soft, warm blows.

Jim asked, "Mac, do you s'pose we could get a leave of absence some time and go where nobody knows us, and just sit down in an orchard?"

" 'Bout two hours of it, and you'd be raring to go again."

"I never had time to look at things, Mac, never. I never looked how leaves come out. I never looked at the way things happen. This morning there was a whole line of ants on the floor of the tent. I couldn't watch them. I was thinking about something else. Some time I'd like to sit all day and look at bugs, and never think of anything else."

"They'd drive you nuts," said Mac. "Men are bad enough, but bugs'd drive you nuts."

"Well, just once in a while you get that feeling—I never look at anything. I never take time to see anything. It's going to be over, and I won't know—even how an apple grows."

They moved on slowly. Mac's restless eyes roved about among the trees. "You can't see everything," he said. "I took a leave and went into the woods in Canada. Say, in a couple of days I came running out of there. I wanted trouble, I was hungry for a mess."

"Well, I'd like to try it sometime. The way old Dan talks about timber——"

"Damn it, Jim, you can't have everything! We've got something old Dan hasn't got. You can't have everything. In a few days we'll be back in town, and we'll be so damned anxious to get into another fuss we'll be biting our nails. You've got to take it easy till that shoulder heals. I'll take you to a flop-house where you can watch all the bugs you want. Keep back of the line of trees. You're standing out like a cow on a side-hill."

"It's nice out here," said Jim.

"It's too damn nice. I'm scared there's a trap someplace."

Through the trees they could see Anderson's little white house, and its picket fence, and the burning geraniums in the yard. "No one around," said Jim.

"Well, take it easy." At the last row Mac stopped again and let his eyes travel slowly across the open. The great black square on the ground, where the barn had been, still sent up a lazy, pungent smoke. The white tankhouse looked tall and lonely. "Looks O.K.," Mac said.

"Let's go in the back way." He tried to open the picket gate quietly, but the latch clicked and the hinges growled. They walked up the short path to the porch with its yellowing passion vine. Mac knocked on the door.

A voice from inside called, "Who is it?"

"Is that you, Al?"

"Yeah."

"Are you alone?"

"Yeah. Who are you?"

"It's Mac."

"Oh, come on in, Mac. The door ain't locked."

They went into the kitchen. Al lay on his narrow bed against the wall. He seemed to have grown gaunt in the few days. The skin hung loosely on his face. "Hi, Mac. I thought nobody'd ever come. My old man went out early."

"We tried to get over before, Al. How's all the hurts?"

"They hurt plenty," said Al. "And when you're all alone they hurt worse. Who burned the barn, Mac?"

"Vigilantes. We're sorry as hell, Al. We had guards here, but they got a fast one pulled on 'em."

"My old man just raised hell all night, Mac. Talked all night. Give me hell about four times an hour, all night."

"We're damn sorry."

Al cleared one hand from the bedclothes and scratched his cheek. "I'm still with you, Mac. But the old man wants to blast you. He went in this morning to get the sheriff to kick you off'n the place. Says you're trespassin', an' he wants you off. Says he's punished for listenin' to guys like you. Says I can go to hell if I string along with you. He was mad as a hornet, Mac."

"I was scared he would be, Al. Listen, we know you're with us, see? It don't do no good to make that old man any sorrier than he is. If it'd do any good, it'd be different. You just pretend to come around to his side. We'll understand that, Al. You can keep in touch with us. I'm awfully sorry for your old man."

Al sighed deeply. "I was scared you'd think I double-crossed you. If you know I ain't, I'll tell him t'hell with you."

"That's the stuff, Al. And we'll give you a boost in town too. Oh, say, Al, did Doc look in on you last night?"

"No. Why?"

"Well, he started over here before the fire, an' he ain't been back."

"Jesus! What do you think happened to him?"

"I'm scared they snatched the poor devil."

"They been pushing you all around, ain't they?"

"Yeah. But our guys got in some good licks this morning. But if your old man turns us in, I guess they'll roll over us tomorrow."

"Whole thing flops, huh, Mac?"

"That don't mean anything. We done what we came to do. The thing goes right on, Al. You just make peace an' pretend you ain't ever goin' to get burned no more." He listened. "Is that somebody coming?" He ran through the kitchen and into the front of the house, and looked out a window.

"It's my old man, I recognize his step," said Al.

Mac returned. "I wanted to see if anybody was with him. He's all alone. We could make a sneak, I guess. I'd rather tell him I'm sorry."

"You better not," Al advised. "He won't listen to nothing from you. He hates your guts."

There were steps on the porch and the door burst open. Anderson stood, surprised and glaring. "God damn it," he shouted. "You bastards get out of here. I've been and turned you in. The sheriff's goin' kick the whole smear of you off my land." His chest swelled with rage.

Mac said, "We just wanted to tell you we're sorry.

We didn't burn the barn. Some of the boys from town did."

"What th' hell do I care who burned it? It's burned, the crop's burned. What do you damn bums know about it? I'll lose the place sure, now." His eyes watered with rage. "You bastards never owned nothing. You never planted trees an' seen 'em grow an' felt 'em with your hands. You never owned a thing, never went out an' touched your own apple trees with your hands. What do you know?"

"We never had a chance to own anything," Mac said. "We'd like to own something and plant trees."

Anderson ignored his words. "I listened to your promises. Look what happened. The whole crop's burned, there's paper coming due."

Mac asked, "How about the pointers?"

Anderson's hands settled slowly to his sides. A look of cold, merciless hatred came into his eyes. He said slowly, softly, "The kennel was—against—the barn."

Mac turned to Al and nodded. For a moment Al questioned with his eyes, and then he scowled. "What he says goes. You guys get the hell out, and don't never come back."

Anderson ran to the bed and stood in front of it. "I could shoot you men now," he said, "but the sheriff's goin' to do it for me, an' damn quick."

Mac touched Jim on the arm, and they went out and shut the door. They didn't bother to look around when they went out the gate. Mac set out so rapidly that Jim had to stretch his stride to keep up. The sun was cutting downward now, and the shadows of whole trees lay between the rows, and the wind was stirring in the branches, so that both trees and ground seemed to quiver nervously.

"It keeps you hopping, keeping the picture," Mac said. "You see a guy hurt, or somebody like Anderson smashed, or you see a cop ride down a Jew girl, an' you think, what the hell's the use of it. An' then you think of the millions starving, and it's all right again. It's worth it. But it keeps you jumping between pictures. Don't it ever get you, Jim?"

"Not very much. It isn't long ago I saw my mother die; seems years, but it wasn't long ago. She wouldn't speak to me, she just looked at me. She was hurt so bad she didn't even want a priest. I guess I got something burned out of me that night. I'm sorry for Anderson, but what the hell. If I can give up my whole life, he ought to be able to give up a barn."

"Well, to some of those guys property's more important than their lives."

Jim said, "Slow down, Mac. What's your hurry? I seem to get tired easy."

Mac did slow his steps a little. "I thought that's what he went to town for. I want to get back before anything happens. I don't know what this sheriff'll do, but he'll be happy as hell to split us up." They walked silently over the soft, dark earth, and the shadows flickered on them. At the clearing they slowed down. Mac said, "Well, nothing's happened yet, anyway."

The smoke rose slowly from the stoves. Jim asked, "Where do you s'pose all the guys are?"

"In sleeping off the drunk, I guess. It wouldn't be a bad idea if we got some sleep, too. Prob'ly be up all night."

London moved over and met them. "Everything all right?" Mac asked.

"Just the same."

"Well, I was right. Anderson's been in and asked the sheriff to kick us off."

"Well?"

"Well, we wait. Don't tell the guys about it."

"Maybe you was right about that," London said, "but

you was sure wrong about what them guys would eat. They cleaned us out. There ain't a damn drop o' beans left. I saved you a couple of cans, over in my tent."

"Maybe we won't need anything more to eat," said Mac.

"How do you mean?"

"We prob'ly won't any of us be here tomorrow."

In the tent London pointed to the two food cans on the box. "D'you s'pose the sheriff'll try to kick us off?" he asked.

"Damn right. He won't let a chance like that go by."

"Well, will he come shootin', d'you suppose? Or will he give the guys a warnin'?"

Mac said, "Hell, I don't know. Where's all the men?"

"All under cover, asleep."

Mac said, "I heard a car. May be our guys coming back."

London cocked his head. "Too big," he said. "That's one of them big babies."

They ran outside. Up the road from Torgas a huge Mack dump-truck rolled. It had a steel bed and sides, supported by two sets of double tires. It pulled up in front of the camp and stopped. A man stood up in the steel bed, and in his hands he held a submachine-gun with a big cartridge cylinder behind the forward grip. The heads of other men showed above the truck sides. Strikers began to boil out of the tents.

The standing man shouted, "I'm sheriff o' this county. If there's anyone in authority I want to see him." The mob approached closer and looked curiously at the truck.

Mac said softly, "Careful, London. They may pop us off. They could do it now if they wanted to." They walked forward, to the edge of the road, and stopped; and the mob was lining the road now, too.

London said, "I'm the boss, mister."

"Well, I've got a trespass complaint. We've been fair

to you men. We've asked you to go back to work, or, if you wanted to strike, to do it peacefully. You've destroyed property and committed homicide. This morning you sent out men to destroy property. We had to shoot some of those men, and we caught the rest." He looked down at the men in the truck, and then up again. "Now we don't want any bloodshed, so we're going to let you out. You have all night tonight to get out. If you head straight for the county line, nobody'll bother you. But if this camp is here at daylight tomorrow, we're going through it."

The men stood silently and watched him. Mac whispered to London. London said, "Trespassin' don't give you no right to shoot guys."

"Maybe not, but resisting officers does. Now I'm talking fair with you, so you'll know what to expect. At daylight tomorrow a hundred men, in ten trucks like this, are coming out. Every man will have a gun, and we have three cases of Mills bombs. Some of you men who know can tell the others what a Mills bomb is. That's all. We're through fooling with you. You have till daylight to get out of the county. That's all." He turned forward. "Might as well drive along, Gus." He sank from sight behind the steel truck side. The wheels turned slowly, and gathered speed.

One of the strikers leaped into the shallow ditch and picked up a rock. And he stood holding it in his hand and looking at it as the truck rolled away. The men watched the truck go, and then they turned back into the camp.

London sighed. "Well, that sounds like orders. He didn't mean no funny business."

Mac said impatiently, "I'm hungry. I'm going to eat my beans." They followed him back into the tent. He gobbled his food quickly and hungrily. "Hope you got some, London."

"Me? Oh, sure. What we goin' to do now, Mac?"

"Fight," said Mac.

"Yeah, but if he brings the stuff he said, pineapples an' stuff, it ain't goin' to be no more fight than the stockyards."

"Bull," said Mac, and a little jet of chewed beans shot from his mouth. "If he had that stuff, he wouldn't need to tell us about it. He just hopes we'll get scattered so we can't put up a fight. If we move out tonight, they'll pick us off. They never do what they say."

London looked into Mac's face, hung on to his eyes. "Is that straight, Mac? You said I was on your side. Are you puttin' somethin' over?"

Mac looked away. "We got to fight," he said. "If we get out without a scrap ever'thing we've been through'll be wasted."

"Yeah, but if we fight, a lot of guys that ain't done no harm is goin' get shot."

Mac put his unfinished food down on the box. "Look," he said. "In a war a general knows he's going to lose men. Now this is a war. If we get run out o' here without a fight, it's losing ground." For a moment he covered his eyes with his hand. "London," he said. "It's a hell of a responsibility. I know what we should do; you're the boss; for Christ's sake, do what you want. Don't make me take all the blame."

London said plaintively, "Yeah, but you know about things. You think we ought to fight, really?"

"Yes, we ought."

"Well, hell then, we'll fight—that is, if we can get the guys to fight."

"I know," said Mac. "They may run out on us, every one of 'em. The ones that heard the sheriff will tell the others. They may turn on us and say we caused the trouble."

London said, "Some ways, I hope they clear out. Poor

bastards, they don't know nothing. But like you say, if they're ever goin' to get clear, they got to take it now. How about the hurt guys?" London went on, "Burke and old Dan, and the guy with the busted ankle?"

"Leave 'em," said Mac. "It's the only thing we can do. The county'll have to take care of 'em."

"I'm going to take a look around," London said. "I'm gettin' nervous as a cat."

"You ain't the only one," said Mac.

When he was gone, Jim glanced at Mac, and then began to eat the cold beans and strings of beef. "I wonder if they'll fight?" he asked. "D'you think they'd really let the guys through if they wanted to run?"

"Oh, the sheriff would. He'd be only too damn glad to get rid of 'em, but I don't trust the vigilante boys."

"They won't have anything to eat tonight, Mac. If they're scared already, there won't be any dinner to buck 'em up."

Mac scraped his can and set it down. "Jim," he said, "if I told you to do something, would you do it?"

"I don't know. What is it?"

"Well, the sun's going down pretty soon, and it'll be dark. They're going to lay for you and me, Jim. Don't make any mistake about that. They're going to want to get us, bad. I want you to get out, soon as it gets dark, get clear and go back to town."

"Why in hell should I do that?"

Mac's eyes slid over Jim's face and went to the ground again. "When I came out here, I thought I was hell on wheels. You're worth ten of me, Jim. I know that now. If anything happened to me, there's plenty of guys to take my place, but you've got a genius for the work. We can't spare you, Jim. If you was to get knocked off in a two-bit strike—well, it's bad economy."

"I don't believe it," said Jim. "Our guys are to be

used, not saved. I couldn't run out. Y'said yourself this was a part of the whole thing. It's little, but it's important."

"I *want* you to go, Jim. You can't fight with that arm. You'd be no damn good here. You couldn't help at all."

Jim's face was rigid. "I won't go," he said. "I might be of some use here. You protect me all the time, Mac. And sometimes I get the feeling you're not protecting me for the Party, but for yourself."

Mac reddened with anger. "O.K., then. Get your can knocked off. I've told you what I think's the best thing. Be pig-headed, if you want. I can't sit still. I'm going out. You do anything you damn please." He went out angrily.

Jim looked up at the back wall of the tent. He could see the outline of the red sun on the canvas. His hand stole up and touched his hurt shoulder, and pressed it gently, all around, in a circle that narrowed to the wound. He winced a little as his exploring fingers neared the hurt. For a long time he sat quietly.

He heard a step in the door and looked around. Lisa stood there, and her baby was in her arms. Jim could see past her, where the line of old cars stood against the road; and on the other side of the road the sun was on the treetops, but in the rows the shade had come. Lisa looked in, with a bird-like interest. Her hair was damp, plastered against her head, and little, uneven finger-waves were pressed into it. The short blanket that covered her shoulders was draped and held to one side with a kind of coquetry. "I seen you was alone," she said. She went to the mattress and sat down and arranged her gingham dress neatly over her legs. "I heard guys say the cops'll throw bombs, an' kill us all," she said lightly.

Jim was puzzled. "It doesn't seem to scare you much."

"No. I ain't never been ascared o' things like that."

"The cops wouldn't hurt you," Jim said. "I don't believe they'll do all that. It's a bluff. Do you want anything?"

"I thought I'd come an' set. I like to—just set here."

Jim smiled. "You like me, don't you, Lisa?"

"Yes."

"I like you, too, Lisa."

"You he'ped me with the baby."

Jim asked, "How's old Dan? Did you take care of him?"

"He's all right. Just lays there mumblin'."

"Mac helped you more than I did."

"Yes, but he don't look at me—nice. I like t'hear you talk. You're just a young kid, but you talk nice."

"I talk too much, Lisa. Too much talk, not enough doing things. Look how the evening's coming. We'll light the lantern before long. You wouldn't like to sit here in the dark with me."

"I wouldn' care," she said quickly.

He looked into her eyes again, and his face grew pleased. "Did you ever notice, in the evening, Lisa, how you think of things that happened a long time ago—not even about things that matter? One time in town, when I was a little kid, the sun was going down, and there was a board fence. Well, a grey cat went up and sat on that fence for a moment, long-haired cat, and that cat turned gold for a minute, a gold cat."

"I like cats," Lisa agreed softly. "I had two cats onct, two of them."

"Look. The sun's nearly gone, Lisa. Tomorrow we'll be somewhere else. I wonder where? You'll be on the move, I guess. Maybe I'll be in jail. I've been in jail before."

London and Mac came quietly into the tent together. London looked down at the girl. "What you doing here, Lisa? You better get out. We got business." Lisa got up and clutched her blanket close. She looked sideways at Jim as she passed. London said, "I don't know what's goin' on. There's about ten little meetin's out there, an' they don't want me at none o' them."

"Yeah, I know," Mac said. "The guys're scared. I don't know what they'll do, but they'll want to scram tonight." And then the conversation died. London and Mac sat down on boxes, facing Jim. They sat there while the sun went down and the tent grew a little dusky.

At last Jim said softly, "Even if the guys get out, it won't all be wasted. They worked together a little."

Mac roused himself. "Yeah, but we ought to make a last stand."

"How you goin' to get guys to fight when they want to run?" London demanded.

"I don't know. We can talk. We can try to make 'em fight talkin' to 'em."

"Talk don't do much good when they're scared."

"I know."

The silence fell again. They could hear the low talk of many voices outside, scattered voices that gradually drew together and made a babble like water. Mac said, "Got a match, London? Light the lantern."

"It ain't dark yet."

"Dark enough. Light it up. This God-damn half-light makes me nervous."

The shade screeched as London raised it, and screeched when he let it down.

Mac looked startled. "Something happened. What's wrong?"

"It's the men," said Jim. "They're quiet now. They've all stopped talking." The three men sat listening tensely. They heard footsteps coming closer. In the doorway the two short Italian men stood. Their teeth showed in self-conscious grins.

"C'n we come in?"

"Sure. Come on in, boys."

They stood in the tent like pupils preparing to recite. Each looked to the other to begin. One said, "The men out there—they want to call a meeting."

"Yeah? What for?"

The other answered quickly, "Those men say they vote the strike, they can vote again. They say, 'What's the use all the men get killed?' They say they can't strike no more." They were silent, waiting for London's answer.

London's eyes asked advice from Mac. "Of course you'll call a meeting," Mac said. "The men are the bosses. What they say goes." He looked up at the waiting emissaries. "Go out and tell the guys London calls a meeting in about half an hour, to vote whether we fight or run."

They looked at London for corroboration. He nodded his head slowly. "That's right," he said. "In a half hour. We do what the guys vote to do." The little men made foreign bows, and wheeled and left the tent.

Mac laughed loudly. "Why, that's fine," he said. "Why, that makes it better. I thought they might sneak out. But if they want to vote, that means they're still working together. Oh, that's fine. They can break up, if they do it by their own consent."

Jim asked, "But aren't you going to try to make them fight?"

"Oh, sure. We have to make plans about that. But if they won't fight, well anyway they don't just sneak off like dogs. It's more like a retreat, you see. It isn't just getting chased."

"What'll we do at the meeting?" London demanded.

"Well, let's see. It's just about dark now. You talk first, London. Tell 'em why they should fight, not run. Now I better not talk. They don't like me too well since I told 'em off this morning." His eyes moved to Jim. "You're it," he said. "Here's your chance. You do it. See if you can bring 'em around. Talk, Jim. Talk. It's the thing you've been wanting."

Jim's eyes shone with excitement. "Mac," he cried, "I can pull off this bandage and get a flow of blood. That might stir 'em up."

Mac's eyes narrowed and he considered the thought. "No—" he decided. "Stir 'em up that way, an' they got to hit something quick. If you make 'em sit around, they'll go way down. No, just talk, Jim. Tell 'em straight what a strike means, how it's a little battle in a whole war. You can do it, Jim."

Jim sprang up. "You're damn right I can do it. I'm near choking, but I can do it." His face was transfigured. A furious light of energy seemed to shine from it.

They heard running footsteps. A young boy ran into the tent. "Out in the orchard," he cried. "There's a guy says he's a doctor. He's all hurt."

The three started up. "Where?"

"Over the other side. Been lyin' there all day, he says."

"How'd you find him?" Mac demanded.

"I heard 'im yell. He says come and tell you."

"Show us the way. Come on now, hurry up."

The boy turned and plunged out. Mac shouted, "London, bring the lantern." Mac and Jim ran side by side. The night was almost complete. Ahead, they saw the flying figure of the boy. Across the open space they tore. The boy reached the line of trees and plunged among them. They could hear him running ahead of them. They dashed into the dark shadow of the trees.

Suddenly Mac reached for Jim. "Jim! Drop, for Christ' sake!" There was a roar, and two big holes of light. Mac had sprawled full length. He heard several sets of running footsteps. He looked toward Jim, but the flashes still burned on his retinas. Gradually he made Jim out. He was on his knees, his head down. "You sure got down quick, Jim."

Jim did not move. Mac scrambled over to him, on his knees. "Did you get hit, Jim?" The figure kneeled, and the face was against the ground. "Oh, Christ!" Mac put out his hand to lift the head. He cried out, and jerked his hand away, and wiped it on his trousers, for there was no face. He looked slowly around, over his shoulder.

The lantern bounced along toward him, lighting London's running legs. "Where are you?" London shouted.

Mac didn't answer. He sat back on his heels, sat very quietly. He looked at the figure, kneeling in the position of Moslem prayer.

London saw them at last. He came close, and stopped; and the lantern made a circle of light. "Oh," he said. He lowered the lantern and peered down. "Shot-gun?"

Mac nodded and stared at his sticky hand.

London looked at Mac, and shivered at his frozen face. Mac stood up, stiffly. He leaned over and picked Jim up and slung him over his shoulder, like a sack; and the dripping head hung down behind. He set off, stiff-legged, toward the camp. London walked beside him, carrying the lantern.

The clearing was full of curious men. They clustered around, until they saw the burden. And then they recoiled. Mac marched through them as though he did not see them. Across the clearing, past the stoves he marched, and the crowd followed silently behind him. He came to the platform. He deposited the figure under the hand-rail and leaped to the stand. He dragged Jim across the boards and leaned him against the corner post, and steadied him when he slipped sideways.

London handed the lantern up, and Mac set it carefully on the floor, beside the body, so that its light fell on the head. He stood up and faced the crowd. His hands gripped the rail. His eyes were wide and white. In front he could see the massed men, eyes shining in the lamplight. Behind the front row, the men were lumped and dark. Mac shivered. He moved his jaws to speak, and seemed to break the frozen jaws loose. His voice was high and monotonous. "This guy didn't want nothing for himself—" he began. His knuckles were white, where he grasped the rail. "Comrades! He didn't want nothing for himself——"